AUGEE

GUARDIAN
of HOHALA

Address inquiries to:
Werner &Lawrence Publishing,
PO Box 381,
Bonita Springs,
Florida 34133-0381

augeeofficial@gmail.com

Learn more at:
augee.com
facebook.com/TheAugeeSeries
twitter.com/TheAugeeSeries
instagram.com/TheAugeeSeries

Library of Congress Control Number: 2020914551
Stuempel, Paul.
Augee: Guardian of Hohala / by Paul Stuempel & Cormac Lambe—2nd ed.

Fantasy—Fiction.2. Action—Fiction.
3. Adventure—Fiction. 4. Dragon—Fiction
5. Forced migration—Fiction
I. Title

Printed in the United States of America

ISBN: 978-0-9996296-1-1

AUGEE

GUARDIAN *of* HOHALA

PAUL STUEMPEL
& CORMAC LAMBE

ACKNOWLEDGEMENTS

This book, since its inception over 40 years ago, has been a project of much labor and love. *Augee: Guardian of Hohala* could not have become a reality without the support and encouragement of so many.

To those who have been involved in the book's development at various stages—editors, Bonny Lemma, Jayne Roberts, and Dr. Graham Price; artists, Damonza and Brian Scheer; consultants, Theresa Ayers and Briget Ayers; website designer and marketing and social media manager, Amanda Richardson; and the countless number of reviewers that followed and guided the book during its development—thank you for all of your efforts. A special thanks to my friend, Debbie Smally, for her extensive editing and formatting of the original manuscript.

My deep appreciation goes to co-author and managing editor, Cormac Lambe. His vivid writing style and expertise have been invaluable to me in the development of this book. My heartfelt gratitude to Dr. Lambe cannot be overstated.

Finally, it is safe to say that *The Augee Series* would not have come to fruition if it weren't for the support of my wife, Rose Anne. Without her tireless dedication, patience, and commitment, I could never have realized this dream. Sincerely, thank you.

Paul Stuempel

Valley of the
Eternal Stream

Hohala Village

Great Bay of Hohala

Hohala

PROLOGUE

MANY LEAGUES ACROSS the oceans of time, space, and everything in between, there was a land known simply as Hohala. Since time immemorial, the country was an idyllic, bountiful place, populated by the Hohalians, a peaceful race of humans who lived in harmony with the natural world around them. The word "Hohala" itself meant "Essence of Heaven," and its inhabitants were a faithful people whose lives were given over in devotion to the Nexus, a divine, unseen network of kindly gods and spirits who guided and provided for the Hohalians as their chosen people.

From an early age, Hohalian children were taught to worship the Nexus with unwavering commitment, while adults were expected to live and work with a special love for the gods in their hearts always. In return for their piety and loyalty, the Nexus provided the Hohalians with crops and fruit and saw to it that their land was perpetually smiled upon by the warm light of the sun.

The village in which the Hohalians resided was, by extension, also known as Hohala. It was an intricate, sprawling settlement of narrow streets, stone cottages, and ancient, grandiose temples. The village itself was largely constructed of sandstone, and when the morning sun cast its light across the rooftops, the very buildings appeared to glint like pale, yellow gold. But the jewel in the crown of the Hohalian homeland was its spectacular royal mansion. The culmination of many generations of artisan builders, the sprawling, oblong-shaped palace was the traditional home of the Hohalian royal family who governed the citizens according to tradition and theology. As if to personify the spirit of the much blessed country, the royal line of

Hohala had always been characterized by benevolence and a humility that endeared them to the people. It was said that Hohala's regal lineage had originated at one time with the gods themselves, and so the people reserved a special fondness for their monarchy always.

Beyond the Hohalian settlement, the natural world flourished as freely and profusely as any other place known man. To the north and south, an expanse of untamed jungle that spread further than the naked eye could see provided a mysterious, natural boundary to the Hohalian village. So thick and inhospitable was the vegetation that parts of the jungle remained scarcely explored by the Hohalians. On its eastern side, Hohala was hemmed in by the coastline which stretched endlessly in either direction, trimmed by majestic, white sands that became increasingly rugged and precipitous as one moved further away from the village. Meanwhile, in the distant west, the snowcapped peaks of a dense, forbidding mountain range rose up against the horizon—a desolate, barely-charted outpost where only a handful of Hohalians were rumored to have ventured in the past. Inhospitable in both terrain and climate, the treacherous highlands marked the outermost limits of the country that the Hohalians lovingly and proudly claimed as their own.

Generation after generation, the citizens lived and worked as a tightly-woven community in which each person shouldered his or her fair share of the common work effort, from the laborers and traders to the priests and teachers. They nurtured and cultivated the land and lived in harmony with all species of the earth, sea, and sky. They neither hunted, nor killed, or even fought among themselves, and it was a cornerstone belief of Hohalian society that no violence ever be committed against another living being.

For those who dwelled within Hohala, thanksgiving to the Nexus was a fundamental part of their lives, as was the emphasis placed on community. Daily, as they went about their routines, the Hohalians prayed and sang the songs of their faith together, and in the evenings, they gathered in the homes of friends and neighbors to share food and make merry. Indeed, life in Hohala was one of blessings and bounty, and as a society, every effort was made to ensure that all citizens felt they belonged. For as long as any living person could remember, Hohalian children had been brought up to appreciate and feel privileged to be part of their community, with each individual understanding his or her own small part in the commonwealth.

And so it was for eons that the Hohalians lived in abundance and pleasure as the chosen people of the Nexus, fulfilled and provided for within the frontiers of their homeland. With little to want or yearn for—either spiritually or materially—the people of Hohala had few reasons to trouble their minds. Their small, blissful world, confined to the hinterland of the Great Bay of Hohala, was all that most men or women could ever desire, and it was a rarity for any Hohalian to cast their imagination beyond the outer limits of their motherland. However, as is often the folly of those who consider privilege to be a birthright, the Hohalians gave little thought to other places or races. Secure within their divinely-enchanted boundaries, the people of Hohala remained content and complacent for countless generations, their plentiful, happy existence untroubled by those who occupied the deprived shadows of creation. But, as is the story of humanity—told time and time again—prosperity and privilege are never eternal, and the frail hands of the broken and impoverished will always, eventually, rise in dissent.

1

NICHOLAS STONE HELD a portion of the sullen bay fixed in his gaze. In the unsettled daylight, forbidding waves punctuated the normally mint-green surface of the water. Nicholas remarked absent-mindedly that the sea that morning looked strangely similar to the day he'd watched the flimsy, leather canoe tumble into the froth and disappear as if it had never been. The memory had shrouded his life ever since, and it marked him deeply.

It was Nicholas's routine around this time of day to visit the obscured portion of cove that offered shelter from the wind and the squinting inquisition of fellow Hohalians. He preferred to rise early and visit the lonely spot before the village stirred for the day's work and trade, hoping to avoid neighborly small talk while the calm of sleep still enveloped him. The short pilgrimage to the water's edge had once been a means of coping with his grief but became a routine as he navigated a haphazard childhood and adolescence.

At 17, Nicholas was by now well-accustomed to his own company, and the other Hohalians regarded him with a mixture of sympathy and suspicion. After his parents drowned in the boating accident, he had been taken in and raised in an unconventional manner by various well-intended neighbors and family friends. As a youngster, he had been considered strange by other children, owing to his aloofness and a robust physique that gave him an unintentionally imposing air and set him apart from most boys his age. He'd had little in the way of solid friendships growing up, and in young adulthood, they counted just as few. But it was a reality he'd become accustomed to, preferring to spend his free time tramping the coastline alone or befriending wild animals he encountered in the jungle that surrounded the Hohalian village settlement on three sides. Even during occasions of worship and tradition, when the entire population of Hohala gathered to partake in community ceremonies, the young Nicholas would be seen standing conspicuously apart from the other children, detached and unanimated. Of course, throughout his boyhood and teenage years, Nicholas sang the traditional songs of thanksgiving and meditated on the Nexus with the other villagers as was expected, but inside, he felt restless and distracted.

While other young men and women of Hohala involved themselves enthusiastically in the life of their community, the introverted Nicholas dreamed of everything that lay beyond the familiar. To his frustration, the Hohalian king and the elders firmly discouraged citizens from travelling away from the village and the surrounding countryside where the protection of the gods did not reach. Folk tales, long handed down through the generations, warned young Hohalians of unknown dangers that lay outside the divine influence of the Nexus, and Nicholas's child-imagination had been captivated by stories of those who had ventured too far and failed to return. He wondered if those journeyers had, like himself, fantasized about what existed beyond Hohala's borders until the lure of the unknown became too intoxicating.

The salt-scented breeze and waking light caused Nicholas's eyes to water, and he rubbed away the tears with the back of his hand. An impatient growl sounded by his hip, and he flashed an affectionate smile in return to the panther's insistence that Nicholas continue petting his head. The big feline, muscular and sleek as marble, purred indignantly as Nicholas fingered the thick, black hair atop its crown.

"Ssh, Nightshade," he breathed absent-mindedly, as the panther stared with intent at the ocean where sunlight shimmied hypnotically on the waves.

Nicholas had always found the feline's rhythmic breathing calming, and its companionship had been one of few constants in his life. He had encountered the panther as a kitten in the uplands that marked the frontier between the Hohalian countryside and the barely charted mountains to the west. He'd told anyone who had enquired about the panther's origins that he'd found it wandering in the jungle. No one but himself could know that he had actually cut the throat of a boar with his fishing knife in order to rescue the helpless kitten from the rampaging hog. According to Hohalian laws on the use of violence, a citizen who had spilled blood should not be permitted to remain part of the community, and so Nicholas had no choice but to keep his slaying of the boar to himself. At the time, he'd been wracked by guilt at his actions, an anxiety that heightened on every occasion the community elders preached about how violent acts offended the Nexus and risked the loss of the gods' guardianship of Hohala. In the years since, however, his mind had explored the possibility of foreign landscapes and people, a notion that Hohalian culture was indifferent to. In truth, it confused him that other citizens of Hohala rarely expressed curiosity about things outside of the comfortable and familiar. As a whole, the community was content to live faithfully by the laws decreed by the king of Hohala whose royal lineage had been the earthly conduit between the Hohalians and the Nexus for millennia. In many ways, Nicholas understood the fervor with which his compatriots happily devoted their lives to the benevolent Nexus who ensured crops flourished, the climate remained pleasant, and who had for eons protected their Hohalian subjects from hardship or danger. As a nation, Hohala had practically every material and spiritual blessing the people could desire; why would any Hohalian yearn for something else? Why would any of them care to imagine what might exist on the other side of things?

Nicholas's moody reflections were interrupted by a sudden flinch of Nightshade's head. The panther's attention had turned to the sand dunes further up the beach where a dark-haired female could be seen stumbling in their direction. As he strained his eyes, Nicholas's pulse quickened to recognize the figure as Caralisa, the only daughter of the country's monarch, King Benjamin, and the much-loved princess of Hohala. Like other young Hohalians his age, Nicholas knew Caralisa well from their school days together, the king having insisted that his child be brought up and educated like any other citizen. When other children had gossiped about the strange boy, Nicholas, who rarely joined in their games, young Caralisa had demonstrated the empathy and non-judgmental nature for which her father, the king, was renowned and respected. They had met when Nicholas was four years old after he had fallen on a crushed-shell path and skinned his palms. Caralisa had seen him sitting at the edge of the trail crying, and by way of some strange incantation sung like a nursery rhyme, she had coaxed a swarm of jungle butterflies to swirl around him in a riot of color simply to cheer him up. Even to this day, he remembered being utterly entranced—by both the butterflies and their conjurer. Little Caralisa had kissed each of his palms and insisted that he stop crying. Even years later, he could recall his shy embarrassment and how he had picked himself up immediately after.

Nicholas gave a self-conscious wave which the girl acknowledged in the distance.

"Relax, Nightshade," Nicholas murmured as the big cat stiffened at the figure's approach, though, subconsciously, the reassurance was as much intended for himself as the panther.

On reaching the foreshore, Caralisa grinned at Nicholas questioningly, prompting his cheeks to flush. Her loose, white gown fluttered in the gentle breeze, showing tantalizing hints of her soft curves. As always, her wavy, black hair and olive complexion appeared to glint in the sunlight, and her eyes, deep and intelligent, were the color of the bay.

"An earlier start than usual today?" the princess greeted cheerily, a measure of teasing underpinning her salute. Although she could not be sure if he intended it, it was a regular occurrence to cross paths with the quiet, but unwittingly handsome Nicholas Stone on her morning walk along the seafront.

"Yeah," Nicholas answered with a smile, clearing his throat. "I thought it might storm, so I figured I'd beat the rain."

"Me too," Caralisa replied warmly. "My father is insisting the ceremony goes ahead today, even though I've told him that the flower crowns and the tapestries will be blown all over. Dear Nexus, he's as stubborn as an old boar when it comes to traditions!"

Nicholas grimaced to himself, his subconscious pricked by her use of the word "boar," and its allusion to the violent act of his past that he could never tell her about. Immediately, he followed up with an exaggerated chuckle which he hoped was enough to disguise his awkwardness as well as the sudden annoyance that rose within him at her reminder of the day's obligation. He had forgotten that it was the beginning of Springtide, a week of prayer and festivities to mark another changing of the seasons which was an important observance in Hohalian culture. All citizens were expected to participate in the events organized by the king and his advisors, and, given his eagerness to remain in positive favor with the hauntingly beautiful princess, he once again put up a positive front.

"Yes, I suppose King Benjamin does love celebrations," Nicholas recovered, clearing his throat. "When is the ceremony?"

"At exactly noon," the princess laughed, imitating her father's officious tone.

It was at that moment that Nicholas detected the slightest twitch of her face muscles, suggesting she was holding something back. She seemed to hesitate for a second before her eyes dropped self-consciously, and she brushed back a strand of hair behind her ear.

"Are you planning to go this time?" she queried, meeting his eyes inquisitively as she referenced Nicholas's absence at the previous ceremony to mark the changing of the seasons which he'd subsequently told her was due to illness.

"Eh, yes, I..." he began before the princess cut across his sentence abruptly.

"Oh, good," she stammered. "It's just that Father suggested that this time I bring a guest to the ceremony for company, and I was going to ask one of the girls, but none of them want to be stuck in the middle of the elders and the royal advisors, and I thought..."

The pace of Nicholas's heartbeat began to increase as she propositioned him clumsily.

"...Well, I thought perhaps you might like to join me?" she finished uncertainly, her eyes barely disguising her tension. "Though, don't feel obliged because I realize you weren't expecting it, and I know you don't really like crowds, but..."

Nicholas again cleared his throat bashfully.

"Uh, yes...I mean, sure," he mumbled before venturing, "Do you mean, together?"

"Well, yes...but only if you want to!" Caralisa blushed, looking away. "It is no problem at all if you prefer to attend with everyone else. It was just a thought..."

For some reason, her obvious nervousness gave him the slightest confidence to drop his own guard.

"That sounds like it could be enjoyable," he replied with a shrug and a soft smile that caused Caralisa's cheeks to redden. "Why not?"

"Are you sure?" she stuttered. "Really, I don't want you to feel pressure…"

He wasn't sure where the sudden confidence came from, but Nicholas found himself reaching for the princess's hand, and it was with a fleeting, but deep relief that he felt Caralisa squeeze his hand in return. He looked down at her, and they exchanged a hesitant smile. Nicholas attempted to steady his breathing, totally taken aback by the forwardness of the princess's request and the realization that she had harbored feelings for him too. He was struck to think that during their brief, but routine morning encounters along the seafront that she had felt similarly the whole time.

"Now, you might hear a little teasing," she resumed, her face flushed. "I did mention to my father that I was thinking of asking you, and, well, you know how he likes to joke around, and…"

Although he did not allow his face to betray it, Nicholas felt a stab of anxiety at the realization that he was an invited guest of the royal family – that the king himself was expecting his attendance at a ceremony he privately had little interest in. Yet, the earnest smile and ocean eyes of the princess filled him with a warmth that momentarily soothed the riot of his thoughts.

"Ha, yeah," he pretended to agree. "I'm sure it will be a great occasion. Thanks for asking me to…"

"Of course," Caralisa jumped in, just about managing to hold back her relived excitement at Nicholas's positive response to her proposal. "I…I'm really glad you want to."

The princess's sentence trailed off as her eyes dropped to the sand by her feet. Nicholas, feeling a clumsy awkwardness rising between them, stumbled about his mind for the appropriate response. However, just as he was about to offer up some hurriedly thought-out platitude, Caralisa made a half-hearted farewell gesture before she stopped and turned back to face him. Before Nicholas could react, the scent of perfume rose in his nostrils as the princess planted a hasty kiss on his face, right on the dimple where his lips and cheek met.

"Well, I shall see you at the royal mansion later, then," Caralisa smiled up at him coyly before throwing a fleeting glance out over the bay and turning in the direction from which she'd arrived.

Nicholas stood stunned and motionless as the wind whipped his hair around his eyes and he reflected on what had just occurred. He felt excited and apprehensive in equal measure, and his mind raced.

Why would Caralisa want to invite him of all people? Had she felt that way about him for a long time? Had she and the king really bantered about inviting him to the ceremony? And what would he wear!

As the panic swirled in his mind, Nicholas's thoughts were interrupted by an impatient growl by his side. Nightshade stared up at him, the panther's surly gaze accusing Nicholas of allowing the time to go too far past breakfast. With a heaving sigh, Nicholas attempted to shake off the daze caused by his eventful encounter with the princess. While he'd never been as passionately devoted to the institution of the Hohalian monarchy as many of his countrymen and women, he felt intimidated by the thought of having to perform unfamiliar airs and graces in the company of the king and his aides. Nicholas knew he didn't belong among them; indeed, he barely fit in with Hohalians of his own age. Yet, the soft pressure of the princess's lips still lingered on the corner of his mouth as did his nervous exhilaration at the discovery of her feelings toward him. As he and Nightshade crossed the mounds of sand separating the beach from the pathway to the village, Nicholas gave a final look over his shoulder at the bay of Hohala in the hope of some vague reassurance.

2

Far beyond the tropical waters of the Great Bay of Hohala, there was another land whose inhabitants knew little of the world beyond their own domain. On the island of Volcaron, freezing winds ensured a cold and summerless climate always, and the country's remote location—a pinprick in a vast, treacherous ocean—often led the natives to believe that they might very well be alone in the universe.

On a haggard, north-facing headland, a man stood alone, gazing across the sea. For well over an hour he had remained there, motionless and unperturbed by the icy spittle that sprayed his face and the outer layers of his animal pleat cloak. In front of him, cold waves broke ceaselessly on the reefs and rocks, rolling and undulating as far as the dim horizon. The sharp-eyed, hard-featured man, for whom the years of youth had long passed by, stared out across the water. His name was Morgoratt, and he too was full of darkness and yearning.

His entire life, Morgoratt had considered himself a cursed man. It had been several years since he'd risen to prominence among his people, and in that time, he had become something of a *de facto* leader of the race known as the Volcarons. Not that this satisfied him, however; Morgoratt despised his own people, ashamed of their slovenly behaviors and non-existent work ethic. Truthfully, his near-daily visits to the bleak sea front, when he would spend hours looking out at the empty horizon, were an escape from the dour reality of his role as leader of a people who had long since let go of hope for a better future. Life on the island of Volcaron—named after its pitiful inhabitants—was one of survival and little else, and the consensus among the people was that they were simply a damned race, doomed to live out their days as gatherers and scavengers, eking out an existence in a place that even the hardiest maritime creatures had long-forsaken. There was little motivation among the despondent Volcaron people to work to improve their lives, and, instead, they spent their days foraging in the island's vast, tangled forests in disorganized fashion for whatever sustenance they could extract from its sparse resources.

However, the Volcarons' grim existence hadn't always been so. They had once been a seafaring people, and for centuries, their ships had plundered coastal settlements on two continents. Generations before Morgoratt's name had begun to be uttered in fearful tones, his great-great-grandfather, a notorious pirate captain, discovered the island that itself became known as Volcaron. There, the captain and his crew found an unspoiled paradise—an island rich in fruit and game, with lush vegetation, fertile soil, and fresh water as clear as crystal. Astonished by the beauty and abundance of the place, the pirates decided to give up their roving ways and they gladly settled there to enjoy a life of indulgence and leisure. However, by nature, the Volcarons were a gluttonous, wolfish race who had little concept of self-control or conservation. Over the following decades, they harvested the island of its riches, taking everything they wanted from the land and the sea without inhibition. Like ravenous locusts, they stripped the place of its natural resources and food, and when the island had been left bare, the covetous nature of the Volcarons drove them to war among each other for dominance and control of scarce food supplies. And less than four generations later, the island of Volcaron that Morgoratt now precariously ruled over was a desolate place, its soil and vegetation too ravaged and abused to ever regenerate and its marine life depleted to the point where only the bitter northern current stirred the dark waters around the island anymore.

In recent times, the population on Volcaron had become divided, and their community had descended into factions of squabbling tribes that fought among themselves and raided each other's ramshackle settlements for food and provisions. Overall, there had been little in the way of organized, structured society on the island of Volcaron for many years until a jaded, but enterprising young man named Morgoratt came to prominence, rising out of tribal obscurity to become a feared authority figure. From an early age, Morgoratt had been proud of what he termed the "noble blood" of his great-great pirate grandfather—a family tie that he believed set him apart and gave him a feeling of superiority over his less-ambitious countrymen. As a boy, he'd been obsessed with the delusions of grandeur he'd assumed from exaggerated yarns told to him about his great-great-grandfather's rampages throughout foreign lands. The old stories had emboldened him and intoxicated him with the sense that he alone—as his pirate grandfather's only living blood heir—could lift his pitiful people out of the mire and make Volcaron great again. When Morgoratt was the tender age of thirteen, the chieftain of his village had been an utterly wretched buffoon—a boorish, violent leader who had presided over the last of the fruit trees being irreparably ravaged of their bounty, the animals disappearing, and the lagoon being overfished until the Volcarons were on the edge of starvation. He'd overseen it all and had done nothing. The young Morgoratt, proud and spiteful, had looked upon the destruction and waste caused by the chieftain's neglect with contempt. After that, he had not dwelt on his eventual decision to kill the elder man, and his hand had been quick and unflinching the night he'd cut the good-for-nothing leader's throat.

As the years passed, Morgoratt gained a reputation for uncompromising ruthlessness, thinking nothing of taking the life of any person who he felt was a challenge to his authority. Before he could barely grow a beard, a fresh-faced Morgoratt had taken complete control of his own village and the surrounding area, and by the time he'd become a man, he had earned the fearful respect of all across the island.

Morgoratt's eventual emergence as the uncrowned leader of the Volcarons had been a result of the one quality that he held above most of the rest of his compatriots, and that was his chillingly focused intelligence. There were few on the entire island that could match him in a dispute—verbally or otherwise—and he was calculated and cold-hearted in all of his dealings. Over a number of years, the young Morgoratt had worked methodically to gain the trust of the various warring factions on the island, placating churlish local chieftains with his charisma, gifts of food and insincere flattery that played to the natural egotism of the Volcaron race. Eventually, after much planning and guileful diplomacy, Morgoratt had, by his thirty-seventh year, managed to unify the island's tribes into a shaky alliance; with much effort, he believed he could organize the clans into a force that might allow him to lead his people out of the squalor of their wretched existence, thereby returning to the glory years of his great-great-grandfather's era. It was an obsession that haunted him—a constant feeling of urgency that clawed at his mind during the day and night and which had given way to a further ambition: to achieve his goal of restoring Volcaron to greatness before the remaining population starved to death. Truthfully, Morgoratt's actual concern was not the welfare of Volcaron's inhabitants. Despite his outward shows of interest, he cared little for the wellbeing of his lazy, wasteful countrymen, the majority of whom he looked upon with indifference. No, *his* concern—practical and sobering—was simply that there was little point in being the ruler of a dead island.

As the briny wind irritated the bare skin on his face and clawed at his long, dirty, black hair, Morgoratt stared out across the grey ocean and contemplated the plan that so deeply consumed him. At sundown that evening, he would host the twelve chieftains of the island to inform them of his plan for the Volcarons' future. Critically, he needed the full cooperation of the leaders of the villages to configure the island-wide work effort that he believed would bring his vision to reality. It was crucial to Morgoratt's ambitions that his authority went unchallenged by the other leaders on the island, and as he surveyed the squalid coastline with disgust, he determined that he would do everything necessary to achieve his victory.

*

That night, as a fragment of the moon fought against the barely-yielding darkness and the ghostly moan of the seaward wind wafted across the island, Morgoratt and the village chieftains gathered in the sullen light of the former's cabin. The twelve guests—a rowdy bunch of cantankerous, bearded men—were seated around a long, wooden table, on top of which rested a flickering candle and a dozen tankards brimming with the coarsest moonshine. At the head of the table sat a glowering Morgoratt, impatient to conclude the evening's important business and for the chieftains to leave from his sight. Before that, however, he needed to be sure of their cooperation. With a grunt, Morgoratt rose to his feet, and the twelve pairs of eyes fixed on him expectantly.

"I do not wish to make merry this evening," began Morgoratt coldly.

"Those of you, who may be of the impression that I have requested your presence for the purpose of drunken foolery, leave my house now."

The chieftains remained silent, each one stealing a skeptical glance at the man beside him.

"Indeed," Morgoratt went on, his tone colorless. "The time has arrived when we Volcarons must cease yielding to the vices that have held us back as a nation for generations. My countrymen, the island is barren and lifeless, and the seas around us are polluted and rotten. Each day, our people—once a proud and feared, dominant race—spend the daylight hours stealing and scavenging like vermin. The little food that remains is dwindling by the week, and once the winter snows set in, there will be many deaths from disease and desperation. The weak union that we thirteen have formed will collapse into war between the villages when the people realize that there is nothing more to eat. And then, the famished people will turn on every one of you. With skeletal hands, they will cut your throats and string you up by the necks, and, eventually, the feeble remnants of our country will be no more."

The chieftains—somber-faced at the starkness of Morgoratt's prediction—murmured among themselves nervously. They knew his words articulated an ominous truth that each of them had preferred to ignore for as long as they could manage; yet, the rumblings of unrest among the people had been going on for some time now, and they knew deep down that it was a matter of time before the island descended into anarchy.

"Now, listen to me carefully, my fellow Volcarons," continued Morgoratt. "I have a vision for our people; a plan for a new beginning that will lift us out of the destitution that our once-proud race has become accustomed to. I want to return Volcaron to its former supremacy—to lift our nation up and make it great again!"

The chatter among the doltish chieftains became more animated and eager, though they all still eyed Morgoratt with a measure of suspicion. They were all too aware of their host's callous indifference to the needs of others and the cruelty that he was capable of when his will was opposed. Nevertheless, every one of them sensed that the level of their compliance with his demands could very likely affect their own tribe's ultimate survival.

"These are very ambitious ideas," piped up one of the men irritably. "Your words are intriguing, undoubtedly. But it isn't clear what it is that you want from us. You would not have summoned us if you didn't need something from us."

The stares of all assembled turned back expectantly to Morgoratt, who wore a feigned wisp of a smirk on his deathly-pale face.

"I simply ask each of you for your loyalty," he answered with a disarming smile and an unsettlingly agreeable tone. "I wish to unite our people around a common goal of achieving the riches and resources that all Volcarons deserve. But I need each of you to convince the people to, in turn, give me *their* loyalty. Many hands will be required to ensure the success of our plan, and I must make it clear to you that the preparations will be long and arduous. However, the rewards, my countrymen, will be greater than anything you have known in your lives—food, clothes, dry houses, women! And you can have all of those things and more, should you choose to follow me."

The chieftains exchanged unsure glances with each other, some whispering mistrustfully with their neighbors.

"Tell us more of your plan then, Morgoratt," the same, gruff-voiced chieftain who had questioned him earlier queried bluntly.

A thin, self-satisfied sneer spread across their host's mouth as he rose to his feet. He realized at that point that he had won the chieftains over. He knew that they greatly feared a possible uprising of their downtrodden people, and such was the lavish nature of Morgoratt's promises, it was unlikely that any of the oafish chieftains would raise objections.

"That's all for now," smiled Morgoratt ambiguously, privately delighted that he had further cemented his place as the unofficial leader of Volcaron. "I wish to retire for the night to think and plan. All of you may take leave now, and when the time is appropriate, I will reveal more to you."

The chieftains looked somewhat taken aback by the sudden termination of their host's hospitality. However, there were no grumbles of complaint as each man tossed the remainder of his tankard greedily down his gullet and stood up to leave. One after the other, they nodded to Morgoratt deferentially before exiting without a further word.

As the creaky, wooden door swung shut with a thud after the final chieftain had left, Morgoratt stood alone in the dying candlelight. He stared around the empty interior of the cabin and reflected on the night's success as he sipped moonshine from a wooden goblet. His plan had been initiated, and his veins coursed with adrenaline and whiskey as he imagined the events that were soon to be set in motion. He was restless and drunk, and he knew that there would be no sleep for him that night.

3

RELIEVED OF HIS guests, Morgoratt fumbled tipsily in the darkness for the steel poker that hung next to his fireplace. A single ember pulsated weakly at the center of the paltry hearth. Roughly, Morgoratt stabbed and prodded at the fire in a vain attempt to stir it to life before eventually tossing the poker across the room in frustration. He lit another crooked, wax candle using the remaining hot cinders and carried it to the far corner of the cabin. Groping in the dim light, Morgoratt lowered himself to his knees and began to feel around the wooden floor until his fingers eventually located a groove about a meter in length. He released a pained groan as he lifted up a section of false wood panel to reveal a rectangular hole in the floor. By the light of the candle, he reached in and extracted a small, wooden chest which was bound in iron and rattled where a padlock kept its lid fixed closed. As was by now his routine, he placed the chest on a flimsily built writing desk and thrust at the lock impatiently with the key that always hung around his neck. As usual, the anticipation rose inside of him as he lifted open the lid and peered inside. The chest had belonged to Morgoratt's great-great-grandfather—the pirate captain who founded the island settlement of Volcaron—and inside of it was an assortment of possessions and papers that had survived since the captain's death more than one hundred and fifty years earlier. It had been in the ownership of various ancestors of the old pirate for generations. However, there had been none, until Morgoratt, who had been astute enough to make sense of the chest's contents.

Most captivating among the captain's trove of yellowing manuscripts, jewelry, old coins, and various nautical implements was a pair of aged parchments that were rolled up and tied with string. With the greatest of care, Morgoratt unfurled the first of the two parchments, and his eyes studied the series of intricate, hand-drawn diagrams that depicted cross-sections of boats and shipping vessels of various sizes. There were numbers, arrows, and letters littered across the extensive document, and together, they presented stage-by-stage instructions on how to construct a fleet of formidable-looking warships. There were battle ships, row boats and supply vessels of differing sizes and complexities, all sketched to scale with impressive precision and symmetry. After several minutes contemplating the elaborate diagrams, Morgoratt unfurled the second roll of parchment on top of the first. By the darting candlelight, his heart began to thump excitedly as the lines of a great map opened up before his eyes. Almost every single night since his great-great-grandfather's chest had come into his possession in his adolescence, Morgoratt had taken several moments to examine the ancient map before retiring for the night. He had studied it obsessively for years and knew every curved angle, every inch of land and every listed location as if he had spent a thousand years exploring the place himself. It was an altogether beautifully crafted map of a distant land that no living Volcaron had ever set eyes on, yet it was one that was deeply seared into Morgoratt's mind. From one end of the parchment to the other, minute ink strokes denoted a painstakingly intricate coastline that marked the boundary between a sweeping expanse of countryside and an even vaster stretch of ocean. The land portion was consumed mostly by markings that indicated a dense jungle, and at the topmost section of the map there appeared to be a substantial mountain range. By the labored glow of the candle, Morgoratt poured greedily over the sweeping lines and curvatures, tracing the outlines and fantasizing about the place as if it was the setting of some dormant memory of his own. Slowly, he ran his finger along the margin of the coast before coming to a halt where a single word stood out from the page. It read, "Hohala."

For many years now, Morgoratt had fixated on the idea of picking up the mantle of his great-great-grandfather and seeking out the place that the old pirate captain had been consumed with for much of his life. The scraps of his journal entries and ship logs that had survived into Morgoratt's possession suggested that the captain had put together an elaborate plan to invade and colonize a bountiful, untouched country that he had discovered by accident, having gotten lost in a storm during one of his voyages. According to his surviving letters, the captain's ship had run ashore, and, to their surprise, the Volcaron crew was assisted by exotic-looking natives who tended to their injuries and allowed them to recuperate in the palatial surroundings of an ancient and stunningly-beautiful village. Included in the captain's notes were descriptions and details of sumptuous fruits and the most delectable brandy, splendid temples and comfortable cottages, as well as a climate more pleasant than any country he'd visited in his long career of pirating. After several days of rest and hospitality, the Volcarons had been astonished to find that the natives had generously carried out the repairs that were necessary to allow their guests to set sail once again. Yet, the tone of the captain's writings suggested that the Volcarons had eventually taken their leave, not with appreciation or gratitude in their hearts, but great bitterness and jealousy. For years afterward, the old captain's entire being seemingly became preoccupied with the magnificent land that the indigenous people there had called Hohala. Having been too ill-equipped and outnumbered to attempt to capture the village following being shipwrecked, he had determined to put all of his energies and focus into building up a pirate army powerful and numerous enough to return and take the country for the Volcarons. However, unfortunately for the captain, he did not live long enough to see his ambitious plan come to fruition, having been murdered by a mutinous crew member. Some of the final letters written before he died suggested that the captain's obsession with finding Hohala had grown so intense that he'd drifted steadily into madness and paranoia, possibly explaining why his men had conspired to cut his throat. In any case, the grand dream of Morgoratt's pirate ancestor was, at the time, discarded by the Volcarons, and his treasured papers had been stored away and forgotten about until, almost a century and a half later, they came into the possession of the old captain's great-great-grandson.

And like his great-great-grandfather, Morgoratt's days and nights had, for a long time, been taken up with the same relentless yearning to find that fabled utopia and to escape the squalor that characterized the island of Volcaron. Until tonight, he had not confided the details of his ambition to any of his countrymen, preferring to have his plan laid out in its entirety before involving others. As far as Morgoratt was concerned, the colonization of Hohala would be *his* triumph, and he was not prepared to have his glory curtailed or compromised in any way by the interference of others. In his dreams, he imagined raising the black flag of Volcaron atop the highest point in the village and building a new empire for his race in the manner that his great-great-grandfather had intended. The prospect was so tantalizing, so far removed from the pitiful existence that he had known his whole life and which he had grown to loathe, that, at times, it stirred him to roar out in fury in the dead of night.

Finally, however, he believed he had successfully secured the cooperation and loyalty of the Volcaron village chieftains who would ensure that the rest of the disenchanted population would commit to the lengthy construction of the elaborate fleet of ships that Morgoratt's great-great-grandfather had meticulously designed in order to negotiate the treacherous sea journey to Hohala. There was, however, one issue that frustrated Morgoratt greatly, and that was his own limitations as an engineer. Unlike his pirate grandfather, he did not possess the knowledge to fully interpret the complex mathematical instructions and obscure symbols that described how to construct the various vessels that would make up the Volcaron flotilla. Essentially, generations of festering laziness and a culture of dismissiveness toward learning had rendered the vast majority of Volcarons illiterate and ignorant, and there were only a small number—Morgoratt among them—who could actually read and write. Fortunately for Morgoratt, however, there was one man among the Volcaron population who he had long since identified as holding the solution to his dilemma. For months now, Morgoratt had kept a watchful eye on the gifted young man from one of the inland villages who he knew as Suma. A manly, stocky lad of about twenty, Suma's reputation as a builder, carpenter, craftsman, and everything in between was known across the island. He was an extreme rarity among the Volcarons in that his parents had placed great emphasis on bequeathing to him the skills and knowledge that had been handed down through many generations of their family. By the time his parents had passed away from malnourishment and fever during his adolescence, Suma had assumed an impressive array of engineering and construction skills. Word of his prodigious talents had gradually spread, and eventually, the young man found himself overwhelmed by requests for assistance with repairs, construction, and all manner of problems. Of course, Suma did give his services gladly and freely to a point; however, he was a highly introverted individual, uncomfortable in crowds, and he generally retreated from the petty quarrels and power struggles that made up life on Volcaron. As a result, he had in recent years chosen to leave his village and had constructed a small, functional cottage and workshop on the eastern fringe of the jungle where he lived alone and untroubled, save for visitors who occasionally arrived to request his services. More often than not, the good-natured Suma would agree to help those who came to his door, usually in exchange for some meagre ration of food, fuel, or some useful raw material. Truthfully, though, Suma wanted little more than to be left to his own devices to think, to build, to create, and—an ambition that he made no secret of—to plan his eventual escape from the miserable country that he frequently lamented he had been born into.

Fatefully for Suma, his talents had been noticed by Morgoratt. Even though the pair had never met, Morgoratt had factored in the young man as a key component in his plan to take Hohala for the Volcarons. He was confident—having spoken casually to a number of people from Suma's village who were familiar with the big man's intent to escape the island—that he would willingly become involved in the work effort if it meant a new beginning elsewhere.

In the shadowy murk of his sleeping quarters, Morgoratt drunkenly pondered the honeyed words that he would speak to Suma when he visited him the following day. He silently contemplated the road ahead and grinned wickedly to himself in the gloom. As alcohol and impatience conspired to stir his emotions, he reached for the serrated dagger that hung from his thick, leather belt and raised it aloft in front of his face. For a time, his mind lingered darkly on the measures that he deemed would be necessary in order to achieve his ambition, until eventually, he closed his fist around the burning wick of the candle, and the feeble light made way for consuming darkness.

4

CRISP, MORNING FROST clung to the weeds and the snares of vines that crunched under Morgoratt's heavy boot soles. The low-rising sun—miserly at this time of year—peeked indifferently through the treetops, providing the sparsest illumination by which to navigate the curving forest path in front of him. The lingering warmth of whiskey still glowed in his belly, providing temporary distraction from the biting numbness across the rest of his body. The temperatures were dropping, and the daylight hours had begun to steadily dwindle. Within a matter of weeks, the dreaded snowstorms would commence, and the entire island would once again be painted a deathly white. He knew that time was of the essence if he was going to quell the growing anger and disillusion among the Volcarons and prevent the total breakdown of order on the island. The cooperation of all was critical to his plan, and any further delay would likely render it too late to enlist the labor of the already famished and dejected masses. With that concern occupying his mind, Morgoratt stole impatiently through the silent jungle toward the secluded riverbank where Suma's lonely cabin was located.

Morgoratt was bothered greatly as he reflected on the unwelcome necessity to proposition a mere pup such as Suma. It needled him, more than almost anything, to be reliant on others to do things that were not within his own capabilities. Moreover, even though he would never admit it—even to himself—he feared, deep down, that his authority could potentially be threatened by men like Suma who were able to think for themselves and who were not seduced by excess and violence like the majority of Volcarons.

Nevertheless, Morgoratt knew that Suma's rare abilities were paramount to his success, and while he would attempt to curry favour with the young man today, he found consolation in reminding himself that he would be able to dispense with him swiftly once the construction work was complete.

A waifish tendril of smoke appeared suddenly up ahead, and a drop-off to the side of the forest path revealed a narrow, frozen river, the ice discoloured by greenish scum. Around a broad bend, a modest, wooden structure surrounded by an assortment of tools and piled building materials suddenly came into Morgoratt's view, and, as if beckoning him onward, the sharp clang of metal on metal told him that he was in the right place. Stepping out of the underbrush, Morgoratt listened as the din became audibly sharper. With a rancorous lumber in his step, he approached the entrance of the cabin, a narrow, hinged door that was faded and dull from the elements. The situation as it presented itself grated deeply on Morgoratt's mind; once more, simmering resentment welled within him at having to solicit the young man's services in a way that he considered to be an open admission of his own limitations. With a peevish sigh that gave way to a growl of annoyance, he rapped on the door with his freezing knuckles and listened irritably. After a moment of hanging silence, the sounds of clashing metal resumed. By this point, Morgoratt's irritableness had grown, and the icy fingers of the forest air had begun to nip painfully at his bones. Unconcerned about the intrusiveness of his early-morning arrival, he pushed the door open to reveal a neat, but unremarkable interior that evidently functioned as both a workspace and sleeping quarters. Tools and masonry were hung in orderly fashion on hooks across the four wooden walls, while a crackling fireplace provided respite from the frigid conditions outside. At the far corner of the cabin, bathed in glum shadow, was a wide-set, broad-shouldered figure bent over a work bench with a thick block hammer in his right hand. For a moment, Morgoratt watched from the doorway as the man, who had clearly not heard or noticed his arrival, continued to strike at a piece of metal. As he observed the figure's muscular arm rise and fall forcefully, he felt his disdain boil up again, and he indulged in the briefest daydream about how he might one day snap the boy's neck.

Morgoratt cleared his throat dramatically, pricking the ears of his unwitting host. The figure shot around at the sound, his eyes full of surprise and irritation. Although he was of prodigious build, his face was bright-eyed and youthful, and his long, straggly hair fell at wild angles around his jawline and neck.

"Hello?" he called out, straining his eyes to make out the identity of his unexpected visitor through the gloom. "Who enters my house unannounced?"

Morgoratt inhaled to steady his smouldering agitation before stepping through the doorway.

"A good morning to you, Suma," he declared, his tone heavy with insincere warmth. "It's Morgoratt. I've come to speak with you on a matter of great importance."

There was no immediate response from the big man as he strode heavily toward where Morgoratt stood, his features cool and unflinching. For a moment, he eyed his uninvited guest with the greatest suspicion, being all too aware of Morgoratt's reputation for deception and ruthlessness.

"How did you find me?" Suma inquired coldly. "And how do you know my name?"

Morgoratt smiled foxily.

"I'm afraid that you are preceded by your reputation, young man," he replied innocently. "Your talents are widely known, and, if I may say, shamefully underused."

Suma stared back distrustfully at the man widely considered by his people to be the most devious and callous-minded Volcaron in living memory, and his instincts screamed at him to immediately cease speaking with him.

"Perhaps you'll listen briefly as I explain my reason for coming here," resumed Morgoratt before Suma could respond. "After I've done so, I will take my leave and allow you to consider my proposal."

"I don't have any interest in what you have to say," answered Suma sullenly. "I prefer to keep to myself. I'm afraid you're wasting your time."

Internally, Morgoratt fumed at the younger man's dismissive rebuke, his hands aching to wrap themselves around his throat; however, reminding himself of the critical need for Suma's expertise, he smiled widely and feigned an apologetic air.

"I respect your preference to be left alone," continued Morgoratt in a placating tone. "I would never wish to impede upon another man's privacy. Indeed, I myself have never been a man of much sociability. However, the proposal with which I come to you today is one that intends to improve the lives of all Volcarons—to lift our nation out of its impoverishment and make it great once more."

There was no hint of interest on Suma's face, no flicker of curiosity in his expression.

"The island is decayed and foul," he retorted moodily, turning away from Morgoratt to pick up the length of metal that he had been hammering at. "It's beyond saving. There is no life in the earth or trees, and the rivers and sea are polluted. There is no future for this island, except as a place for hopeless, hungry people to scavenge until sickness or starvation relieve them of their torment. I haven't heard your proposition, but I can tell you that, whatever you are planning, you're wasting your time."

At that, Suma turned back to his workstation and waved dismissively for Morgoratt to leave.

"I ask now that you leave me be," he added without looking back. "There is nothing that can save this land, and I have no desire to listen to you further. Now, please, go from my house."

Enraged by his host's insolence, Morgoratt stood in furious silence, his teeth grinding as he fought to resist the burning temptation to plunge the blade of his dagger into the boy's spine; nevertheless, the many, many nights of planning, plotting, fixating, and fantasizing had stiffened his resolve over time, and he was unwilling to endanger his ambitions.

"I couldn't agree more," announced Morgoratt with forced agreeableness. "Before our eyes, our island is indeed dying, and, in turn, many will perish—if we remain here."

At Morgoratt's words, Suma halted his arm mid-air as he began to strike down on the metal. Slowly, the big man set his hammer down on the worktable and turned to face his visitor.

"What do you mean by 'If we remain here?'" he asked gruffly.

Morgoratt's heart quickened as he realized he had finally piqued his young host's interest.

"Like you said," replied Morgoratt, now emboldened to test Suma's mental resolve. "The island is all but dead. There is no future here. And therefore, we must build a new Volcaron nation away from this wretched place."

Suma watched with uneasy disgruntlement as his smirking visitor strode, uninvited, over to a stool by the fireside. To Suma's surprise, Morgoratt proceeded to sit down and drink lustily from a metal whiskey canister that he'd removed from his pocket.

"Now," resumed Morgoratt nonchalantly as Suma surveyed him with a measure of disbelief at his forwardness. "As I tried to explain, I wish to lead the Volcarons out of their misery and hardship. I want to acquire for our people new, unspoiled lands where food and resources are plentiful, and where we will establish a *new* Volcaron nation that will last for a thousand years."

"Nonsense," guffawed Suma. "No living Volcaron has ever set foot beyond this hideous island. We have no proof of the existence of any place that is within the reach of the pitiful fishing boats falling apart down on the beach. And in any case, there's not one person on the island that's capable of constructing a vessel that can make lengthy sea journeys. Give it up, Morgoratt. Go and use the time left between now and when the snows arrive to gather what provisions you can before the people come demanding help that you cannot give them."

Morgoratt peered at him spitefully, composing himself just enough to resist physically lashing out.

"You see, that is where you're wrong, Suma," he persisted, rising to his feet with a serpentine grin. "There *is* one person on the island who has the skill and talent to direct the construction of the ships that will carry our people to a new land of promise—and that is *you*, dear boy! I have the necessary plans and instructions in my possession, but I need a mind as capable and efficient as yours to lead the effort. You were given skills that, sadly, no other Volcarons possess, and the time has come for you to properly put them to use. You have a responsibility not only to your fellow countrymen, but also to yourself to join in the effort to build up a new and great Volcaron empire."

Suma eyed Morgoratt sceptically, his senses warning him not to be easily corralled by beguiling words and vague promises. He was unsure whether or not to believe his guest's claims of the existence of a distant, plentiful land across the ocean, yet, deep within himself, he wanted nothing more than for those words to be true. He despaired at his own unfulfilling existence, and he looked on in shame at the tragic, worthless conditions in which his people festered. As he stared warily into the grinning visage of Morgoratt, with his greasy hair and sharkish eyes, Suma became deeply conflicted, to the point where his head started to ache.

"I need time to think," he responded guardedly. "You have given me much to contemplate, and I must reflect on it all."

"Of course," replied Morgoratt sheepishly. "I understand that it is no small commitment, and, indeed, on very short notice, considering that the preparations must commence without delay if we are to depart before the island freezes over. I ask only that you give what I have said your full consideration."

"Honestly, Morgoratt," returned Suma matter-of-factly after a moment's pause. "I don't know if I can trust you. I don't know you personally, and from what I've heard from others, you use cruelty and fear to get what you want."

Morgoratt considered the boy's outburst with a knowing smirk. He knew, at that point—just like with the village captains the night before—that Suma's subconscious had already begun to ruminate excitedly on the prospect of finally escaping the island.

"My boy," he answered plainly, replacing the cork on his whiskey flask and tucking it back inside his thick cloak. "There are those who do what is necessary for the common good, and there are those who drift aimlessly and powerlessly to their own graves. The snow and ice is coming. You must decide whether you wish to use your talents for the betterment of your people, or to wait around until death arrives to sneer at all of us in the face. Think hard about the type of future you want to see, if, indeed, any."

At that, Morgoratt gave Suma a last, lingering look, which served to unsettle the younger man considerably. Without a further word, the Volcaron leader turned coldly and stepped out into the daylight. For several hours, Suma sat in the silence of his cabin and reflected, long and hard, on all that had been relayed to him during Morgoratt's intrusive visit.

The next morning, as ominous flecks of sleet and hail fell sporadically from the sky, Suma made the long trek to the most northerly village on Volcaron to inform Morgoratt that he was at his service.

5

FOR TEN, LONG weeks, the people of Volcaron toiled and labored to the limits of their famished bodies. They gathered, every day before dawn, on the shore by the northern village, and remained at work until sundown each evening. Over that time, the temperatures on Volcaron fell steadily, and the increasingly freezing winds were a spiteful promise of the torment and suffering that awaited the demoralized Volcarons should they fail to escape the island before the impending snows. Before long, the sleety wind would give way to merciless, daily ice-blizzards, and it was a certainty that, if they did not leave, a great many of them would not live to see the snow recede again.

Under the watchful, impatient supervision of Morgoratt and the twelve chieftains, the people of Volcaron set to the back-breaking work, each man, woman and child of age submitting to the punishing effort out of the twin fears of starvation and Morgoratt's wrath. Unlike any time in their recent history, the people of Volcaron—unified by both terror and desperation—worked as one to create the vessels that they were promised would carry them away from the skeletal island that their own emaciated bodies had begun to personify. Along the wind-beaten seafront, they toiled relentlessly, and it was not long before the frames of seven towering, wooden ships had sprung up along the coastline.

At the center of the work effort was Suma who, indeed, turned out to be a master engineer and an even better organizer. Unlike Morgoratt and the chieftains, who the majority of the Volcaron people regarded with a prudent measure of fear and suspicion, Suma was acutely aware of the limits to which the workers could be pushed. He had objected in strong terms to the involvement of pre-adolescent children in what was often back-breaking and perilous work. He had also challenged one of the chieftains who had cruelly proposed that the workers relocate their families to the exposed shoreline where they could work longer hours to avoid using up time journeying each day to the construction site. On those two matters, he had gone to speak with Morgoratt himself and had threatened to withdraw his offer of help if the already miserable working conditions of the people decreased any further.

Unsurprisingly, these demands had privately angered the Volcaron leader, but, obstinate and dogged in his ambitions, he had elected not to risk losing Suma's allegiance, at least until the shipbuilding was completed. After that, Morgoratt didn't care if the young man lived or died; if he was honest, he was very much attracted to the idea of snapping Suma's neck for the boldness of his demands.

Yet, despite his rancor toward Suma, Morgoratt was soon delighted by the standard of the work, the speed of the construction and, most pleasingly, the likeness that the seven, steadily-developing ships bore to the sketches in his great-great-grandfather's parchments. As the weeks trudged on and the weather grew slowly more inhospitable, the formidable vessels rose higher and higher into the air, and by the close of the tenth week, an impressive armada lined the northern shore of Volcaron. Among the fleet, there were two supply boats, two larger, steep-sided vessels that would be used to ferry the majority of the passengers, a pair of gunner ships that were—just like those depicted in the old pirate captain's ancient papers –lined on each side by an assortment of catapult-like devices for launching rocks and long, spear-shaped projectiles made from the hardy jungle tree limbs. Unsure of what resistance they would possibly encounter, the Volcarons also gathered all of the weapons and implements of violence that they could find. They filled the bowels of the ships with every morsel of food that they could manage to scour from the miserly land, hoping desperately that the meagre rations would be sufficient to see the majority of the several-hundred-strong population through the unknown sea journey. In all, the Volcaron work effort during those ten weeks was a staggering feat—an almost tragic example of what they were capable of achieving as a unified people when it was, essentially, too late to save their homeland.

With the flotilla ready to set sail, there was one important matter left for Morgoratt to address. Although his great-great-grandfather's journal entries contained extensive details about the beauty and bounty of the place he'd recorded as Hohala, there had been little in the way of information about the natives themselves, other than the fact that they were an attractive, exotic-looking race that treated their shipwrecked guests with the utmost hospitality and kindness. However, that was many decades in the past, and Morgoratt had no intention of risking his efforts to take Hohala by arriving there to find a well-armed and organized local resistance. So, for the week prior to their planned departure from Volcaron, Morgoratt turned his attention to training an army. He had become privately obsessed with crafting an effective brigade of fighters out of his enfeebled countrymen. Methods of attack were skills that few on the island were better qualified to instruct in than Morgoratt, who, even in his youth, had built a reputation for his ruthless conduct during altercations with those who challenged him.

Early each morning, Morgoratt assembled groups of men, and with the assistance of the other Volcaron chieftains, they aggressively organized squads of fighters. For seven days, they worked under the cold, grey sky; they trained in weaponry, hand-to-hand combat, and survival techniques. Morgoratt and the chieftains were relentless and brutal in their shaping of the men into soldiers. They abused them viciously, breaking their spirits and bombarding them with exaggerated tales of Volcaron supremacy in generations gone by. The training routine continued incessantly and, by the time the Volcaron flag was hoisted atop the towering mast of the first-assembled warship, the fighters had submitted completely and were restless to fight. Finally, the Volcarons were ready to begin their journey.

On the day of their departure from the island that had been the cradle of their people for over a century and a half, the entire population of Volcaron gathered on the northernmost beach where their imperious armada stood out against the dull horizon. They assembled—men, women, and children of every age—in regimented lines across the beach, shivering as the freezing sea wind, bitter and salty, harassed their creaking frames. They carried no possessions other than the clothes on their backs, it having been Morgoratt's insistence that only items essential for their mission be permitted to take up space on board the ships. At the front of the crowd, in the shadow of the largest of the ships, the chieftains congregated together where they eagerly discussed the impending voyage. They sensed a great relief and some measure of excitement among the exhausted people that the work was done and that they were about to escape the slow, inevitable demise that awaited them if they stayed; however, each of the chieftains—Morgoratt himself included—were all too aware that their people teetered on the knife's edge of starvation, and it would take very little for mutiny to set in.

With the Volcarons assembled on the beach, Morgoratt anxiously paced across the upper deck of the largest of the ships. Looking around him at its neat sails, impressive rigging, and the towering mast that rose into the sky like an enormous javelin, he felt impatient to depart. However, first, he wished to mark the momentous occasion by delivering some final words to his people as they prepared to leave their island purgatory forever. With a long exhalation of breath, he strode intently toward the edge of the deck that overlooked the beach. Below him, the teeming throng of Volcarons stood shivering in their uniform lines, and a ripple of commotion stirred among the people as they noticed Morgoratt looking down at them. When the crowd's interest had been sufficiently roused, the Volcaron leader raised his hand authoritatively to quench the chatter, and an obedient hush descended.

"My people!" Morgoratt hollered, his animated roar echoing across the beach. "I want you to think for a moment about Volcaron, the land that we are about to leave behind. Think about the color of the earth, dusty and grey, and the trees, withered and choked by the pollution from its rivers. Think about the dried skeletons of the animals that litter the beaches and pathways. And visualize the creaking, damp shack that each of you once called your home."

Down on the beach, the people exchanged subdued, knowing glances with each other as they contemplated the wretched place that they had all been born into.

"Now, I want you to ask yourselves, do you *believe* that you deserve better?"

After a moment of mumbling and murmuring, there came a staggered, collective reply in the affirmative from across the beach.

"We, my fellow Volcarons," continued Morgoratt, "have achieved something that none of our ancestors could manage since the founders of the island arrived here over one hundred and fifty years ago. For too long since then, our people have worked and slept and lived among the waste and decay handed down to them by previous generations of incapable Volcarons. But now, *we* are the generation that has the opportunity to alter Volcaron history; to rebuild—to *redefine* what it means to be a Volcaron!"

Morgoratt brought his fist down with a thump on the ship's wooden bow rail, his emotion rising steadily. The crowd grew more animated in response; some of them shouted up excitedly in agreement, and Morgoratt sensed that he had begun to awaken within them some measure of long-dormant, latent pride. He knew they were his to command completely now.

"Well, let me share this with you," he continued wildly. "The place, where we will achieve the noble future we deserve, lies far beyond the faint line of the horizon. This land that I have spoken to you of, where there is wealth and abundance greater than any living Volcaron has experienced, was trod on a long time ago by our great sea-faring ancestors, and now it is time for *us*, their descendants, to take the country for ourselves. It is there—in beautiful, plentiful Hohala—that we will make the Volcaron race proud and powerful once more."

He had his audience captivated. None of them spoke a word. Even Suma, who stood discreetly to the fringe of the crowd, was enthralled.

Morgoratt's voice quickened as he grew increasingly impassioned. It was as if the reality of the words he uttered had long been smouldering within him, and now, finally, the time had come for them to be given voice.

"Too long we have festered in a wasteland," he continued at a shout. "Too long we've been exiled to the margins of nature's wealth. Today, we right this injustice!"

By now, the pitch of Morgoratt's tone had developed into a growl, and the knuckles of his tightly clenched fists had turned white.

"Hohala and all of its riches await us, my brothers and sisters, and soon we will raise the black flag of Volcaron to the top of its highest tower. Are you ready to fight for what you deserve?"

"Yes!" the entire crowd shouted.

"Are you ready to build a proud Volcaron legacy?" Morgoratt went on dramatically.

Once more, the electrified mob roared in agreement.

"Then, my people, ready yourselves!" cried the Volcaron leader as he reached for the dagger that hung by his belt and thrust its blade to the sky. "And, when the time comes, be prepared to do whatever we must to take Hohala in the name of Volcaron. Our future begins, now!"

At that, the crowd burst into a fever of cheering and riotous chanting. Many of the men among the multitude began to stamp their feet and beat their chests like violent, frenzied gorillas, and as one, they chanted thunderously, "Volcaron! Volcaron! Volcaron!"

A smirk snaked its way across Morgoratt's mouth in response to the fervour that he had instigated among his people. Hohala, and the greatness he craved, seemed close enough to taste.

6

By MID-MORNING, THE sails were raised across the flotilla that it was hoped would deliver the Volcaron people to a new era. In each of the passenger ships, every possible inch of space was taken up with anxious Volcaron adults and children. In the dark bowels beneath the deck, they huddled uncomfortably and tried to ignore the nauseating rocking of the boats on the waves that beat against the vessels' sides. For the majority of unassuming Volcarons, the conditions on board were dirty, dark, and severely cramped. The only light that managed to penetrate the gloom of each of the ships' bellies was through a trap door that led onto the top deck by way of a ladder. In the darkness, families shivered helplessly and clung to each other for warmth as the sickest among them wheezed and coughed, and small children cried out in distress.

Above deck, however, Morgoratt, the chieftains, and the choicest of their fighters looked out upon the mysterious horizon as the bluster of the sea breeze stung their faces and caused their eyes to water. Positioned across the seven ships, the chieftains had been directed by Morgoratt to ensure that absolute order was maintained on each of the vessels, and that any whisperings of mutiny among the passengers were to be dealt with in the swiftest and harshest of manners. Morgoratt knew that the journey would be lengthy and arduous and that some among their numbers would likely perish from disease or exhaustion; nevertheless, there could be no dissent tolerated if his grand ambitions were to be realized, and he had left the chieftains in little doubt about what was expected of them should any person pose the threat of upheaval.

As his armada began to sail out from the shore, Morgoratt stood on the deck of the largest war ship and stared back at the bleak island of Volcaron with its gnarled jungle and jagged, forbidding coastline. He wished to never set eyes on the place again, and as the empty landmass began to slowly fade from sight into the mist that perpetually encircled it, he pledged to himself once again that he would not allow anything to prevent him from realizing his goals.

For the remainder of the day and through the freezing ocean night, the caravan of Volcaron ships sailed west, moving silently through the darkness like a pack of jackals closing in on some unsuspecting prey. Then, in the morning, the chieftains rose from their own more comfortable sleeping quarters to observe that the color of the ocean was clearer and more spar-kling-blue than any waters that they had witnessed in the vicinity of the island they'd left behind. To the jaded Volcarons, weary of their lifeless homeland, it was a stunning, spiriting sight, and the mood among the people was lifted significantly at the promise it yielded.

As they sailed onward, the progress of the voyage pleased Morgoratt. They maintained a straight course, moving in a resolute, westward line that continued across a vast ocean where there was not a single hint of dry land in any direction. Had it not been for the deep faith that he placed in his great-great-grandfather's ancient maps, the Volcaron leader might easily have panicked at the sheer immensity of the seas that surrounded them. However, for five days, he drove them relentlessly onward as they sailed blindly into the distance with only the old pirate captain's aged parchments to serve as assurance.

Then, on the morning of the sixth day following their departure from Volcaron, just as the dawn light had begun to conjure a spectrum of regal colors across the sky, Morgoratt was woken from his uneasy slumber by a yelp of excitement outside of his private cabin. Springing to his feet, he burst through the doorway to the top deck. As he shielded his eyes against the blinding morning glare, his heart began to thump, and he dropped to his knees in stunned disbelief. There, in the distance straight ahead, set against the palette of the dawn sky, lay a sprawling landmass that stretched further than Morgoratt's naked eye could see. The young, male crew member whose cry had alerted him stood next to him, gesturing wildly toward the rolling coastline ahead.

"Is that it, sir?" he inquired excitedly. "Have we made it?"

Morgoratt gave no reply. Instead, he reached inside of his matted, fur robe and withdrew a sheet of parchment. For a moment, he studied the document intently.

"Yes, boy," he responded colorlessly, fighting to maintain his measured demeanor. "I believe that is indeed Hohala."

As the commotion above deck grew, the rest of those on board woke and congregated excitedly to look out at the land that pure desperation had led them to. Across the entire fleet, the sea-weary passengers emerged into the sunlight—many of them for the first time since they'd departed Volcaron days before—and wept in relief at the sight of the unknown world before them.

*

A dawn chorus of birdsong from outside in the gardens of the royal mansion filled Princess Caralisa's ears as she made her way down to the banquet hall to eat breakfast with her father, King Benjamin. Through the expansive window of the mansion's third floor atrium, she saw that it was to be another glorious late spring day in Hohala. She smiled at the confirmation of fine weather, given that her father was to address the people that evening as he always did to mark the beginning of a new Hohalian season. She had agreed to be by his side during the public gathering just like she had done throughout her childhood, but on this occasion, she was particularly excited to have persuaded Nicholas Stone to stand with them during the address. Nicholas had been highly reticent to put himself into a situation where he was the focus of so much attention, but Caralisa had gently chided him for weeks about making it known publicly that they were now a couple. In the past few weeks, the princess and Nicholas had enjoyed a whirlwind romance, having finally admitted their true feelings for each other. Caralisa had always regarded Nicholas as a special friend growing up, appreciating his unassuming, gentle manner and the way he could make her laugh without even trying. However, now on the cusp of his eighteenth year, Nicholas was the subject of much whispering among the females of Hohala, having grown into a ruggedly handsome young man. Indeed, his development into the strapping lad he'd become had, for a long time, not escaped the attention Princess Caralisa, and it was to her delight that Nicholas had returned her nervous kiss that day on the beach. Now, weeks later, Nicholas found himself in the unexpected position of being invited to stand alongside the royal family during King Benjamin's seasonal address, and, being a person who preferred to shun the limelight, he felt a measure of nervousness at the prospect.

"Who knows?" Caralisa had teased him with a mischievous glint in her eye on the day she had invited him to join her for the ceremony. "You might be standing up there addressing the Hohalians as their king one day!"

Although he knew she was largely poking fun, the very notion of such a public role unsettled him, and his only response to the princess's joshing had been to laugh it off awkwardly. As far as Nicholas was concerned, if there was a person who had it in them to be Hohala's king and spiritual shepherd, it was certainly not him.

Descending the spiral, stone staircase that led to the ground floor banquet hall, Caralisa hummed to herself happily as she thought of the fun that always followed after her father's end-of-season address. There would be dancing and feasting, and the entire Hohalian population would throw open their doors to each other in one grand celebration of their community and of the divine Nexus that provided for them so generously. As she'd gotten older, Caralisa had grown to love socializing and interacting with the ordinary Hohalians, and in turn, they'd come to love her, both as their princess and as one of their own. Although the people revered her father, King Benjamin, they adored Caralisa for her straight-talking, kindly manner. She lacked the airs expectant of her royal title, and by the time she had turned seventeen, she'd become known throughout the village as "the people's princess."

The aroma of fresh baking invaded her nostrils immediately as she pushed open the heavy, banquet hall door. The chamber—a cavernous space with stone walls, a plunging, arched ceiling lined with candelabras, and a long, ancient dining table—was brightly lit, and at the head of the table the king himself was seated, dressed smartly in one of his most elegant purple robes. Caralisa smiled as she approached her father who, to her surprise, wore a somewhat haggard expression. With his furrowed brow, he appeared to be deep in thought, and a plate of fresh fruit lay on the table in front of him, untouched.

"A blessed morning to you, father!" Caralisa greeted him cheerily. "Such a beautiful day awaits us—the perfect weather for your address!"

The king started at the sudden sound of her voice, and it seemed as if he had been jolted out of some unsettling day-dream.

"Good morning, my dear daughter," he replied with forced brightness, rubbing his forehead in a seeming attempt to compose himself. "I didn't hear you approaching."

Caralisa touched her father concernedly on the shoulder as she seated herself down next to him. The king, a usually twinkle-eyed, white-haired gentleman of seventy, looked at her wearily, his long, thick beard frayed at the edges where he had been rubbing at it.

"Father?" the princess inquired. "Are you alright this morning? You seem worried or unhappy. Is something the matter? Are you anxious about speaking to the people this evening?"

King Benjamin smiled at his daughter with tired affection.

"I apologize, my love," he answered softly. "Of course, I am quite looking forward to speaking to the villagers. My mind has been distracted all night. Nothing to worry about, I'm sure."

Caralisa eyed him curiously. Her father was clearly apprehensive about something, and it bothered her to think of him upset.

"Are you sure, Father," she pressed. "I can tell that there is something troubling you—I can see it in your eyes."

At that, the king broke eye contact, and his gaze fell to the floor.

"Father, please," insisted Caralisa quietly, placing her hand on his. "We've talked about the need for you to keep me informed and to not shelter me. I'm an adult now and will one day be queen. As I've said a thousand times, you have a duty to teach me and to really expose me to the work you do and the decisions you make—good or bad. How else am I going to be ready when the time comes for me to lead Hohala?"

King Benjamin stared at his beloved daughter, stunned—as he often was—at her maturity, her youthful beauty, and the eloquence with which she articulated herself. Although he had always wanted only to protect and cherish her—particularly since her mother, the late queen, passed away when she was a child—he knew that her assertions were correct; one day, his young princess would be charged with guiding their entire population, and it was crucial that she was ready when the time came.

"Oh, it's just an old man's tired mind, my dear," he smiled at her weakly, though her dubious stare immediately indicated she knew otherwise, to which he responded with a long, resigned sigh. "I did not sleep much last night. My mind was troubled by dark thoughts."

"Dark thoughts?" the princess questioned, unnerved by her father's uncharacteristic fretfulness. "What do you mean?"

The king cleared his throat awkwardly as he attempted to verbalize the worry on his mind.

"It is difficult for me to explain," he sighed. "As I lay awake in the darkness, I could sense that the Nexus was troubled. It was as if the very spirit of Hohala had been disturbed; I could feel the presence of something dark and unknown penetrating our borders, and it made me fear for the harmony of our land."

"Father," responded Caralisa softly after a moment's reflection on his words. "You're probably just a little anxious about speaking publicly. The seasons are changing over, and there is much preparation to be done for the summer harvests. It is a lot to organize and direct, and, forgive me, but you're not getting any younger. If you would just allow me to have a greater responsibility in the running of the village! It's become a lot of work for you to do alone, and you should let me help you."

King Benjamin beamed lovingly at his daughter, appreciating her enchanting smile and the earnestness that lingered in her eyes always.

"My dear girl," he answered. "You are wise, decent, and kind beyond your years. You will make an excellent queen one day."

"Only, though, if you *let* me help you," she scolded gently. "I really mean it, Father. I am more than capable of carrying out the royal duties."

"Of course!" chuckled the king, finding his daughter's persistence endearing. "I will teach you all of the good and bad habits that I have learned through my many years as king."

"Don't joke, Father," replied Caralisa with a hint of sternness. "I'm very serious."

"I'm sorry, my love," he responded tenderly. "You will learn it all in good time—indeed, starting this evening at the public gathering. And, I've heard whisperings among some of the servants that a young Master Stone is to join *us* tonight for the festivities. Is this correct?"

Caralisa blushed instantly, slightly flustered by the teasing expression on her father's face.

"Um, yes," she said with a wry grin. "Nicholas is joining me at the celebration."

"Excellent!" replied King Benjamin, his earlier dreary demeanor overtaken by the good-humoured exchange with his daughter. "Nicholas is a very fine young man. We'll be delighted to have him by our side. In any case, it would be good for him to be involved in the workings of the royal family on important days like this—you know, so he can see it all for *himself*."

"Oh, you stop it, Father," laughed a rosy-cheeked Caralisa as she swatted the king's shoulder playfully. "I *am* very happy that Nicholas is coming. He's…great."

King Benjamin smiled, amused.

"Then let us prepare ourselves for tonight and have no more talk of worries today," he chortled, rising determinedly to his feet. "This day marks a fresh new season for the Hohalians, and, as always, is an occasion to look forward to with the joy of promise in our hearts. I must retire to my chamber now to collect my thoughts for the address. I will see you later this evening, my princess."

For a moment, Caralisa sat and watched as her aging father shuffled slowly through the chamber doorway, and she suddenly felt an inexplicable sense of unease well up inside of her too.

"It's nothing," she whispered to herself firmly as she grabbed a handful of purple grapes from her father's abandoned plate and rose to go help direct the preparations for that evening.

7

THE SANDS THAT fringed the coast in an endless line seemed like white snow to the awestruck Volcarons. All along the shorefront, hospitable waves of the most striking turquoise kissed the land's edge gently as the sun smiled its soft rays across the entire country, and a gentle current of warm air filled the place with the most pleasant and soul-soothing aroma of sea-salt and jungle blossoms.

Amid a racket of cheering and clamorous excitement, the Volcaron ships crept slowly along what Morgoratt was convinced was the Bay of Hohala, searching for a place where they could discreetly dock their fleet. For a lengthy spell, they hugged the coastline, scouring the indented inlets and the rocky, maritime landforms that increased in height and jaggedness as they travelled further south.

After some time, the morning fog began to subside, and a lone rock formation that bore an uncanny likeness to that of a screaming monkey or ape towered above the water like a sentinel. To Morgoratt's delight, the bizarre landform appeared almost identical to a marking on his great-great-grandfather's map that indicated the mouth of the Bay of Hohala. Clenching his fists in anticipation, he composed himself with an intake of breath.

Impatiently, Morgoratt's eyes explored the seafront as it opened up before them. He marvelled at the vivacious colors of the plant life and the dazzling flecks of light that danced on the waves like winking diamonds. Lost in his thoughts, he was entranced by the quiet serenity that seemed to be intrinsically present within every rolling wave, in the call of unseen birds from the forest beyond, and in the caressing warmth of the morning sun. As the ships drifted along the untouched coastline, the Volcaron leader hungrily surveyed the topography of the land. After some time, his eyes caught sight of a great, raised mound of earth several miles inland. Surrounded by profuse, dark green jungle, the towering landform was steep-sided in every direction, curving upward to where the sharp angles quickly evened out into a vast, flat summit like that of a plateau or tableland. As Morgoratt examined the enormous landform, his heartbeat began to hasten, his impatient mind evaluating the surrounding countryside intently. After several minutes of deliberation, he strode to the front of the ship, shoved a trio of chattering crewmen roughly out of his way and leapt nimbly onto the wooden railings that ran the length of the vessel. The boisterous discussions across the Volcaron armada fell silent as Morgoratt's voice cut harshly through the pristine morning.

"Volcarons!" he hollered so that his voice carried to every set of his compatriots' ears. "Let all who hear my words bear witness to this most prominent day in the history of our race. We, who have suffered, toiled and persevered in the hope that we might one day find a new home in a place where the waste and destruction of our ancestors can no longer curse us, have been rewarded at last for our endurance. You have kept faith in the promises that I made to you, and I now reward you for that good judgement. Finally, I welcome you to Hohala!"

Immediately in response, a thunderous cheer went up all around as the Volcarons thrust their fists in the air and stared longingly at the virgin countryside that lay open before them. Pleased at the fervor that he had whipped up, Morgoratt smiled darkly to himself.

"Indeed," he continued with a sweeping arm gesture that focused the attentions of his audience on the giant, flat-topped rock formation in the distance, "Each one of you is now a part of the greatest day in Volcaron history. *This*, my brothers and sisters, is the point where we will make land-fall, where I will lead you as we together follow in the esteemed footsteps of the Volcaron voyagers that discovered this paradise a century and a half ago. Once we dock, we will make our way to the highest elevation in the area and fully survey the countryside to identify the presence of any natives that we may have to deal with, for, my friends, unlike those Volcarons who journeyed here before us generations ago, *we* shall not abandon our earthly right to enjoy and to possess the riches of nature while weaker, less-deserving peoples live in comfort and abundance."

Once more, the frenzied Volcarons roared out in their hundreds as they stamped their feet and slapped each other on their backs and shoulders. As if by instinct or impulse, the entire contingent of men, women, and children began to chant the name of their race repeatedly and with the intensity of a people who had long-anticipated their moment of triumph.

"Now, fellow Volcarons," Morgoratt went on once the cheering had died down again, "Let us venture onward and explore the paradise that we'll shortly call our own. Gather your weapons and tools, and let us waste no further time in marking the soil with the imprints of our boot steps. From today onward, this land shall be known as New Volcaron!"

When the ensuing riot of whooping and applause subsided, the Volcarons did as their leader had instructed, and they worked under the hot sun to unload the necessary provisions from their ships. Like an uncompromising swarm, they poured onto the white beach, many of them charging madly across the sands like wild animals suddenly escaping from captivity. Before long, the ships were unloaded and, between them, Morgoratt and the chieftains had restored some measure of fearful order among the exuberant Volcarons. As the noon sun settled above, Morgoratt gave the order for the majority of the people to head out into the jungle while a small band of dagger-clad fighters stayed behind to stand guard over the ships. In single file, the Volcarons tramped and fought through the tangled forest, using the distant sight of the plateau through the treetops as their guide. For much of the afternoon, they wheeled and hauled the lightweight, sturdy carts that Suma had designed specifically for transporting supplies efficiently across distances. It was, however, an exhausting, energy-sapping trek; the jungle itself was overgrown and humid, and there was little talk among the Volcarons due to Morgoratt's strict command that they avoid making unnecessary noise that could draw the attention of any living creatures of the countryside—human or otherwise. In a winding procession, they hacked and stomped for hours through the trees and the thorny coils of vines until, at long last, the vegetation grew less dense, and the stark, overhanging slopes of the plateau appeared in front of them.

At the head of the cavalcade, Morgoratt looked up longingly at the looming walls of the gigantic formation. He was weary from the sun and his exertions during their long passage from the coast; yet, inside, he was impatient and restless for quick success. Without a further word, and to the bemusement of those around him, the Volcaron leader took off at a determined sprint and began to ascend the gravelly slope. Prompted by his example, a number of the chieftains followed suit, pursued then by the perplexed men and women behind them until, eventually, every one of the exhausted Volcarons was involved in an *en masse* scramble to the top of the plateau.

At last, as the late afternoon sky gave way to a blushing evening pink, Morgoratt staggered tiredly up over the crown of the slope and found himself atop the plateau's vast, flat surface. To his satisfaction, he had made it to the top well before any of the others, owing to his tenacity and superior athleticism. Taking time to catch his breath, he strolled curiously from one end of the colossal landform to the other until he was overlooking an almost-sheer drop that plummeted down into the treetops of the jungle below. For several moments, Morgoratt stood alone, drinking in the undulating view of a beautiful, untamed countryside. He could see a great mountain range that ran along the western horizon, while the deep blue of the ocean shimmered and foamed moodily to the north. And then, Morgoratt's pulse stuttered, and his eyes grew wide as he noticed, no more than about a mile below where he stood, the unmistakable sight of a smoke column. Straining his vision, his anticipation heightened as he began to make out an assemblage of small, thatched cottages and amber-colored buildings that sprawled along a sandy portion of the coastline, sandwiched to the south by the dark, infinite jungle. The settlement—more handsome and beckoning than Morgoratt had ever imagined—seemed to have developed outward from a majestic palace or mansion that dominated the skyline, and, along much of its periphery, the colony was enclosed protectively by an ancient-looking wall that glinted the color of honey in the evening sunlight. However, it was the throngs of people that lined the streets that captivated the Volcaron leader; in their thousands, tall, bronze-skinned, graceful-looking men and women of every age were gathered and appeared to be waiting for some expected occurrence. On the swirling, high-altitude breeze, the sounds of cheerful laughter and good-humored yelps could be heard, prompting the enthralled Morgoratt to inch as close to the edge as he could. For a spell, the Volcaron leader watched transfixed as the crowds grew even more numerous in the vicinity of the grand palace that appeared to be the centrepiece of the village, before eventually, a chorus of dramatic trumpet sounds struck up. In the dusk light, Morgoratt could see that the focus of the massive crowd's attention was an aged-looking male with a profuse, grey beard and purple robes, while by his side stood a radiant young woman, the sight of whom caused his face to flush desirously. He could not hear anything the older man was saying, but his words appeared to thrill the crowd who responded to his ebullient hand gestures with cheers and collective chanting. As the man kept his audience enraptured, Morgoratt watched enviously as the girl by his side took the hand of another young man and kissed him on the lips, drawing good-natured cheers from some of the onlookers.

So, these are the Hohalians, he thought to himself spitefully.

He could not say exactly why, but in that moment, Morgoratt hated the Hohalians; whether it was their elegance, the prosperity of their village, or the togetherness of their community—the likes of which the Volcarons had never known—he wanted nothing more than to burn it all to the ground, then and there. He felt his anger rise further, and his thoughts simmered with resentment as a band of fiddlers struck up a lively tune to which the delighted Hohalians responded with gleeful cheers and laughter.

"Sir!" came a young voice from behind him, abruptly interrupting his dark musings. "Sir? We saw people! A village full! There's hundreds of them—thousands maybe!"

Morgoratt turned to the eager-faced youth with a snarl of contempt.

"Do you think I'm blind?" he spat hotly, causing the boy to retreat backward a couple of steps. "Where are all the others?"

The young man looked petrified by the Volcaron leader's sudden turning on him.

"They're coming, sir," he responded in panic. "Some of them stopped along the slopes to rest and take a look at the village down there. It's amazing! I've never seen a place like it."

Morgoratt glowered at him.

"You're impressed by the Hohalians, are you?" he rasped, his tone deadpan and dangerous. "You like what you see of them, do you?"

"I mean, their village looks very pretty, sir," came the boy's stammered answer as Morgoratt's formidable frame loomed over him. "And, well, those women…"

The youngster hadn't the opportunity to finish his reply before he felt the Volcaron leader's long, bony fingers wrapped around his throat. With terrified gasps, the unfortunate young man began to flail his arms and legs in a frenzied attempt to escape from Morgoratt's choke hold, but despite his desperation, he could not break free, and it was a matter of seconds before his eyes rolled back in his head, and his entire body went limp.

"Pathetic scavenger!" hollered Morgoratt as he released his grip on the blue-faced corpse which dropped to the ground with a thump. "Is simpering to those feeble Hohalians the extent of your pitiful ambitions?"

There was no response from the boy's motionless body except for the cold, vacant stare that looked up at the Volcaron leader accusingly. With a snort of indifference, Morgoratt reached down and with both hands hauled the lifeless, young man up by the collar of his tunic, before carrying him to the precipitous edge of the plateau that overlooked the village.

"Bloody fool," he muttered as he coldly tossed the young man over the ledge where he fell like a stone into the overgrown jungle foliage far below. "You couldn't keep your mouth shut. Not like anyone will even notice."

At that, the sounds of excited, approaching voices punctuated the grim moment, and drawing in a long, shuddering breath to compose himself, Morgoratt turned to greet his newly-arriving followers with a deceitful, disarming smile.

8

WHILE THE HOHALIAN celebrations continued outside, a sleeping Nicholas Stone tossed and writhed uncomfortably in the darkness of his cottage. It was late, and his slumber had been broken and restless for hours. A normally heavy sleeper, Nicholas usually reserved his dreaming for lengthy afternoon walks along the seafront, yet, tonight, in his unconscious state, he found himself being visited by the most vivid and disconcerting images. In his sleeping mind's eye, he visualized that he was standing on a white sand beach in the moonlight. He could hear the sounds of the inbound tide lapping gently at the shore, and behind him, he recognized the dense snarls of brambles and thick vegetation as being part of the outer fringe of the Hohalian jungle. Puzzled at his awareness of his dream state, though sufficiently anchored by his familiarity with his surroundings, Nicholas was initially more curious than fearful. He decided to venture along the shorefront, listening to the passive whisper of the waves and appreciating the velvety texture of the sand beneath his bare feet. Suddenly, he sensed a presence nearby; to his surprise, his enthusiasm immediately gave way to an arresting impulse to hide. As if he was no longer in control of his own faculties, Nicholas found himself diving into the thick underbrush of the jungle before hunkering down as low and as quietly to the ground as he could. For several minutes, he lay within the shadows of the jungle scrub, daring not even to flinch. More seconds passed without incident; however, for reasons he could not himself discern, Nicholas remained rigid and alert beneath the tangled foliage. Some moments later, his heart leapt in his chest at the sound of faint whispering from some distance away.

Patiently, he listened with trembling breath, keen to avoid making his presence known in any way. The voices began to increase in volume and number until it was apparent that there was some large gathering or congregation approaching along the beach. He felt a gnawing unease that he could not shake, but convinced himself momentarily that the voices surely belonged to a group of Hohalians who had ventured out for a night-time stroll; yet, as he listened, he noticed that the accents of the speakers were foreign-sounding and strange, and there was a coarse boisterousness in their laughter that made him further wary. It appeared that they were, for the most part, adult males, and it seemed to Nicholas that they were probably drunk.

Alone, and rigid with concern and suspicion, he listened intently to the sounds of some kinds of canvas tents being erected across the beach, and he felt his blood run cold as he heard the hammering of steel stakes into the ground just a few yards from where he lay. Through gaps in the foliage, he could see the outline of two figures who were busy setting up a temporary hut for themselves.

Without warning, an angry exclamation sounded further up the beach. There were frantic, stammered cries of apology, followed by a volley of curses and threats.

"Please, Morgoratt!" came a pleading voice that seemed to belong to an older, weary-sounding male. "I'm sorry! I didn't think. It's just that I'm not very well, and I find it so cold at night…"

"Do you think that I give a curse about you, you old skeleton?" hissed the old man's aggressor. "If I'd had my way, I'd have left decrepit burdens like you to rot back on Volcaron."

"Sir, please!" begged the man once more. "It won't happen again—I swear!"

"You're a very fortunate fellow that you didn't manage to light that fire before I got here," came the growled reply. "If you or anyone else is careless or stupid enough to alert the Hohalians to our presence before we've the chance to strike, then rest assured the punishment will be severe."

"Yes, sir! Yes, sir!" spluttered the old man in terror.

And then, the respondent turned his attention to the others around him.

"Is that clear to every damn one of you!" he hollered with a venom that was deeply perturbing to the eavesdropping Nicholas.

"Yes, Morgoratt!" answered a chorus of voices in unison.

Nothing more was said as the previously lively mood among the congregation dampened. Wide-eyed, Nicholas listened as the strangers settled themselves down to rest for the night. By the tent nearest to him, a male and a female voice giggled to each other as they rolled and shuffled around on a blanket.

"That's the wildest I think I've seen him," whispered the young male voice. "I was sure old Terrowin was about to get his neck broken."

His female companion appeared to scoff in response.

"He deserved to get his throat slit for what could've happened, the stupid old fool," she sneered. "Morgoratt was right to be furious. We could very nearly have been discovered."

"I mean, I knew he had a temper," replied the young man with an exhalation, "But I didn't know he was that bad."

"I've heard stories of the things he's done to people that go against him," returned the girl in a hushed voice. "They say he has no mercy in him, and that killing comes as easy to him as breathing."

The response from her companion was a long, disbelieving intake of breath.

"You realize he plans to kill them all, don't you?" whispered the young woman after a moment's silence.

"The Hohalians?" answered the boy.

"Yes," she breathed, as if she was fearful of their conversation being eavesdropped on. "I've overheard the chieftains saying things—laughing about who they would make clean up all of the blood. And what do you think that all the weapons and training was for? Not self-defense, that's for sure."

There was another pregnant pause as the pair reflected on the severity of their leader's plans.

"They won't know what's hit them, will they?" murmured the young man.

"It's going to be really bad," replied the girl. "He won't stop at anything."

At that point, the pair ended their conversation, and before long, the drone of low snoring filled the empty silence.

In the darkness, Nicholas was filled with horror as the couple's words reverberated through his mind. He felt nauseous and immobilized with rage. The question as to whether or not there were other races that existed beyond the boundaries of the Nexus's embrace—a mystery that had burned in his mind his entire life—had, it seemed, been answered in the strangest of ways, but it was a revelation that enraged and terrified him. From all he had seen and heard, it was obvious that the unknown foreigners were ruthless mercenaries, intent on invading Hohala and murdering its citizens.

As fear and fury rose within him, Nicholas felt a rare and unsettling sensation of bloodlust, followed by an overwhelming compulsion to spring forth from the jungle and kill the one named Morgoratt whose plan it was to plunder their home. With his balled fists quivering angrily, he leapt to his feet and tore wildly out of the jungle.

A sharp, painful sensation like that of a sudden impact caused Nicholas to jolt awake, and after several disoriented seconds, he realized that he was lying on the floor next to the creaky, wooden bed where he'd fallen asleep just a few hours before. As he rubbed his head confusedly, he could hear drunken merriment and laughter from the street outside, indicating that the Hohalian end-of-season celebrations were continuing well into the night. He had left the ceremony at the royal mansion early—much to Caralisa's disappointment—having felt suddenly and inexplicably unwell. He'd not been able to explain why, but there had been something at the back of his mind that had caused him to feel troubled, and he'd explained to the unconvinced princess that it was best if he turned in early for the night.

Now, Nicholas sat alone, anxious and confused on the hard, wooden floor of his cottage, his mind struggling desperately to make some sense of the distressing scenes that had haunted his dreams that night. It had seemed too real—too uncannily lucid—to ignore. He tried to convince himself that it was just a particularly vivid nightmare, maybe brought on by his discomfort at having to stand with the royal family in front of the whole community earlier that day. However, he had rarely, if ever, experienced a dream so tangible and disturbing, so specific in its details, and, eventually, he came to the reluctant conclusion that he had a responsibility to share it with King Benjamin and the elder Hohalians. With a sigh of fretful resignation, Nicholas hurriedly dressed to go and find Caralisa.

*

In the Hohalian royal mansion, a late-night commotion was underway as a handful of harried-looking advisors to King Benjamin congregated around the semi-conscious monarch who rested uncomfortably on a chair in the banquet hall. To the distress of the people, the king had taken ill that evening during the celebrations, complaining of dizziness and mumbling incoherently about some great, imminent danger. As one of the village nurses mopped perspiration from King Benjamin's drooping forehead with a cloth, the chief royal counselor—a wise, white-bearded man named Lawson—speculated sombrely with the other advisors about the king's sudden and dramatic turn. As he spoke, the king's trusted confidant paced back and forth across the chamber, his wise face drawn with concern.

"There is something deeply wrong," said Lawson flatly. "The king has sensed a threat to the harmony between ourselves and the Nexus. The spirits have been disturbed, and the king, as the Nexus's anointed shepherd in this realm, has felt the discord most strongly. The deep affliction we can see in his eyes is a sign that the gods are aggrieved by some menacing force that has penetrated Hohala's borders."

"But what is it?" questioned Conal, one of the king's younger aides. "Who or what could possibly wish to cause harm to Hohala?"

"We only know what His Highness has already told us," sighed Lawson. "Something about a 'great danger' and 'dark strangers.' We have no choice but to wait until he regains full consciousness."

Together, the troubled counselors deliberated among themselves as they attempted to make some tentative sense of King Benjamin's uncharacteristic ravings. A short time later, the company looked up in surprise to see the banquet hall door swing open and Princess Caralisa appear in the doorway, followed by a solemn-faced Nicholas Stone.

"Princess Caralisa," greeted Lawson awkwardly, so protective was the counselor of the king's young daughter. "Please, I told you already that you should not be here. I don't wish for you to see your father like this. We're looking after him well, so you need not worry."

"I am the future queen of Hohala," shot back Caralisa heatedly, taking Lawson by surprise. "I don't wish for you to shelter me."

"Your Highness..." he began consolingly, but his words were smothered by the fiery interjection of the princess whose worried eyes were lined with tears.

"Nicholas has something important to tell you all," she exclaimed. "He too knows of some danger to our people."

For the first time, Lawson and the advisors peered quizzically at the anxious-faced Nicholas, their eyes betraying their annoyance at his and the princess's sudden intrusion.

"Very well," answered Lawson with a sigh. "What is this danger you know of, Master Stone?"

It was the first time that any person of authority had ever asked Nicholas for his thoughts or input on a matter of importance, and he suddenly felt very self-conscious as he stood among the royal family and their closest aides dressed in the same, tattered tunic that he'd worn to bed earlier that night.

"I, um, saw people," he declared, clearing his throat.

"You *saw* people?" pressed one of the advisors with an impatient roll of his eyes. "Where did you see these people, and who were they?"

Nicholas hadn't had the chance to give much prior thought to what exactly he was going to say to the king and his company, and his response was a long-winded, off-the-cuff description of the dream that he'd had about the shadowy figures on the shorefront. He told them hurriedly of the familiar setting of the beach outside of Hohala, of the violent and dangerous man that appeared to be the leader of the foreign intruders, and of the ominous predictions that he'd overheard the young couple in the tent discussing. When he finished, he was almost breathless, and all around him, fearful faces studied him in disbelief.

"This is indeed both troubling and mystifying," said Lawson in a low, grave tone as he halted his pacing in the middle of the grand chamber. "Your descriptions, Master Stone, are quite similar to the vision that visited itself upon King Benjamin. I do not know why, but it appears the Nexus has channelled some cautionary message through both you and His Highness. While this would not be the first time the king has been spoken to by the spirits, it is, admittedly, a mystery as to why they chose you too as a conduit."

Nicholas had no immediate reply. He was as confused as any of them, yet there was something about Lawson's incredulity that bothered him deep down—as if he was reaffirming Nicholas's own perceived unworthiness to be touched by the Nexus. As the counselors argued among themselves, Nicholas brooded morosely once again on the detachment he felt from the rest of the Hohalians, and with a tired glance at Caralisa, he decided he might as well take his leave.

As he turned to slip off toward the doorway, he heard one of the aides question, "So if our borders have been trespassed by some force that wishes us harm, whatever can we do?"

Then, before anyone present could reply, a weary voice spoke up unexpectedly.

"We will evacuate the village," rasped King Benjamin doggedly. "There is no time to spare. Every one of us must leave Hohala—tonight."

9

King Benjamin's face was serious and harassed-looking as he spoke. The counselors and royal aides, with their concerned expressions, swarmed around the monarch protectively.

"Young Master Stone is correct," resumed the king gravely, his eyes flicking toward Nicholas appraisingly before returning to his advisors. "There are, indeed, intruders in our land. At this moment, they have penetrated our borders and they linger like eager predators in the shadows beyond the lights of the village. Unfathomable to us as it may seem, I sense that they do intend to bring us harm."

Closing his eyes, King Benjamin paused momentarily, breathed in deeply, and then exhaled at length. Eventually, his eyelids flickered open, and his eyes were wrought with worry as he turned to his trusted advisor, Lawson.

"There is no time for deliberation," asserted the king flatly. His voice still commanded authority, but there was a darker note underlying his words that betrayed his fear. "The air grows heavy with the threat of ruin and violence. I have sensed the spirits of the invaders by way of the all-seeing Nexus. They will not be reasoned with, and they will not make peace. They wish to take and destroy. They plan to feed and consume like locusts, and they intend to butcher our animals and tear the roots from Hohala's sacred soil. These men are hostile and come armed with both weapons and a hunger for violence. If we remain, our people will be slaughtered and our way of life extinguished."

The king then turned to the gathered assembly of awe-struck advisors with a look of deep foreboding, as if he was himself in shock at the starkness of his own words.

"Order the immediate evacuation of the village," he commanded decisively. "We must move swiftly and without delay. Daylight will be upon us within a few hours, and we must be gone from here by that point. Instruct the villagers to gather only the most essential provisions and to leave all else behind. Then, lead everyone westward through the jungle and into the foothills where we will assemble and regroup from there. Is that understood?"

"Yes, Your Highness," replied the advisors in unison before turning frantically to go and organize the unsuspecting Hohalians as instructed.

However, the counselors were stopped in their tracks by a sudden interruption from the other end of the dining chamber.

"Wait!" interjected Nicholas, the words escaping from his mouth before he had even realized what he was saying. "Couldn't we stay and fight?"

A sea of eyes turned to gape at him, each pair wide with a mixture of irritation and appalment. Suddenly, Nicholas felt very self-conscious. The faces of all present, from the counselors, to the king, to even Princess Caralisa herself, looked at him in stunned silence, as if he'd uttered something foul or blasphemous. King Benjamin opened his mouth to respond, but his words were cut short by the highly-strung voice of one of the other counselors.

"Fight?" scoffed the middle-aged advisor that Nicholas knew as Tristan. "Have you been struck down by some manner of fever that has caused such a nonsensical outburst, Master Stone?"

"Not at all," replied Nicholas, stony-faced and resentful at Tristan's haughty dismissal. "My mind is fine. It is the suggestion that we abandon our home—that we surrender it unquestioningly to a band of robbers—that appears most ludicrous to me. Why can't we stand and defend ourselves?"

"Foolish boy!" thundered Tristan, rising to his feet. "That you would even suggest any person of Hohala should tarnish their soul and jeopardize their connection with the Nexus is blasphemy."

Nicholas was incredulous as the peevish advisor rounded on him.

"So, you want to lead several thousand defenseless men, women, and children into the wilderness like beggars?" he shot back, his anger rising at Tristan's pompous demeanor which was an obvious power play by the uppish politician. "The Hohalians aren't equipped for that type of life. We've nowhere to go—no roots in the world beyond our native soil."

Nicholas looked around at the silent congregation of Hohala's most respected leaders who themselves appeared thunderstruck by his forthrightness in their company.

"You'll be condemning our people to starvation and suffering," he accused them heatedly. "And for what? To appease the Nexus? To leave your pure, white souls unblemished?"

The final sentence Nicholas uttered with a note of bitterness. He knew all about the clandestine, night-time rendezvouses on the beach that the married Tristan routinely enjoyed with the village blacksmith's eldest daughter, so to have the advisor speak down to him so piously was more than he was prepared to tolerate. It had always greatly irritated him—even as a child—when the Hohalian elders, such as Tristan, acted so dismissively toward ordinary people like him.

"How dare you speak to your superiors with such insolence and disrespect," snarled Tristan as he rounded on Nicholas with an imperious swagger. "Just because King Benjamin's daughter has for some reason taken a liking to you doesn't give you the right to interfere in things you know nothing of and have no place knowing about. Away with you now, and do as you were instructed, like a good lad."

Nicholas stared back at Tristan with disdain, fighting hard against the urge to lay the advisor's extra-marital activities bare for all to hear.

"Enough, Tristan," interrupted the voice of Lawson who ushered his posturing colleague to the sidelines. "There is nothing to be gained from quarrelling at this time."

As Tristan took his seat indignantly, Nicholas turned to King Benjamin whose vacant expression indicated that he had barely taken notice of the testy exchange.

"Your Highness," implored Nicholas firmly as he searched the wise ruler's eyes for any glimpse of his former determination. "You can't tell us that abandoning our home is the right way to face this threat. We have nowhere to go! Our people know no other life than here. We *must* stay and defend ourselves. Surely, you can see that."

The king peered at him tiredly.

"I appreciate your input, Nicholas," he replied slowly. "I really do. But I stand by what has been the enduring cornerstone of our race. The Hohalians are not a war-like people. We are protected by and bound to the Nexus by virtue of the fact that we have always looked away from the path of violence. You know as well as anyone that no Hohalian hand should ever cause blood to spill from another living creature, and that is not a convention I will allow to be overturned, no matter how trying the circumstances. The curse of violence will never be permitted to take root among our much-blessed race, and it is our sacred responsibility to continue to place our trust and faith in the hands of the ancient spirits that have so lovingly protected us till now. The Nexus will guide us into whatever future it has determined for us. We shall merely follow the path of righteousness in order to arrive there."

Nicholas listened to the king in awe. He was well-aware of the Hohalian belief in non-violence against other living creatures, but he could not believe that the monarch would have them willingly abandon their beautiful homes, their proud heritage, and their prosperous way of life out of blind, uncertain faith.

"Your Highness," he stuttered pleadingly. "We can't just…"

But before Nicholas had finished, the impertinent voice of Tristan interrupted him.

"You heard the king, boy," he barked. "There's no time to indulge in such foolishness from the likes of you. Go now, and make your preparations to leave, and stop wasting your energy; you'll need it for the long journey ahead."

Nicholas stood seething with anger and bewilderment. He'd expected that the king would be reluctant to command the Hohalians to take up armed defenses, but he'd never imagined that they would concede to the enemy so willingly.

"So that's it then," Nicholas spat furiously, forgetting in the heat of the moment that he was among venerable company. "We should just give up? Is that it, Your Highness?"

"How dare you speak to the king in such a manner!" roared Tristan, his face red with enmity and self-importance. "Have you gone mad, boy?"

Nicholas ignored the advisor's bombastic rebuke, instead switching his gaze to each of the assembled advisors in turn.

"Have *you* all really gone blind?" he stammered almost breathlessly.

"Are you actually prepared to uproot our entire population and lead them into the wilderness—of which you know nothing?"

None of the counselors gave a response, other than to return his stare morosely.

"Your Highness?" persisted Nicholas, his focus turned back to King Benjamin. "Is this really what you believe is the way forward?"

"Enough, Nicholas," the king cut across him sharply. "The decision has been made. You would do very well to fall into line with the rest of your countrymen."

At that point, the monarch turned back toward the counselors and continued to deliberate with them in a serious tone. Feeling well and truly dismissed, Nicholas looked defeatedly at the one person in the room who he was sure would care to listen to him; however, to his dismay, he knew immediately from her quivering bottom lip and tear-strewn eyes that the princess had made her mind up about what side she was on.

"Caralisa," he pleaded, moving back toward her. "You can't agree with this?

Caralisa shook her head sadly and reached out for his hand.

"Nicholas, my father and the elders are right," she insisted reluctantly. "We're not a violent race, and we must not stain our souls by contributing to bloodshed in times of trial. Above all else, we must retain our purity—even if we have to make sacrifices."

"Running away is not a sacrifice for the greater good!" shot back Nicholas, his voice heavy with emotion. "It's cowardly! I can't believe that you would accept a path of exile and hardship rather than stand up for what is just."

"Don't make this difficult, please, Nicholas," implored the princess, her cheeks by now lined with tear streaks. "Come with me, and help me with the evacuation. Do what you *know* is right, deep down."

Nicholas stared at her blankly for several seconds, mulling deeply on her words and on the extraordinary circumstances that had suddenly befallen them. He thought of the raucous, drunken laughter of the invaders that he'd witnessed in his dream. He reflected on the sinister coldness of the words spoken by the one they had referred to as Morgoratt. He deliberated on the dismissal of his views on the matter by the overbearing Tristan. Finally, his mind lingered on the pleas directed at him by the young woman that he loved to submit to her father's orders.

"In that case, I will not do what I know in my heart is *wrong*," Nicholas answered her, coolly as he pulled his hand away from hers, his eyes piercing and narrowed with bafflement. "I'm sorry, Caralisa, but I can't agree to the surrender of our land without resistance. I've always listened to your father and the elders and heeded their teachings, but I won't be a willing part in the abandonment of our home out of fear."

And then, as the lines of the princess's face began to crumple into a pained sob, he added a final remark that he regretted almost immediately.

"I knew your father was completely blinded by the Nexus," he muttered bitterly. "But I never thought you were."

Princess Caralisa's now steely-blue eyes bored into his, her face turning stony and tight-jawed for the first time.

"Very well," she murmured, almost at a whisper. "You've offered your opinion, and it's clear that we're not in agreement. We don't have time to argue on the matter any further. My father has given the decree that we shall evacuate Hohala, and my presence is required in the village. Do what you see fit, Nicholas; if I'm so blind to this foolhardy reality that you alone see, then leave me out of your un-Hohalian ideas."

"Are you serious, Caralisa?" gasped Nicholas in exasperation. "Are you really going to go along with this—this—*suicide?*"

"Enough, Nicholas!" interrupted the princess sharply, raising her hand to halt his outburst. "I've said all I need to say—as have you. I think it would be best if you leave, now."

As his dearest friend's hard words reverberated in his ears, Nicholas felt his face begin to burn and his heart to ache.

"Very well," he replied tonelessly as he fought to smother the rising emotion in his chest. "I'll not delay you any longer, Your Highness."

Without a further word, Nicholas turned on his heels coldly and marched briskly toward the exit at the far end of the chamber. As he swung the heavy, wooden door shut behind him, he could hear Caralisa call to him angrily. He hurried down the corridor, ignoring her cries—desperate to escape the confines of the mansion.

As he burst angrily through the gate that separated the palace grounds from the village, he could see that the evacuation effort was already under way. In every direction, crying, wild-eyed Hohalians tore past him, each one laden down with the simplest of possessions—various foodstuffs, clothing, small animals, and children. As his mind swam amid the chaos, Nicholas felt an urgent need to be alone.

Ducking out of the crowd, he sprinted along the exterior walls of the village until he came to an opening that led onto the beachfront. In the pallid moonlight, he stomped across the sands to where the foam of the tide lapped impatiently at the shore, and he walked along the water's edge until the hysteria from the village could be heard as little more than muffled warbling. After some time spent trying to make sense of it all, he turned and looked back at the ancient settlement. Along the jungle fringe just outside the village walls, he saw that a large group of Hohalians—many of whom held flickering lanterns above their heads—had already gathered. As he watched, it pained him greatly to think of all of those families quietly and obediently gathering up their belongings, shutting up their cottages, and walking away from their homeland without option. Within minutes, a line of Hohalians had begun snaking along the edge of the jungle before eventually disappearing into the lightless trees further up the beach. As more and more emptied out of the village, the faint sound of children crying filled the cold night air, and Nicholas, finding himself almost on the verge of tears, lifted his head to the sky and let out a roar of impotent rage.

Standing beneath the light of the waning moon, Nicholas had never felt so alone, and as the stream of fleeing Hohalians swelled along the jungle's edge, he held his head in his hands and coughed out bitter, helpless sobs.

10

NICHOLAS FLUNG THE wooden door of his cottage shut with such force that the clay tankard atop his mantelpiece crashed to the floor. With frustration simmering in his mind and a heavy sadness weighing on his heart, he stared down helplessly at the shattered fragments. The tankard had contained remnants of the rich wine that he'd drunk before the ceremony earlier that evening, and now the floorboards around the hearth were spattered with the dark, crimson liquid. Nicholas cursed through gritted teeth as he lit a candle which quivered feebly in the gloom of the cottage. In the corner, a pair of piercing, green eyes stared back at him, wide with concern. Immediately, Nicholas felt a stab of guilt at his hot-tempered arrival home, having clearly startled Nightshade who looked up at him, unsettled and rigid. The panther rose to his feet and padded across the room to his master with a cautious gait. Seeing how unsettled the sudden commotion had made his companion, Nicholas crouched down with a weary exhalation and stroked him gently behind his ears.

"I'm sorry, Nightshade," he cooed as the panther purred back reassuringly. "It's been a difficult night."

Nightshade buried his great head, black as the thickest ink, into Nicholas's midriff and purred supportively. As he wrapped his arms around the panther's neck, he thought again about how lucky he was to have him for a friend, particularly now at a time when such uncertainty surrounded relationships with his own kind. With Nightshade's heavy chin resting on his knee, Nicholas gave quiet thanks for his companionship—one of the only constants in his life at that point.

Outside, in the cobbled street, the sounds of panic-stricken villagers indicated the evacuation effort was ongoing. Carts and wagons rattled noisily by, joined by the terrified crying of children and urgent exclamations from adult Hohalians.

"They're all leaving, Nightshade," Nicholas growled, as if it pained him to articulate the words. "There are intruders in our land who've come to colonize Hohala for themselves. The whole village is being evacuated, and no one will stay to defend it because King Benjamin is too damn stubborn to permit us to fight back. None of them, not even Caralisa will hear otherwise. The fools…"

He uttered the last two words with a resentful purse of his lips. For a moment, his mind lingered on the furor in King Benjamin's dining hall, and he asked himself if he had been out-of-line by speaking so freely in the company of the king and his advisors. Nicholas had always shown the appropriate respect toward the royal family and elder Hohalians, but he did not believe the king to be infallible as many in the community did. Tradition and ceremony were one thing, but he had never given over to the absolute deference that the rest of his people reserved for the monarch. He was aware that many Hohalians were generally less free-thinking than him, and he reassured himself over and over in his head that he had done the right thing by objecting to what he truly believed was a disastrous course of action for the Hohalians. Nevertheless, in this time of crisis, the young man was reminded how different he really was from the rest of his kind. His wild ideas had finally separated him from his own people, who were now obediently gathering to be led away from their homes like good, compliant citizens.

"I refuse to live as a tramp, Nightshade," he murmured determinedly to the panther. "This is my home, and if none of the others will defend it, then I will."

With that, Nicholas rose to his feet and picked up a sharp-bladed shearing knife as Nightshade's green eyes followed him warily.

*

The moonlight shimmered on the dark waters of Hohala Bay as two warships, laden with implements of violence and Volcaron fighters thirsty to use them, drifted silently along the coastline. As they approached the portion of the bay where the Hohalian village was situated, a cool, dawn fog encircled the ships, making visibility poor.

On the top deck of the larger of the two ships, Morgoratt stood in silence, drinking in the misty, coastal view as the wind tousled his hair about his face. By now, he was almost manic with anticipation, having commanded that the Volcaron army arrive at the village before daybreak to retain the element of surprise. To the expectant leader's satisfaction, the outline of the settlement appeared suddenly from out of the fog, just as the night sky was giving way to a rose-pink dawn. Before long, the ships carrying the expectant Volcarons drifted into the wide-set inlet where a stretch of pristine, white beach ran up to the Hohalian village on either side. Morgoratt's heart hammered with anticipation, and the long, serrated knife that always hung from his belt seemed all the more heavy that morning.

So, this is what destiny tastes like, he thought to himself with a baleful smirk.

His features taut with suspense, Morgoratt turned to one of the chieftains with a silent nod. Immediately, the chieftain set about alerting all on board to their arrival, and within minutes, several hundred restless, pike-wielding soldiers emerged from the bowels of each vessel to congregate on deck and survey their target from a safe distance.

"My soldiers are ready, Morgoratt," one of the chieftains reported, his back straight as a general, but his mouth curved as a crook's.

"Ensure that you control your soldiers, and understand that if any one of your men jeopardizes the attack, your entire tribe will face the consequences," Morgoratt replied without turning from the horizon, his banal tone unnerving the chieftain into a hurried exit.

The Volcaron leader strained his eyes to peer through the thinning haze that obscured the new lands he'd long considered to be his birthright and bounty. As the mist subsided, the village came into clearer view, and in the early light its quaint architecture took on a peculiar, gilded glow. However, unlike the day before, there were no visible signs of life: no early-morning fishermen, no animals on the beach, no birds wheeling in the sky. Everything was still and silent, the quiet punctuated only by the slap of the waves against the Volcaron ships.

Suddenly, the first of the vessels gave a shudder as it began to run up on the seabed around fifty yards from the beach, and moments later, the second ship also docked with a thud. The Volcarons had trained well for this moment, and in bands of five, they lowered themselves with ropes into the shallow water and waded to the shore. They assembled in groups along the fog-shrouded beach. A far cry from the disorganized swarm they once were, the soldiers stood together in well-drilled formations, tense with purpose and anticipation. As an eerie blend of fading moonlight and glowing sunrise glinted off the blades that the Volcaron horde held poised for use, Morgoratt looked upon his army with a boastful, leering countenance.

What great wonders one can achieve when fear is wielded wisely, he pondered to himself maleficently.

Without a further word, he began to lead his skulking army in a silent march. The pointed steeples and rounded towers of the village became visible through the trees as the parade of Volcarons advanced along the jungle border that fringed the beach. Beneath his cloak, Morgoratt gripped the hilt of his dagger tightly. As he strode purposefully toward a broad, arched opening in the perimeter wall of the village, the Volcaron leader stopped, closed his eyes and drew in an extended breath that caused his lungs to rattle in his chest. Then, with the long-awaited moment upon him, he turned to the silent Volcaron pack, removed his dagger from its rusty sheath and raised it to the sky imperiously. As they had drilled for months, the fighters moved forward across the sand and filed into the soundless village.

With a riot of curses and battle cries, the Volcarons burst into the Hohalian streets, eagerly anticipating shrieks and mayhem from the terrified natives; however, to their wide-eyed surprise, there was nothing. The interior of the town was perfectly still with not even a light breeze to shake the leaves of the trees. With trepidation in their steps, the Volcarons spread through the village, weapons at the ready. They stalked through the convoluted warren of ancient streets that curved to reveal yet more tightly packed dwellings and splendid, cobblestone roads. It was an utterly perplexing scene to the Volcarons; there was no one to be found, no terrified faces looking out of the windows, not so much as a stray cat to glare at them accusingly. And yet, the streets were littered in every direction with ribbons, goblets and brandy jars, trampled flower blossoms, and various other implements of merry-making.

At a grandiose plaza near the center of the village, a waspish Morgoratt shoved his way aggressively through a throng of Volcarons who stood taking in their enchanting surroundings and puzzling as to where all of the tall, honey-skinned inhabitants that they'd observed the day before had vanished to. With his fists balled in frustration, Morgoratt surveyed the place and attempted to fathom an explanation for the disappearance of the Hohalians. Were they all hiding somewhere? Could they be ensconced in some underground shelter? Were they watching him at that very moment, laughing at his confusion and rising anger? With the fury of a man who suddenly realized that he'd been severely duped, Morgoratt rounded on one of the fighters, a young twenty-something who was misfortunate enough to be standing too close to the Volcaron leader.

"Where are the cowardly maggots!" he hollered into the hapless face of the soldier, grabbing the young man's front collar in his quivering fist. "Some slithering vermin among our ranks must have come here during the night to warn them! Which one of you betrayed me?"

"It wasn't me!" cried the boy. "Please, I swear! I know nothing about the Hohalians!"

The terrified young man began to hyperventilate as the Volcaron leader searched his face with a long, vacant stare like that of a snake inspecting its prey. The unfortunate soldier began to plead breathlessly as he felt Morgoratt's white, bony fingers creep up around his neck and begin to squeeze tightly.

"Sir!" came a panting voice approaching from behind.

Morgoratt lingered dangerously over his young victim for a few seconds before tossing the choking soldier aside. With venom in his eyes, the vexed leader turned to the voice that belonged to Alvis, one of the chieftains.

"What is it?" snarled Morgoratt through clenched teeth, spraying the heaving-chested chieftain with hot spittle.

Fighting to catch his breath, the rotund Alvis raised his arm aloft to display a metal-framed lantern from which a miserly wisp of grey smoke rose into the air.

"Look!" gasped the chieftain who had clearly run some distance. "I found it at the edge of the jungle, just a few minutes ago..."

Before Alvis could complete his sentence, he felt the lantern being ripped from his grip. The surrounding crowd of Volcaron fighters watched speechlessly as their leader lifted the lightly smoking lantern to his face, closed his eyes slowly and inhaled the sulfuric fumes. After a moment, Morgoratt's eyes blinked open, and the lantern dropped from his hand with a sharp crack of glass.

"They were here!" hissed Morgoratt, his eyes glazed murderously. "They were *just* here!"

The packed plaza became a throng of commotion as the Volcaron fighters argued loudly about the whereabouts of the Hohalians. Wild-eyed, Morgoratt swept hurriedly through the confounded soldiers in the direction of a wooden bandstand at one end of the plaza. Cat-like, he clambered onto the platform, and with a wrathful swing of his foot sent a pile of abandoned woodwind instruments flying through the air.

"Listen, all of you!" he roared, more frantic and crazed-looking than any of the dumbstruck Volcarons had ever seen him. "The Hohalians are still here! Move, all of you, and rip them out of whatever rat hole they've crawled into. Leave no house or cellar unsearched! Burn the damn village to the ground if you have to, but find those spineless vermin!"

At his command, a collective roar went up, and the riotous Volcaron soldiers began to charge out of the plaza and into the streets. Immediately, their frenzied war cries were joined by the sounds of shattering glass and crashing masonry as they rampaged through the defenseless, old village like crazed barbarians. They toppled trees and set fire to thatched roofs; they broke down doors with heavy, stone-headed hammers, and they ransacked the exquisite Hohalian temples, pillaging their bejeweled statues and religious icons of precious metal.

Back in the plaza, Morgoratt called to the portly chieftain who had discovered the smoking lantern.

"Alvis," he growled. "Bring me to where you found it!"

Before the chieftain could respond, Morgoratt had leapt down from the stage and had begun to haul him like a dog by the scruff of his collar. Composing himself out of sheer fear, the awkward-footed Alvis led the Volcaron leader hastily in the direction from which they'd first entered the village. They exited onto the white shorefront and began to sprint as Morgoratt hauled the chieftain forward with wild, uncompromising impatience.

"There, sir! There!" wheezed the exhausted Alvis as he fought with all his might to regain his breath. "It was lying just there by the trees!"

With a powerful whip of his arm, Morgoratt tossed the chieftain to the ground dismissively. He studied the foliage by the edge of the jungle where Alvis—who now lay spluttering pitifully in the sand—had pointed to. After several minutes examining the thick underbrush, Morgoratt's temple twitched as he spotted a company of delicate, low-growing blossoms whose stems were snapped and broken from where they had been trodden on. Morgoratt's eyes prowled through the vegetation up ahead, and narrowed to see a distinct trail of trampled grasses, vines and branches leading into the jungle. Then, to the watching Alvis's bewilderment, the Volcaron leader suddenly burst into the trees and began to dash through the forest; within seconds, he was out of sight.

Morgoratt raced along the freshly trodden pathway, his movements quick and agile as he darted through the forest and sprang across felled trees and rocks in his way. He could sense the presence of the Hohalians in the distance ahead; he could almost smell them, and the thought of finally snaring his prey was overwhelming. He tore madly through hanging vines and thick, barbed brambles that ripped at his clothing and skin; yet, the pain of those abrasions barely registered in his mind so fixated was he on hunting down the Hohalians.

All of a sudden, the clawing vegetation began to thin out and Morgoratt found himself standing in a large, dimly illuminated clearing. The sound of running water filled his ears instantly, and across the clearing he saw a towering rock formation from the top of which a roaring waterfall cascaded into a foaming rock pool below. Hawk-eyed, Morgoratt scoured his surroundings for any sign of movement, his knife drawn longingly. Advancing forward, he searched the undergrowth and the treetops at every angle, but there was no indication of Hohalians. He stole toward the bellowing waterfall, stopping by the edge of its plunge pool where the spray spat irritatingly at his eyes and cheeks. Morgoratt knew the Hohalians were close by—he was *convinced* of it!

"Where are you, you spineless bastards!" he roared through the gap in the trees high above him. "Come out and face me!"

The Volcaron leader's murderous cry reverberated all around the clearing as he listened intently for even the slightest footfall or snapping twig. For a spell, there was no further sound, save for the din of the waterfall and Morgoratt's own rasping breathing. However, a dull growling caused his ears to prick and his limbs to flinch. He searched around quickly for the source of the noise, and his eyes were drawn to an overhanging rock ledge to the right of the waterfall. Staring at him menacingly was a large, coal-black panther with eyes as green as emeralds. It peered at Morgoratt distrustfully, and the sharp, low tone of its growl suggested it considered the Volcaron leader a threat. With a disinterested snort, Morgoratt returned his dagger to its sheath and made to turn back the way he'd come. However, something caught his attention as he threw a parting glance back up at the panther: there, standing behind the giant cat, partially obscured by a veil of hanging willow branches, was a lithe, dark-haired young man who glared down at him with the hostility of an old adversary. Hostility was chiseled across his youthful face, and armed with a glinting knife in his fist, he looked poised for confrontation.

Morgoratt recognized the young man's face at once, and his mind instantly returned to the day he had spied on the Hohalians from the top of the plateau overlooking the village. He remembered watching enviously as the alluring Hohalian princess had embraced the boy during the gathering of Hohalians outside of the grand mansion. Once again, the Volcaron leader's resentment began to rise.

Morgoratt and the youth stared at each other momentarily, and it was the latter who eventually spoke first, raising his voice to a shout so that his words could be heard above the rush of the waterfall.

"Leave this place today," the young man warned coldly. "Your kind isn't welcome here, and you have no right to trespass on our homeland. Turn around and go, or I promise I will kill you where you stand."

Morgoratt sneered up at him. He felt his breath quicken with anticipation, and he moved his hand back onto the handle of his resting dagger. Attempting to disarm the young stranger with faux casualness, he cleared his throat, slowly and dramatically.

"Greetings to you, boy," he saluted innocently. "And who might you be?"

The young man did not utter a reply. Instead his nettled expression hardened into one of bitter contempt.

"Oh, let's not be so needlessly hostile," chided Morgoratt with a forced chuckle. "My people and I have travelled a great distance across the ocean, and I wish to meet with the natives of this place. May I ask your name?"

"I'm Nicholas Stone," answered the youth bluntly. "And I'm aware of who you are. You're the one they call Morgoratt, and I know all about your intentions. Neither you nor your people have a right to be here. I'm warning you again to turn around and sail back to wherever it is you came from."

The fact that the boy knew his name mystified and aggravated Morgoratt greatly, as did his irreverent words, the type with which the Volcaron leader was not accustomed to being spoken to.

"Very well," replied Morgoratt darkly, the faint grin disappearing from his purple lips. "I suggest that you stop talking now and listen very carefully to me: we are people of Volcaron, the proud descendants of a great, pirating tribe that landed at this place many generations ago. Today, I return to claim this country for my kin and I, who have long suffered in a wasteland while a weak and feeble race like yours lives in abundance. I am here to right that injustice and take this land for *our* superior nation."

In response, Nicholas pointed the razor tip of his knife in Morgoratt's direction as the panther stood rigid by his side, his hackles raised threateningly.

"I'm warning you one last time," barked Nicholas. "You have no right to come here to claim what isn't yours like some shameless robber. This country belongs to the Hohalians, and if you refuse to leave, I *will* kill you myself."

"You stupid boy," snarled Morgoratt finally. "The Hohalians will never see the sun rise above this place again. Your people are feeble and cowardly, as is obvious by their desertion of their home. They neither deserve nor have earned the right to enjoy the riches of this land. You Hohalians are weak and useless; like cockroaches, you scurry under a rock at the first sign of danger. All the prosperity that you have known, you received without condition; yet now, when the shadow of ruin arrives on your shores, your people flee like mountain sheep? What a pitiful race you belong to!"

The latter sentence, Morgoratt uttered so belittlingly that it stung Nicholas to his soul.

"You seem very certain that the soldiers of Hohala haven't already surrounded your men, ready to cut them down where they stand," he retorted, a sudden crack in his voice betraying the insincerity behind his bold words.

Morgoratt responded with a dismissive chortle that made Nicholas instantly feel foolish. For all his bravado, he knew with certainty that there would be no Hohalian resistance, and that the parasitic invaders would be free to pillage and ravage the country until they reduced it to a boneyard.

"What nonsense!" cackled Morgoratt, his lungs rattling loudly as they always did on the rare occasions he was prompted to laughter. "There's no resistance coming. The Hohalians have abandoned this place. They are passive and cowardly—too submissive to defend themselves. No, my boy; it has become clear to me that bloodlust is a gift that has not yet been passed down to the natives of this place."

"I'll prove you wrong when you feel my knife against your throat," returned Nicholas through gritted teeth.

Next to him, Nightshade growled warningly, as below, Morgoratt contemplated the situation; it was just him, the boy and the panther—hardly a challenge. Yet, the idea of returning to the village with the bloodied corpse of the Hohalian princess's lover dragging behind him in the dirt was a tantalizing prospect—a symbolic triumph which would provide a further example to any of his own who might be tempted to question his authority.

"Then, why wait?" suggested Morgoratt icily. "Come down here, and let's settle this now."

However, Morgoratt had scarcely finished his sentence when he unexpectedly flinched at what felt like the hot flash of metal against his cheek. The salty taste of blood on his lips immediately followed and raising his fingers to his jaw, he was filled with disbelieving rage to feel the deep, stinging slash wound. His heart pounded violently, and an explosive anger filled him as he realized that the boy had thrown the knife at him. Morgoratt's eyes grew bulging and bloodshot. With a roar of fury, he charged in Nicholas's direction, his dagger poised murderously.

Though almost breathless with rage, the Volcaron leader's body was as lethal as his calculating mind, endowed with quicker, sharper instincts than any adversary who had challenged him in the past. In his peripheral vision, he could see the flitting movement of the black panther as it bounded down the rock face in defense of its master. As Morgoratt anticipated, the panther leaped at him, emitting a piercing roar that reverberated through the clearing.

"Nightshade!" Nicholas hollered in alarm, having not foreseen his companion's sudden attack on the dangerous intruder.

The huge cat twisted in the air as he prepared to strike down his target, his enormous claws bared. However, with an effortless-looking flick of his arm, Morgoratt made a rapid, upward motion that would have been missed in the blink of an eye. An anguished, feline cry rang out as Nightshade crumpled to the forest floor with a thud. As Nicholas screamed his name in horror, the panther began to writhe and contort in pain. To his master's immediate devastation, his body jerked and convulsed to reveal his bloodied underbelly, from which the shank of Morgoratt's dagger protruded nightmarishly.

"No!" bellowed Nicholas in horrified disbelief. "You bastard!"

Without a thought, he leapt down from the rock ledge with a single bound and threw himself at the sneering Volcaron. With the taste of violence already fresh on his lips, Morgoratt had anticipated Nicholas's attack, and with almost unnatural timing, he caught his challenger's knife-wielding wrist at the critical moment and attempted to plunge its blade into his abdomen. However, Nicholas, nimble and well-built himself, was not to be so quickly outdone, and with all his might he defied the Volcaron leader's demented attempts to stab him. In the ensuing struggle, both tumbled to the ground, each one trying to administer the critical blow to the other.

Then, without warning, a concerned, male voice caused both men's focus to break, and they could hear Morgoratt's name being called out frantically. Recognizing that the approaching individual was not a friend and intuiting that his rival was a superior fighter to him, the grief-stricken Nicholas realized that he had only a fleeting opportunity to avoid being overpowered by the two men and any other Volcarons that might be nearby. Taking advantage of the momentary distraction in Morgoratt's eyes, he mustered every ounce of his strength, and with a forceful swing of his right knee, he connected square with his enemy's abdomen. With a painful splutter, the winded Morgoratt tumbled backward, clutching his midriff.

"Sir! Morgoratt, Sir!" came the frantic voice of the chieftain, Alvis, as he grabbed his gasping compatriot under his shoulders. "Are you okay?"

Wincing, Morgoratt took a second to compose himself before springing to his feet combatively, knocking Alvis on his backside.

"Where is he?" roared the Volcaron leader at the top of his lungs as he scanned the clearing breathlessly.

There was no longer any sign of Nicholas.

"Where did he go?" Morgoratt stammered, hauling the startled Alvis off the ground by the throat. "Quick, you fool!"

"I didn't see where he went!" coughed the chieftain in panic. "I went to help you up, and when I turned around…"

"Damn it!" howled Morgoratt with such fury that his outburst momentarily drowned out the clamor of the waterfall behind him.

Wrathful, mad-eyed, and bleeding heavily from his face, he scanned the entire area again for any indication of Nicholas's whereabouts; however, there was no sign or sound of the young Hohalian, and with one more infuriated outburst, he cursed himself for his own fleeting lack of focus.

The echo of Morgoratt's exclamation faded, and the clearing was still again with the rush of the waterfall and the Volcaron leader's heaving breath the only remaining sounds. As he regained his poise, he looked around to see Alvis trembling, too frightened to even inquire about his leader's well-being. Morgoratt turned away from the chieftain with indifference, and as he did so, he spotted the sunken form of Nightshade, the grass around his body shining from his trickling wound. Without a word, Morgoratt stomped toward the dead panther, lifted him up and flung him over his shoulder. As Alvis watched dumbfounded, Morgoratt marched back into the jungle, ignoring the steady dripping of the panther's blood down his skin and clothes. The chieftain, fearful of being alone in such unfamiliar surroundings, followed behind from a safe distance.

Eventually, with the sweat rolling off his forehead, Alvis emerged from the jungle onto the beach where he once again spotted Morgoratt with the giant panther across his shoulders. Onward he scuttled, trailing the Volcaron leader through the arched entrance to the Hohalian village and toward the center of the now-heavily-vandalized settlement. As Morgoratt went by, startled and bemused Volcarons called to him, speculating animatedly about the bleeding wound across his cheek and the curious sight of the dead panther across his back. Within a short time, a sizable crowd had joined Alvis in following after their leader, and by the time Morgoratt reached the entrance to the great, Hohalian mansion, an unruly gang of Volcarons had congregated around him.

Upon entering the garden of the mansion, a stony-faced Morgoratt turned to his audience and dumped the beast's body on a stretch of manicured lawn. Without a word, he abandoned the panther and ascended the steps of the mansion before stopping and turning to the crowd of Volcarons that now filled the grounds. There was a chilling menace in Morgoratt's eyes as he gestured toward the body of Nightshade.

"Any of you who may have doubted my leadership," he glared down at his gathered followers. "I invite you to look upon the body of this once-powerful beast in front of you. This fine animal was a guardian of this land and was sent out by one of the Hohalians to kill me, your leader, in the hopes that you, my fellow Volcarons, would crumble and accept defeat."

The listening fighters murmured to each other in outrage and bewilderment.

"But—and heed this when I tell you," Morgoratt continued in a steely tone. "I prevailed."

And then, he spoke his next sentence through gritted teeth and with the most chilling note of warning to his audience: "I will *always* prevail!"

Again, the crowd whispered nervously among each other.

With a sharp intake of breath and a new surge of animation in his voice, Morgoratt exclaimed, "I hereby declare a new nation of Volcaron! From here on, this land is *ours!*"

With that, he raised his bloody dagger to the sky in triumph, and the Volcaron crowd united in a hideous roar of celebration.

11

ON THE NIGHT the bewildered and terrified Hohalians fled their beloved village at King Benjamin's command, they followed a path that was well-trodden by their people throughout the centuries. In their thousands, they headed westward toward the furthest point of safe ground that they knew of. Their intended destination, just at the point where the lush slopes west of the jungle extended into inhospitable mountain crags, was a place known to the Hohalians as the Valley of the Eternal Stream. Hidden at the conclusion of a mountain path, beneath a dense canopy of trees, the Eternal Stream wound gently through the valley, amid exotic plants and flowers that grew nowhere else except within its enchanted boundaries. When it reached the end of the valley, the stream poured gracefully over a young waterfall which emptied into an oblong pond of glassy water. A perpetual, radiant mist clung to the water's edge, and there was an air of serenity all around.

The Eternal Stream was considered a most sacred place by the Hohalians. It was the holiest of their shrines, situated at the furthest extremity of Hohala's hinterland and tied directly to the powers of the Nexus. As was customary, on the occasion of the death of a Hohalian, the community would gather and carry the body up the long, mountainous trail to the Eternal Stream. At dawn the next day, there would be a departing ceremony on the shore of the glassy pond, and the king would place the body on the water. The mist at the water's edge would glow brighter and brighter as the body of the departed drifted across the water and closer to the exiting stream. As the body left the pond, the glow would grow as bright as the noon sun, and the deceased would then disappear into the radiant mist to finally become one with the spirits of the Nexus.

Just hours before the Volcarons surrounded their village, the Hohalians began the long walk to the Eternal Stream under the direction of King Benjamin who believed that the divinity of the valley would protect them from the invaders. Throughout the starless night, the terrified Hohalians navigated their way through the tangled jungle before winding their way up into the highlands, carrying meager belongings on their backs or pulling small, two-wheeled carts. Larger wagons, hastily hitched and loaded, carried as many supplies as the villagers had been able to gather up, while the last of the Hohalians to leave the village did everything they could to quickly obscure the trail from the dangerous intruders. It was King Benjamin's hope that the Volcarons, having had all of the bounty of Hohala forfeited to them, would have little inclination to follow them.

On this occasion, just as they did when carrying the body of one of their own to the Eternal Stream, the people of Hohala walked in silence and grief. A funereal air surrounded the procession as the Hohalians mourned the certain desecration of their sacred homeland and carried its remnants toward the Eternal Stream.

Though internally lost himself, King Benjamin attempted to project a demeanor of control and assuredness in the tragic course of action that he now felt was unavoidable. During the short, panicked period that he had deliberated the evacuation with his advisors, the king had privately agonized about the consequences of either abandoning Hohala or remaining to defend it against the insidious invaders. He had not, deep down, disagreed with Nicholas Stone's argument for taking up arms against the intruders, yet dogma and tradition absolutely forbade the use of violence. Such was the acute importance attached to the divine laws of the Nexus, King Benjamin had reluctantly deduced that the only choice available to the Hohalians was to surrender their homeland and place their faith entirely in the guidance of the Nexus. Feeling otherwise helpless and afraid, the king had held out the hope that by praying and meditating near the spring, he would receive direction from the gods.

The cumbersome journey took the Hohalians most of the night. By the time they reached the valley, many were weak with fatigue, and such was the collective confusion and fear that disgruntled voices began to protest in the darkness. Sensing their exhaustion, King Benjamin instructed everyone to stop and rest, and the adult Hohalians set up a temporary camp on a rugged hillside above the Eternal Stream.

As the sun rose above the treetops, King Benjamin gathered his closest advisors, and together they made their way down the overgrown trail to the mystical pond. The mist, swirling at the edges of the water, glowed brilliantly in the first rays of the sun. The grass near the pond was lush and verdant, and the air was filled with the scent of wildflowers. At the end of the pond, the waterfall poured in a smooth sheet over the rock face above, and prismatic colors danced in the spray. The king looked upon the serenity of the scene and tried to comprehend the notion that, at that moment, the invaders were running wild through their cherished home. Wearily, he knelt down in the grass by the edge of the stream and placed his hands on the ground. In silence, his counselors stationed themselves in a line on either side of him and took up the same position on the grassy forest floor. Together, they prayed to the Nexus and asked for guidance.

Minutes, then hours passed by, and eventually, the noon sun rose high in the sky, and its light dazzled the men, disrupting them from their meditation. In the past, the king had been able to connect with the Nexus with ease, but now he was wholly unsuccessful in his attempts to speak to the ancient guardians who appeared to have gone mute in the moment of the Hohalian's greatest need. King Benjamin opened his eyes and lifted his hands from the earth, feeling shaken. To the advisors, the monarch's manner appeared changed. Absent were the voices of the Nexus that had spoken to the king freely, whispering to him and inspiring him in all of his royal duties. Throughout his entire reign, the gods had guided him when he needed direction. Now, however, those voices were worryingly silent.

The counselors searched each other's eyes with unease. In the hours since they had fled from the village, they had held out all of their hope that the Nexus would indeed speak to the king, and that its guidance would direct them to safety. To their distress, the monarch's lengthy silence and forlorn demeanor told them that their prayers had gone unheard.

"My most trusted friends," King Benjamin addressed them with quivering emotion in his tone. "Let us not give up our humble petition to the Nexus. We *must* persevere in our attempt to reconnect with the gods."

The counselors buried their hands in the thick grass once more, concentrating all of their energies. Desperately, they strained their minds in the hope that the kindly spirits of the Nexus would come forth to offer a solution to the dire plight of their people. Hours passed, and there came no response from the Nexus. It was as if the violence and negativity cultivated by the Volcarons' spirits had corrupted the purity of Hohala and disrupted the king's connection. One by one, the advisors' mental energy faded, and they retreated mournfully from the pond until King Benjamin remained alone amid the silence of the shrine.

King Benjamin's determined vigil continued into the following days. During the daylight hours, he remained at the bank of the Eternal Stream, kneeling silently in the dew-soaked grass as he implored the Nexus to respond to his prayers; and yet, there was still no response. Princess Caralisa visited him often, bringing him food and joining him in prayer. The futility of her father's attempts to communicate with the gods distressed her greatly, and her heartbreaking estrangement from Nicholas Stone had only deepened her misery. Each night, as the sun set behind the crooked peaks of the nearby mountains, the princess lay down in her canvas tent and wept in despair.

The days turned into weeks, and gradually, the temporary camp on the hillside began to develop into a settlement of sorts. On one particular morning, Caralisa was woken from her restless sleep by the sound of hammering against wood. She peaked out of her tent to see a team of Hohalian men constructing a number of wooden frames for huts. A single tear rolled slowly down her cheek as she recognized that the Hohalians had given up their faith in the king's ability to deliver them from hardship, and had concluded themselves that they would not be returning to Hohala. For Caralisa, it was a heart-wrenching realization. However, her father was still the king, and therefore she, heir to the Hohalian throne, had a responsibility to lead her people to the best of her ability. She took a few moments to compose herself before dressing in her robe and tiara and emerging from her tent to help orchestrate the building construction. In her quiet, assured way, she began giving orders, inspecting the plans for a new village and did what she could to ensure that everyone worked together efficiently. Patiently, she organized groups to gather firewood, find sources of food, and to begin clearing land to grow crops. As the building commenced, the foundations of a new settlement were set down, and the Hohalians' era of exile had begun.

12

Five years later

ON A BLACK, moonless night, with only the light from a smattering of stars, Nicholas Stone stole through the jungle in the direction of the original village of Hohala. Accompanied by a small band of trusted Hohalian men, Nicholas followed one of several obscure routes to the village. In the pitch darkness, they crept through the twisted jungle, taking great care to avoid creating a trail that could lead back to the Valley of the Eternal Stream. Some of the men carried lanterns equipped with adjustable metal screens that enabled them to hide the flame quickly without having to douse and re-light the lantern.

Under the cover of darkness, they moved silently, at all times remaining alert for even the slightest sign of Volcaron presence. Despite their abundant caution, Nicholas knew that there was little likelihood of there being much activity around. By this hour, the slovenly Volcarons had usually drunk themselves unconscious.

As they had done many times, Nicholas and his men approached the frontier of the sleeping village. Entering and returning from the village undetected was their foremost objective. For several years now, they had made periodic excursions to the village in search of supplies. However, for Nicholas, still bitter and humiliated by his people's submission, there was a rare feeling of autonomy in knowing that the sleeping Volcarons lay unaware of his presence among them; and, as on every occasion he returned to the village, Nicholas took solace in the simple thought of Morgoratt lying unconscious and vulnerable, his exposed neck begging for a vengeful knife's edge. Nicholas drew his dagger from the sheath on his belt and fingered the blade, the old anger smoldering in his heart. It was a small flame he carried with him now after so many years, the passing of time having slowly dulled the ache of grief at Nightshade's death. Nevertheless, memories of that terrible day did linger with him always and drew Nicholas to wonder if the burden would ever be lifted.

On this particular night, however, Nicholas forced those memories to the fringes of his mind as he and his men made the perilous journey to the Volcaron-occupied village with one specific goal.

After emerging from the jungle on the edge of the sleeping settlement, Nicholas and his men stole their way toward an old, weather-beaten cabin situated on one of the lesser-trodden parts of the village's outskirts. Moss-covered and forlorn, it lay silent and long neglected. Before the Hohalians abandoned the village, the cabin had functioned as a storehouse for drying timber and stocking carpenters' tools. These days, however, the din of the woodworkers' hammers and nails no longer rang out with the music of an honest day's work—such things being of little importance to the Volcaron population.

Cautious in their movements, the chances of Nicholas and his men being spotted were slim, but, as always, they remained alert to the remote possibility of a trap. On approach to the lightless cabin, Nicholas paused in his tracks and signaled back to his companions who followed a slight distance behind. Immediately, the men stopped in their tracks, their dark-clad forms melting back into the shadows of the trees. Barely daring to breathe, Nicholas surveyed his surroundings guardedly. Cupping his right ear with his hand, he listened intently. The only sounds at that point were the chattering night insects and the rustling leaves. A gentle breeze wafted by, bringing cool, sea air to Nicholas's nostrils; however, when the wind dropped, the faint stench of rotting food and abandoned garbage infused the otherwise muggy air.

Satisfied that they had so far gone unnoticed, Nicholas signaled to his men to join him by the gable end of the cabin.

"Remember, all of you, don't let your guard down for a second," he reminded grimly.

Nicholas shot a cautioning glance at the men he had come to trust with his life on these moonlit missions, before turning to a hulking introvert named Hamar who shared his objection to the Hohalian policy of inaction.

"Hamar, come with me," Nicholas instructed flatly. "Everyone else, keep watch, and signal if you see anything unusual."

Leaving three of the men in the cover of the trees, he and Hamar stepped out of the shadows and approached the entrance door, their knives drawn and ready for use if necessary. Even after five years, the innate Hohalian guilt at wielding implements of violence still lingered in Nicholas's subconscious. Indeed, although he and his small band of like-minded followers did not openly admit to them, rumors had become rife among the rest of the Hohalians that certain members of their community had broken King Benjamin's decree on the use of weapons. These whisperings caused a large number of Hohalians to shun Nicholas and his companions, to the point where they became outcasts among their own people. However, on dangerous excursions such as on this particular night, the reassurance of a freshly sharpened dagger went a long way to assuaging Nicholas's ill-ease.

Allowing himself a final glace around him, Nicholas lifted the wooden bar that secured the door, slid it aside, and pushed it open. The hinges appeared to have been recently oiled, and the door made no sound. Normally, that would be a sign of danger—an indication that the structure was not abandoned as appearances suggested—but tonight, it was exactly what Nicholas had hoped for: his contact had been here.

Once inside with the door closed, Nicholas was satisfied that the light from his lantern would not be noticed through the cabin's moss-blinded window. Opening the shield on his lantern, Hamar stepped quietly to where a waist-high pile of logs was stacked. Placing the lamp on a nearby shelf, he and Nicholas grabbed the ends of the top logs and heaved them up together. Like the lid of a chest, the entire first layer of the stack lifted up, and setting it to the side, the pair peered inside with intrigue. The interior of the stack was hollow, with logs fastened to the sides and sawed-off rounds glued to either end to make the deceptive container look like real firewood. Inside was an assortment of smaller boxes and various other implements. Keen not to linger, Nicholas hastily rifled through the imitation wood stack and compared its contents to a scribbled list of items in the pocket of his breeches. Inside the crate, there were rolls of fine silk, still in their protective woven sacks from five years ago; machine parts, and fittings, and the molds to make more of them; bags of masonry nails; clocks and other useful objects; and a plethora of assorted implements that were difficult to reproduce or required specialist knowledge to make. They were all items that the Hohalians had left behind, things that Nicholas's contact—after months of tentative, secretive communication between them—had discreetly gathered and agreed to trade to Nicholas and his men; for a price, of course. Pinned to the underside of the false lid was a tattered sheet of parchment on which the contact had indicated—in surprisingly ornate handwriting—what it was that he wanted in return. With a satisfied nod of his head, Nicholas pocketed the note before returning to the doorway of the shed and poking his head out gingerly. With his fingers to his lips, he gave a brief, whistle that sounded like that of a parrot, but which the others waiting outside knew to mean the way was clear. Discreetly, the other three Hohalians slipped silently out from the nearby trees and joined Nicholas and Hamar inside the cabin. Hurriedly, they divided the supplies and stowed them in the woven cloth bags that they had slung across their shoulders. Within minutes, the sacks were filled and all were eager to take their leave while undetected.

Before exiting, Nicholas removed another sheet of thin parchment from his pocket and put it in the same place the contact had left the note for him. On it was written a single word: "Agreed." Pulling the cabin door quietly behind him, he signaled to the men to move out without delay. It would take the rest of the night to get back to the new Hohalian settlement, and it was important that their nocturnal activities went unnoticed by prying eyes there also. As he watched the other four creep along the jungle border before slipping back into the foliage, Nicholas indulged in a longing glance at the lightless village. He knew every inch of the place intimately, like the distinct lines and furrows on a lover's face: every curving lane, every ancient tree and every corner, alcove and alleyway he'd spent his youth exploring. In these new and trying times, Nicholas longed to return to his home—not so much because he yearned for the ordered life that they had left behind, but because the sheer injustice of the Volcaron victory still tormented him. And despite having learned over the course of his community's exile to refocus his anger into more useful endeavors, his hatred of the invaders had subsided little in that time. It was more than his still-grieving heart could endure to imagine the one named Morgoratt—the killer of Nightshade and architect of all of his people's upheaval—sleeping comfortably on the silk sheets and soft, feather blankets in King Benjamin's personal chamber. Once again, the knife in his clenched fist seemed more conspicuous. With a sigh of resignation, Nicholas turned away painfully in pursuit of his men.

*

Some six hours later, as the rising sun cast a flush of crimson across the sky, Nicholas stood at the doorway of his cottage in the hillside settlement of Haven. As he ruminated on the previous night's visit to the old Hohalian village, he sipped from a cup of hot, elderberry tea while the early rays crept across the cottage's façade. The word, "cottage" was, in effect, a generous description for his one-room log cabin, with its hard-packed dirt floor, thick layer of dried rushes and roughshod arrangement of rag rugs. The furniture consisted of little more than a wood-framed bed, a kitchen corner with a hearth, a simply built table, and two rocking chairs which sat in front of the dimly-glowing fire. Most of the cottages in Haven were similar in size, and, suffice to say, were worlds apart from the well-built stone homes in which the Hohalians had once lived so pleasantly.

Nicholas turned his gaze to the south. On the hillside across the valley, he could see smoke beginning to rise from chimneys across the larger village of New Hohala where the Hohalians had first settled and the majority of the community still lived. Faintly, he could hear the peal of a hammer against metal. Abil, the blacksmith, was already at work, likely with the intent to come and barter with Nicholas over the tools taken from the storage shed in the old village the night before. It would, however, be a discreet transaction between himself and the blacksmith; as it happened, there were few Hohalians outside of Nicholas's circle who knew of his and his men's secret dealings with one of the Volcarons. Indeed, the people of Haven—Nicholas's men and the wives and children of the few who were lucky to have them—were outcasts among the Hohalians. They were known to keep weapons, were rumored to hunt wild animals for food and were openly prepared to defend themselves against attack from the Volcarons. Their ways were unacceptable to the king, his advisors and the many Hohalians who still clung to their nonviolent ideals. Nicholas, who had drawn the blood of another on two occasions—once to save Nightshade from the wild boar and again against Morgoratt—abandoned those ideals when he lost his home and his dearest friend.

Five years previously, when King Benjamin heard reports that Nicholas had actually attacked Morgoratt, he had flatly blamed Nicholas for damaging the Hohalians' connection to the Nexus, causing the voices of the spirits to go silent. In an uncharacteristic fit of rage, he'd banished Nicholas from New Hohala in the hope that the Hohalians' favor with the Nexus would be restored. Whether or not that was actually the case had never been truly determined, nevertheless, Nicholas had been shunned as a result of his admission that he'd injured the Volcaron leader—a circumstance that filled him with the most stinging sense of betrayal. For nearly a year Nicholas lived separate from the Hohalians, lost in his grief and isolated in his anger.

And then, of course, there was Caralisa, whose relationship with Nicholas was never the same after their heated dispute on the night of the evacuation. With emotions raw and loyalties uncertain in the aftermath of the Hohalians' upheaval, the pair's relationship had deteriorated, the king's condemnation of Nicholas serving as their breaking point. Eventually, Caralisa did manage to persuade her father to allow Nicholas to at least associate with the Hohalians, her heart unable to bear the thought of the man who she had at one time adored wandering the hills like a vagrant. She had pleaded with her father to show leniency until the monarch finally conceded that Nicholas could interact with Hohalians who chose to do so. However, the king had made it very clear that if Nicholas did return to live among the people, then it would be without his blessing. Nicholas, proud and himself disapproving of King Benjamin's own stubborn stance regarding the relocation of their people, had elected not to return to New Hohala, but was shrewd enough to realize that the king's permission to communicate with its inhabitants could aid his survival. On that stated basis, he set up his camp on the steep hillside that overlooked New Hohala, and over time, he built himself a meager cabin.

Life was lonely in those early days, and Nicholas's spirits dwindled in the oppressive solitude. However, during the first winter of the Hohalian exile, following the deaths of several children from fever, a number of men from New Hohala went to him to ask if he would teach them to hunt for food, to make weapons, and to use them. Nicholas, convinced of the necessity for ample self-defense in the new reality they inhabited, obliged them and equipped the disenchanted Hohalians with fighting and weaponry skills. In the cases of several of Nicholas's trainees, the trauma of their exile had resulted in foreign feelings of resentment and anger. Newly possessed with combat skills and weapons, they had dismissed their ideologue king's decree on non-violence in order to feed themselves and their loved ones. They caught fish in the mountain streams and took to eating wild goats and small, woodland creatures. Tired of the judgement of their neighbors, these disaffected Hohalians soon decided to leave New Hohala and settle near Nicholas. Before long, Nicholas had become the de facto leader of his own village—a community of hunters and raiders—which they christened "Haven"—a fitting name in their eyes.

With tired eyes and the satisfaction of a successfully completed expedition, Nicholas looked out over the wakening valley below. The Eternal Stream was just visible from his vantage point, and its permanent mist glowed radiantly in the distance. Nostalgically, Nicholas contemplated how, far off to the east, the waters of Hohala Bay were by now turning pink and gold, and how the first rays of light would soon wash the sandstone cottages in morning colors—or, at least they used to. It had been a long time since Nicholas had seen Hohala in the light of the sun, but he knew from his late-night incursions that the clean, yellow stone of the village's ancient dwellings had been turned a dingy brown by the neglect of the new inhabitants. The narrow paths that had once been lovingly maintained with sparkling, crushed seashells and the finest, white sand were now a filthy mess of mud and run-off from an overflowing sewer drain which caused the place to stench dreadfully at times. To Nicholas, there was a sense of tragic irony in the knowledge that the secluded, ramshackle settlement of Haven was almost in better condition than what the Volcarons had now reduced Hohala to.

Nicholas lifted his arm to shield his face from the young sun's glare. While he surveyed the horizon absent-mindedly, his eye caught sight of a lone figure emerging from the misty, hillside forest that separated Haven and New Hohala. A thin, young woman, dressed in a rough shawl that hung down to her knees, was walking his way, her long, dark hair loosely braided over one shoulder. Nicholas watched as Princess Caralisa traversed the steep slope with a familiar grace that momentarily put him in mind of happier times. Gone from her face, however, was the girlish innocence that had once marked it, replaced by a hard resolve and weary sadness that reflected a difficult life. In the days before their exile, Nicholas would have run to meet her, but that morning, he sipped his drink, and waited for her to come to him.

They had never agreed on the basic principles of Holalian philosophy, but he had been too afraid to admit that before. Now, though, despite being an outcast from his people, he knew that he was being true to himself and, over time, Nicholas had accepted his vocation as a hunter and vigilante. He knew Caralisa didn't approve; although she had explained to him numerous times that he and any of the others from Haven would be welcomed back to New Hohala if they renounced violence and bloodletting and pledged never to return to that way of life. However, it was this fundamental point that had resulted in a further cooling of Nicholas's relationship with the princess. What Caralisa and the other Hohalians denounced as violence, Nicholas defended as survival.

As Caralisa approached, the rising sun struck her face. She paused briefly and raised her eyes to the sky, reveling in the sun's touch. Her skin was still alluringly tanned, unlike most of the Hohalians who were several shades paler now that they lived in the forest instead of the sun-kissed bay. In that moment, Nicholas caught a glimpse of the girl she had been— free-spirited and innocent. Now, with the king's withdrawal from active life, she had effectively assumed the responsibility of governing New Hohala. She had become lithe and strong, with a quiet steel to her demeanor. Today, though, Nicholas saw something different in her body language.

She approached his cabin slowly and stopped a few feet away before making eye contact with him. Without smiling, she slid a small pack off her back and let it dangle from her hand.

"Hello, Nicholas," she greeted primly. "It's good to see you."

13

NICHOLAS'S FACE REMAINED expressionless. When he met the princess these days, he kept his emotions hidden, and on this occasion, he acknowledged her with a courteous nod.

"Caralisa," he saluted colorlessly, intentionally omitting her royal title which he had refused to use since his banishment.

The princess stared at him intently but did not smile. Despite Nicholas's show of cool indifference, her mere presence caused familiar emotions to come flooding back to him. In particular, a sudden recollection of the tender moment when she kissed him for the first time on Hohala beach caused his stony demeanor to soften. He felt the warmth of blood rushing to his cheeks as the taste of her delicate lips came back vividly to him.

Sensing his distraction, Caralisa's expression grew immediately concerned.

"Is something wrong, Nicholas?" she inquired, her tone guarded, yet still considerate. "Your face looks flushed. I brought the fever medicine for your neighbor that you requested last time we spoke. Perhaps you're in need of some *yourself*?"

He dropped his eyes to the pack she carried, forcing the past from his mind.

"I'm fine," he replied, nodding toward the steaming, clay cup in his hand. "It's probably just the tea warming my veins. It's quite cold out here this morning. Would you like some?"

Caralisa rubbed her hands together in agreement with his assessment of the weather and inclined her head.

"Please, I would," she nodded.

She sat on the uncomfortable, wooden bench beside the cabin front door as Nicholas disappeared inside to pour her tea. While he rattled by the stove, the princess's eyes wandered over her surroundings. She frowned sadly as she examined Nicholas's paltry dwelling and the small cabins that the other exiles lived in. A few moments later, as Nicholas's footsteps approached, Caralisa tightened her expression and tried to mask her sympathy.

"Do you have the goat wool I asked you for?" she inquired as he handed her the piping-hot tea which she wrapped her fingers around gladly.

"Of course," Nicholas replied, "You can send one of the men over to carry it back for you—that is, if you can provide the dried fruit and whiskey I asked for."

Her lips pursed slightly at this. Even after five years, Caralisa and the New Hohalians were still uncomfortable bartering with their estranged compatriots. Despite King Benjamin's slightly thawed stance on their separation from the rest of the Hohalians, the Haven-dwellers were still firmly out of good favor. There were also the unsubstantiated—yet, nevertheless, scandalous—rumors about some of Nicholas's men secretly raiding the Volcaron-occupied village for supplies and goods for trading—rumors, the princess had told him in very clear terms that she hoped were untrue. Although Nicholas did not admit the truth to her, he cared little for her warnings. The people of Haven—*his* people now—were hungry and had little, and they certainly did not have the luxury of charity. They'd learned, in the severest manner, the difference between prosperity and poverty, between living in a land of plenty and eking out a grim existence on a wind-swept mountainside. The Hohalians, both in New Hohala and Haven, had become possessive and competitive of the little food and resources that their haggard surroundings were capable of yielding. Against such hardship, the traditional Hohalian inclination toward charity and neighborliness had, in large part, given way to the instinct for survival. There was still kindness and generosity to be found among them, but the Hohalians—particularly the inhabitants of Haven—had developed a dispassion that ensured all dealings between members of the two factions were matter of fact and short-lived.

"Of course I'll keep my end of the bargain," Caralisa responded stiffly, before falling silent.

Even in her coolness, Nicholas could sense that there was something troubling the princess. Her eyes shone with worry, and the furrow in her brow suggested suppressed emotion.

"Caralisa," he inquired with a slip of warmth in his tone. "Is everything all right? You look…"

As she raised her eyes solemnly to his, he hesitated briefly before adding, "I can tell you're upset."

"It's nothing, really," she sighed, her head dropping as she cleared her throat. "I'll just get some of that wool from you and let you get on with your day."

"Caralisa," he pressed, his voice faltering self-consciously as he spoke. "You know that you can still confide in me, don't you? I know what it's like to have to pretend to be strong for others, even when you feel lost yourself."

Caralisa averted her eyes awkwardly. She knew all too well the pretense of publicly putting on a show of strength and composure, and she was aware that it was a responsibility that she and Nicholas had in common in these changed times. She took a sip of her tea before lowering the mug to her lap, toying with the handle. Finally, she looked him in the eyes and spoke in a low, subdued voice.

"Nicholas, I'm really worried," she admitted. "You know my father has been wasting away ever since we left Hohala. He barely ever leaves his camp by the Eternal Stream. He hardly eats, and when he does sleep it is only out of exhaustion. He spends day and night trying to restore our people's connection with the Nexus."

And then, her voice dropped to a quivering whisper as she added, "It's been five years—and I don't think that he ever will."

Nicholas hesitated for a moment, before drawing a thin breath and placing his hand lightly on hers in a timid gesture of comfort; in response, she wrapped her slim, strong fingers around his.

"The people are beginning to give up," she sighed as she went on, her voice quivering. "It's as if my father's decline has spread through the whole population like a disease. The people are depressed and indifferent. They take no pride in their work and little joy in their families anymore. They've stopped singing the songs of praise, and even the children rarely laugh anymore. Disagreements have turned into outright quarrels. There isn't enough food to go around, and people are getting sick. They're frightened, and that makes them even more angry and hostile toward each other."

Nicholas frowned.

"I'm sorry," he consoled. "I know it's difficult for you. But you know what I think you should do."

It was no secret to her that Nicholas believed the rest of the Hohalians should do as the villagers of Haven did to survive, and that, essentially, was to hunt and to raise animals for sustenance. Without the blessings of the Nexus, which had in the past made their farms and forests bountiful, their previous way of life was unsustainable, and it seemed to Nicholas that the stubbornness of the king was holding them back from lifting themselves out of their miserable lot.

Caralisa cleared her throat and after a brief pause replied, "I never thought I would hear myself say this, Nicholas, but I'm beginning to think…"

She broke off, and Nicholas waited for her to gather her thoughts.

"I'm beginning to think that maybe you were right after all," she conceded sadly, meeting his eyes. "Maybe we should have stayed and fought for Hohala."

Nicholas felt the shock of her words jolt through his entire body. Of all the Hohalians Nicholas had known, Caralisa had always been the gentlest by nature, the most innately attuned to the Nexus and resolutely steadfast in her belief that violence damaged the soul. And, indeed, Nicholas had not forgotten that she'd stood next to Lawson, as the counselor—acting on behalf of King Benjamin—banished Nicholas from New Hohala for what he'd termed "acts of sacrilege and violence." He'd felt ambushed at the time, and had been left astounded and stung that Caralisa had not opened her mouth in his defense, as all the while she'd stood with tears rolling down her cheeks.

He dropped her hand at the thought of those bitter memories, his mood darkening instantly.

"I *did* fight," Nicholas returned gruffly, rising to his feet with resentment. "I fought alone with Nightshade, and he was killed. And your father banished me from the village for standing up to the Volcarons and said that Nightshade's soul would be punished for his part."

Nicholas felt his face go red again, and his voice shook as he recalled that fateful night.

"Nightshade was protecting me, and I was protecting our home," he continued, his voice thick with emotion. "How would it have been wrong to fight in order to protect what was right and good?"

Caralisa didn't answer him, and after a pause, Nicholas added ruefully, "And you turned your back on me."

At this, she rose to face him, her eyes glaring.

"Maybe I'm not the same person I was then," she defended, a tearful rattle in her throat. "It's been a long time since I have had enough faith in the Nexus to justify your exile. As princess, I've tried to keep my people safe and in strong spirits while we've been cursed with starvation and disease in the wilderness, as all the while my father spirals into madness. And I don't know if I can stay strong for much longer."

There was a moment where it seemed as if the princess was on the cusp of breaking down, but she coughed to distract herself and proceeded to look Nicholas in the eye unapologetically.

"In any case," she added sternly. "I don't need you to lecture me on choices I made five years ago. I'm here to ask for your advice and your help."

Nicholas stared at her, noting the new conviction in her stance and the fiery emotion behind her features.

"Maybe you're not the same," he replied after a moment's contemplation. "But do you really think that you're ready to arm the Hohalians and lead an army to take back our home? To leave the security of this place? To risk lives?"

And then his voice dropped as he added, "To maybe even kill?"

"You risk your people's lives when you take them hunting," Caralisa challenged.

"Yes, I do," he returned flatly. "And some of them *have* been hurt. But they all know the risks and do so willingly"

"Sometimes, I don't know what it matters anymore," she confessed bitterly, tears now forming in her eyes. "The people are dying—of diseases, of accidents, of depression, of hunger."

"Hunting and war are not the same," Nicholas retorted moodily, not yet ready to accept the princess's professed motives. "Leading people into combat and asking them to give up their lives; do you really think you can do it?"

Caralisa dropped her eyes, and suddenly, the realization of why she had come to him dawned on Nicholas.

"Or, is it that you want *me* to do it for you?" he questioned with a sharp note of inquisition.

The princess did not reply or look at him.

That was it, and he could see it in her face; Caralisa knew nothing about weapons or combat, and now that Nicholas had turned from Hohalian ways, she hoped that he and his men would lead an uprising and fight on the front line. Perhaps she thought he and his men might even save *her* people from the necessity of shedding blood, the way he saved them from the involvement of stealing from the Volcarons and, yet, allowed them to enjoy the benefits of his risk through trade. In that moment, he wondered to himself what the spirits of the Nexus thought about the morality of trying to keep one's soul pure by allowing others to carry the burden of so-called sin.

"There are not enough of us here in Haven to mount a challenge," he answered coldly. "All the Hohalians would have to be prepared to fight."

"Some of them are," she replied quickly. "In the last year, I've seen more and more unrest and unhappiness. Those of my people who have not sunk into complete depression have a growing anger in them, and I believe a number of them would be willing to fight to retake our land. But they need weapons, training and leadership. What if we could do this together? Reunite Haven and Hohala, and regain our true home?"

Despite his anger at her willingness to use him, Nicholas felt a tiny flicker of hope kindle in his heart.

"Do you *really* think there are enough people willing to fight?" he demanded skeptically. "And what will your father say?"

Caralisa sighed.

"He'll say what he's always said," she conceded. "I've spoken to him about this, and he's always adamant. The gods are testing us, and we will never regain their favor if we abandon our ways simply because life has grown more difficult. When he speaks to me that way, I feel ashamed—as though I'm trying to take the easy way out. I feel like I should be doing more to help our people spiritually. But I don't have *time!* Father isn't the one trying to care for the sick, and mediate disputes, and organize a school, and maximize food production. *He's* just sitting by that damn stream all day, staring into space and wasting all of his energy trying to connect with the Nexus. *He* doesn't have to watch his people slipping into despair. He may not have abandoned our ways, but he's abandoned *us*. Still, the people won't rise up against the Volcarons without his blessing—not enough of them, anyway."

Then, she took a deep breath before adding, "Would you try to help me persuade him? Perhaps together we…"

Incredulous, Nicholas turned away from her at her brazen suggestion, wondering how she had the gall to ask him to even approach her father after all that had occurred, let alone reason with him.

"He'll never listen to me," he returned with a surly wave of his hand.

"He might," Caralisa replied hopefully. "You're the leader of this village, of Haven. You can speak to him as an equal, a man with leadership experience. He may well be ready to listen."

As Caralisa's face implored him, he once more saw a hint of the vulnerable, beautiful girl he'd fallen in love with so long ago, and his heart ached.

"I'll think about it," he relented as he gulped the last of the tea down his throat sullenly.

14

THE QUIET SERENITY of the morning had dissipated by the time Caralisa left. The magnitude of her proposal reverberated in Nicholas's mind and caused his head to swim. It was a brazen request considering the betrayal that Nicholas had felt when the king had ostracized him for being "tempted" into committing violence by Morgoratt. To this day, Caralisa and her father's denial of him stung deeply.

On the face of it, the princess's blunt plan of a Hohalian offensive against the Volcarons seemed to him poorly thought-out and over-simplified. While it was clear that the Volcarons had become complacent and lazy in the five years that had passed, they were still a formidable and numerous enemy. It undoubtedly would require a sizable army with strong numbers and a water-tight strategy to drive them away. All of the Hohalians would have to fight, and it was a near-certainty that lives would be lost.

Nevertheless, as Nicholas had argued ever since the Volcaron invasion, some blood sacrifice was likely to be necessary, and that the taking up of arms was the only means by which the Hohalians could regain what had been divinely theirs. As far as Nicholas and his like-minded men were concerned, it was honorable to risk one's life for his people and country—better to die fighting to defend what was right than to allow evil to flourish through fear and inaction.

While Nicholas had responded with reservation to Princess Caralisa's request for help, admittedly, the idea did intrigue him. For so long, his attempts at insurrection against the Volcarons had been limited to mere trespass and robbery. He and his men had wrestled often with the idea of embarking on a guerilla-style campaign of attack against the invaders but had always withstood that urge out of fear that the Volcarons would resolve to hunt down the exiled Hohalians in retaliation. However, if he could persuade the rest of the Hohalians to commit to an uprising with the blessing of the princess, then the expulsion of their enemy might actually be possible. Deep-down, the idea thrilled him, and he mulled the prospect of avenging the many wrongs he and his people had suffered. As Nicholas fantasized darkly, a swell of unfamiliar bloodlust rose up inside of him, and he imagined himself standing over Morgoratt's cold, dead body. Truth be told, Nicholas—hardened by experience, loss and destitution—cared nothing for the wellbeing of the Volcarons. As the frequency of his nighttime incursions into the captured village had increased, so had his contempt for them as a people. From the shadows, he had spied on them as they went about their nightly routines of drinking, gorging and debauchery. To Nicholas, they were a deplorable race with no respect for the fragility of nature. Like parasites, they had leeched on the life-force of the countryside and had plundered its resources voraciously. The lush farms had grown fallow; the abundance of livestock that the Hohalians had been forced to leave behind had all been butchered and consumed with no consideration given over to sustaining herds capable of producing dairy or wool for clothing. In addition, the once-bustling workshops of the village now lay gathering dust, and the great central plaza that once hosted a teeming Hohalian market had had its marble statues vandalized and many of its ancient cobblestones ripped out of the ground. Most offensively, however, the shrines and temples of the village that had always been maintained and tended to with such deep reverence by the Hohalians had been purposely desecrated by the spiteful invaders.

He did not know how long he'd sat on his chilly porch ruefully contemplating the Hohalian tragedy, but his musings were unexpectedly interrupted by the sight of movement within the trees leading into Haven. It was a stocky, male figure whose face was as grey and burdened-looking as a winter sky—a visage that Nicholas recognized instantly.

Guardedly, Nicholas rose to his feet, unsure if he should greet the man with hospitality or hostility. It was a visitation that he had not ever expected, and he immediately felt ill at ease. When the man emerged from the trees, he spotted the watching Nicholas outside of his cabin and saluted him with an unceremonious wave. Nicholas returned with a subdued nod as he watched the interloper stomp tiredly up the steep gradient toward him. He was dressed in an uncomfortable-looking hide cloak and to Nicholas's bemusement, a small, yellow-beaked parrot was perched on the man's shoulder, its head cocked in curiosity at its surroundings.

Leg-weary and with a disgruntled air, the man approached the steps of the cabin without a word as the parrot returned Nicholas's perplexed stare mischievously.

"What is this, Suma?" Nicholas asked his visitor briskly, his tone tinged with suspicion and concern.

"Pardon my intrusion," replied the big man indifferently. "May I enter your home and rest my feet awhile? The journey from New Volcaron is a long one, and I've matters of importance that I must speak with you about."

The sudden arrival of Suma, his contact from the occupied village, was unsettling to Nicholas. Not in a million years would he have predicted that the obsessively secretive Volcaron would turn up in Haven, an onerous half-day's journey through the thickest portion of the jungle, followed by a gruelling trek through the western uplands.

"How in the world did you find your way here?" pressed Nicholas impatiently, highly alarmed that the big Volcaron had actually managed to find his way to their settlement. "This is not what we agreed, Suma."

The big man returned a doleful, disinterested stare.

"You Hohalians have gotten complacent about leaving evidence of your movements," he answered curtly. "You didn't even bother to cover your tracks through the jungle properly. Although it's not much concern of mine, I should warn you that such carelessness could be very, very foolish."

Nicholas felt himself blushing at the accusation from his guest, but knowing that his point was valid, he opted not to argue. If he was honest with himself, he and his men had, over time, become a bit sloppy in hiding their trails during those night-time expeditions to the old village, and inwardly he admonished himself for this negligence.

"In any case," Suma went on. "I've travelled for hours to come here and speak with you, and I didn't do so for my own benefit. So, again, I ask that you let me enter your house so that I can say what I need to and return to the village before my absence is noticed."

Nicholas peered at him dubiously for a moment before stepping to the side of the doorway and ushering his guest inside. As Suma passed, the parrot on his shoulder squawked at Nicholas noisily.

"Danger is coming! Danger is coming!" it croaked loudly, twisting its head at Nicholas portentously. "Run while you can!"

"Hush, you old windbag," scolded Suma, batting the bird with the back of his hand to which it responded with another impetuous squawk. He made eye contact with Nicholas as he added, "Sorry about Goldbeak here; he doesn't know how to shut up."

Nicholas, rattled further by the parrot's ominous outburst, sighed as he handed his guest a tumbler of steaming tea from the same batch he'd given to Caralisa earlier.

"I don't mean to be rude, Suma," he said bluntly. "But you can imagine I'm confused to see you. Was there some problem with what we took from your store last night? I removed only what we'd agreed on, so if you've come to dispute our agreement, then I'm afraid you're wasting your time."

"Perhaps if you weren't so quick to presume, I'd have a moment to tell you why I'm here," came the sullen reply.

Nicholas looked at his visitor warily.

"Very well," he conceded. "What then has prompted you to chase after us, hours after we returned from the village?"

Suma's expression hardened as he uttered the grim words that he'd journeyed to Haven to deliver.

"Well, as the bird said, you're all in danger," he revealed darkly.

"In danger from what?" Nicholas shot back impatiently.

Suma glanced around him—bizarrely, as it seemed to Nicholas—as if he was checking to ensure that he wouldn't be overheard by anyone. Then, after a minute of searching Nicholas's puzzled expression, he coughed to clear his throat.

"If Morgoratt knew I was here, telling you this, he'd have my arms and legs torn off and my head stuck on the gate of his mansion," he informed his host fearfully.

"He's *your* leader," Nicholas replied somewhat sarcastically. "It's not like I'm going to run to tell him whatever secrets you have."

Suma returned a warning sideways glance—one of his annoyed, dangerous looks that Nicholas recognized from the occasions when Suma was anxious about their clandestine arrangement being discovered.

"This is serious," he grunted irritably before shaking his head and muttering to himself. "I don't know why I even came here."

"But you did," Nicholas shot back testily. "And I presume you're eventually going to tell me why?"

"Here's the thing," Suma divulged moodily. "Morgoratt held a council of the Volcaron chieftains last night. I was present at that meeting as I've recently been burdened with finding ways of conserving our remaining food sources—which was the reason I wasn't able to warn you while you were in the village. There is increasing discontent among the Volcarons from hunger and their disgust at the polluted state of the village."

Nicholas was totally incredulous at what he was hearing.

"And you're here to complain to me about this?" he spluttered disbelievingly. "We're working ourselves to the bone here—all of us—and we're barely surviving.

By this point, Nicholas's voice had risen to an angry shout.

"You—you *barbarians*—have managed to poison the most bountiful, plentiful land imaginable in five years," he continued to rail at his brooding guest. "The dregs of what you bastards have left is still more than we have! How dare you come up here and…"

Suma barely shifted in his seat, but Nicholas suddenly felt himself being thrust backward against the bench with Suma's knife at his throat. Then, the big Volcaron calmly took another sip from the cup in his free hand, the blade at Nicholas's throat never wavering.

"Awwk," Goldbeak squawked. "Dead man walking!"

"Not yet, bird," Suma answered calmly. "Though, who knows if he doesn't relax himself?"

"Dead men don't talk," the parrot twittered menacingly in response.

Taking the parrot's prompt as a warning of his current vulnerability, Nicholas relaxed his muscles and raised his hands in concession. In response, Suma lowered the knife and returned to sipping his drink.

"Morgoratt doesn't think like you," he proceeded calmly. "Sustaining a colony takes hard work and organization, and I'm the only Volcaron who is really willing to work. And even I don't grub in the dirt and grow things; I only build them."

Nicholas didn't bother to point out that the hard work required to cultivate food from the land seemed to him to be beyond the capacity of the parasitic Volcarons.

"When Morgoratt brought the Volcarons to this land," Suma went on, "They celebrated him as a savior—especially after he killed that panth –"

At that, Nicholas shot Suma a dangerous glance. The big Volcaron had struck a nerve too many, and he wanted to know nothing about how killing Nightshade had further aggrandized the Volcaron leader.

"Right," Suma cleared his throat, acknowledging the hint. "Anyway, late last night, Morgoratt announced a plan."

A dull foreboding began to ferment in the pit of Nicholas's stomach. Whatever this new information was, it had prompted Suma to immediately make the journey to Haven.

"And this plan of his is?" he inquired tensely.

"Morgoratt wants to sweep the land for resources." Suma answered.

Nicholas's heart pulsated in alarm.

"He's going to divide the Volcaron fighters," continued Suma. "Hundreds of them—into search parties and send them out into the countryside."

At that point, he looked Nicholas directly in the face and exhaled quietly before adding:

"They're going to scour the jungle and hills and mountains until they find your people. They want to enslave the Hohalians and will massacre anyone who resists. They will terrorize your children, ravage your women, and hang your royal family from the tree branches. And then, they will take everything of value that you possess."

Nicholas was frozen in shock. With nausea rising in his throat, he sat in horrified silence for a moment before getting to his feet slowly.

Finally, with a note of icy resolve, he declared, "I need to go and see Princess Caralisa."

15

It was with a subdued air that Suma departed Haven, and Nicholas had been left numbed by the Volcaron visitor's revelation. Although the Hohalians' years of exile had been a perpetual struggle, they had always been consoled by the knowledge that they were secure and hidden from the murderous Volcarons. Nicholas had taken solace in the notion that the invaders had been too self-absorbed and lazy to search for his people; after all, the great bounty that had been forfeited to them had left Hohala's foreign occupants with little motivation to search for the natives in the rugged, harsh terrain.

But now that the Volcarons—according to Suma—were growing desperate and agitated, the Hohalians were again in grave danger, this time of enslavement and oppression. Indeed, given what he knew of the tunnel-visioned Volcarons, Nicholas felt sure that if Suma had information they were planning to hunt down the Hohalians, then they could be quite sure that it was their enemy's sole plan—one that Morgoratt would be relentless in driving to fruition.

In the fog-filled air, Nicholas frantically contemplated the situation: if the Volcarons came looking, would the Hohalians be able to defend themselves? Would they even be willing? He knew that his comrades in Haven would be eager to fight, but their numbers would never be enough without the support of the rest of the Hohalians. It was clear to Nicholas that there was no room for hesitation or uncertainty. The Hohalians had already sacrificed their home, their way of life and their identity, and in return, they'd been cursed to a life where survival was their displaced community's main ambition. Now, if Suma was to be believed, that very survival was under threat. With the Hohalians faced with the very annihilation of their nation, Nicholas concluded to himself that the time for passivity was over.

It had been many months since Nicholas had set foot in New Hohala. Even though he had not strictly been prevented by King Benjamin from engaging with the village, he felt uncomfortable and particularly detached from its inhabitants. Ever since he'd rejected their conservative way of life, he saw judgement in the eyes of the people there when they looked at him, as if he was someone to be pitied. However, their ostracizing of him had hardened Nicholas over time, and whatever desire to win back their approval had once lingered with him was now replaced by awkward indifference.

With the urgency of Suma's warning at the forefront of his thoughts, Nicholas set out for New Hohala to speak again with the princess. It was a relatively short distance, yet the trek across the rocky mountain trail seemed long and arduous to him on this occasion. It was just after noon by the time he reached the village. A subconscious trepidation gripped him as he approached the demur settlement, and immediately, he could sense an unsettled atmosphere. A smattering of Hohalian women were browsing at a line of flimsy stalls offering scrawny, root vegetables, while a group of subdued-looking men stood smoking from pipes. There was little chatter or activity, and overall, the industriousness that had characterized the village in the past was replaced by a cheerless gloom. Around him, the faces appeared sunken, dispirited, and restless.

New Hohala was considerably larger than Haven and consisted of an assemblage of wooden-framed houses that overlooked the trail leading down to the Eternal Stream. Winding paths between the houses linked to a central thoroughfare that was slightly wider for the movement of supplies by cart.

Although he had never been inside, Nicholas knew Caralisa's house was located at the very western edge of the village. It was larger than the dwellings of the other Hohalians, but a world apart from the splendid mansion in which she had once lived. It was one of the few buildings with two stories, and it was home to Caralisa, King Benjamin, and their loyal counselor, Lawson.

Nicholas's heart thumped in his chest on approach to the house. As he rounded the building *en route* to the main entrance, he spotted Caralisa through a ground floor window. She stood hovering over a table with an expression of deep concentration. Nicholas started as she turned suddenly and noticed him. Her eyes looked weary and preoccupied, and there was something prickly in her body language as she rose from the table to let him in.

The door groaned open and Caralisa stood in the entranceway, her eyebrows raised at seeing him for a second time that day.

"Nicholas?" she greeted, her suspicion apparent.

"Hello again, Caralisa," Nicholas replied. "I need to talk to you."

Without a further word, the princess stood to the side and gestured to him to enter. As he closed the creaking door behind him, she turned away and walked into the room to her left. The tension between them disconcerted Nicholas, but he followed her lead without speaking.

Caralisa sat down on a wooden stool by the window, and with an irritable air she shuffled pieces of parchment into a bundle before looking up at her visitor expectantly.

"So, what is it that you've come here for, Nicholas?" she inquired. "Have you thought more about my proposal? Or are you just here to trade again, because if that's the reason then I'm afraid you are…"

"I have grave news, Caralisa. Listen to me, please," interrupted Nicholas impatiently.

Caralisa, taken aback, looked at him worriedly but said nothing.

"I'm sorry," returned Nicholas. "But I need to tell you something urgently."

In a somber tone, Nicholas reiterated everything that Suma had told him as Caralisa listened in horrified silence. When he had finished, the princess's face was drawn with worry.

"Is this man's word reliable?" she asked with a tremble in her voice. "Can you trust his information?"

Nicholas shrugged and sighed.

"Suma's loyalty is to himself, like all of the Volcarons," he replied. "But I don't see why he would have journeyed all this way to lie to me; if it *was* all lies or a trap, he could have just met me in the village when I was there last night."

His face reddened slightly as he revealed that detail to her. Caralisa nodded solemnly.

"How much time do we have?" she stammered, intentionally ignoring Nicholas's admission of his visit to the occupied village.

"A couple of weeks, maybe, according to Suma," Nicholas revealed. "From what he told me, Morgoratt is trying to reorganize the Volcarons into an army. He's going to divide them into teams and they're going to sweep the jungle and the mountains until they hunt us down."

Then, Nicholas's eyes dropped to the floor as he added, "Suma said Morgoratt intends to round up and enslave our people, Caralisa. They want to use us like animals. If we're unprepared, many will die, or worse."

The color drained from the face of the princess, and Nicholas knew that the severity of their situation was fully dawning on her. It was horrifying to her to even fathom the idea of her people—once a proud, divinely-blessed race—in chains, penned up like beasts and forced to work so that the Volcarons could prosper from their labor.

Caralisa closed her eyes, and her voice became low and shaken.

"Giving up the sea, our holy land, and our deep bond with it," she sniffed, her expression and voice tired beyond her years. "Sometimes I feel physically ill with homesickness and the desire to feel that connection to the place again."

She opened her eyes and looked up at Nicholas. Her striking gaze now pleaded to him, and the deep sadness in her sea-blue irises filled him with sympathy.

"Can I tell you something? I still go down to the Eternal Stream and sit alone in the mist," she revealed with a sigh. "Actually, I walk there nearly every day. I can still sense the spirit of the Nexus there, but it feels so faint and distant—as if we've been abandoned by the gods."

Nicholas didn't reply. The disenchantment in her voice made his heart ache, knowing how lost and unhappy she'd been all these years. He realized that he'd never really appreciated until now the true spiritual loss to the Hohalians that had occurred when their connection with the Nexus had been severed. Seeing how devastated Caralisa had become by the gods' apparent abandonment of them, it also dawned on Nicholas that he'd been uniquely prepared for the life they were living now, having spent his youth on the periphery of the Nexus's circle of comfort.

The princess looked at him with tears in her eyes.

"I don't know if we can ever get that connection back," she confessed, shaking her head. "But fighting and killing? It just seems impossible to me that facing down the Volcarons with violence could yield any return to the peace and harmony we once knew."

Nicholas couldn't stand to see her hurting so much, even as she struggled with an issue he saw as an obvious choice. He moved to the window and put his arms around her, protectively drawing her close to him in an embrace that made him yearn for days gone by. She leaned into him, and he felt her taut body trembling.

"I've tried so hard to make the most of our lives here," the princess lamented in a near-whisper. "But now the Hohalians are slowly perishing. Day after day, another starving old person or newborn is found dead. The people are scared. And angry…"

She swallowed back a sob and wiped the tears from her eyes before continuing.

"Our traditions teach us to place our faith in the Nexus—that if it's our destiny to be enslaved by the Volcarons, then we should peacefully accept that fate as the will of the gods until they show us otherwise. But I know that to become slaves under the Volcarons would mean the certain end of our nation."

Nicholas gently stroked her hair, which filled his nostrils with the scent of jasmine. His deep affection for her—long-smothered by his pain—felt reanimated. In that moment, he wanted nothing more than to help her, to save her—to give her back her home and the life of beauty and fulfillment that she deserved.

"Then we have to fight," he declared gravely. "If Hohala is worth fighting to regain, then our choice is obvious. Had we stood our ground when the Volcarons first arrived, maybe the Nexus would have come to our aid. But we withdrew; we abandoned our homeland and all the values that were sacred to our people without making a stand. I sincerely believe we've suffered because of it ever since."

Caralisa looked up at him once more. Although tears trembled on her lashes, he could see that newfound strength in her intent stare, a hardness developed through difficult times. Perhaps, over generations of plenty, the Hohalians had lost their fortitude, but maybe now, in their time of greatest trial, there was a chance to recover it.

Nicholas gazed down at the princess's face, and he saw both the sweet, gentle girl he'd fallen in love with and the resolute leader that she had been forced to become. Caralisa stared searchingly into his eyes, and without thinking, Nicholas lowered his mouth to hers in a kiss. Her lips were as soft and warm as he'd remembered, and to Nicholas's joy, she wound her arms around his neck and returned his embrace. Breathless, Nicholas drew back after what seemed like an age, and he rested his forehead against hers.

"We'll do this together," he promised her. "Can you gather the Hohalians? Find out how many are willing to fight. We won't turn them into warriors in such a short time, but we'll give them as much training as we can. We will divide them into groups, each with one of my men as its leader. We can –"

However, while he was mid-sentence, Caralisa pulled away from him, worry still marring her face.

"Nicholas," she sighed quietly. "I agree with you, but you've forgotten; I'm not the queen. There's no way I can mobilize the people to fight without my father's approval."

Nicholas dropped his arms and stepped away from her. He understood what Caralisa was saying, but she simply wasn't used to rebelling, or acting against the will of her father.

"He'll never agree," he murmured with a shake of his head. "You know he won't. He's spent five years sitting by the Eternal Stream, looking for a message from the Nexus that will never come. He's trying to justify making the wrong decision by claiming it was morally and spiritually correct. When was the last time he even came up here and spoke to any of the people?"

"It's been over a year," Caralisa admitted. "He just stays in his hut, praying and meditating. Lawson is the only one he really talks to anymore."

"Then maybe it's time King Benjamin gave up his crown," Nicholas answered flatly. "He's not in his right mind, and everyone knows it. He's not fit to rule."

"Maybe not," said Caralisa. "But he's still the king, and we have no laws that allow us to remove a monarch from the throne. We never thought we'd have to. The Nexus always took care of and guided us—we thought it always would."

"Then it's time you took matters into your own hands," Nicholas replied, knowing his words were harsh but necessary. "The people will follow you, Caralisa."

The princess averted her eyes.

"I at least have to talk to my father," she responded, shaking her head. "I have a responsibility to explain to him what's going on and to give him the chance to change his mind."

She put her hand on Nicholas's arm as she added hopefully, "Will you come with me?"

Nicholas gave a strained smile and nodded in agreement.

*

A short time later, Nicholas and Caralisa made their way down to the Eternal Stream. Although he had visited the place before in years gone by, the peace and silence that surrounded them—broken only by the faint rush of the waterfall and the birds calling in the trees—mesmerized his senses. It seemed as if this was the only place on earth where the spirit of the Nexus might be felt, even though it had been silent for five years. Suddenly, amid the tranquility of the sacred place, Nicholas understood why the king had been unable to leave. If Caralisa felt so lonely and bereft from having been cut off from the Nexus, he wondered how much more painful it was for King Benjamin, clinging desperately to the last shreds of everything he had once believed in.

As they made their way down the forested slope, a host of vividly colored butterflies appeared from out of the foliage. Caralisa stopped briefly, a fleeting smile on her face, and spread her arms out as if to touch the sunbeams that peeked through the gaps in the leaves. To Nicholas's enchantment, the butterflies swirled around her in a riot of color.

This was how she should be, carefree and happy, Nicholas thought to himself, and for a brief moment, he was taken back to the time as a child when Caralisa had enticed the butterflies to dance for him.

Eventually, the kaleidoscopic swarm dispersed, and Nicholas saw that the sadness had returned to Caralisa's face. As the princess dabbed the corners of her eyes with her sleeve, he could tell she was coming to terms with the realization that the Hohalians' time of innocence was truly at an end.

16

A THATCH-ROOFED WOODEN shelter was perched by the water's edge. It was three-sided and curtained at the front where it overlooked the crystalline pool. The sheep wool curtain was drawn almost halfway, and as they approached, Nicholas could make out a stuffed straw mattress and blankets inside. On a wooden table by the entrance there lay a plate of untouched fruit which had attracted a swarm of flying insects.

The king's counselor, Lawson, stood a few feet off from the shelter, smoking from a long, clay pipe. His tunic was grubby and frayed, and he appeared much gaunter than when Nicholas had last seen him. Upon noticing their arrival, Lawson self-consciously brushed away scattered flakes of pipe residue and dirt from his clothes.

"Princess Caralisa," he greeted, with weary, yet genuine animation in his voice. "I wasn't expecting to see you here today."

As always, Lawson took Caralisa's hand and kissed it respectfully. It was only at that point that he seemed to become aware of Nicholas's arrival, and the mildly startled look on the counselor's face suggested that he was taken aback by his presence. Nonetheless, he nodded cordially to Nicholas, curious as to his reason for coming to the Eternal Stream.

"Nicholas Stone," he greeted uncertainly. "It's a surprise to see you, I must admit." There was the subtlest hint of scolding in Lawson's tone, but Nicholas caught it easily.

The counselor then turned back to Caralisa.

"Princess, I am not sure that this is a good time," he began hesitantly.

"The king is…resting in his cabin after a long night of prayer, and I just don't know if unexpected visits are the best idea at the minute."

As he spoke, he glanced skeptically in Nicholas's direction.

"Lawson," Caralisa replied with exasperation. "We need to speak to both you and my father, right away."

Lawson replied, "My dear girl, I don't know about this. The king is tired and hasn't been very responsive for several days now. He's been increasing his meditation time, and that saps his energy, so I just feel that…"

A labored, rasping voice from inside the shelter cut across Lawson's protestations.

"Let them approach, Lawson," it called.

Lawson closed his eyes and exhaled, before replying politely with, "Yes, Your Highness."

A moment later, the curtain was drawn back, and a gaunt frame of a man emerged into the daylight. Although he resisted showing it on his face, Nicholas was startled by King Benjamin's appearance; he was not merely thin, he was emaciated. His limbs were stick-like, and the outline of his ribs could be seen underneath his dirt-stained, white robe. His unkempt, silver hair fell in a tangled mess almost to his waist, as did his beard. His sunken eyes squinted in the daylight, and it was noticeable that it tired him to raise his hand to his face.

Caralisa firmed her lips as she took Nicholas by the hand and led him toward her father. The monarch's eyes were still struggling with the sunlight, and he seemed anxious and distracted. Caralisa hugged her father very gently and looked at him worryingly.

"Father," she addressed him affectionately, taking his hand in hers. "You haven't been eating."

"I'm fine, I'm fine, my love" the king waved dismissively without looking her in the eye. "The Nexus sustains me. It speaks to my soul and nourishes me. I have little time for earthly distractions like food."

As Lawson and Caralisa exchanged dubious glances, Nicholas wondered to himself if the Eternal Stream really was speaking to King Benjamin. By their expressions, the princess and the counselor seemed to doubt it. He felt a pang of dread in his chest as he wondered if the king really was still sane enough to understand the seriousness of the unfolding situation.

"Father," Caralisa repeated more firmly this time. "I've brought Nicholas Stone. You remember Nicholas, don't you?"

King Benjamin glanced in Nicholas's direction for a moment before turning his stare to the water without a response.

"Father!" Caralisa spoke impatiently for a third time. "You have to listen to what Nicholas has come to tell us. He has information that the Volcarons are planning to attack our settlement. They have already stripped Hohala of everything and are now in need of new resources and labor. They want bring us back to Hohala in chains so that they can put us to work while they live idly."

The king returned no answer; he simply sat in silence, squinting at the winking ripples on the water. Nicholas looked at Caralisa exasperatedly.

"King Benjamin," he interjected. "There is a great threat hanging over our people. The Volcarons are panicking, and when they are this desperate, they'll have no restraint in their use of violence. They'll come here, and they will spill Hohalian blood. They'll burn New Hohala and Haven, they'll kill or imprison our menfolk, and then, finally, they'll drag our women back to old Hohala and share them among their barbaric soldiers."

The king flinched slightly and directed a concerned glance in Caralisa's direction before switching his gaze self-consciously.

"And, sir," Nicholas continued. "They will come here, and they'll destroy the Eternal Stream, just as they did to the holy shrines in Hohala. They will defile the sacredness of this place and reduce it to a swamp."

Having lowered himself onto the grass by this point, the weary king spoke directly to Nicholas.

"I have prayers to attend to, boy," he snapped irritably. "Be quick and tell me what it is you're looking for."

"We have to fight," Nicholas retorted, resentful of the king's condescending tone. "The Volcaron army is coming, and we can't afford to wait here for them to find us. We must take the fight to them—*all* of us. We need to arm ourselves and drive them out of Hohala, for good."

The king remained silent for a lingering moment before replying tiredly: "The creed of the Hohalians has always directed that no violence should ever be used against any other human or living creature. That is what the Nexus has taught us. That is why our ancestors long before us were blessed with Hohala. We cannot suddenly abandon our ways and expect to regain our home."

Nicholas eyed him with despair.

"That creed served the Hohalians well for countless generations," he responded agreeably in an attempt to placate the stubborn king. "But the world changes; circumstances change. Why can't we move with these changes too in order to defend what is right?"

The king didn't answer or look at him, preferring to stare absent-mindedly ahead.

"That which is good and noble is worthy of protection," persisted Nicholas. "Are you willing to see the Hohalians butchered and enslaved? Because that's what is going to come to pass if we don't act. And, forgive me, sir, but the stain of that blood will be on your hands if you dismiss this warning."

With a note of bitterness in his tone, Nicholas then added, "What use will your deference to the Nexus have been if you are hung by the neck from Morgoratt's window."

Once more, the ruler was stubbornly silent as Nicholas pressed on, addressing Lawson now as much as the king.

"We must drive the Volcarons out," he urged vehemently. "The people of Hohala have been suffering from this injustice for five years too many. It's our responsibility and our last chance to save our way of life. Your people are ready and willing to fight. Please, King Benjamin, give us your support."

"With fighting, there will be loss of lives, and loss of lives cannot be justified," the king answered disinterestedly. "Violence against the Volcarons is no less evil than them killing Hohalians."

"No less evil?" Nicholas scoffed, unable to mask his disgust at the king's refusal to consider his plea. "Evil has no respect for life. We must rise up—all of us!—otherwise the Volcarons will prevail."

"Father, the people are already dying," Caralisa chimed in before the king could speak again. "Even if the Volcarons were not coming for us, our race will have died out within a generation should we remain here. And if they do manage to enslave us, the Hohalians will die of broken hearts and crushed souls. I know the people are willing to take the risk."

Then, she paused before adding, "And I'm ready to take that risk also."

The king turned to her with a disarmed look in his eyes.

"What good is saving Hohala if we pollute our souls, girl?" he replied sadly.

"What good is the purity of our souls, if the country we have a divine responsibility to protect is reduced to a wasteland?" Caralisa countered softly.

King Benjamin rose shakily to his feet, and Nicholas, Caralisa and Lawson watched in confusion as he stepped into the water's edge and slowly began to wade out into the center. Caralisa gasped, aware that only dead bodies were ever placed in the pool.

Immersed to his waist, the king splashed the water over his head and suddenly cried out, "Dear Nexus, our guidance and deliverer, please speak to us! Tell these children that we must not succumb to the temptation of violence!"

Nicholas turned disbelievingly to Lawson, who had taken a step forward and was now looking on with incredulity at the king's bizarre behavior.

"How can you let this go on?" Nicholas questioned the counselor with a low, accusatory tone. "Responsibility for the Hohalians' safety has fallen to Caralisa, and yet you willingly allow all authority to rest in the hands of a madman—one whose mind is lost in the past. The Volcarons have no care for the balance of life, for the Nexus, or the natural world. They give nothing and destroy everything. And we have allowed their destruction to prosper up to now! How can that be what the Nexus wants?"

Lawson looked troubled and sad as his soul ached for the leader and dear friend he had lost. The old advisor turned away from where the king still stood waist-deep in the water, as if it anguished him to see the king so apart from reality.

"I don't know what to do," he admitted, his voice choking. "King Benjamin was coroneted by the Nexus, and the gods have given no sign that he should cease as the leader of the Hohalians."

"Except that we've lost our land, our abundance, our joy, our culture, and we now may lose our lives." Nicholas pointed out heatedly. "How many more signs do you want?"

Lawson opened his mouth to answer, but he was cut across by a sudden and exultant exclamation from King Benjamin.

"My dear fellow-Hohalians!" he cried, throwing his hands in the air excitedly, sending a spray of water all around him. "The Nexus has not abandoned us!"

He turned with shining, smiling eyes to Caralisa, Lawson, and Nicholas by turn.

"The Nexus has spoken to me at last! I've heard the gods whisper to me, and they are to send a savior to deliver us from ruin!"

"What?" exclaimed Nicholas, Caralisa, and Lawson in unison, all three bewildered by the king's sudden and dramatic declamation.

"Yes!" thrilled King Benjamin delightedly. "At last, our prayers have been answered! The spirits have informed me that this savior will be one who is outside of Hohalian ways; an outcast who knows what it is to stand between two worlds but belong to neither; one who has known violence, but who will become a vehicle for peace. This savior will fight the Volcarons on behalf of our people!"

The monarch then waded back toward shore, dripping with holy water as his eyes shimmered fanatically.

"We are saved!" he exclaimed deliriously.

To the shock of the on looking trio, the king then staggered onto the grassy embankment and broke into a convulsion of delirious laughter.

"We are saved!" he continued to rave breathlessly. "Oh, praise the Nexus, we're saved!"

Lawson sprang forward and caught the king just as he was about to collapse.

Nicholas was filled with dismay as he realized fully what had become of the king. It was clear that he was unhinged, driven to madness by the weight of time and shrinking hope. He turned to Caralisa who looked utterly devastated. With Lawson's pleas to the hysterical king to return to his shelter ringing in their ears, Nicholas placed his arm around her supportively.

"I'm sorry, Caralisa," he consoled. "Your father's mind is weary and drained. He needs our help, but first we must accept that he is no longer able to rule. I really think..."

"Wait," Caralisa interrupted, and Nicholas could see that her expression had become fixed on the pool of water which sparkled brilliantly having been stirred by the king's raving.

Stepping toward the edge of the water, she knelt down in the grass and began to stare at something that Nicholas could not make out himself.

"Caralisa?" he inquired warily.

The princess did not answer him; instead, her eyes continued to fixate on the center of the pool, her features tense and distracted. For several minutes, Nicholas watched in perplexed silence as she continued to gaze into the resplendent mist and water. Eventually, Caralisa's eyelids fluttered open, and she wore the look of one who had been woken abruptly from a deep slumber. Slowly, she appeared to regain focus, and she looked up at Nicholas, wild-eyed and dazed looking.

"Nicholas!" she gasped, with a tremble in her voice. "My father's right. I heard the Nexus speak too. It *has* told of a savior who can deliver us from our suffering.

Nicholas looked at her in bewilderment. It was preposterous to believe that the Nexus had all of a sudden decided to speak to her and her father after five years of silence. Surely, she too couldn't have gone mad.

Caralisa rose to her feet and squeezed Nicholas's hands intently in hers. A quivering, excited smile had by now crept across her mouth.

"It's obviously you, Nicholas!" she exclaimed at a gasp. "You're clearly the chosen one. It all makes sense now! The Nexus has sent you to save Hohala!"

Taken completely by surprise by her feverish outburst, Nicholas's mind could form no reply other than to stare back at her in utter disbelief.

17

NICHOLAS'S DISBELIEVING STARE moved first to Caralisa, then to Lawson, and finally to the tent in which the king now lay rambling to himself incoherently. His mind scrambled to make sense of it all. Had the ordeal of exile driven all of them insane? Had he lost his own mind? It was an utterly confounding situation that unnerved him greatly.

And then, a thought occurred that appalled and infuriated him equally: what if it was all a ruse? What if the real intention behind their visit to the Eternal Stream had been to dupe him and his followers in Haven to rise up against the Volcarons? Had Caralisa—the woman for whom a flame had always flickered in his heart– and her father and Lawson conspired together to deceive him? It seemed all too convenient—too absurd—to believe that after five years of total silence, the Nexus had suddenly spoken to both Caralisa and her father in his presence. As Nicholas's mind raced, his confusion turned to rage. Years of anger and pain began to stir within him, and the outburst that followed surprised even him.

"You are liars, all of you!" he roared, prompting dumbfounded stares from Caralisa and Lawson. "This is what you've planned all along; to use me to save your own souls—just as you've been doing for years! Stealing is wrong, but you'll happily barter with me for seeds and cloth as long as no questions are asked about where they came from. Apparently, fighting for survival is wrong, dying for what is right is wrong, and now, in his wisdom, the king decides that our people's basic, natural right to defend themselves is wrong. So, your ingenious solution? Convince Nicholas that organizing an uprising against the Volcarons is his sacred duty, divined by the Nexus itself! Better yet, have him lead the rest of the sinful outcasts from Haven into battle. Why not? They're all tainted by violence already, aren't they? Ready-made martyrs who can risk their lives to save good, upstanding Hohalians like yourselves from polluting your pure, white souls!"

Caralisa stepped forward heatedly.

"Stop it, Nicholas!" she remonstrated defiantly. "That is not fair. The Nexus *did* whisper to me. It spoke of a savior that will lead us to freedom, and I'm convinced that savior is you, Nicholas! It all makes sense!"

Growing evermore convinced that he was the victim of conspiratorial dealings, the princess's remonstrations only served to heighten his distrust.

"Nonsense," he growled. "This is all a plot to convince me to risk myself and my men in a rebellion against the Volcarons so that the rest of you can continue with your souls unblemished. *That* is what makes sense! Well, I refuse to take on that burden. You can fight by yourselves, or you can wait here until the Volcarons drag you away in chains. But I'm done with all of you!"

"Nicholas, stop!" implored Caralisa placing her hand on his shoulder, her eyes freshly lined with tears. "You must listen to me!"

"Leave me be!" Nicholas shot back angrily, shrugging her hand away. "Do not try to make contact with me again. You are frauds, the lot of you. You betrayed me once before, Caralisa, and you've no idea how deeply it cut, but I won't be deceived a second time. I never want to see any of you again."

"Master Stone!" Lawson broke in defensively. "This is most inappropriate! Cease this ridiculous talk at once. You do not understand the workings of the Nexus. You must stop and listen to what…"

"Don't insult me, Lawson!" Nicholas retorted fiercely. "You had no interest in what I had to say five years ago when I came to warn you all about the Volcarons. Back then, I was just an upstart to you, and you dismissed the notion that the Nexus could choose to connect with someone like me. However, that's all changed now that you realize that you can use me. Well, you can forget about that."

Without another word, and with Caralisa's tearful pleas calling after him, Nicholas stormed away from the Eternal Stream. As he stomped through the trees, his heart pounded relentlessly in his chest. Cold beads of perspiration streamed from his forehead, and his mind was a whirlpool of anger, confusion, and uncertainty. All that made sense in that moment was to disappear like the outcast he was.

With rancor in his every step, he strode past New Hohala and Haven and up into the hills beyond, paying little attention to where he was going. His anger drove him aimlessly onward, his reason and judgement clouded by a panicked rage. The Nexus hadn't spoken of him. The very idea was ridiculous! He'd never been good enough for either the gods or the Hohalians. And now he was expected to believe that the Nexus had chosen him to save the community who had shunned him? A savior, indeed!

For what seemed an age, Nicholas trekked aimlessly through the mountainous terrain, his mind occupied by all of the betrayals and injustices that he had known in his life. The terrain became rockier and more precipitous, and the evening air brought with it a stinging chill. At one point, as he rounded an upland peak, he was able to make out the demure outline of New Hohala in the distance below. Suddenly, the hopelessness of his situation became too much for him to smother any longer, and with tear-filled eyes and the cold, infinite sky above him, he roared into the wilds of the mountains.

"If you're so keen for me to do your bidding then speak to me yourself!" he challenged the Nexus.

He listened breathlessly as his words echoed off the surrounding mountaintops, but the response from the gods was empty silence.

"I didn't think so," he whispered through gritted teeth.

Nicholas drove through the rugged mountain range, marching through a great, forested valley that swept up to the sky on either side, until the topography ahead began to slope upward again. He didn't know for how long or how far he had climbed, but the darkening sky indicated it had been hours since his outburst at the Eternal Stream. His legs burned as he pushed on blindly, desperate to put as much distance between himself and the Hohalians as he could manage. His breathing had become labored, and he was dizzy with exertion. Then, just as he felt himself about to succumb to the weight of exhaustion, his path ended at a steep rock face with no visible way forward. He leaned against the wall, his energy spent. As he stood panting, Nicholas's ears suddenly pricked at the sound of footsteps and the rustle of underbrush. Cautiously, he drew his knife and scanned around for whatever predator or wild beast he was about to have to defend himself against.

Just then, he was stunned to hear a soft, familiar voice call his name which he recognized instantly as belonging to Caralisa. He scoured his surroundings frantically, his mind struggling to comprehend that she had followed him all this way, but sure enough, a minute later, the princess stumbled out of the foliage, breathless and disheveled. Her hair was torn out of the braid she had earlier worn so elegantly, and her white sandals were broken from hours of struggling to keep up with Nicholas. In her hand, she carried a glowing lantern that dazzled Nicholas's eyes. They faced each other across the overgrown valley, and Caralisa's expression was one of sorrow as Nicholas returned an unapologetic stare. The silence was broken by the princess.

"Nicholas, I'm so sorry," she pleaded.

"For what?" Nicholas called back indifferently, his faith in her too shaken to be moved by her obvious upset. "For trying to use me? Or for being so desperate that you'll believe anything that avoids going against your creed—even if it means putting me and my men in danger? I don't know why you bothered following me."

Caralisa flinched at the bitterness in his tone.

"I don't blame you for being angry," she conceded. "I realize we have been using you, trading with you for bartered goods while at the same time saying it's wrong to have dealings with the Volcarons. Your actions have helped us survive all these years, and I suppose, in a way, we've looked down on you unfairly."

Yes, you have, Nicholas thought to himself, but as he noticed Caralisa's trembling shoulders, he couldn't bring himself to reproach her aloud.

The princess's voice choked as she tried to compose herself.

"You didn't deserve to be shunned or mistreated," she stuttered as she stepped toward him, closing the distance between them. "I don't care what my father or Lawson have said. *I* know you're a good man. You're kind and brave and honorable…and Nicholas… I should have…"

Nicholas felt his own eyes heavy with tears as Caralisa's sentence was muffled by a sob. Her impassioned words had disarmed him, and he felt the fury within him subsiding. Sadly, he extended his hand and raised the princess's chin with the edge of his index finger, searching her eyes intently.

"Please believe me," she resumed, as if encouraged by his small gesture. "The message I heard from the Nexus was real. I *did* hear the spirits speak of a savior that would liberate the Hohalians, and it all points to you, Nicholas! But it is wrong—*we* were wrong—to expect that you to do it alone."

She moved closer to him, not breaking her stare.

"I wouldn't blame you if you decide never to return to us," she went on quietly. "What has the guidance of the Nexus ever done for you except make you feel like an outsider among your own people? Indeed, I now agree with you in wondering why the Hohalians should be your responsibility after everything that's happened."

Her eyes grew intense as she went on, "But, Nicholas; it's possible that you *are* the only one who can save our people. If you'll consider trying, then I promise I will stand with you, through every difficulty and danger."

Then, she took his hand in hers and added, "We'll do it together."

Nicholas sagged against the towering rock face and felt a combined ache of guilt and empathy as he searched the princess's face. She was so beautiful and impassioned, and yet still so naïve and unaware of the real cost of survival. A moment ago, he'd been furious with her, wanting her to understand the pain and darkness that existed within him. But, as he looked at her, her eyes clear and unwavering, he realized that he wanted nothing more than to save her from any further distress.

After placing the lantern on the ground, Caralisa closed the remaining distance between them and put her hand over his throbbing heart. At that instant, Nicholas felt a sudden jolt of energy pulse in his veins, and an unfamiliar image flashed across his mind's eye. He saw himself surrounded by a dismal, barren landscape of jagged rock and smoke-filled air. It was a lifeless place, absent of purpose, other than to pass through. In his mind, he watched himself climb with determination high up into a sierra of mountain peaks until eventually, just as he sensed he had reached his unknown destination, the thick smog made it impossible to see any further. But then, from somewhere within the smoky haze, a whisper called to him by name and urged him onward:

"Nicholas…Nicholas…Nicholas…"

He was woken from his daydream by Caralisa's far away voice calling his name. Abruptly, he became aware of her presence, and he returned to reality. His mind raced as he struggled to fathom what he had just experienced, and looking into the princess's concerned eyes, he was filled with an unexpected sense of certainty and determination. At last, for the very first time in his life, Nicholas felt the warm, assuring touch of some otherworldly hand. His veins coursed with adrenaline, and he felt as if he knew exactly what he needed to do, even if he could not explain for the life of him why.

Off to his right, at the top of the rock wall, a fleeting movement caught Nicholas's eye and prompted him to scan the rocky overhang. To his amazement, he was presented with a sight so incredible that it caused his knees to falter; standing atop a ledge, looking directly at him, was a large, black panther. He could see its brilliant, green eyes—unearthly and striking in the dusk light—fixed on him, but its form appeared semi-transparent, like that of a specter. Astonishingly, Nicholas could sense it calling to him— entreating him to venture after it.

He turned back to Caralisa—who clearly had not seen the ghostly animal—staring at him, puzzled.

"What's the matter?" she whispered, concerned at Nicholas's sudden distraction. "Did you see something?"

"Look!" Nicholas stammered as he pointed to the ledge where the panther stood, watchful and brooding. "Up there. Can't you see it? The panther; it looks just like…"

"What?" replied Caralisa confusedly. "Nicholas? What panther? I don't see anything."

"Nightshade!" breathed a dumbstruck Nicholas, perplexed that the princess could not see what he was pointing to. "It looks exactly like him, but it can't be! Nightshade is dead. I watched that savage, Morgoratt, kill him."

He looked back up at the ledge where the panther still stood making eye contact with him, staring impatiently as it swished its tail.

"It couldn't be," reasoned Nicholas to himself, shaking his head.

But the more he stared at the lithe feline, the more comforted and reassured he felt.

"I have a feeling that I need to go with it," he exclaimed to the princess suddenly.

"What? With whom?" she queried confusedly. "You mean the panther? Nicholas, there's nothing up there."

Nicholas continued to fix his gaze up at the rock ledge where he could see for himself—beyond any doubt—the same pair of spectral, green eyes staring back at him. Why, though, he wondered to himself, was Caralisa unable to see the panther? Had she really grown that short of sight in five years? Was she lying to him? Had his *own* sanity have deserted him? Or was he looking at ghost?

"You really can't see it?" Nicholas inquired to the princess one more time as he observed the big cat pacing the ledge restlessly.

She shook her head, worried by his bizarre claim.

"There's nothing there, Nicholas," she admitted to him gently. "You're weary and probably starving. Our minds can play tricks on us when we're not feeling ourselves."

However, her well-intended reassuring barely registered in Nicholas's mind as he continued to gape transfixed at the panther's majestic, near-translucent form.

"I think the Nexus sent the panther to find me," he declared, his natural pragmatism at odds with the bewildering comfort that now engulfed his spirit. "I feel I should follow it."

As Caralisa searched his face bewilderedly, Nicholas looked down at his hands and aching body, and he began to feel a rejuvenation spreading from a warm place in his chest. He clenched and unclenched his fists, wondering at the new power he was feeling after his angry and arduous flight across the highlands. Was it possible that the Nexus had sent the panther to present itself to him? Could it be that the gods actually wanted to work through him—the parentless child, the disgraced rebel, the tainted sinner?

"This is my one chance to know if what you've said is true," he breathed. "That the Nexus has chosen me to carry out its work. I have to follow the panther."

The words brought on a rush of intensity that Nicholas couldn't explain.

I'll come with you," replied Caralisa, increasingly worried by Nicholas's bizarre change of demeanor, and she wrapped her fingers around his hand as if to let go, even for a second, might mean to lose him forever.

Nicholas put his arms around her and grimaced as he felt tears prickle in the corners of his eyes once more. It had been one of the most confusing and upsetting days of his life. He felt uncertainty of the way forward—of blindly continuing onward through the wilderness, guided by nothing but intuition and the black panther that, for all he knew, was a manifestation of his own imagination. No living Hohalian had travelled further westward than where they stood now, and the folk tales that the older people told to children warned of terrible dangers that awaited those foolhardy enough to journey that way. If there turned out to be any truth in those legends, then there was the very real possibility that that moment could be the last time he embraced Caralisa who, despite the cooling of their relationship, he had never stopped loving.

"More than anything, I wish you could come with me," he told her softly, his voice faltering. "But, Caralisa, you can't. The Hohalians need you, and your first responsibility is to them."

He took a deep breath as he added, "Please, will you do something for me? Speak to Hamar and ask him to look after Haven while I'm gone."

She pulled away from him, her lips pursed.

"You're leaving now?" she exclaimed. "You don't even have any food or supplies! You have no plan or preparation, and you're exhausted and weak! Damn it, Nicholas. A martyr is no use to any of us…to me! I can't bear this…"

Upon hearing her point out the facts of the situation, the immensity of his decision hit Nicholas hard. He stroked the princess's hair, memorizing her scent and the feel of her cheek on his chest. Suddenly, Caralisa gripped him tighter, as if she could sense that he had made his decision.

"I know it's crazy to travel into the unknown with nothing…" Nicholas murmured into her hair.

He looked up to the top of the rock wall again where the black panther was still lashing its tail expectantly.

"…but it's what has to be done," he finished determinedly. "Tonight, for the first time, I've felt the connection you've told me about so often, and I know I have to place my trust in it if Hohala is to be rid of the Volcarons. But I swear, Caralisa, whatever happens I will return to you."

His voice wavered, and he paused to look into the princess's eyes, reflecting on the years they'd spent separated as he prepared to leave her again.

"And that will be the greatest reward I can imagine," he added with a smile that trembled with emotion.

A heavy stillness befell the scene as Caralisa broke their stare to wrap her arms around him.

"I'll have faith that you will," she whispered. "I'll pray for your safety every day until you return."

He smiled and kissed her again, softly and tenderly.

"Go," he urged when they finally parted. "Get back to New Hohala and prepare the people without delay. Regardless of when I return, they will need to be ready to evacuate again if the Volcarons do come that way."

Caralisa slowly and tearfully pulled away, memorizing his face for the comfort she knew she soon would rely on. Fumbling in the glare, she picked up her lantern and began to walk away, turning back only once to mouth the words, "I love you."

Nicholas watched until she was out of sight, and with a sigh, he turned his face once more toward the wall of rock before him. Suddenly, he felt alone and uncertain again, frightened by the unknown nature of the journey and, for a split-second, he contemplated following Caralisa back to New Hohala.

As if it had read his thoughts, Nicholas's waiting guide, the strange panther, snorted impatiently, and he shook the doubts immediately from his mind. Composing himself, Nicholas breathed in deeply and began to climb.

18

THE MUSK OF spilled brandy infused the air of the dining chamber in the Hohalian royal mansion. It was late, and the lanterns that lined the walls had by now burned to blushing embers. In the dim light, Morgoratt sat at the head of a long banquet table. The twelve Volcaron chieftains were seated around the table, grumbling and bickering drunkenly with each other. Remnants of the night's indulgences were scattered across its surface, and the fare that evening, as it had been on recent occasions, had been conservatively portioned and underwhelming. The generous amounts of fine meat and seafood that Morgoratt and his inner circle had long grown accustomed to had steadily decreased in abundance and quality. That night's offering, which Morgoratt's cook had nervously sworn was the best food that he'd had available to him, had consisted of a platter of stringy meat from a nest of parrot chicks that had been recovered from the jungle. It had been insufficient and unsatisfying, and the lack of food lining his stomach had made Morgoratt irritable and drunker quicker.

The food stocks were dwindling, and the Volcarons were restless and agitated. Many were ill from undernourishment, and scuffles were breaking out between rival factions. In recent weeks, Morgoratt had overseen the burial of a number of Volcaron men who had died following late-night skirmishes in the village. On a handful of occasions lately, his own authority had been called into question in the form of subtle quips of criticism of his reign thrown from within huddled crowds as he walked the streets. The first time this occurred, Morgoratt made an example of a young, male bystander—who may or may not have been the source of the remark—by publicly and painfully snapping the fingers on one of his hands. Yet, despite the boy's public punishment, a detectable air of animosity toward Morgoratt's leadership now lingered in the streets, and in recent weeks, he had spent an increasing amount of time shut away in the mansion. While he still had authority over the Volcarons, he now acknowledged that his hold on that power was at risk as a result of their rapidly deteriorating living conditions.

On several nights of late, Morgoratt had experienced unsettling, recurring dreams where he wandered endlessly on the dusty beaches of the old island of Volcaron. The sea water was grey and viscous, as if lined with a layer of grease. Everywhere, the beach was littered with dried-out, crumbling bones. The sunken corpses of his men were scattered all across the sand dunes, and as he passed, each of them turned their rotting visages his way to insult him and mock his impotency as a ruler.

Morgoratt had never been one to place stock in dreams, yet the jeering corpses that visited him in his sleep haunted him during the day too. The idea of a future uprising by the disaffected Volcarons occupied his thoughts constantly and had persuaded him to increase his guard detail at the entrances to the mansion. Aware that he needed to quell the bubbling unrest, Morgoratt resolved to expand the Volcaron sphere of influence beyond the village. He needed fresh resources, skills, labor, and women to resuscitate the rotting Volcaron settlement, and he had begun to obsess about seeking out the whereabouts of the Hohalians who he could use to those ends.

Now that the modest banquet was at an end, Morgoratt sensed the assembled chieftains were growing impatient. Keen to be rid of their company, he addressed them abruptly with a thump of his fist on the table. The squabbling around the chamber ceased, and twelve pairs of eyes turned toward him.

"How was the food?" Morgoratt inquired with an upward tone of agreeableness. "Did you get enough to eat, Finn?"

"I could eat that meal five times over," grunted Finn, the most portly of the chieftains. "Your feasts have lost their impressiveness, Morgoratt. I can't remember the last time a banquet consisted of picking flesh off the bones of a canary."

Morgoratt leered at him silently. He had expected such a response from Finn, yet he continued to stare him down until the chieftain averted his eyes submissively.

"I am sorry to hear that, Finn," answered Morgoratt scornfully. "In that case, maybe you'll listen closely to what I have to say."

Finn and the others watched as Morgoratt rose from the table and retrieved a rolled-up parchment from a cloth bag by his feet. With an intoxicated sweep of his free arm, he cleared the food, dishes, and cups off the table with a clatter that startled the other men. Morgoratt unfurled the parchment on the table in front of them. The men recognized it as a map of the village, and in the top left corner, in dark, cursive scrawl, were written the words, "New Volcaron."

"Brothers," he addressed them. "This is the plan for a fresh beginning for our colony. You are aware that supplies are running out, and the people are growing impatient. There is unrest in the streets, and if we remain passive, it won't be long before the same anarchy we feared back on Volcaron is brought to our doors."

The men exchanged worried glances.

Morgoratt's pale, outstretched index finger directed their attentions to a section of the parchment that none of them recognized as being part of the village. There were sketches of an assemblage of huts and a fenced enclosure that encircled the expansive site, open at one end to a vertical cliff edge.

"We are going to need some fresh blood to get our settlement up and running again," he continued imperiously. "The Hohalians are hiding somewhere in the countryside, and I am proposing we bring them safely back home."

The chieftains easily detected the sinister facetiousness in Morgoratt's tone, and they listened with curiosity.

"As you can see here," he went on, directing the attentions of all back to the parchment. "There will be ready-made sleeping quarters for the Hohalians. Here, they will work for us, build for us, farm for us, prepare food for us. It will be a life of routine and work, and it will be a much more valuable use of their time than cowering in the wilderness."

"So, this is a slave colony?" piped up one of the chieftain's interestedly.

"If that is your choice of words, then yes," replied Morgoratt with a thin smirk. "We'll put the strongest of the Hohalian males to work on the land. The women, well, they'll prepare our feasts, and in the evenings... they can be our *guests*."

The men chortled heinously as they envisioned the scenario.

Their mirth was suddenly broken by the dining chamber door creaking open. The chieftains turned in unison to see the unmistakable frame of Suma appear in the entrance way. Their sneering eyes followed him as he approached the table and found an unoccupied stool.

"Sorry I'm late," he mumbled in Morgoratt's direction. "I had some important work that needed to be finished tonight and got delayed. Have I missed much?"

"Suma!" greeted Morgoratt with a hearty tone that unsettled the big man. "The most important one in all of this! We've been discussing some exciting construction work that we are going to need your expertise for. You're going to be a busy man for a while."

Suma looked around the table with fearful confusion as the chieftains guffawed in agreement with their host. The carpenter glanced down at the sketch laid out on the table and the meanings of the denotations registered with him ominously. The sinister laughter grew as Morgoratt approached the seated Suma and slapped him forcefully on the shoulders. All around the table, the countenances of the watching chieftains were buoyant and contorted with wickedness.

Suma smiled nervously, and a pang of dread began to grow in his stomach as the full purpose of Morgoratt's plan dawned on him. As the blood drained from his face, he looked around the table in silent horror, and the manic expressions worn by Morgoratt and the chieftains seemed like those of excited devils.

19

THE PANTHER DISAPPEARED from Nicholas's sight moments after he began the daunting ascent of the rock face, but he could still sense its presence ahead of him. A series of ledges spiraled upward like an uneven stairway, which appeared to lead to the summit. Although the journey appeared foolhardy, the brief, otherworldly sensation that he had experienced during his conversation with Caralisa had filled Nicholas with a sense of determination and confidence which he could not explain. Bewilderingly, it was if his hands and feet knew where they needed to go, and the ease with which he was able to locate footholds in the dark was a surprise to him. The slope became increasingly precipitous, but Nicholas continued to advance up the craggy mountain. The movements of his limbs were relaxed and instinctive, responding to some new and inexplicable climbing dexterity.

The full moon moved steadily across the sky as the night grew later and Nicholas climbed higher and further. He had no comprehension of how long he had spent scaling the daring slope, but dawn had woken by the time he gratefully hoisted himself onto the topmost ledge. Sure enough, he found the black panther sitting with an expectant gait, and it growled encouragingly at the appearance of Nicholas.

Exhausted, Nicholas took a moment to compose himself and peered over the edge. The steepness of the drop below and the realization of the distance that he had climbed took his breath away. In the far-off distance, he could just make out the winking lights of Hohala village. He gritted his teeth as he envisioned the odious Volcarons asleep in the beds that once belonged to the Hohalians, and his determination to continue the journey was strengthened further. Nicholas surveyed the mountainous terrain ahead of him. In the rising dawn light, he could make out that he was standing atop a great, forested plateau. With his limbs aching, he rested for a few minutes and deliberated about the direction to take. All around him, his eyes met with an unbroken, mountaintop forest, thick with undergrowth and trees that obscured the horizon. There was no trail or visible path, but the panther, now standing upright and alert, appeared almost insistent that he follow.

Nicholas continued after the panther all morning, tramping his way through the dense foliage of the forest, frequently having to climb over ditches of rock and briars. By noon, as the sun beat down intensely through breaks in the trees, his body was pining for water and rest. Doubt and uncertainty began to interrupt his thoughts for the first time since he had set out from Haven, and he suddenly became anxious about his lack of provisions or a discernable plan.

After some time, the forest gradually began to give way to brush and a dusty, rock-strewn surface. On and on, across the increasingly rugged terrain, the panther scampered, and on and on Nicholas remained in determined pursuit. Fixated on keeping pace, he soon lost his sense of direction and of the passing time.

Before he realized it, the darkening sky indicated to the delirious Nicholas that he had been aimlessly following the panther at a distance for hours, and his joints howled from his exertions. Dusk crept in, and the scrubby trees darkened around him. Nicholas felt as if he could continue no further and looked ahead to see if the panther was still in sight. Sure enough, he could just make out the black tail waving restively in the darkness.

"I'm sorry," Nicholas called to it in defeat. "But I'm done; I can't go any further."

As if it understood, the panther returned a very impatient-sounding growl before hopping up onto a pile of large boulders and then out of sight on the other side. The forest was dark and still, and it was at that moment that Nicholas noticed the delicious sound of trickling water coming from behind the boulders. Exhausted, Nicholas followed the delicate, tinkling melody. To his delight, a small clearing revealed itself, and he could see where a clear, fresh spring bubbled up among a tumbled pile of rocks. The forest here was less dense, but a copse of bending palm trees lined the perimeter of the clearing where profusions of berries weighed down the moonlit branches. With the very last store of energy he could muster, Nicholas gathered several handfuls of the fruit and after eating until his stomach no longer pined, he collapsed thankfully on top of a pile of fallen palm leaves. As his eyes began to surrender to fatigue, he caught a fleeting glimpse of the black panther's gliding movement a few meters away.

Feeling reassured by its presence, Nicholas smiled appreciatively and whispered, "Thank you," before succumbing to his exhaustion.

*

A thunderous howl split the silence of the clearing, and Nicholas woke with a panicked start. The area, now bathed in morning light, reverberated with the clamorous echo, and a shower of loose berries trembled from the branches above his head. A sulfuric odor that Nicholas had not noticed the night before clung to the air, and the clearing—previously shrouded in darkness—was now fully visible. It was a dusty, barren place, and Nicholas observed that the fruit-bearing vegetation of the clearing was greatly outnumbered by gnarled, spiteful-looking trees.

The booming roar sounded once more, and Nicholas felt the ground vibrate beneath him. Bewildered, he leapt to his feet. Without thinking, he bounded through the forest in the direction of the sound, stumbling through the dry underbrush. As he sprinted, he was startled by his own eagerness to inspect the source of the noise when fleeing in the opposite direction should have been instinctive. The roar went up yet again as Nicholas approached a dense copse. Fearful of losing the direction of the sound, he ran at top-speed through the foliage and burst through a thicket of branches.

All of a sudden, an immense, screaming ravine appeared in front of him, and he flailed his arms frantically at the surrounding foliage as the ground disappeared beneath his feet. He pulled a trail of briars and vines downward with him, and thrashed wildly in an attempt to catch hold of anything that might cease his fall. His entire body jolted painfully as he grasped a thick, thorn-covered vine, and he hung breathlessly from the lip of the canyon. Nicholas's arms began to ache immediately, and thin streams of blood rolled down his wrists as he clutched at the vine for dear life. The pain and the strain on his arms were immense, and after a defeated glance at the yawning chasm below, Nicholas resigned himself to his end and indulged in a brief thought of Caralisa.

Suddenly, he felt himself being tugged at by the vine from above, and his innate will to survive jolted him into regaining his composure. He continued to be hauled by something unseen above him, and the alleviation of the strain on his arms afforded him the opportunity to swing his foot into a pocket in the ravine wall. With the pressure spread more evenly, Nicholas was able to hoist one hand over the other, and he heaved himself up onto the ledge where he collapsed in a breathless, panting heap.

Some minutes passed before Nicholas had composed himself enough to take stock of what had just happened. His hands and arms throbbed, and his fingers and palms were torn and bloodied. He cursed in pain and annoyance at his own stupidity for charging recklessly through the trees. Then, in the corner of his eye, he noticed the familiar flick of the black panther's tail. The beast, which he now saw up close for the first time, was a magnificent animal, and it stood watching him intently. Its eyes, emerald and intelligent, reminded him strikingly of Nightshade, and the cat's purr was unsettlingly reminiscent of his old friend's. Then, it suddenly dawned on Nicholas that it was just himself and the panther on the ravine ledge.

"Was it you who hauled me up?" he stammered disbelievingly.

The panther simply purred in response.

Nicholas shook his head, attempting to comprehend how he had just cheated death and doubting his own sanity for suggesting that a wild animal could have saved him from certain doom.

"Well, I guess I must thank you again," he continued bewilderedly.

The panther just purred contently, its eyes fixed on the ravine ahead of them. Nicholas sat up, and he stared out at the surrounding landscape for the first time. The view before him, washed in pale light, consisted of a vast, lunar-like terrain, uneven and mountainous. There were few trees in sight, and the jagged peaks threw ominous shadows across the land. Most notably, the earth appeared to be charred and blackened, as if it was the aftermath of some great inferno. As he scanned the topography, the same fury-filled howl that had drawn him to the chasm emitted piercingly from somewhere in the distance. Startled, Nicholas tried to make some sense of the sight before his eyes. Never in his life had he encountered a scene so desolate, so forbidding.

"What is this place?" he whispered fearfully to the panther who stood beside him in solemn silence.

At that moment, a booming eruption sounded from somewhere within the ravine, and a massive cloud of black smoke billowed violently out of the precipice. Nicholas's skin began to burn, and his windpipe spluttered from the acrid fumes. Behind him, he could hear the urgent growl of the black panther, and he turned to see its waving tail beckoning him back from the ledge. As he shuffled to a safer distance, another demonic howl erupted from within the bleak abyss. Whatever it was that lurked down in the recesses of the canyon, it struck a fear into Nicholas that was more strange and acute than any he had ever experienced.

20

AFTER SOME TIME, the smoke began to disperse, and Nicholas felt it safe enough to more closely investigate the canyon. Lying flat on his chest, he crawled across the ledge and attempted to peer down through the hanging smog. The drop was sheer and dizzying, and the canyon stretched for miles. A purplish haze obscured the horizon, and Nicholas wondered to himself whether he had in fact journeyed beyond the limits of the world touched by human feet. A combination of instinct and the guidance of the ghostly panther had taken him to this point; but now, as he lay looking down across the fiery netherworld, he suddenly felt confused, fearful and very much alone.

As the air cleared further, the canyon came into closer perspective. Below him, Nicholas's eyes were met by the most extraordinary and alien landscape. The terrain was jagged and uneven, littered with gaping craters and wizened rock formations that appeared to defy physics. There was a dark, copper-like hue to the rocks and soil, and while there was no great abundance of vegetation, the plant life that dotted the land was exotic and unearthly-looking. Towering, cactus-like plants, each adorned with a blaze of flowers, provided respite from the brutally barren landscape. Nicholas was mesmerized by the otherness of the place, so unlike anywhere he had known in his life.

Yet, as the haze dispersed, his wonder abruptly gave way to alarm. Far down, he could see that the canyon floor was a flurry of activity, alive with the movement of creatures, the like of which Nicholas had only encountered in his most absurd nightmares. In every direction, hideous, winged, reptilian beasts swooped through the air or clambered frenetically along the canyon walls. They were all manner of colors and shades, and their bodies were sleek and muscular. Their spines and long, thin necks were studded with pointed cartilage, and their whip-like tails swished menacingly like those of furious cats. But it was the fire that filled Nicholas with breathless dread. In bursts of every intensity, the creatures snorted and spat torrents of rock-scorching flame and evil, black smoke. Right then, the source of the smog that enveloped the land became clear to him.

For some time, Nicholas looked on, stunned. As he struggled to make sense of it all, he recalled the fireside stories from his childhood in Hohala that told of a far-off place filled with deadly creatures that were born of fire and darkness. But these old tales, handed down from previous generations, were assumed to have been myths only, regaled to young Hohalians to dissuade them from wandering away from the village. He remembered his late grandfather in particular, filling his child mind with fantastic, exaggerated descriptions of terrifying beasts that lived beyond the borders of man, which he had always assumed to be make-believe. Yet now, before his eyes lay that same, forbidden land of fire that his grandfather had transfixed his imagination with all those years ago, and Nicholas began to regret his compulsion to have ventured this way.

As he observed the nightmarish spectacle, Nicholas's eyes took notice of what appeared to be a layer of translucent light, like an almost-invisible film that spread across the entirety of the ravine, about three quarters of the way up the canyon walls. The swooping monsters below the shimmering layer all appeared to avoid flying too close to it. The creatures tumbled and rolled in the air, spitting fiery trails and snapping at each other indiscriminately, but as far as Nicholas could make out, none dared to fly near to the strange barrier.

Just then, Nicholas spotted a large, reptilian bird that was being pursued by a trio of screeching dragons. The predators howled as they shot clouds of flame in the fleeing bird's direction and appeared to round on it like a baying pack. Attempting to escape the circling flames, the bird rose higher in the air, and seemingly driven to the greater altitude by its pursuers, it glided into the glimmering film. In horrified awe, Nicholas watched as the bird's body was incinerated in an eruption of blood and flame.

Nicholas was nauseated and terrified. It was apparent to him now why past Hohalians who had travelled the mountain path west of Hohala had not been seen again. He had never known of a person who had ventured this way and returned, and his blood ran cold at the thought that he would meet his end too. Nicholas had no idea if the transparent layer of light was a permanent impediment to the beasts' escape from the canyon, or if the arrival of night would extinguish the shimmering barrier.

Whatever changes the coming darkness might bring to the place, Nicholas was unwilling to stay and find out.

There's been some mistake. There is no meaning in this dreadful place, he concluded to himself as he moved away from the lip of the ravine.

But, just as Nicholas had begun to inch to his feet, a monstrous, deafening roar caused the ground beneath him to tremble. He sat up with an alarmed start as the thunderous howl echoed like the reverberations of an explosion. The source of the dreadful roar had come from within the canyon, and judging by the sheer intensity of the cry, seemed to be in severe distress. Suddenly, something inside of Nicholas's mind whispered to him to investigate the sound. Adrenaline and curiosity coursed through him as he cautiously lowered himself onto his belly. With a grunt of exertion, he pulled his body up to the end of the ledge and peered over it once more.

21

As HE STRAINED his eyes to see through the translucent barrier below him, Nicholas could make out the bulky form of a hunched creature, much larger than the other beasts he had observed with horror moments before. It was an enormous, dragon-like animal with a wingspan of at least thirty feet and a spiked tail as thick as a tree trunk. Its cries became increasingly anguished, and Nicholas could see that it had wrapped its considerable forearms around a giant boulder. The creature was alone, and the canyon was empty and otherwise still, the rest of the demonic occupants of the ravine having fled at the tremendous din.

As he observed its pain, Nicholas became saddened by the creature's obvious distress. He watched with growing concern as the beast collapsed onto its knees. Such was its pain, Nicholas began to assume that it was mortally injured, and that he was witnessing the creature's death throes. The beast's bulging grip tightened around the boulder, and the fearsome, reptilian face became contorted as flames spluttered from its nostrils. Then, it threw its head backward, tensed its forearms and roared with such ferocity that the great boulder split with an audible crack. With its energy and endurance exhausted, the dragon collapsed in a heap on the canyon floor. There were no more howls or bursts of fire as its body succumbed to the strain of whatever dreadful excruciations it had been experiencing.

As Nicholas watched from the canyon ledge, frantically deliberating his next move, the limp wings of the creature appeared to twitch and jerk. The convulsive movements of the wings continued for several moments before a small flap of skin near the beast's abdomen began to gape. All of a sudden, the head of a much smaller creature emerged. An expression of astonishment spread across Nicholas's face as it dawned on him that the tormented cries of the animal had been cries of labor as she gave birth. Entranced by it all, he watched as the offspring struggled its way into the world. It too was sleek and reptilian, with wild, crimson eyes and jaws lined with teeth that snapped wildly. Before long, its thin, skeletal body, with disproportionately large wings and menacingly sharp claws emerged fully, and Nicholas saw that it was a miniature version of the monster that had birthed it. The ghastly infant stood upright on its hind legs, its eyes demented and thirsty for violence. It thrashed its head wildly and sputtered small bursts of flame from its mouth. With an instinctive flutter of its wings, it jolted a few feet above the ground where it bobbed confusedly. As it flapped and flailed, the creature seemed to grow increasingly confident in its movements and, before long, it had begun to flit through the air almost effortlessly. While it was small—no larger than a young deer—its venomous snarls and wild, thrashing jaws told Nicholas that he had just witnessed the birth of a being that could be no friend to humans. He watched as the monstrous infant, growing ever-more assured, shot upward through the canyon at surprising speed. Just as it was approaching the shimmering barrier above it, it wheeled away instinctively and avoided the gruesome fate of the bird-like creature whose incineration Nicholas had witnessed.

By now, the mother had raised her head to observe her offspring's new-found flying abilities, and Nicholas intuited that there was a sense of maternal pride in the way she watched it zip through the air. Her gaze remained fixed on the movements of the young dragon, and she growled encouragingly as the infant spurted a ball of swirling flame that dramatically obliterated a towering rock arch. A moment later, Nicholas watched as the newborn creature propelled itself toward the barrier a second time before diverting its course at the last possible minute. Looking on mesmerized, Nicholas was grateful for whatever force safeguarded his world from the pit of demons below him.

The power and fury of the creatures was unfathomable, and Nicholas resolved that this was a place not meant for the passage of humankind. He felt weak and confused, having been so hopeful of uncovering some means of salvation for his people; instead, he found himself looking down at what he imagined the underworld itself must look like. Was it for *this* that he was to believe the Nexus had led him this way? Could it really have been the will of the gods to guide him blindly to a gateway that opened only to fire, smoke, and wild savagery? Looking down upon the scene, so brutal and barbaric, Nicholas questioned angrily if he had been duped by the Nexus; had his abandonment of Hohalian laws damned him to the demise of some terrible sinner? Was this some divine punishment for having left behind nonviolent ways during the years of exile?

He decided he had seen enough. There was nothing for him here, and he was mindful that Caralisa was anxiously waiting for him back in New Hohala. Without further reflection, he turned and lunged back into the foliage, determined to abandon his foolhardy expedition and never again step foot in this nightmarish land.

Then, after only a few steps, Nicholas's stride was broken abruptly. The afflicted wails of the mother dragon began to echo again, and something deep inside of Nicholas inexplicably called him back. It was an overpowering sensation that immobilized his better judgement and filled his body and mind with a compulsion to bear witness to the extraordinary scene below him. Helpless to resist, the urge to take a final glance over the canyon edge consumed him, and he turned back once more in the direction of those vociferous roars.

22

THROUGH THE MURKY haze, Nicholas craned his neck to peer down into the ravine one last time. To his surprise, he saw that the mother dragon had resumed her stance by the boulder and had locked her powerful forearms around it as before. Her muscles were taut and her limbs rigid. Nicholas was thoroughly confused; despite his instinctive fear, he was saddened by the thought that he was now witnessing the slow demise of the awe-inspiring creature. Although these *were* monsters, he appreciated the terrible magnificence of their species. The creatures frightened him greatly with their chaos and violence, but Nicholas's natural inclination toward the well-being of animals now presented a conflict in his mind as, despite his revulsion, he found himself willing the anguished creature to be released from her pain. As the mother groaned loudly and struggled to remain upright on her hind legs, he winced and resigned himself to her demise.

However, Nicholas's pity quickly gave way to dumbfoundment as he watched the fold of skin below the mother dragon's abdomen twitch and flap yet again. Then, just as had occurred a few moments before, a diminutive head and forearms appeared, and a second infantile creature began to grope its way into the world. After several minutes of struggle, a plump, green form tumbled limply onto the canyon floor. It landed with an awkward thump and lay disorientated as its newborn eyes adjusted to the light. As Nicholas observed the young creature, he could make out that it looked very different from its mother and its terrifying sibling. This infant animal did not resemble a dragon at all; it was wingless and stout, with chubby limbs and a thick, domed skull. As it came fully into view, Nicholas could tell that it was somewhat smaller and much pudgier than its sibling, and its huge eyes—a glistening, ocean green—had a strikingly more benevolent appearance to them. The creature wobbled confusedly as it tried to raise itself to a standing position, and from his viewpoint on the canyon ledge, Nicholas was taken aback by its innocent, almost charming appearance. He could not say exactly why, but he immediately felt gripped by a strange feeling of attachment to the newborn, and he became filled with concern for its welfare. Having emerged from the security of its mother's womb into the fiery chaos of the canyon, the timid creature was undoubtedly overcome with fear. High up on the ledge, Nicholas's heart quaked with unexpected affection for the strange, little being, and all thoughts of leaving the ravine were momentarily dismissed.

The infant lay on its side, staring up beseechingly at its mother, who by now had used the nearby boulder to raise herself to her feet. Nicholas's distress heightened, and his heart leapt as the mother let out a roar of intense rage at the first sight of her latest offspring. She towered menacingly over the infant, and something about her stance suggested to Nicholas that the affection with which she had observed her first fledgling was now replaced by a murderous demeanor. With a burning wrath in her eyes, the ferocious mother pounded her feet vehemently while the little offspring lay stupefied in front of her. As she glowered down at the struggling infant, the mother dragon's eyes narrowed into sharp slits, and her nostrils flared threateningly. With a sudden spread of her wings, the beast threw back her head and emitted a roar that seemed to shake the entire canyon. Nicholas was panic-stricken as it became clear to him that the infant—so feeble and dissimilar to its parent and sibling—had not, for some reason, roused the maternal instincts of the monster that had spawned it. Almost unable to watch, he was filled with dread as it appeared that the little creature was about to be taken from the world just as quickly as it had entered it.

Dark gusts of smoke fumed from the mother dragon's nostrils as she bared her teeth, but the strain of double-birth had taken hold of the beast. She stumbled from one hind foot to the other as she prepared to strike at her offspring, which by now had raised itself to a standing position and stared up imploringly at its mother's unforgiving presence. From above, Nicholas winced in horror as the mother dropped her head in a rapid movement and chomped her jaws down toward the infant. A cloud of loose ash and dust rose up, and the panicked Nicholas struggled to see the creature. To his great surprise, the dust cleared, and he could see the mother hunched over in obvious pain, holding her snout with her forearms. The dragon's strike against the infant had been hindered by her disorientation, causing her to wallop her head against the ground and affording the infant an unlikely opportunity to evade her. Meanwhile, the newborn had begun to stagger away, terrified, yet unharmed. It waddled toward a pile of boulders a short distance off in a desperate attempt to find refuge. As fast as its legs could carry it, the newborn lumbered desperately toward the shelter of the boulders. As it staggered, a shrill wail cut through the air, and Nicholas saw the young creature's screeching sibling appear in the distance. With ghastly precision, the demonic sibling shot a long jet of flame from its open jaws, striking the pile of boulders with an eruption of black smoke. Such was the force of the blast, the traumatized newborn was thrown violently into the air, and it dropped to the ground with a smack that made Nicholas grimace. His heart beat wildly, and a rush of anger stirred within him at the brutal assault on the helpless creature. As the dust and smoke cleared, Nicholas's eyes scoured the canyon for the infant, and to his utmost relief he saw it slumped helplessly against a rock. Its pale-green skin was charred and bloodied, and one of its legs was bent at an awkward angle. From high above, Nicholas listened to its anguished whimpers with dread, and, as the malevolent squawks of its sibling cut through the canyon, his conscience propelled him to act.

Nicholas's searched his surroundings with a growing panic for the infant's safety. The sheer vertical walls offered little indication of a route down into the ravine. His thoughts grew more desperate as he watched the little creature drag itself into a low cavity in the canyon wall opposite. Through the dissipating smoke, he saw the mother dragon and the swooping sibling grunt angrily at each other as they hunted for their prey through the smog. Nicholas felt utterly helpless; at a loss for a better idea, he contemplated tossing rocks down into the canyon as a feeble attempt at distracting the mother and her hideous offspring. But just as he made to pick up a loose stone by his side, his heart skipped a beat at a familiar and very welcome sight. Perched upon a ledge, just a few feet below, was the enigmatic, black panther. Its tail swung restlessly, and its brilliant, green eyes appeared to beckon to Nicholas as they had before. He hadn't noticed the ledge, and he saw now that a perilously narrow pathway snaked its way from the point where the panther stood and continued down along the canyon wall at hair-raising angles. The panther growled up at Nicholas demandingly. At the ghostly cat's insistence, his mind was jolted to attention, and he responded with a refocused nod.

The drop to the lower ledge was not far, but the sheer depth of the canyon itself caused Nicholas's entire body to tremble as he lowered himself down with the help of some overhanging branches. Using a foothold in the rock face, he slowly inched himself onto the ledge. When he had gained his bearings, the panther snarled urgently and took off down the narrow pathway. Gripping the canyon wall with quivering fingertips, Nicholas followed the panther as quickly as he possibly could. As he went, parts of the pathway crumbled beneath his boot soles and dropped with ominous cracks onto the rocks below. Inching forward, Nicholas suddenly became aware of the shimmering barrier further down the ridge. The panther, by now considerably ahead, approached the point in the canyon where the pathway merged with the translucent light, and Nicholas yelled out warningly to it as it disappeared from his sight. Frozen in fear, he was almost unable to watch as he waited for the panther to fall victim to the same gruesome obliteration as the reptilian bird. However, several moments went by, and the expected grisly aftereffects never materialized. Curious, and concerned for the panther's welfare, Nicholas stole guardedly down the curved pathway toward the barrier, shuffling gingerly around the bend in the path where the panther had disappeared from his sight. As he turned the corner, he saw to his relief that the curve led to an opening in the canyon wall. While Nicholas had by now grown somewhat conditioned to the extraordinariness of the place, it was with astonishment that he saw there was some manner of a crude, low tunnel that seemed to have been bored into the canyon wall. It was pitch dark inside and impossible to see more than a few feet beyond the tunnel mouth. The hole itself was small but sizable enough for the large panther to stand in. As Nicholas stood deliberating whether or not to investigate the opening, he looked down warily into the canyon below him. To his surprise, he caught a sudden glance of the black panther gracefully navigating an extension of the descending pathway. Realizing that he had few other options, and with beads of sweat dropping from his temple, Nicholas crept guardedly through the dark entrance of the tunnel.

Inside, the passageway was low, confined, and as lightless as the deepest ocean trench, and Nicholas felt increasingly aware of his own vulnerability as he groped his way through. After several minutes of wearisome shuffling, Nicholas's eyes were met by the welcome sight of light ahead. Buoyed that he had almost reached the end of the passage, he squirmed enthusiastically toward the light. Just then, his elbow brushed against something solid and cool that made the tunnel walls resonate with a hollow rattling. Intent on reaching the end of the passage, he continued disinterestedly; yet, the loose clattering persisted as his movements seemed to have dislodged some kind of fragmented matter along the tunnel floor. As the light from the tunnel exit grew brighter, Nicholas's curiosity overtook his trepidation, and he strained his eyes to inspect the scattered debris around him. Lying on the confined tunnel floor, he picked up a rather large, rounded object in his right hand and held it in front of his face with curiosity. Aghast, Nicholas cried out in repulsion as he tossed the object away wildly, and a subsequent rattle echoed through the tunnel. In the gloom, Nicholas fought back the vomit rising to his throat as he saw the dead, black eye sockets of a human skull returning his horrified stare. He yelled out in horror as he hauled himself down the remainder of the passageway and tumbled out into the light of the open canyon. Lying on the narrow pathway to compose himself, Nicholas swore aloud repeatedly as cold perspiration soaked his skin, and his heart palpitated in his chest. Nauseated, he contemplated what he had just encountered: human remains, lonely and forgotten—the remnants of some fellow traveler of old who met a wretched demise at this lonely, uncharted frontier. Nicholas shuddered at the possibility that those bones may belong to the Hohalians of the past who traveled this direction, never to return—and, indeed, the prospect that he may well be following them to a similar doom.

It took several anguished moments before Nicholas was able to focus his attention properly on his new surroundings. He had emerged further down the pathway and, sure enough, the tunnel had led him to a point just beneath the deadly canyon barrier. Above him, the overcast sky was all but a blur, and he was forced to keep his eyes averted from the glare of the shimmering veil. His eyes searched again for the panther, and spotting it perched on a ledge ahead of him, he breathed in and continued on his way.

He wasn't fully aware of how long it had taken, but upon reaching the canyon floor, Nicholas dropped to his knees in grateful relief. A film of tear-inducing fog was present in the air, and it appeared to have thickened as he'd descended further down the side of the chasm. Nicholas surveyed the area: scorched boulders and piles of rocks littered the ground, and the entire area was fringed with haggard, desert plant life that loomed threateningly all around. The walls of the ravine towered overhead with the sky now visible as little more than a crack of pale light, and he wondered fearfully to himself if he would soon join the ranks of those long-forgotten explorers for whom the place became a tomb. With the blank stare of the human skull still impressed on his mind, every one of Nicholas's instincts screamed at him to abandon his foolhardy expedition, the end-goal of which he didn't even understand. And yet, his inexplicable determination to come to the aid of the helpless creature propelled him onward.

All of a sudden, Nicholas heard the pitiful whimper of the newborn further up the canyon passage, and he took off at a cautious sprint. The black panther led the way, darting between boulders and throwing repeated backward glances at Nicholas to spur him onward. The choking smog continued to thicken, and irritated tears streamed from Nicholas's eyes as he searched for any sign of the young creature. The roars of the mother dragon and the shrieks of the other infant thundered in his ears. Assailed from every angle by the smoke and deafening bedlam, Nicholas's senses threatened to be overcome for a second time. He tried to concentrate on the swish of the panther's tail up ahead as he fought to remain lucid. And then, somehow, he spotted the pale, green form of the helpless creature through the smoke, shivering and cowering within a cleft in the canyon wall. The terrified newborn lay curled up in a fetal position, and it appeared to have become aware of Nicholas's presence. It moaned sadly, and its brilliant eyes gazed at him imploringly. Nicholas returned a sympathetic stare; something in the creature's beseeching eyes set his heart astir, and he was filled with increased concern for it. It was clear that the creature was injured, its skin charred and grazed and its eyes shining with tears of obvious pain. All of a sudden, a familiar, stomach-churning roar ripped through the canyon, and Nicholas whipped around to see the returning silhouette of the mother dragon in the distance.

There was no time for hesitation, and before he fully realized what he was doing, Nicholas found himself running to the injured creature. He heaved its limp body across both of his shoulders, and with the bawls of the infant creature's terrible parent approaching rapidly, Nicholas took off sprinting down the canyon in the direction he had come. Blindly, he tore down the smoky path with the furious roars of the mother dragon ringing in his ears. Nicholas knew he would never outrun the giant beast. He scoured the ground hurriedly for anything that might shield himself and the infant from the crazed monster's inevitable onslaught. Before Nicholas even knew it, a colossal claw swiped through the haze from above them, and he and the infant creature were walloped to the ground. The creature tumbled from his grip and began to struggle in terror as Nicholas lay winded. Despite its injuries, the creature stumbled in the direction of a grove of cactus trees, desperate to get out of the sight of its murderous mother. The infant was inches from the shelter of the thicket when, without warning, its sibling appeared from above with a vindictive rasp. A gust of spinning flame tumbled from its mouth, instantly igniting the cacti into a ferocious inferno. The petrified infant, narrowly missed by the blaze, was blown backward by the force of the explosion, and Nicholas cried out in alarm to see it lying motionless and bloodied. The roar of the mother dragon echoed all around, and she spat a scalding cloud of flame at her winged offspring which snarled back indignantly and flew off. A sweltering wind swirled around Nicholas, as the mother dragon took to the air once more in search of her unwanted offspring. Through a veil of dust and smoke, he watched as her gigantic frame hovered above the unconscious infant, and her low, satisfied growl suggested she had spotted her defenseless target.

Nicholas's mind raced; he searched frantically for anything he could use as a weapon, but nothing caught his eye. Both his heart and his mind cried out to him to help the unconscious newborn who appeared to be on the cusp of death, its body streaked with gashes and its leg sticking out at an eye-watering bend. His subconscious was ablaze with desperation as if there was nothing more urgent in the world than the rescue of the little creature.

"Please," he whispered to the spirits of the Nexus who he could not know were even listening. "Help me save it. Please, don't let it die. I beg you, please…"

Before he had even finished his prayer, Nicholas watched in dismay as the mother lowered her neck and snapped up the infant in her jaws, before raising its frail body triumphantly. Suddenly, Nicholas's muscles tightened and his eyes focused. He saw the crazed eyes of the mother dragon and the fading light in those of her drooping infant. All external noise became blocked from his senses, except for the dull thump of his heart. All of a sudden, he felt inexplicably purposeful, and his senses grew calm and focused. In the back of his mind, a faint voice whispered to him, and he became aware for the first time of a nearby boulder, similar in size and shape to the cauldron that hung above his hearth back Haven. He glanced at the hunk of rock and then back to the mother dragon who stood shaking the infant in her jaws. Without a further thought, Nicholas bent his knees as low as he could and wrapped his taut arms around the boulder. With a cry of pure exertion that caused the mother dragon's blood-crimson eyes to dart in his direction, he launched the enormous rock above his head before dropping exhaustedly to the ground. Sprawled on his back, he watched as the boulder soared across his eye-line before striking the mother dragon's head with a gut-churning crack.

Sprawled on his back, Nicholas observed the beast collapse to the ground, causing a cloud of ash to flare up, obstructing his view. His ears were ringing, and the burning grove of cacti had thickened the smog, disorientating him further. His arms were numb, and his entire body felt like it had been stretched and beaten. He called out, yet he could not hear the sound of his own voice. He picked himself up as he deliriously scanned his surroundings for the infant creature and clawed the dust from his eyes, pleading that he would spot the little green figure. However, when his vision finally cleared, Nicholas was stunned to observe the motionless body of the mother dragon, prostrate on the ground before him. Her eyes were lifeless, and her serpentine neck was contorted horribly, Nicholas's boulder having delivered an impact that was instantly fatal. And, wheezing by her side in the ash, was the infant, dazed and bloodied but miraculously still alive.

Nicholas climbed to his feet and staggered toward the creature, his arms slack from the strain of his extraordinary exertion. Despairing at the thought of losing the infant to its injuries, Nicholas hurriedly considered his options;

the fledgling animal was not of his world, and he knew nothing about its species. The other beasts that he had encountered in the fiery canyon were malevolent and deadly, yet he could not imagine abandoning the creature to the mercy of its terrible sibling which was sure to return soon.

"Don't give up!" Nicholas urged as he got close enough to see his own face reflected in the creature's sparkling eyes, fearful that its remaining life-force might give out at any moment.

Taking the greatest of care not to brush against the creature's damaged leg or the bleeding puncture wounds inflicted by the mother dragon's fangs, Nicholas lifted it slowly and carefully into his arms. Then, for the first time, he noticed that the canyon was now in silence. Like the eye of a storm, there was no sound to be heard, no movement and no sign of anything living other than himself and the whimpering creature. After a short, pre-cautionary pause, he was reassured that they were alone in the immediate vicinity, and he crept quickly back through the ravine in the direction of the way that he and the panther had first entered. It didn't take long and despite the haze, he easily found the point at which he had descended into the canyon. Eager to escape before any other dangers presented themselves, Nicholas slowly and gently hoisted the creature across his shoulders. It gave no resistance, other than to quiver whenever Nicholas moved too suddenly. For a moment, he stopped to look for the black panther which had not appeared again since the mother dragon's attack. Resigned to making it on his own, Nicholas gritted his teeth and began the laborious trek back up the sloping pathway.

How long it took, he could not be sure, but Nicholas was utterly exhausted by the time he emerged into the cool, night air at the top of the ravine. With a long groan of fatigue, he lifted the ailing creature onto the ledge before hoisting himself up as well. By now, Nicholas was distressed for the creature's welfare, and he cried out to it to regain consciousness as he caressed its blood-soaked skin.

Come on!" he implored through distraught tears. "You did not come into the world today to be ripped out of it again. Keep fighting! Do you hear me? Keep fighting!"

However, to Nicholas's growing anguish, there was no response from the creature; no whimper of acknowledgement or any sign of improvement in its dire condition. Instead, its breathing had only become shallower, and for the first time since his companion, Nightshade, had been taken from him all those years ago, Nicholas felt a familiar grief return.

"This can't be it!" he roared out at the dark sky, his voice filled with a depth of rage he had not felt since that terrible day five years before.

"You can't have led me all this way just to watch this poor creature die!" he called out to the Nexus. "What is it that you want? Please, just…"

And with that, Nicholas broke down, his tears dropping onto the creature's blood-stained scales. There was no sound or movement from the infant, its respiration barely detectable.

"Was it for *this* that you brought me to this place—to witness this… *barbarity*?" Nicholas ranted at the Nexus a second time, unaware if the gods were even listening. "It can't end like this!"

To Nicholas's dejection, the only reply to his outburst was the shrieks of the creature's hideous sibling echoing mournfully from the canyon below. With his energies utterly depleted, and his emotions overwrought, Nicholas let out a howl of despair and finally collapsed in a heap next to the unmoving creature. As he too slipped into unconsciousness, Nicholas held the infant in his arms, and his senses finally succumbed to exhaustion.

23

NICHOLAS'S NOSTRILS TWITCHED with irritation from the sulfuric fumes that hung on the air, and it was with a choking splutter that he regained consciousness. Panicked by the burning sensation that filled his throat and windpipe, he shot upright with a dramatic wheeze. Glaring sunlight stung his eyes, and his entire body was covered in beads of grimy perspiration. Rubbing his forehead, Nicholas glanced around him in order to recover some sense of his bearings. Just off to his side, the canyon lay gaping and smoking like the crater of a volcano, while through the murk, the wild, reptilian shrieks were still audible from deep within the ravine.

Nicholas's heartbeat began to quicken as he spotted to his right a familiar, green form, motionless and caked with soot and encrusted streaks of blood. Almost not daring to breathe, Nicholas leaned across the creature's body and placed his finger to its neck; after several tremulous seconds, he discerned the faintest throbbing beneath the skin along its windpipe, and the presence of a pulse reassured him that life still stirred in the creature's poor, battered body.

Nicholas gently shook the creature's slack frame in the vague hope that he might rouse it. Several seconds passed and there was no response. Fearing the worst, Nicholas rubbed the top of its head and called to it urgently.

"Come on," he pleaded as he shook the creature with greater desperation. "I know you're not gone. Don't give up. Come on!"

Suddenly, the creature jerked awake, its eyelids so encrusted with soot that they could barely open halfway. At the dazzling light, it groaned feebly, its babyish snout busted and bloodied. The creature opened its mouth to reveal two rows of infantile teeth and a pointed tongue that writhed about its jaws in distress. It gasped and retched, and a gurgling noise in its throat told Nicholas that it needed water immediately. Without a further thought, Nicholas wrapped his own weak arms around the creature's body and, with a grunt of fatigue, hauled it across his right shoulder.

"Be strong, and give me a chance to help you," he whispered to the creature as its breathing became barely audible.

Groaning with exertion, Nicholas turned away from the canyon and stomped through the arid scrubland in the direction of the jungle spring the panther had led him to the day before. The sun beat down relentlessly through the sparse, mountainous foliage, and Nicholas could feel his own breathing become strained from the humidity that lingered like an oppressive weight. With each shuddering step, Nicholas was forced to fight back his own exhaustion, grunting through the pain with only the thought of getting the ailing creature to water driving his own defeated body forward. For what seemed an age, he plodded onward, listening warily to the weakening rhythm of the creature's breathing. The jungle began to thicken once more, and drooping, thorn-covered vines clawed at Nicholas and the creature's exposed skin. As he trudged through an overgrown portion of the forest floor, Nicholas tripped over an obscured hollow, and his ankle twisted painfully underneath the creature's weight, causing him to drop to his knee with a growl of frustration. He felt his whole body go weak, and his arms trembled with the burden of the creature. His energy was sapped, and his every muscle screamed at him to give in to his exhaustion; yet, at that moment, a familiar distant voice somewhere in the back of his mind whispered to him. As before, his mind was instantly soothed, like cool balm on burnt skin.

"We *can* do this," he growled to himself breathlessly as he forced himself back into a standing position and resumed his trek.

Nicholas continued straight ahead at an arduous plod, his senses of time and direction all but deserting him. Onward he drove himself, pursing his eyes in anguish as he tried with all his remaining energy to block out the searing pain across his body. His arms howled out in pain, and he was forced to vomit into the bushes as nausea and exertion began to overwhelm him. Amid the creature's fading gasps and the sound of his own retching body, Nicholas's mind turned again to the possibility of meeting his own ignoble end in the jungle wasteland, starving, broken, and forgotten in the loneliest, most wretched of places. He thought of Caralisa and imagined her watching the mountain path from her window, waiting for the day of his return that she knew might never come. He felt tears run down his face, and he coughed out a sob as his vision grew dim and blurred.

"I can't...I'm sorry," he gasped dejectedly to the creature across his shoulder. "I can't..."

However, just then, the faintest, most welcoming sound of tinkling water danced in Nicholas's ears, and so stunned and grateful was he to hear it that he took a deep breath and drew upon his last reserve of energy to rise to his feet once more. With a roar so impassioned that it rose up from deep within his stomach, Nicholas resumed his unsteady slog toward the spring, fighting with all of his strength to drive his body forward. At long last, just as he felt like his knees would give in at any moment, he stumbled through a low-hanging canopy of palm branches, and a wide, verdant clearing revealed itself like a gift from the heavens. It was indeed the place that Nicholas had previously been guided to by the black panther, and, sure enough, at its center was the babbling rock spring that trickled into a pool of the most deliciously crystalline water.

As he began to stagger toward the pool's edge, Nicholas felt the creature slumped across his shoulder begin to flinch and jerk. Alarmed at its sudden distress, he lowered it to the ground. To Nicholas's surprise, the creature's shimmering, green eyes—now wide and dilated—were fixed intently on the spring, and its forepaws dug into the soil of the clearing floor as it tried to drag its own way toward the water.

"Stop!" rasped Nicholas as he went to hold the creature still, all too aware that it was gravely injured. "You're too hurt. Wait, and let me help..."

However, the rest of his frantic plea was cut short by a sharp, unexpected exclamation from the flailing creature.

"Auuuu-gheeee!" it cried out in a shrill, determined tone that was so piercing it caused Nicholas to lose his balance and falter backward.

"Wait!" cried out Nicholas again weakly, but the creature paid him no heed; instead, it continued to claw its way through the thick grass in a seemingly desperate bid to reach the spring.

"Auuuu-gheeee!" it shrieked a second time as it thrashed madly with its blood-smeared limbs and tail.

Nicholas—by now terrified that the creature's crazed movements would cause it serious harm—scrambled toward it on his hands and knees and wrapped his arms around its thick midriff. Beneath Nicholas's grip, the creature quivered in agitation and fear, but continued to try and shuffle away to reach the spring.

"Auuuug-heeee!" it wailed a third time.

"Stop, you're bleeding all over," Nicholas implored. "You need to calm down!"

To his surprise the creature ceased its struggling and grew still at his words. With a sad, tired moan, it turned its head to face Nicholas, and its enormous eyes looked up at him, glinting in the sunlight like the most flawless emeralds. Nicholas stared into the creature's brilliant eyes, transfixed by their forlorn and beseeching beauty. Without a further word, Nicholas gingerly lifted its battered frame in his arms, and, slowly, he carried it to the bank of the pool. As they stood next to the water's edge, the creature's face visibly brightened once more at the sight of the glittering ripples on the water that rolled gently and invitingly across the limpid surface.

Again, the delirious cry of "Auuuu-gheeee" filled the empty clearing as the creature jerked in Nicholas's arms, its eyes filled with longing for the glassy water. Nicholas attempted to set the creature down on the grass, but it began to lash its tail in a bid to get free.

"Okay!" conceded Nicholas, struggling to contain the infant's excitement. "I'll let you go. Just stop for a moment."

Weak to the point of collapsing himself, Nicholas could no longer keep a firm hold on the writhing creature, and as it thrust its weight toward the pond, it slipped from his grasp. With an awkward thud that made Nicholas wince, the creature landed on the grassy edge; however, it seemed barely unperturbed by the sudden landing, and with wild cries of "Auuuuu-geeee! Auuuu-gheeee!" it shifted its weight and rolled clumsily into the dark water.

"No!" hollered Nicholas in alarm as the creature's outline disappeared from sight, consumed by the deep pool.

He splashed at the water in panic, trying desperately to disperse the obscuring froth that had accumulated where the creature had fallen in. For what seemed like an eternity, his frantic eyes scanned the dark water, but he could see nothing of the plump little body within the ripples. A moment or two later, he began to fear the worst. Banishing his gnawing exhaustion, Nicholas tore off his boots and prepared to jump in after the creature. But just as he was about to dive, the pool's surface shuddered, and without warning, a cascade of water erupted into the air like a ferocious geyser, drenching him and the surrounding pool edge. Stunned, soaked and gasping for breath, Nicholas rubbed the water from his eyes and looked up in shock, struggling to comprehend what had just happened. To his amazement, he watched as the creature twirled and splashed carelessly in the spring, rejuvenated and very much enjoying the new sensation of the water.

Nicholas rubbed his dripping eyelids in disbelief; he had witnessed so many strange and surreal things of late, but watching his new, otherworldly companion luxuriating in the crystal pond, as if he had not suffered a scratch, was utterly bewildering. Nicholas looked closely at the infant creature's body and realized that its injuries were all but healed. Its skin still glowed an angry red where its mother's teeth had punctured the deepest. However, the grazes and burns that ravaged it were now all but invisible. The little creature sparkled with a healthy coat of glistening, green scales. As it indulged playfully in the vitalizing water, it cried out, "Aug-heee! Aug-heee!" even louder and with increasing joy, and Nicholas's addled brain attempted to fathom what manner of extraordinary creature he had removed from that dark and fiery netherworld.

"Au-gee?" Nicholas mouthed to himself absent-mindedly as he gazed in wonder at the beaming creature, absent now of any visible pain or discomfort. "What *are* you?"

24

FOR OVER AN hour, Nicholas remained seated in dumbfounded silence on the edge of the pool as he watched the creature play in the water. He marvelled at how only a short time earlier, he had been convinced that its battered body would give up. Bizarrely, now that same creature appeared perfectly healthy, as it mischievously sent strong, rolling ripples up against the bank of the pond, splashing the area where Nicholas sat watching. The spray against his skin was cool and refreshing, and Nicholas's aching limbs were grateful for the opportunity to rest on the soft, damp grass. The all-consuming fatigue that had gripped him since he awoke next to the battered creature had begun to ease in the light of the sun and the spray of the pool.

Before long, the afternoon daylight began to dim, heralding the rapid onset of darkness across the strange and dangerous country that Nicholas and the creature now found themselves stranded in, both of them vulnerable and displaced from their native places. Considering how much enjoyment the creature was getting from his playful exertions in the rocky pool, Nicholas was reluctant to interrupt its fun, but the fall of night unsettled him, and his body and mind begged at him for food and rest. Grimacing as he raised himself to his feet, he waved and called to the creature.

"It's getting late," he called to it, as if he was speaking to an infant or young child. "We should find some food and shelter."

In response, the creature paused its playful thrashing in the water and cocked its head at Nicholas impishly.

"Auu-gheee!" it chirped in response as, to Nicholas's astonishment, it darted through the water like a salamander, clambered up onto the overgrown embankment, and proceeded to shake its body vigorously to dispel the droplets that had clung to its now-glowing, green scales.

Nicholas stared at the creature in amazement as it stood looking up at him. The fact that the spring water had somehow relieved it of what had—certainly, at the time—appeared to have been mortal injuries, was mystifying to him. However, the creature's ability to understand his words and intentions bewildered Nicholas even more. He had witnessed it come into the world only hours before, and to Nicholas's addled mind, there was no possible way that a new-born creature –entirely unacquainted with human language and expression—could somehow understand verbal communication; yet, despite his disbelief at the notion, he *had* just witnessed his new companion act on his request to come out of the pool, and by its body language, it was evident that the creature was indeed now ready for the food and sleep that Nicholas had suggested.

"You're a very strange little fellow," mused Nicholas. "And what was that sound you were making when you saw the water? 'Aug-gee, aug-gee?' Whatever does that mean?"

The creature peered at Nicholas curiously and chirped once more in amusement.

"Do you have a name?" Nicholas queried, feeling a little silly.

As if to underscore the absurdity of his question, the creature emitted a shrill, rolling sound with its tongue that to Nicholas almost seemed as if it was responding to him in the negative.

"Bit of a foolish question, I suppose," conceded Nicholas, his cheeks growing slightly pink. "Well, I do like that sound you made: 'Au-gee!' It's… *different*. Maybe that should be your name."

This time, the creature gave an affirmative-sounding chirp and looked up at him earnestly.

"Well, *Augee*," continued Nicholas, placing slow, hard emphasis on both syllables of the creature's new name. "I think we should get moving. I know a place that's not too far where we'll be safe for tonight. But we have to get moving if we want to make it there before dark."

In reply, the creature clicked its tongue good-humoredly, prompting an affectionate smile from Nicholas.

From there, he and Augee made their way together through the tangled jungle, relying on Nicholas's vague memory of the way to guide them. Augee, now sufficiently recovered from his wounds, walked upright on his portly hind legs. It was apparent that the creature was still in some discomfort, his gait slightly labored and uneven when he stepped with his right foot. Otherwise, Augee appeared healthy, and in a standing position, the creature measured almost to Nicholas's shoulders. Although he argued to himself that it couldn't possibly be the case, it actually appeared to Nicholas that Augee had even grown a little in the hours since they'd encountered one another in the canyon.

Nonsense, pondered Nicholas unconvincingly. *You're imagining things.*

Whatever the case, Augee was tall enough to reach for the plump forest berries that hung from the loftier branches above their heads, and, encouraged by Nicholas, the creature nibbled at a selection of the fruit with the utmost seriousness. Such was the look of solemn preoccupation on Augee's countenance as he sampled the new tastes, Nicholas was forced to stifle an impulsive chuckle at the mess of berry stains around his reptilian mouth and paws.

"Good, huh?" Nicholas grinned, to which Augee returned with an exuberant chirp that made him beam even wider.

Before dusk had fully descended on the jungle, they arrived at the aperture in the rock face where Nicholas had taken refuge the night before. It was cramped and drafty, but the hollow was obscured by enough thick vegetation that Nicholas was content to forgo comfort for the reassurance that they were unlikely to be discovered by any beasts of the extraordinary countryside.

In the gloom of the cave, Nicholas lit a sparse fire, and in the furthest corner, he fashioned makeshift bedding from some wide palm leaves and soft foliage. It was a cool evening, and a light breeze whistled intermittently through the entrance of the hollow. Still mindful of the dire physical state that Augee had been in prior to immersing himself in the curative jungle spring, Nicholas removed his outer tunic and placed it carefully over the sleeping area. Augee, weary and confused, had by this point propped himself up against the cave wall.

"Come here, Augee," Nicholas ushered to him softly. "You need to rest now. We'll figure out a plan in the morning, but now we rest."

Augee cocked his head in response, before tottering toward the rough-shod bedding and settling himself down gratefully.

"You sleep peacefully, my friend," Nicholas smiled. "You're safe now, and I'll make sure you come to no harm."

As if acknowledging Nicholas's assurance, Augee made a long, purr-like noise that suggested his comfort, and he curled his pudgy feet and forearms into his sea-green midriff. His large, round eyes, heavy with fatigue, fluttered and then closed as his breathing became lighter, and finally he drifted into slumber for the first time.

By the firelight that dimly illuminated the cave's interior, Nicholas surveyed the curious little creature with wonderment and affection. The remnants of the berry juice still smeared his infantile snout, and every few minutes, his body made slight jerking movements as Augee dreamed about whatever occupied the minds of his strange species as they slept. Nicholas felt a great warmth toward his peculiar, new companion, and he was certain that his decision to risk everything by descending into the canyon had been entirely justified by his rescuing of Augee.

As he settled himself down on the cave floor, Nicholas contemplated solemnly whether or not the Nexus *had* actually guided him to Augee. He glanced at the peacefully-slumbering form beside him and tried to fathom how on earth such a docile, unimposing animal could be an answer to the Hohalians' plight. Surely, there was no possibility that the stout, good-natured creature—so utterly different from its cruel dragon-mother and its beastly, winged sibling—could be of assistance in rising up against the Volcarons. Yet, something within Nicholas's subconscious whispered to him to be patient and to have some faith in the infant Augee.

"Maybe you *are* the miracle," he murmured in the darkness.

Nicholas smiled as Augee grunted softly in his sleep, and then he too succumbed to his tiredness.

25

THE FEEBLE GLOW of the rising sun intruded into the cave and invaded Nicholas's senses. He was disorientated at first, but the feel of cool rock beneath him triggered his recollection of the past day's events. With a gasp, he bolted upright and, remembering the presence of Augee, and he saw that the flattened, makeshift bedding next to him was empty. He rose to his feet and ducked out of the cave into what was a still, overcast morning. To his great relief, he didn't need to search far; just outside the entrance of the cave Augee sat hunched over in the grass, deep in concentration. Nicholas stifled a laugh upon seeing that Augee, having clearly enjoyed his feast of berries the previous evening, had been foraging for more and was now gorging on an array of jungle fruit. The little creature hadn't noticed Nicholas's approach, and he jumped when Nicholas rubbed his domed head in greeting from behind. Augee spun around with a self-conscious expression and a splatter of purple fruit juice stained around his mouth. It was with growing affection that Nicholas laughed to himself as Augee innocently extended his paw, nudging a handful of slightly bruised blueberries in his direction to share.

For a while, Nicholas lay contently in the grass, watching in silence as Augee greedily devoured the remaining fruit. The forest floor was cool and comfortable beneath him, and for a rare moment he felt at ease. He watched in amusement as Augee licked the remnants of berry pulp from the end of his claws with an absorbed, contented look in his eyes. Nicholas laughed to himself as Augee's enjoyment of the fruit put him in mind of Caralisa's love for jungle berries. That thought, however, caused his mood to darken as he remembered the grim uncertainty of Caralisa's circumstances as she waited for him back in New Hohala, and he wondered in frustration when, if ever, the purpose of his own blind trek into the wilderness would reveal itself.

Without warning, the quietude of the morning was punctured by a shrill, blood-chilling shriek in the distance. Nicholas's heart leapt, and immediately he could see that Augee had turned rigid and alert as he scanned the clearing for the source of the noise. The sky had quickly darkened over with surly storm clouds, and off beyond the forest, from the direction of the canyon, the ghastly chorus of roars and howls ripped through the countryside. The dreadful, thunderous wails appeared to have visibly distressed Augee, and his eyes were dilated with fear. Nicholas placed his hand gently on his berry-stained claw and offered him a forced smile of reassurance.

"They can't harm you now," he consoled the trembling creature. "It's a good idea if we get a move on, though. New Hohala is a long way off, and the journey will take a couple of days. What do you think? Are you ready to go?"

Augee scrambled to his feet, glancing back nervously in the direction from where the pandemonium of the canyon had emanated. Keen not to delay further, Nicholas stomped out the last of the blinking cinders from the campfire and gathered up his cloak and boots. He peered at Augee who stood trembling at the demonic bellowing that continued to echo intermittently in the distance, and he concluded that it was time for them to leave.

Abandoning their makeshift shelter, Nicholas and Augee began their hasty trek through the jungle. As they fought through convolutions of trailing vines and clambered over briars and brush, Nicholas discreetly monitored Augee's movements. It was with a measure of uneasiness that he noticed the creature still walked with a visible limp in his right foot. The mysterious curative properties of the jungle spring appeared to have rejuvenated his life force and healed the wounds on his skin; however, the injury that he'd incurred to his leg had been only partially healed, which could present a considerable problem in making the lengthy trip to New Hohala.

"Does it hurt?" he queried after a few minutes of observing Augee hobble across the overgrown terrain in obvious discomfort.

In reply, Augee gave what sounded like a defiant chirp and continued on his way; yet, the infant creature's tightened facial features indicated to

Nicholas that he was persevering through the pain. His leg clearly needed to be treated, but it was too much of a risk for them to stay so close to the ravine.

"Let me help you," suggested Nicholas softly, concluding that Augee was currently unfit to continue on such a difficult journey unaided.

Before Augee could react, Nicholas placed his arm across his infantile shoulders to prop him up. In tandem, they waded clumsily through the undergrowth with Nicholas supporting Augee's weight as the creature took each step with nervous uncertainty. As they tramped over unseen rises in the terrain, Nicholas could see that the exertion was taking its toll on Augee, although the spirited youngster endured the discomfort without complaint. Unfortunately, it was soon clear that Augee was in no condition to make it all the way to New Hohala, and Nicholas's thoughts turned to the rejuvenating jungle spring that had already once cured Augee of his ailments.

"Do you think you can make it a bit further?" he inquired gently to the creature as a rumble of thunder sounded above them and thick rain droplets began to spit through the leaves overhead. "The spring's not too far, and we can rest there until we decide what to do next."

Augee replied with a labored, yet determined-sounding, grunt, and together they tramped on defiantly through the rapidly increasing rain.

By the time the trickle of spring water greeted them like welcoming birdsong, the storm clouds overhead had opened, and a downpour had begun. The heavy rain plummeted through the dense treetops, soaking Nicholas, Augee and the jungle all around them. Augee, who was witnessing rain for the first time, stared up at Nicholas with a combination of bemusement and apprehension.

"Come on!" shouted Nicholas over the growing deluge, supporting the creature's forearm to where the pressure on Augee's bad leg was lessened. "Let's get to the clearing and find shelter!"

Together, they lumbered across the remaining distance until, at long last, saturated vegetation gave way to the relieving sight of the clearing and its rejuvenating pool. Amid the torrential rainfall and dangerous flashes of forked lightning, Nicholas rubbed the relentless globules of rain away from his face as his eyes combed the clearing for a place to take refuge. He contemplated taking shelter underneath a willow tree whose branches spread out like a leafy dome, but an explosive crack of lightning in the near distance warded him off that idea. Full of confusion, Augee looked up at him miserably as the rain pricked his exposed skin.

"Let's look over here," Nicholas proposed as he pointed to the shapeless, sprawling rock formation from which the spring bubbled up from the ground and flowed into the adjoining pool.

Together, they stumbled into the open clearing as Nicholas willed the jagged forks of lightning to encroach no further. The elegant spring that they had encountered the day before was now replaced by a gushing, ungainly torrent that tumbled and spilled noisily into the deep pool.

"Stay right here, okay?" instructed Nicholas to Augee, patting him comfortingly on the head. "I'll be back in a moment."

With that, Nicholas hopped up onto a shoulder-high ledge that stuck out from the rock formation and overlooked the pond on the other side. He climbed a little further and higher along the extensive landform to where an overhanging ridge created a sweeping, arch-like effect, under which lay a dry, sheltered hollow that was large enough to accommodate both of them. As a crash of thunder erupted overhead, he gestured triumphantly to Augee to take his hand. Augee reached out and allowed Nicholas to hoist him up, and moments later the sopping-wet pair were huddled together in the hollow at the center of the rock formation. As they sat in silence, listening to the torrential thunderstorm, Nicholas began to feel Augee shivering. He looked drained, and his green scales had taken on a sickly, greyish tinge. His eyes appeared sunken, and he had begun to sniff and wheeze from the rain. Concerned, Nicholas removed his cloak from his own shoulders and wrapped it around Augee. In response, Augee glanced up at him in surprise at the kind gesture before nuzzling his head affectionately under Nicholas's shoulder. Soon, Augee eventually drifted off to sleep while Nicholas stared out tiredly at the formidable downpour. It was a strange feeling to Nicholas, to have, for the first time since Nightshade's death, another vulnerable, wild creature place such absolute trust in him. He glanced down at the dozing creature—so benign and vulnerable—and he pondered to himself doubtfully as to the likelihood of Augee being the miracle that the Hohalians so desperately needed. What was discouraging to Nicholas was that—other than the creature's exceptional intelligence and his surprising capacity for empathy—there was little else about Augee that suggested he *could* be the miracle for which the whispering voice of the Nexus had implored Nicholas to commence his journey through the mountains. Despite the fact that Augee had been born of a dragon—spawned by a beast of ferocity and violence the likes of which Nicholas had not even encountered in his most disturbing nightmares—there was no aggression in his demeanor, and, physically, he was uncoordinated, lumbering, and rather clumsy. Although Augee was charming and endearing, Nicholas found it impossible to fathom how he could offer any real assistance in an uprising against the sheer numbers and violence of the Volcarons. Augee displayed no signs that he could breathe fire like his fearsome mother and sibling, and most curiously, he was wingless with no apparent capability to take flight. Without a doubt, Augee was a creature of gentleness, not aggression; of meekness, rather than malice. His instincts, personality and spirit were so unlike the vicious beasts of the canyon, and Nicholas came to accept that his new friend would be of little use in the looming war against the Volcarons. Indeed, Augee may have been born into a world of monsters, but he was certainly not one of them.

After some time, the rain began to subside, and the familiar sounds of the jungle clearing replaced the clamor of the storm. Noticing that Augee continued to shiver underneath the damp cloak, Nicholas gently rose to his feet, taking care not to wake the slumbering infant. From there, he began gathering up twigs and tree limbs that had been scattered throughout the clearing by the storm. Within a short time, Nicholas had gathered up a substantial bundle of firewood which he piled into a campfire.

At the sound of the commotion, Augee yawned awake and stared at the firewood with curiosity as Nicholas set to work with a flat piece of rock and a pointed flint stone, smacking the point of the flint down hard to create sparks. He had built fires in the past, but on this occasion the firewood was saturated from rain, and the meagre sparks that Nicholas managed to produce failed to latch on to the wet bark. Several minutes passed, and frustration began to get the better of him. Exasperated at his unsuccessful efforts, he swore aloud and tossed away the stones angrily. Irritated, Nicholas looked back at Augee, who by now, awake and alert, was trembling violently in the draughty hollow. He was clearly unwell from the wet weather, and Nicholas began to feel increasingly concerned for the creature's health, being so far removed from the dry and arid conditions of his birthplace.

"Let's get you warm," Nicholas suggested soothingly as replaced the cloak around Augee's hunched-over back.

However, just then, Augee made a sudden jerking movement with his head that made Nicholas take a cautious step backward.

"Are you okay, Augee?" he questioned, the concern in his voice poorly disguised.

Once again, Augee made the same sudden thrust with his head, his nose pointed upward. Nicholas made to put his arm around him, but an uncharacteristic snort from Augee suggested to him to stay back. A third time, Augee's head twitched and jerked, until, without warning, he emitted a booming sneeze which, to Nicholas's astonishment, was followed by a rush of white-hot flame that illuminated the hollow and sent up a flash of sweltering heat. Nicholas stumbled backward from the shock and was awestruck as Augee followed up with three more equally forceful flame-accompanied sneezes. A moment later, all was still, except for the sound of Augee's panting and the faint crackling sound of scattered embers—the remnants of his sudden bursts of flame. Nicholas stared in silent wonder at Augee who averted his gaze and rubbed his blackened snout self-consciously.

"My goodness!" Nicholas whispered in stupefaction.

Augee shuffled nervously in response, clearly taken aback himself by what had occurred. Without a further word, the quick-thinking Nicholas picked up a wide, flat palm leaf from the ground, swept up a scattering of glowing embers and dropped them into the damp skeleton of the fire that he had been attempting to build. Seconds later, it ignited with a dull roar, and the hollow with a swell of heat.

For a spell, Nicholas and Augee simply sat together in silence, staring into the dancing flames.

26

THE NEW, UNEXPECTED development left Nicholas with much to reflect on. Given the species from which Augee had been birthed and the fiery underworld that was his native place, it should have come as little surprise to Nicholas to learn that he possessed such a formidable capability. It was, nonetheless, a shock to discover that such a docile, gentle, water-loving creature as Augee could wield the destructive ability to create fire. For Augee's part, he seemed equally perplexed, rubbing his blackened, irritated nostrils and glancing up at Nicholas as if he was just as flabbergasted by the unexpected flaming sneeze.

"Wow," Nicholas breathed, running his hands through his hair as he realized the danger that existed in Augee's unassuming form.

The creature looked up at Nicholas as if he was in agreement.

"Aaauug," he whimpered, rubbing his nose again, still shaken from his unexpected, fiery outburst.

In the aftermath of the extraordinary occurrence, Nicholas was reluctant to press Augee on his newly realized ability, seeing how confused and self-conscious the creature had become. His enormous eyes lingered on the crackling fire, and he seemed to Nicholas to be afraid of a repeat of the explosive sneezes, cautiously rubbing his nose as if to reassure himself that it was a once-off. Truthfully, the new development privately intrigued Nicholas. The benevolence that he'd observed from Augee since their escape from his dreadful birthplace had, to that point, convinced Nicholas that he lacked the same fiendish traits as his mother and sibling. It appeared now, however, that the strange creature shivering by his side might not be so far removed from his beastly kin as Nicholas had first assumed.

For the rest of that day, they remained in the rocky hollow by the jungle spring, listening to the twitter of the birds and the thrum of insects. The storm clouds had by now drifted off, and the peace left in their place was soul-soothing. In the calm after light, the sleepy clearing had an enchanting appeal, and Nicholas wondered if it would be prudent to remain there until such time that Augee was fit to make the trek to New Hohala. His leg obviously required recuperation and rest, and besides, the sudden discovery that Augee was capable of producing fire had piqued Nicholas's curiosity. The more he thought about it, the more it made sense that Augee would be a fire-breather, considering the devastating infernos that he'd witnessed down in the ravine, and he wondered if such a skill could somehow be harnessed to aid the Hohalians in their fight against the Volcarons—even if the timid Augee himself seemed an unlikely warrior.

With the sun drawing in, Nicholas made the decision to set up a more permanent shelter in the rock hollow where there was ample shade, water, and jungle fruit close by. Augee, for his part, seemed more than content with the decision to stay put. As Nicholas constructed some improvised bedding and collected berries and pears to eat, the creature wasted no time in revisiting the sparkling spring pool.

Three days passed in the quiet clearing as Nicholas and Augee's bond continued to flourish. They were entirely comfortable in each other's company, and in an uncanny way, Nicholas felt as if he could implicitly understand Augee by his actions, sounds, and movements, despite the fact that the creature could not communicate with him verbally. Inexplicably, Nicholas felt he could discern Augee's moods and wants before they were even apparent, as if the youngster's disposition and feelings were instinctively perceptible to him.

Nicholas was also struck by the extraordinary pace at which he observed the young Augee growing. In the short time since they'd escaped the canyon, Augee had shot up to almost seven feet tall when upright on his hind legs, and his features had matured rapidly all around. The spiked abrasions on his back had become thick and pointed, and his forearms and legs had filled out, giving the creature a less infantile appearance. His jaws had grown rows of jagged, serrated teeth, lending him a slight measure of ferocity. Nonetheless,

Augee's most distinguishing feature, his crystalline eyes—as profound and deep as the forest pool in which he and Nicholas swam together daily—remained unchanged and betrayed his benign, kindly nature.

As Augee's injured leg continued to heal slowly, the days wore on, and he and Nicholas formed a comfortable routine. By day, they swam together and foraged in the jungle for food, and at night they ate by campfire while Nicholas regaled Augee with tales of his people and the home the Hohalians had left behind. He told his new friend more about Caralisa and the sad course of their relationship; he described the pitiful conditions of the people in exile and his own tragic isolation from the rest of his community; finally, he told Augee of the Volcarons—of how they had arrived like a plague under the cover of darkness, how they had plundered Hohala, and how the one they called Morgoratt had slain Nightshade the panther in cold blood. As he listened, Augee's expression remained attentive and solemn, as if he could truly perceive the gravity of Nicholas's words and the raw emotions that ran behind them.

Each night, when the campfire had crumbled to glowing ash, the pair bundled Nicholas's cloak around them and slept within the comfortable curve of the rock hollow with the gentle gurgle of the spring as their lullaby. Still only days old, Augee was quick to drift off to sleep, and it made Nicholas smile on each occasion he felt the creature's domed head nuzzle under his arm like a child grateful for their parent's protection.

Although Nicholas was convinced that they were hidden from the eyes of any passing beasts of the jungle, he remained alert and watchful while Augee slept. Most of the time, the nights went by silently and without event; however, on occasion, the drowsy Nicholas was alerted to what sounded like low growls in the jungle beyond. The first time, his blood had run cold at the noise, but after the distant sounds continued into a second and third night, Nicholas's unease lessened, and he concluded them to be the nocturnal calls of foraging jungle animals.

And while their first nights together in the jungle went undisturbed, Nicholas found himself continuing to agonize about failing in his quest to find an answer to the Volcaron threat and returning to Caralisa with no further answers. Most chillingly, on a number of occasions, he'd woken with a frantic start following a recurrent dream where countless chain-clad Hohalians, both young and old, were forced to march in a line through the nighttime jungle, led by cloaked figures with flaming torches. The images unsettled him greatly, and he prayed silently that the dream was not a prophetic one.

It was on the fifth morning since their encampment at the spring that dwindling amounts of tree-hanging fruit in the vicinity prompted Nicholas and Augee to venture deeper into the surrounding jungle. By now, Augee's injured leg had improved significantly, and he was capable of walking limited distances without a pronounced limp in his step. The pair hiked about an hour from their camp to where the jungle fruit grew riper and in more abundance. Nicholas carried his cloak across his shoulder, the four ends tied together as an improvised sack for hauling as much fruit as possible. The vegetation in that part of the forest was heavier, and the treetops arched just above their heads like an overbearing ceiling indifferent to the light of the sun. As they picked greedily at the plump, sticky plums and overripe berries, Nicholas chattered absent-mindedly to Augee about life in Hohala during the good times, the travesty of their upheaval, and about how he hoped more than anything that his people might someday soon retrieve their home and their freedom.

"We just need a miracle, Augee," Nicholas lamented as he reached forlornly for a low-hanging pear.

In response, Augee paused his fruit-picking and afforded Nicholas a soft, knowing glance that indicated to him the remarkable young creature's empathy toward the Hohalians' plight.

"Thanks for the support, Augee," he sighed. "We'll figure out what to do eventually, I hope."

Suddenly, a violent snarl cut through the somber moment from somewhere within the jungle. The pair froze in alarm, and Nicholas held his breath in dread, knowing that they'd trespassed upon a territory in which they were not welcome. A second menacing growl sounded from behind them, followed quickly by another to their right. The cries sounded feline, unwelcoming, and full of threat. Suddenly, in the corner of his eye, Nicholas caught the flash of a quick-moving creature through the tree trunks to his left. The chorus of snarls continued as another darted between the trees in front of them. Again, Nicholas and Augee both spun around defensively as a sharp howl was emitted from within the trees behind them. As his heart thumped in alarm, Nicholas held one arm in front of Augee protectively, and his eyes darted across the forest floor for anything at all that he could use as a weapon. His panicked search was halted as, from out of the dense foliage in front of them, stepped a sinewy, brown tiger, imposingly large and with sullen menace in its gait. It was sleek and muscular with sharp, pearly teeth protruding like icicles over its heavy bottom jaw. Without warning, a second, identical tiger leapt out beside it and growled menacingly at Augee who stumbled backward in trepidation. Then, another thick scrub of nearby bushes rustled, and slowly, out stepped a third tiger, darker and heavier-set than the others. This third creature growled as it advanced toward them, entirely unperturbed by the intruders in its midst. A cold sweat broke over Nicholas as he stared into the largest beast's deep, glaring eyes.

Although shaken himself, Nicholas was immediately terrified for Augee's safety. He knew that Augee—still ungainly from his growth spurt and the effects of his injured leg—would never outmaneuver the power and agility of the tigers, and, given the manner in which the three predators had begun to surround them, it was apparent that Augee was their preferred prey.

One of the smaller tigers sprang to within a couple of feet of them. Without hesitation, Nicholas leapt out in front of Augee and directed a hard, swinging kick at the tiger's head. With a dull crack, his boot connected with the beast's jaw and it was thrown backward by the sheer force of the kick. At that moment, Nicholas realized his mistake. Furious roars went up from the other two tigers in response to the sight of their pack mate sprawled and barely conscious on the jungle floor.

"Stay back!" cried Nicholas angrily, and he grabbed a thick branch that lay by his foot, brandishing it defensively. With his other arm, he held on to Augee's shoulder, preparing to shield him if an attack came from behind.

The two tigers that remained on their feet began to circle them, both growling in anticipation. With the blood coursing in his veins, Nicholas swung the branch forcefully at the head of the largest tiger. Unlike with the first beast, the expected connection never materialized as the branch missed the tiger's head by a fraction, and with a thump that winded him, the powerful animal threw itself full force at Nicholas. A white-hot sensation flashed across his chest as he was thrown to the ground, and the back of his head knocked against the trunk of a nearby tree. His head spun as he wrestled with the urge to drift into unconsciousness, and looking down at his torso, he could see that his skin had been slashed by the tiger's claws.

Grimacing through the pain, Nicholas's eyes searched frantically for Augee who had disappeared from his sight. But, before he could get a proper look around, he felt himself being dragged violently backward. From behind, Nicholas could hear the tiger snarl savagely as it shook him, and, in that moment, he resigned himself to a most gruesome fate.

An immense roar exploded in Nicholas's ears, and instantly, he felt the tiger release its grip on him. He felt dizzy with pain, and his blurred vision struggled to focus on his surroundings. The booming howl was quickly followed by shrill cries of attack from the tigers nearby, and Nicholas struggled to make sense of the chaos. Without warning, a deafening crash assailed his eardrums, followed by a violent, orange flash that stung his eyes and made him wince. A wave of raging heat swept past him, and, to his disbelief, when he opened his eyes, the surrounding forest was awash with flame and blustering, black smoke. Nicholas bolted upright in alarm, darting his head in every direction in terrified awe as his mind swirled with fearful thoughts of the monsters from the canyon. All around him, the trees, grasses, bushes, and briars writhed and sank beneath the blaze. Fierce clouds of smoke and dust rose up to obscure Nicholas's vision, and he could not make out any sign of the tigers or, to his heightened distress, Augee.

"Augee!" he roared out in panic, his ears ringing and his lungs choking from the carbonic fumes.

Nicholas staggered to his feet and, with tears in his eyes, cried out again desperately for his friend.

All of a sudden, a dark form plummeted from above and struck the ground near him with a nauseating crack. Awe-struck and almost afraid to look, Nicholas peered down to see one of the three tigers slumped in the charred, black grass, its body twisted and lifeless. Before his mind could begin to register what had happened, a second tiger's body plunged from the sky and landed with a similarly dramatic thud.

Just then, a sweeping, swirling wind whipped up all around Nicholas, causing the smoke to partly disperse and the surrounding treetops to bend. He stared open-mouthed as an enormous silhouette swept out of the sky and came to rest on the forest floor. The smoky haze parted further, and Nicholas looked on in awe as the form came into greater focus. A monstrous, charcoal-skinned beast towered over him, standing upright on a pair of muscular hind legs. Spreading several meters outward from its torso was a set of enormous, semi-transparent wings, and raised threateningly by its sides was a pair of forearms that concluded with terrifying, razor-like claws. Nicholas was struck with horror at the power and strength of the beast before him, and he resigned himself to the same grisly fate as the tigers. Bracing himself for the monster to make its move, his heart pounded violently. Breathless and frozen, he gazed into the creature's piercing eyes which were tinged with a sanguine, red glow that was as entrancing as it was terrifying. However, as the petrified Nicholas waited for the attack that he was sure would come, he sensed something familiar about the beast—something that he could not immediately pinpoint. The feeling left him with little doubt that he had somehow seen the gargantuan creature before.

And then it dawned on him.

"Augee!" he gasped breathlessly. "It's—*you!*"

27

THE RAGING BLAZE had devoured the surrounding forest to a point where all that Nicholas could make out through the haze was the gigantic form that towered over him, its awesome wings spread out wide like ship sails caught in a tempest. The beast's prodigious, charcoal frame was rigid and taut, its great muscles as pronounced as chiseled rock, and it loomed over Nicholas, lashing its massive tail. As the noxious smoke billowed about him, Nicholas's gaze lingered on the pair of pulsating, blood-red eyes that glowered down at him with such intensity that it felt as if his very spirit had been brutally shaken.

After their time spent together, Nicholas had quickly come to the conclusion that Augee was an utterly timid and placid soul who lacked even the slightest inclination toward violence; yet, the monstrous creature before him—terrible and magnificent in equal measure—was most certainly his dear friend. It was as if Augee's essence was somehow evident to him even beneath the dreadful form that he'd suddenly assumed.

Engulfed by suffocating smoke, Nicholas remained rooted to the spot, unable to break away from the hypnotic light that radiated from the searing, red eyes. In every direction, howling brushfires spat and burst like lanced boils, and the trees and bushes groaned under the oppression of gyrating flames. In the midst of the scorching maelstrom, Nicholas's senses began to dull, and he felt his endurance wane along with his consciousness. His legs began to quiver as an uprising of vomit welled in his throat. The fire, the destruction, the smoke, and Augee's unfathomable metamorphosis had all conspired to disarm him, and his consciousness began to blacken. As he clung to the remaining sliver of his lucidness, Nicholas felt himself sink to the ground, the foul smoke enveloping him until he could see nothing but smothering darkness.

"Augee!" he rasped, his voice barely audible over the deafening roar of the inferno. "Go! If you can hear me, get yourself away to safety, now."

At that, Nicholas's eyes rolled back in his head, and his body finally began to surrender.

Without warning, he was thrust violently back to consciousness as he felt his entire body being yanked upward with a forcefulness that caused his remaining breath to catch painfully in his lungs. He could feel a tight grip around his midriff, and he had the alarming sensation of weightlessness as he was hauled up from the ground at full-speed. Everything around him was pitch dark in the smoky haze, and the brutal heat made him roar out in fear and pain. All of a sudden, the smog parted and cool air licked deliciously at his skin. To his astonishment, Nicholas opened his eyes to the striking, welcoming blue of the sky above him. He realized that he was hurtling higher and higher, and as the stinging tears in his eyes dissipated, he could make out the green blur of the jungle far below him. In complete panic, he flailed his head all around to make some sense of what was going on, and the sight that met him was one that rendered him stupefied: wrapped around his waist was a huge, reptilian limb, jet black and tipped with claws that curled into acute points. Startled, he whipped his head around, and it was with a fearful gasp that he realized he was being carried high above the countryside by the terrifying, black-scaled Augee.

"What in the name of the gods is happening?" he yelled out in panic, but it drew no response from the titanic creature.

With Nicholas's heart hammering and his lungs struggling for breath, he and Augee hurtled through the sky, soaring above the sweeping jungle. Below them, a solid square mile of the forest looked to have collapsed in on itself, the remaining trees mangled and blackened, while an ungodly cloud of smoke billowed into the air like a brooding funeral pyre.

Moments later, Nicholas could see the western mountains far off to his right, and on his other side, he was just able to make out the Bay of Hohala where the ocean rose to kiss the line of the horizon.

When his awe had marginally subsided, Nicholas looked up to see a pair of enormous, leathery wings, and above them, the sharp, pointed features of the creature who held his life in its claws. With a furrowed brow, the transformed Augee stared determinedly ahead, his skin tinged a wicked black and the muscles on his limbs still tense and tightly drawn. But despite, Augee's new and frightening form, Nicholas noticed that the fearsome, scarlet light that had burned in his eyes below in the jungle was by now absent, replaced once more by a familiar, emerald green. It was at that moment that Nicholas knew he had nothing to fear. He was utterly bewildered by Augee's metamorphosis, but it seemed apparent that it had taken place after they'd come under threat from the prowling tigers.

"What manner of creature are you, Augee?" Nicholas breathed silently to himself as he gazed in wonder at the beauty of the landscape far below.

28

Princess Caralisa's concentration was broken by a deep boom reverberating in the distance. Seconds later, the sounds of chatter and shouting met her ears from outside, and, concerned by the commotion, she rose from her desk to inspect what was going on. Peering through the window of her cabin, she saw Hohalian men, women, and children gathered at the edge of the village, their attention collectively focused on something high above the horizon. Caralisa opened the cabin door and stepped out into the bright afternoon. All around, people were shouting in uneasy voices and pointing to the westward sky. A wave of fear swept over the princess as she raised her eyes and saw the source of the crowd's interest. Far off in the distance, an immense, spiraling smoke cloud stained the clear, blue sky. It tumbled in dark, threatening plumes that obscured the far-off mountain peaks and dulled the light from the sun. All around her, the Hohalians deliberated in anxious, confused tones about the source of the smoke. As the rolling column continued to rise higher, a number of men and women called out for their children to retreat to their cabin homes.

As the crowd bustled around her, Caralisa was rooted to the spot, her pulse racing and her throat tight with fear. The sight of the ominous eruption in the distant west filled her with a grim foreboding, and her heart told her that it had something to do with Nicholas. She sensed, somehow, that the appearance of the sinister cloud was no coincidence, and she felt sick to her stomach at the thought that Nicholas had gotten caught up in something disastrous out in the wilderness. Fighting back tears of defeat, she acknowledged to herself that the time had come for her to abandon the remaining shred of hope for his return that she'd so desperately clung to since his departure. Tears swelled in her eyes as she concluded that there was likely to be no great Hohalian uprising, no deliverance from their exile, and no triumphant return of the man who she'd always deeply loved. She had no idea as to the cause of the towering pillar of smoke, but deep down, she took it to be an indication that the Hohalians needed to ready themselves for difficult times ahead.

As she moved through the throng, the worried eyes of the Hohalian people pleaded at her for an explanation or guidance, but Caralisa had none to give.

"Princess, please tell us," implored one man who held a crying toddler in his arms. "What is happening? Are we in danger? Are we to abandon our homes once more?"

"Was it the Volcarons who caused it?" cried another as he pointed toward the smoke cloud.

"After this, are you and your father *still* going to tell us that we shouldn't fight to protect ourselves?" raged a tired-looking middle-aged woman.

From every angle, distressed faces looked to her for some sign of leadership, but all that Caralisa could muster were short, feeble apologies.

"Sorry. I'm sorry," she mumbled helplessly as she shuffled her way through the animated crowd.

Eventually, Caralisa reached the far edge of the village where the trail to the Eternal Stream began. Tears dripped from her cheeks as she agonized over her people's dire circumstances and the uncertainty of the road ahead. In silence, she walked the long, sloping path toward the pond where she knew her father would be resolutely stationed. As she entered the shady clearing, Caralisa breathed in the peace and stillness of the place, a complete contrast to the frightened hysteria back in New Hohala.

As Caralisa had expected, her father was ensconced in his usual position by the bank of the Eternal Stream next to the tiny hut in which he spent his nights. The king was crouched low on his knees with the palms of his hands flat on the grass. His eyes were closed in concentration as he whispered prayers to the Nexus.

"Father," the princess interrupted abruptly.

King Benjamin looked up at the sound of his daughter's voice.

"My dear!" he croaked hoarsely. "I—I wasn't expecting to see you."

Caralisa stared imploringly at her once-dignified father, his hair and beard unkempt and the corners of his eyes matted with grime and dirt. He looked weak and undernourished, despite the plate of fruit and homemade bread that Caralisa had gathered from the village's scant resources the night before, which sat untouched.

"Father," she sobbed, the strain on her resilience too great for indulging in pleasantries with the increasingly unhinged king. "I've come to beg you one more time to reconsider your stance on our people's future."

The king looked up at her wearily as she continued.

"The people are frightened and restless. They are arguing among themselves, and nobody seems to know what it is that we should be doing or planning for beyond the day-to-day routine of the past five years. There is great discontent in the village, and now something very worrying has happened beyond, in the highlands west of here. Today, there was a huge explosion in the mountains, which you had to have heard, and I am afraid that…"

Caralisa's outpouring was halted mid-sentence by the king raising his hand with assured calmness.

"My dear," he began in a hushed tone. "I know what you are coming to ask me. I am aware that there are events in motion that will profoundly affect our people."

Caralisa stared at her father in confusion.

"I am aware that I have not been as present among the people as I was back in Hohala. But I placed my trust in the Nexus, as I have asked all Hohalians to do, no matter how trying the circumstances. However, I do admit that my leadership has been lacking as of late, and I realize that the people need their shepherd in such bleak times."

"Father," Caralisa interrupted. "The Volcarons are coming this way. It could be any day or night; we just don't know. We have to do something. We cannot continue to ignore the threat. Everyone is angry and scared, especially after the eruption in the sky today."

"Yes, my dear," resumed the king softly. "I know that I must advise the Hohalians, and looking at you right now, my beautiful daughter, has convinced me that I must not wait another moment to speak with them."

Caralisa looked at her father with a mixture of surprise and relief.

"Really, Father?" she questioned with a lingering hint of skepticism. "You'll come up to the village and address the people, today?"

The king nodded with a watery smile, and Caralisa responded by throwing her arms gratefully around his neck.

"You must trust me, my dear," he continued with a weak chuckle. "I know you are afraid, but after all of this time praying and reflecting, now I am sure what the correct path ahead is for the Hohalians. So, come; help me dress properly, and we'll go to see the people."

However, as she helped her father to his feet, Caralisa could no longer restrain her emotions.

"Nicholas is gone, Father," she blurted out, her words stinging and absent of hope.

The king looked at her inquisitively out of the corners of his eyes.

"He's gone, Father," she repeated, whimpering as tears streamed down her face. "He believed that the Nexus spoke to him, and that he had to make a journey westward beyond our lands. But that was days ago, and now today after the eruption in the mountains, I just have a terrible feeling that he's…"

"Caralisa," responded the king soothingly. "Your energies are not best spent anguishing over things that are not clear. Nicholas chose to place his faith in the Nexus, and we must be respectful of that choice."

The king rubbed his daughter's tear-stained cheek with the back of his fingers before adding: "Now, I don't wish to see any more tears. You must show that you are strong for the sake of our people. We must not concede to our emotions in times of trial."

"Yes, Father," nodded the princess with a sniff as she linked the king's arm and led him slowly back up the sloping path to the village.

*

Later that evening, the Hohalians congregated in the area of New Hohala that was usually reserved for morning market stalls. A raised platform had been hastily constructed, and atop it stood King Benjamin, flanked on either side by Caralisa and his counselor, Lawson. It was twilight, and a sea of weary faces waited anxiously for the king's address. The news of their leader's unexpected return had spread quickly, and even some of the disaffected men of Haven loyal to Nicholas Stone had made the short journey to hear what the monarch had to say.

When the entire village had gathered, the king raised his hand to hush the crowd, and he raised his voice as loudly as his diminished body would allow.

"Dear friends and citizens," he began, "I know you have all suffered in these years away from our homeland. I see that you are frightened, but I am here to tell you that we are to return to Hohala."

The crowed murmured in unison, some excited, some skeptical, while the men of Haven stood at the back of the crowd with their arms folded, listening intently.

"The Nexus has at last spoken to me," he resumed. "And in return for that privilege, I have decided to place every trust in its guidance."

Confused whispers rippled through the crowd.

The king went on, this time with his voice lowered to a graver tone:

"As you stand before me now, there are dark forces conspiring against us. The strangers who drove us from our home five years ago are no longer content with the wealth and resources that were not theirs to plunder in the first place. Now, they plan to persecute our race as well."

Gasps and cries of fear broke out among some of the less-informed members of the crowd in response to the king's grim pronouncement.

"The Volcarons will come for us—that seems certain," he declared. "And it is clear what we, as Hohalians, must do."

At that, the men from Haven nodded.

"We must remain true to ourselves. We must retain our dignity and composure," insisted the king.

He then paused for a moment, breathed deeply and declared: "We will *not* respond with sinful violence. We will *not* have our Hohalian purity sullied by violent acts. We *will* remain true to our souls and to the glorious Nexus that loves and guides us. The Volcarons intend to take us home, and we must have faith that the Nexus's divine will is being done."

A deafening silence filled the clearing.

"You mean take us home, in chains!" someone remonstrated from the back of the crowd.

"As slaves!" another person cried out.

The king smiled, misty-eyed.

"It does not matter," he asserted dreamily. "Once we have returned to Hohala, all will be well. There, we will be able to connect *fully* with the

Nexus, and the Volcarons will be expelled before long. *How*, it is not yet clear, but I believe this to be the divine will of the Nexus—the righteous way, and thus it shall be done."

King Benjamin then closed his eyes and faced up to the twilit sky as the incredulous Hohalians looked around at each other in despondence. Caralisa sat in appalled silence, and an acute feeling of defeat enveloped her as she listened to her father's rambling. She could not believe that he was speaking in earnest about allowing the Hohalians to be taken as slaves without putting up resistance. Five years ago, she had been complicit in the king's decision to abandon Hohala, rather than cause affront to the Nexus by calling on the people to defend themselves. At least in that situation, the Hohalians had remained in control of their destiny, and they had, through sheer perseverance and grit, preserved their community and culture by forging a new existence in the mountain wilderness. But the king's insistence that the Hohalians surrender without question to the Volcarons, that they blindly accept slavery as the *righteous* path, was to her a concession too far. As she watched King Benjamin raise his hands aloft in a naïve attempt to quell the unrest of the crowd, a tear fell from her eye, and she finally allowed herself to admit that her father was no longer of sound mind. She glanced in the direction of Lawson who stood nearby, and he exchanged a look with her that suggested he too questioned King Benjamin's capacity for good judgement.

"We shall not fight, and there are to be no more utterances of such blasphemy," asserted the king once more, as he closed his address. "Place your complete faith in the Nexus, my dear people, and you will be saved."

Then, King Benjamin turned his back to the crowd and calmly stepped down from the platform, passing Caralisa and Lawson without a glance. As the gathered Hohalians yelled out protests, the king coolly made his way through the tumult back in the direction of the Eternal Stream. Within a few minutes, he had disappeared from sight, and the attentions of all gathered immediately turned to Caralisa.

The princess looked helplessly at Lawson. Some within the crowd had begun to argue, and it was clear that the king's address had served to rile the Hohalians, rather than reassure them.

"You must speak to them, Your Highness," Lawson whispered to her. "If your father can no longer lead them, then that responsibility falls to you."

"Lawson, I'm not equipped to make such decisions," replied Caralisa, her tone brimming with distress. "I don't have the answers to all of this."

"Just do what your heart and your conscience tell you," he advised, touching her warmly on the hand. "*That* is what is most important."

Caralisa stared the counselor's face for a moment before releasing a quiet sigh and stepping hesitantly to the center of the platform. She opened her mouth to speak, but her uncertain words caught in her mouth. After taking a further moment to compose herself, she raised her hands, and an expectant hush went over the crowd.

"Hohalians," she began. "I know that you are afraid. I am too."

The princess's voice shook, and her hands trembled as she looked down at the swell of people. To her right, Lawson nodded in solemn encouragement, and she resumed her address.

"Truthfully, I do not know how to advise you," she continued, her voice steely and dispassionate this time. "I disagree with my father's decree, but, the fact is I am not yet your queen."

"We don't even have a king that can lead us!" shouted one irate onlooker.

Remaining composed, Caralisa declared, "As I cannot knowledgeably advise you of the correct path forward, I am advising each individual Hohalian to listen to his or her own conscience and decide what the right path is for themselves and their families. Those who choose to take up arms should not be impeded; those who wish to evacuate should be given the opportunity to do so. And, those who decide to allow themselves to be taken by the Volcarons…"

Her voice broke, and she breathed deeply before resuming, "…let no one stand in their way."

Without a further word, Caralisa stepped down from the platform and walked decisively through the congregation of flustered and frightened Hohalians. As members of the crowd shouted frustrated objections after her, the princess sobbed a quiet, desperate prayer for Nicholas Stone's unlikely return.

29

It was just before nightfall when Nicholas and Augee swooped down into the jungle clearing where they had made their camp. With surprising grace, Augee perched himself on the rocky embankment by the spring and lowered his back to allow Nicholas to alight. Still breathing heavily, and with his heart pounding from adrenaline, Nicholas clambered onto the rocks. The still gloom of the clearing instantly had a calming effect on his soul. He was still trembling from the exhilaration and shock of Augee's unexpected metamorphosis, and the quiet, familiar surroundings went some way to helping him regain his composure.

For his part, Augee seemed to have suffered no lingering distress from his dramatic transformation. With Nicholas watching on in wonder, Augee wasted no time in immersing himself gladly in the dark water of the pond. By now, the monstrous guise that Augee had assumed back in the jungle had all but subsided; his eyes had returned to their usual, enchanting green, and his frame again seemed slighter and less imposing. His scales had also returned to a shimmering emerald, and the bulging muscles in his forearms and legs appeared to have relaxed completely.

Nicholas looked on bewildered as he tried to make some sense of the incredible events of that afternoon. As far as he could reason, it had to have been the attack by the wild tigers that had provoked Augee's transformation from his docile, unassuming self to the furious colossus that had ravaged an entire portion of the jungle. Not even down in the depths of the fiery ravine had Nicholas seen such terrible power. Augee had it all—flight, fire, ferocity, and fearlessness—and Nicholas's mind raced with excitement at the realization of what he now knew his friend to be capable of. It was a stunning revelation, and as he reflected on the awesome power that he had witnessed, he bowed his head and whispered thanks to the Nexus. Just a few days ago, he had felt so discouraged, so alone and so helpless, never dreaming that the gods even knew of him, much less would direct him to do their work. As he ruminated on the discovery of Augee's new abilities, he determined then and there to devote his every energy to dispelling the Volcarons and fulfilling the mission that he was now sure the Nexus intended for him.

The sheer challenge of rising up against the Volcarons filled Nicholas with the darkest foreboding. However, now the Hohalians had a potential weapon and ally. He day-dreamed to himself about the terrified reactions of the Volcarons as he imagined himself and Augee sweeping down upon the old Hohalian village at the break of day, sending their enemies into hysteria with gigantic bursts of flame. He fantasized about chasing them all out of their homeland and watching gleefully as they fled to their ships in panic. Finally, he imagined his and Augee's triumphant arrival back to New Hohala to proclaim the defeat of the hated invaders amid the cheers of his people and the warm smile of his beloved Caralisa.

A torrent of cold water cascaded over Nicholas, disrupting his day-dreaming and bringing his mind firmly back to the forest clearing. With a stunned gasp, he looked up to see Augee submerged to his snout, his eyes glinting playfully. Sopping wet, Nicholas gave a belly laugh before picking himself up from the ground, tearing off his boots and cloak, and throwing himself into the pool with an exhilarated yelp. The silver moon rose into the sky as Nicholas and Augee wrestled and played together in the glimmering pond. For the first time since their unlikely union, both felt completely at ease and carefree. However, when the pair eventually climbed out of the pond to turn in for the night, Nicholas paused by the water's edge to speak to Augee seriously.

"Before anything else, Augee, I want to talk to you about something," he began. "What happened today was incredible. I mean…it was unbelievable! Breathtaking; Terrifying! I've never seen such…*power*!"

Augee looked at him bashfully from the corners of his serenely green eyes. Nicholas was almost certain that his fire-breathing and flying abilities had instinctively come upon him when they had been confronted by danger.

He wondered for a moment if Augee had been aware of his capabilities all along, but his coy demeanor suggested that it had all been just as much of a surprise to him.

"Look, Augee," Nicholas went on, apprehensive about sharing his true feelings regarding utilizing his friend's newly discovered powers in the fight against the Volcarons. "I'm not going to lie to you. I admit I'm now convinced that the Nexus intended me to find you. I believe that you are the miracle that can help lead the Hohalians out of their suffering."

Augee stared back earnestly as he listened.

"But," Nicholas added seriously, looking intently into Augee's eyes. "I don't want you ever to think that there's an expectation of you to serve me or the Hohalians. I took you to this unfamiliar world without your consent. You didn't really have a choice in the matter. But there is a war coming with the Volcarons, and *I* must lead the Hohalians in that battle."

Augee tilted his head thoughtfully as Nicholas continued.

"Please, Augee," he requested solemnly. "I want you to realize that it is not your fight, and there is no obligation on you to subject yourself to danger. You've become my dearest friend, and I'm blessed to have found you. Our friendship won't be affected if you choose not to be involved in what happens next. I really want you to know that."

At that, Nicholas stretched out his arm and touched Augee on the shoulder. Augee remained silent for a moment, looking at the ground as if he was carefully contemplating his friend's words. He turned to face Nicholas, then, with a roguish look in his eyes and a flick of his jaw that almost seemed like a grin, he sent a determined-sounding snort of flame into the air that told Nicholas he didn't need to worry about Augee's willingness to participate in the looming confrontation with the Volcarons.

"Thank you, Augee. You'll be the toast of New Hohala when we arrive, you know that?" smiled Nicholas as they retired to the shelter of their cave.

*

It was full of anticipation that Nicholas woke the following morning. The tentacles of the dawn sun had barely penetrated the entrance to their shelter, but he was anxious to prepare as swiftly as possible. While Augee was immensely powerful, with abilities that the Volcarons could surely not defend against, his aim when breathing fire was certainly haphazard, as evidenced by the incredible destruction that his fiery outburst had caused in the jungle the day before. Indeed, the expulsion of the Volcarons from Hohala would be of little benefit if the village and the surrounding countryside were destroyed by Augee's wild fire blasts. Moreover, although his hatred for Morgoratt and the Volcarons had plagued his dreams throughout the five years since the invasion, Nicholas was still, at heart, a son of Hohala, and to any Hohalian—no matter how lapsed their faith—wanton violence and destruction were still anathema to the soul. As far as Nicholas was concerned, if Augee's recruitment was to be the spur for his people's return to their rightful land, then it would require practice to refine his extraordinary abilities.

After they'd eaten, Nicholas climbed onto Augee's spine, and they took off into the sky. The wind felt cool on Nicholas's face as they ventured higher into the air, and Augee roared out with enjoyment as the welcoming glow of the sun enveloped them.

Eventually, they reached a height at which Nicholas felt Augee could practice his flame-throwing without fear of causing unnecessary destruction. As the swirling wind howled in his ears, Nicholas took a deep breath and cried out, "Fire!" In quick response, Nicholas felt Augee's muscles tighten. His long neck thrust backward, and, abruptly, a cloud of flame bloomed out in a dense, patternless projectile. Nicholas felt the sensation of scorching heat as the wind blew the flame back toward them, and Augee howled out in surprise as the blowback swept up against him.

"Drop lower, Augee!" Nicholas hollered, and immediately, Augee stiffened his wings, causing them to swoop downward in a diagonal fashion. As their altitude decreased, the whistling breeze quietened, and it was possible for Nicholas to speak to Augee without having to roar.

"Okay," he called out, pointing toward a nearby encirclement of mountaintops. "Straight ahead!"

Before long, they were soaring just meters above snow-capped peaks that glistened icy silver against the morning sky.

"Let's try it again, Augee," commanded Nicholas as they approached an immense, oblong-shaped glacier nestled between the crests of two mountain peaks. "Concentrate. Take your time, and pick your target…now!"

Once again, Augee's muscles tightened, his neck swung back, and his jaw opened wide in a deafening roar. Once more, a blanket of flame filled the air, but on this occasion, there was no blowback, and Nicholas's veins pulsed with exhilaration as the smoke cleared; the once-enormous glacier was now reduced to mist and wet ice.

"Good job, Augee!" he whooped as they rounded the steaming mountain peak. "Now, let's give it another go."

Augee replied with a jubilant growl and they were off again.

For the remainder of the day, Nicholas and Augee journeyed across the countryside perfecting Augee's fire-breathing. It came as no surprise to Nicholas that Augee was an exceptionally fast learner, and his determination to master his own power was relentless.

At the cusp of nightfall, the pair decided to finish their training for the day. Both were tired—Augee especially so—but were highly satisfied with their progress. It had taken Augee mere hours to turn his indiscriminate blasts of flame into accurate and concentrated beams of fire. As they wheeled through the air, they left behind a host of smoke spires across the barren highlands, and they flew back to their camp in content silence as both relived the highlights of their momentous day.

"If only Morgoratt could see what he's got coming to him," pondered Nicholas with a smirk as he stared into their crackling campfire that night, to which Augee responded with an emphatic growl.

The next morning and into the following days, Nicholas and Augee travelled high into the mountains to continue Augee's training. It didn't take long for them to become attuned to each other's movements and body language so that one could read the meaning in the other's slightest flinch or shift in weight. Nicholas could not believe how, within such a short time, Augee's dexterity in both flight and fire had increased immeasurably. He could glide and hang in the air with a grace reserved for the most majestic birds of prey, and he was able to shoot everything from spitting embers to tiny electrical threads and any configuration of fire, all with beautiful accuracy.

Five busy days later, as night was falling across the jungle, Nicholas and Augee glided down into the clearing. It was the final evening they would do so. One last time, the pair reenergized in the moonlit pool, before retiring to their shelter to eat and rest. As the full darkness of the night enveloped them, and they settled down inside the rocky hollow, Nicholas expressed another prayer of gratitude to the Nexus. After that, he drifted off to sleep, clutching to renewed hope for the times ahead.

30

BEYOND THE NORTHERN perimeter of the village of New Volcaron, sandwiched between the jungle frontier and the southernmost cliffs of the Bay of Hohala, a network of wooden structures and fencing was under construction. It was an elaborate structure, consisting of a collection of outbuildings, four tall, wooden towers, and a perimeter fence that obscured the interior completely from the outside. The site of the new development was the most windswept and desolate place in the vicinity of New Volcaron, an elevated point at which the most vindictive storms of the bay came ashore, and a portion of the coast that was avoided by even the staunchest wildlife.

Against a billowing gale wind that stung his ears and face, Suma stood directing the construction of an incomplete tower at one corner of the wooden perimeter fence. His parrot, Goldbeak, was perched uncomfortably on his right shoulder, the bird's feathers ruffling as it attempted to shelter itself from the relentless ocean wind. A trio of red-faced Volcaron men were attempting to raise a heavy beam using a pulley mechanism as they wrestled with the coastal wind. Against the din of the howling breeze, Suma roared out instructions to the men in his charge. For weeks now, he had supervised the construction of the complex practically by himself, as had been Morgoratt's insistence. Suma had been praised highly for the quality and efficiency of his designs, and in public, Morgoratt had promised that he would be well-rewarded. But it was not a project that Suma had submitted to willingly, and his conscience berated him when he was alone in his workshop or in the silence of his sleeping quarters at night.

Lately, as food stores and resources depleted, and Volcaron stomachs had begun to grow hungry, Suma had witnessed brutal acts reminiscent of those during the miserable days of "Old Volcaron." The old culture of waste and greed had again started to take root within their society. Indeed, such was the deplorable violence that Suma had observed from the increasingly unhinged Morgoratt and the chieftains, that he had quickly become desensitized to the infighting. Yet, despite the normalization of the oppression he had witnessed under the cruel regime, Suma's awareness of the sheer inhumanity of the project he now led burned in his conscience and filled him with a guilt that weighed heavily night and day. With the completion of every watchtower, holding cell, fence, and punishment chamber, he was haunted by the fact that this place would soon play grim host to the suffering of countless, innocent Hohalians.

Nevertheless, the big man did his best to banish his own feelings of culpability, reminding himself that in order to survive, he had little choice but to adhere to Morgoratt's wishes. With Suma's remarkable skills in construction and carpentry exclusive to him among the Volcarons, he was unofficially regarded as New Volcaron's architect-in-chief. Attention from others was something that he had always done his best to avoid, and he soon found that the faster Morgoratt's projects progressed, the less direct interaction he had with the Volcaron leader and the chieftains. So, Suma reluctantly continued supervising the new project. He did take some solace in the knowledge that he had been able, at the very least, to give ample warning to Nicholas Stone so that he and his people could take preemptive precautions and maybe even escape further into the wilderness beyond the reach of the Volcaron army. He knew Nicholas to be a sharp, resourceful man, capable of acting decisively. In his brief encounters with him when they'd traded goods, Suma had built a reluctant respect for his acquaintance's determination in the face of the Hohalian exile. Moreover, Suma convinced himself repeatedly that he had risked enough by having already travelled to Haven to warn Nicholas, and that the fate of the Hohalians was no longer his responsibility. But despite his feeble attempts at indifference as the slave complex—perversely dubbed "the plantation" by Morgoratt—moved toward completion, Suma found it increasingly difficult to shrug off his deep unease.

On this particular day, he had supervised the completion of a large sleeping quarter that consisted of uniform rows of narrow benches, each one barely sizeable enough to hold a small adult. There were no blankets, and heavy chains hung ominously from every bench. In truth, Suma had not, until now, contemplated that there were plans to incarcerate children, and the completion of that mass prison cell had shaken his conscience and reminded him, yet again, of all that he had been complicit in. Faced with that sobering reality, he was unable to deny his own culpability in the ghastly plans that were underway.

Later that evening, as dusk descended on the Bay of Hohala, Suma bid a curt farewell to the Volcaron men in his charge, and he and his parrot moved discreetly down the winding cliff path that led to the village. On this occasion, Suma bypassed the usual turn into the settlement that he took nightly, and he ventured beyond the village, westward in the direction of the jungle. Before he'd finished up for the day, he had resolved that he could no longer just assume that Nicholas that the Hohalians were acting on his earlier advice to evacuate their mountain settlements. The sight of the completed children's prison cell that day had rattled him, and he was determined to ensure that he would have as little blood on his own hands as he could manage.

For over four hours, Suma and Goldbeak stole through the dark jungle, following a familiar route. As he tramped through the underbrush, Suma contemplated what he would say to Nicholas. He knew that Nicholas and his comrades would be horrified to know the elaborate details of Morgoratt's plan, as well as the true extent of Suma's involvement in the design and construction of "the plantation." In reality, the men of Haven were little more than acquaintances with whom he did business, and, for all he knew, they may well decide to cut his throat on the spot once he informed them of the dark dealings that were afoot in New Volcaron. Nonetheless, Suma's conscience drove him onward through the forest to bring fresh warning to the Hohalians. After that, he hoped that he might sleep a little easier knowing that he had done what he could to undermine Morgoratt's plot.

It was close to midnight by the time Suma rounded the steep, upland path on approach to Haven, and they found the tiny village in silence. At the highest point of the slope-side settlement, Nicholas's cabin stood lonely and lightless. The usually cluttered porch area was notably less disorderly, and Suma got a sense that the place hadn't been disturbed in some time.

"No one at home, dead or alive," squawked Goldbeak, and Suma shushed the bird with his finger.

"Maybe they were wise enough to leave," he whispered in hope rather than expectation.

Goldbeak responded, more quietly this time, "Awwk! Leave or be taken. Leave or be taken."

Suma had begun to wonder if maybe the Hohalians had heeded the first warning he'd given to Nicholas to abandon the area when he noticed a faint, flickering glow from the window of one of the cabins further down through the settlement. Bereft of other ideas, Suma crept quietly in the direction of the dimly lit cabin. The scent of the evening's cooking fires hung faintly in the air, so it was clear there were still people living in the village. Suma sighed at the stubbornness of the Hohalians. A feeling of irritation crept through him at the thought that he may have come all this way a second time for Nicholas and his people to ignore his warnings about the imminent danger.

Arriving at the cabin with the glowing window, Suma whispered, "Whatever happens tonight, Goldbeak, nobody can say that we didn't do the right thing."

The parrot responded with a rolling of its tongue and tucked its head under its wing. Suma's knock on the door met with no response. He held his breath and leaned his head against the door to listen. For several minutes he stood in silence, but there was no sound or movement to be detected. Exasperated, Suma swore quietly as he turned to leave.

Without warning, he felt the cool sensation of metal against his throat, and he froze instantly. Alarmed, Goldbeak leapt from Suma's shoulder and began squawking and flapping panickedly in the air.

"Move, and you die where you stand," rasped a male voice in the darkness.

Suma's body went rigid as he slowly raised his hands above his shoulders. In the moonlight, he could make out the outline of a sizeable figure next to him, and the blade that was held dangerously against his Adam's apple glinted in the pale gloom.

"You have one second to identify yourself," the figure warned. "Wait another second, and I'll cut you down on the spot."

"It's Suma! I know your leader, Nicholas Stone," the big Volcaron stammered, rattled by the violence in the mysterious man's voice. "I came to speak with Nicholas. I came with a warning for him—for all of you."

Suma breathed a sigh of relief as the blade was removed slowly from his throat. However, he became unsettled again as he rubbed his neck gingerly and felt that the pressure of the knife had caused a thin trickle of blood to run down to his collarbone. Suma heard the figure beside him sheath his weapon, and he felt the stranger shrug past him in the darkness before stepping up onto the porch of the dimly lit cabin. The figure opened the creaking front door and gestured impatiently to Suma to follow him.

The cabin interior was grubby and roughly furnished. There was a bench with some untidily arranged bedding and a crude, functional table with two equally roughshod stools. Matted-looking animal pelts lined the walls, and, in the corner, was a hearth fireplace that had been the source of the glow through the window.

"Sit down," instructed Suma's host, suddenly hospitable. "Do you want a drink of something? I've a cask of apple brandy that'll warm your gut."

"I'm fine," responded Suma reservedly.

He surveyed the man who stood before him and saw that he was a great hulk of a fellow, broad shouldered and more muscular than even Suma himself.

"Suit yourself," the man sniffed and proceeded to pour himself a generous measure from the clay jug on the table.

"Hamar's my name," he continued. "I know Nicholas Stone well. I wouldn't call him a friend exactly, but I trust the man entirely. If there's something that is of enough concern to him that it has brought you here in the dead of night, well, it must be important."

"What I have to say to Nicholas is very important," replied Suma. "It's crucial that I speak with him now, tonight."

Hamar set down his tumbler of brandy and looked Suma in the eyes. "I'm going to have to disappoint you, sir," he frowned. "Nicholas hasn't been seen in Haven or New Hohala for quite some time. Weeks, as a matter of fact."

Suma narrowed his eyes in confusion.

"He headed westward across the mountains," continued Hamar, gesturing out the window with his arm. "Some folks from New Hohala told me that he'd gone off that way, claiming that the Nexus had told him to do so—at least, that's according to the princess who was the last person to see him. Other than that, I don't know what's going on with that fellow or what he means to do. He's a good man, but a strange one, I tell you."

Suma swore aloud angrily, drawing a perplexed glance from Hamar.

"Sorry for the profanity," he added a moment later, slightly embarrassed at his outburst in a stranger's home. "I just really needed to speak with Nicholas."

Hamar smiled to himself before extending his finger toward Goldbeak who had hopped onto the table and was foraging in the cracks for crumbs.

"Swear all you want here, sir," he replied jokingly. "I'd just hate to think that this pretty fellow here might start twittering all sorts of things, and then I'd probably have to cut his throat too."

Hamar laughed to himself at his own joke and poked teasingly at Goldbeak's breast.

"Awrrk! Morgoratt will cut your throat," squawked the parrot in response. "Morgoratt is coming!"

Suma flinched as he saw the mood in Hamar's eyes change.

"What did that damn bird say?" Hamar challenged dangerously.

"Hey, relax," responded Suma, raising his hands defensively. "Nobody's going to cut anyone's throat. Goldbeak's just a bit mouthy…"

"He used the word, 'Morgoratt!'" thundered Hamar. "What do you know of Morgoratt? Who are you? What is your business here?"

Suma paused for a moment. He knew that there was little benefit to being secretive at this point, and, given the threatening leer in Hamar's eyes, it was likely to be less risky for him to be open with his host. Suma sighed resignedly.

"I came from New Volcaron tonight," he revealed.

Hamar's eyes narrowed dangerously, and Suma fingered the handle of his own blade under the table in readiness for a confrontation.

"You're one of them?" growled Hamar, his voice becoming animated.

"I just walked for four hours in the dark to come and warn Nicholas of the danger your people face," Suma interrupted moodily. "I've had business with Nicholas for months, and he trusts me—so, either *you* trust me as well, and you keep quiet while I speak, or you should just go ahead and cut my throat now—your choice."

Hamar eyed his visitor suspiciously.

"You mean *you're* Nicholas's contact from the old village?" he probed with a raised eyebrow.

Suma nodded without speaking.

"Go on then," Hamar conceded, the skepticism still lingering in his voice.

"You shouldn't be here," stated Suma bluntly. "None of your people can stay here."

"Why?" pressed Hamer impatiently.

Suma sighed once more.

"Morgoratt and his army are preparing to scour this area for miles around," he revealed somberly. "If you stay here, or if you move anywhere within a day's journey of this place, they will hunt you down. They are going to enslave your people and burn your settlements to the ground. Those that are spared death will wish they had been killed. They will make your young men toil until they drop dead from exhaustion. They'll violate your women and use them as surrogates for the next generation of Volcarons. They'll force your children to work in the fields and on fishing boats until they are of age, and then they too will suffer the same fate as the adult men and women. You'll be treated as beasts, used only for labor and breeding. Believe me, the cruelty of Morgoratt and his followers is such that you cannot even imagine. You need to go—far away from here—before you no longer have the choice."

Hamar stared back at Suma in silence.

"I told all of this to Nicholas the last time I was here, but I see that he didn't take my advice seriously," the big Volcaron added sternly.

"It seems that you are quite knowledgeable about the specifics of Morgoratt's plan, Suma," began Hamar, rising slowly to his feet. "May I ask *how* exactly you know so much about it?"

Suma swallowed hard, immediately hoping that Hamar hadn't noticed.

"Because I helped him plan it," he admitted, looking directly at Hamar to convey his honesty. "I had no choice. I was given orders, and I would have been killed if I'd refused."

"You're a filthy, treacherous Volcaron," snarled Hamer as he slammed his fist down on the table. "I should have known by your accent. You have some audacity to…"

"I'm a Volcaron who wants to make amends," interrupted Suma gruffly.

"I'm ashamed of my race for what we've done to the Hohalians. I've seen the suffering of your people since we arrived, and I don't want blood on my hands once Morgoratt comes to look for you."

"Do you know that one of our men has gone missing?" Hamar inquired darkly, not ready to accept Suma's profession. "Weeks ago, during one of Nicholas's raids on the village. He got separated from the rest of us in the jungle on the way back here, and we haven't seen him since."

"I received Nicholas's note," Suma nodded grimly. "Unfortunately, I know nothing of the man you speak of, I swear."

Hamar shot his visitor a dubious glance before giving an unconvinced snort.

"We discussed going back several times to search the village for him," he resumed. "But the risk of compromising the rest of our people's whereabouts and safety was too great."

"If indeed Morgoratt *has* taken your companion," responded Suma in a low tone, "Then I fear there is little you can do for him."

He then faltered for a moment before adding to the pale-faced Hamar, "Please. Heed my warning and go. If Nicholas is dead or has disappeared, then you need to lead the Hohalians away from here."

There was a glum pause for a moment before Hamar spoke:

"Princess Caralisa said that Nicholas has a plan. He's gone off—where, nobody knows—supposedly under divine instruction from the Nexus, which is supposedly going to lead him to a miracle that will save the Hohalians. Nicholas apparently told Caralisa that we should wait until he returns before doing anything further."

Suma found himself slightly bemused at Hamar's mention of the Nexus. He was not inclined toward the worship of divine beings, especially given the squalor and shame that he and his fellow Volcarons had known their entire lives.

"Do you actually believe in all of that?" asked Suma with a furrowed brow.

Hamar shrugged.

"I grew up believing," he said. "Obviously, since I'm no longer living by all the precepts the Hohalians follow, I have my doubts. But Nicholas asked me to take care of Haven and to be ready to fight for the Hohalians— because *they* believe, and so they're not going anywhere."

"If it was me, I'd leave anybody that gullible to fend for themselves," Suma scoffed.

Hamar chuckled darkly to himself.

"Maybe," he said. "But you walked all the way here to warn us, even though we didn't listen to you the first time."

"Anyway, it doesn't matter," replied Suma self-consciously, "I've done my part tonight. That's all I can do. I can't stop Morgoratt and his army. It's up to you and your people from here."

Hamar's face grew thoughtful.

"True," he replied slowly. "But you *could* slow them down. Morgoratt is counting on you to help him get ready, right? Cells? Chains? Weapons? Those kinds of things take time to prepare, don't they? Things could go wrong. Tools and materials can be faulty or get damaged. If you could help things to go wrong for long enough, it might give us Hohalians more time... maybe even Nicholas too."

Suma stared at Hamar in silence.

"If Morgoratt found out I've been helping you, he would cut out my heart and feed it to the vultures. Do you realize the huge risk that I am taking by just speaking to you, let alone sabotaging his grand plans?"

"Well, I suppose that you have an opportunity to further atone for the sins of your people, don't you Suma?" responded Hamar matter-of-factly.

Suma stared at him tensely but did not respond. His embattled conscience was creating even more problems for him than he thought possible, and he scolded himself for his recklessness. With a shake of his head, he extended his arm to Goldbeak who hopped off the table and clambered onto his shoulder. Suma then rose from the table and walked toward the door in silence. As he made to leave, he stopped for a moment and looked back at Hamar who stood tall against the dancing shadows thrown up by the fire.

"Not all of us Volcarons are like *him*," added Suma bitterly.

Without waiting for Hamar to respond, he and his parrot exited the cabin and set off on their long return journey.

31

FROM THE ROOFTOP of the Hohalian king's former mansion, Morgoratt surveyed the land before him. His eyes wandered across the landscape, along the white fringe of the bay and upward toward the rocky cliffs that lay exposed to the harsh, maritime elements. The newly constructed slave complex loomed as the highest point along the southern landscape. It appeared on the horizon as a lightless, sprawling monstrosity—an unnatural feature on an already inhospitable, windswept portion of the Bay of Hohala.

After a protracted construction, beset by unforeseen delays and disruptions, Morgoratt's plantation was at last ready to receive its first occupants. On this particularly somber day of sullen, grey clouds that were full of the threat of rain, Morgoratt had gathered the chieftains to the mansion for an important briefing of the Volcaron leadership. Among them, acting as inconspicuous as possible, stood Suma. As a result of his impressive engineering feats over the course of the construction of Morgoratt's prison, Suma had been forced further into the Volcaron inner circle. He'd become privy to the highest level of preparations for the enslavement of the Hohalians, his input critical to the success of the grand Volcaron plan. As a result, Suma had grown increasingly disturbed as the specifics of Morgoratt's ambitions regarding the Hohalians were gradually revealed to him. He was appalled by the cruelty of the leader's vision, the arrogance of his despotism, and the sheer inhumanity in his motivation. Privately, Suma remained deeply ashamed of his barbaric people. It was for this reason—as well as his secret affiliation with Nicholas and the men of Haven—that Suma had done as much as he possibly could to sabotage and delay the progress of Morgoratt's plan without raising the suspicions of his fellow Volcarons. As suggested by Hamar during his recent visit to Haven, Suma had intentionally inserted subtle flaws into the structural design for the plantation, necessitating extensive revision and reconstruction of certain aspects of the complex. This had slowed the building process considerably, which Suma solemnly hoped would buy the Hohalians enough time to make the necessary preparations to defend themselves or, better yet, disappear.

Morgoratt had dubbed his nefarious vision, "The Harvest," whereby the exiled Hohalians would be hunted down and rounded up, and, eventually, would be either enslaved or exterminated, depending on the perceived usefulness of each Hohalian and the level of their cooperation. The once-lush meadows south of New Volcaron had grown dusty and fallow, and it would take much toil to rejuvenate the pastures to the point where they could once again support crops. There was also a need for extensive repairs and construction work throughout the village which had begun to fall apart due to the Volcarons' neglect.

Particularly, however, it was Morgoratt's belief that the Volcaron bloodline had grown stale. Great men were no longer emerging from within the Volcaron race, and Morgoratt had long concluded this to be the result of the shallow breeding pool among his people. He believed that enslavement of the Hohalians—a tribe of industry and vitality—would enable new blood to be injected into the next generation of Volcarons and rejuvenate their race. Morgoratt, as Volcaron leader, believed that he was deserving of the fairest of the Hohalian females He'd wondered for some time now if the king's daughter, whom he'd admired from a distance all those years ago, was still as alluring as he remembered. Morgoratt's mind fantasized darkly at the prospect of taking the young princess for his own, and a riotous excitement coursed through his body as he prepared to address his men for the final time before the commencement of the Harvest.

The assembly of Volcaron chieftains stood together in expectant silence as Morgoratt turned his gaze from the rugged coastline to address them. There was a dazed, almost manic glint in his eyes as he surveyed each of the men slowly, searching their faces for any hint of weakness or hesitation.

As the disruptions to Morgoratt's plans had continued, the Volcarons saw their ruler grow increasingly distrustful and violently unpredictable.

Even those within his closest circle were left in no doubt that the leader sensed there were treasonable dealings afoot, and that the discovery of any acts of betrayal would be met with a brutal response. Suma's close involvement in the process, in addition to his expert cover up of his own sabotage, had led Morgoratt to be less suspicious of him. Nevertheless, as the Volcaron leader's eyes moved on to Suma, the big engineer couldn't help sense that there was a hint of cold skepticism in the way Morgoratt examined him. However, Suma was not a man who easily betrayed his own emotions, and he remained sullen and stony-faced until Morgoratt's attention moved on. Eventually, when he had scrutinized the visage of each man, Morgoratt cleared his throat to speak. His voice was agitated and icy, and his top lip was curled into a faint snarl.

"So, we've made it to this point, at last," he lilted with a thin smile that was as chilling as it was insincere. "Yes, my brothers, despite strange, inexplicable—and, dare I say, severely punishable—but failed attempts to vandalize our plans for Volcaron progress, the time is at last upon us to make Volcaron great again."

The chieftains—self-serving sycophants whose continued loyalty to Morgoratt was down to a combination of fear, ignorance, delusion, and greed—cheered compliantly.

As Morgoratt continued his monologue, his tone switched to one of mock-hurt.

"Yes," he went on coolly. "It has been sobering to know that all this time, there has been one among us who would rather conspire with the cowardly Hohalians than see his own nation prosper. It pains me to think that one of you—whom I have counseled and kept among my closest allies—would undermine the achievement of Volcaron greatness."

Morgoratt's lips twisted back into a thin, menacing grin as he added, "It also leads me to believe there is a person among us who has a very urgent death wish."

Suma's heart pounded in his chest.

"Not to worry," continued Morgoratt. "A rat will eventually reveal itself when cornered."

The Volcaron leader then indulged in a final, interrogative gaze at each of the assembled faces around him, before adopting a more buoyant tone.

"Now, my friends, the time has come for you to play your part in the next momentous chapter of the Volcaron story," he asserted with a sweep of his arm that gestured toward the jungle of Hohala and beyond. "The countryside is yours. *You* are the harvesters. Go now and bring in the harvest that will sustain our nation into the future. Leave no rock uncovered, no pool of water unsearched, and no tree unfelled in your hunt for the Hohalians."

The men hung onto Morgoratt's every word as he paused to remove his dagger from its sheath and finger the razor-sharp blade softly, but precariously.

"Remember, brothers. Let there be no mercy shown to resistance or pleading from the enemy. Where blood must be spilled, then spill it with a steady hand and a cold heart. The greatness that we strive for dictates that there is no room for indecision or feeble-mindedness. Is that clear to each of you?"

"Yes, Morgoratt!" came the collective reply from the men.

"However, I want you to understand that this 'harvest' is not simply to capture the Hohalians and force them to work. No, our goal is to cleanse this land of that weak, gutless tribe to make room for the expansion of our own naturally superior and more deserving race. The sun is about to set on the age of Hohala."

At that, Morgoratt's jaw stiffened as he clenched his teeth, his eyes narrowed hatefully, and his knuckles turned white as he gripped the handle of the blade in his hand tightly before continuing slowly.

"I want you to crush them so that they will never contemplate rising up," he snarled lustily, as if merely uttering the words brought him gratification. "Burn their homes and possessions until they are ash on the wind, desecrate anything that they hold sacred, shed the blood of the old and infantile, as well as any who are not suitable for work or breeding. I want you to humiliate and demoralize them so that they become little more than the beasts that work in the field and that, in the future, there will be no prospect of revolt."

Suma's eyes darted around at the other chieftains, and he could tell that even some of the most hardened of them felt uneasy about Morgoratt's deranged intentions. His focus then returned to the Volcaron leader himself whose eyes were bloodshot and demented-looking and whose arm quivered as he gripped the knife handle.

"As I have said many times before, my brothers," Morgoratt continued with an imperiousness that caused Suma's disgust to rise even further. "We

Volcarons have too long settled for the scraps of nature, the leftovers of races weaker than ourselves. Let us no longer live as locusts, as anchorless nomads wandering the world in search of survival. Our race has long been forsaken by the gods of creation while the pitiful Hohalians have always been blessed with abundance. Now, let us decide for *ourselves* what we are worth. Let the other races of the world serve *us*!"

Morgoratt paused, and his voice turned to a heartless growl as he continued, "Yes, my brothers, we *will* make Volcaron great again! Today, you go forward to determine our future as the master race of these lands. Now, let us recover our glorious Volcaron past and once and for all assert our supremacy."

At that, Morgoratt turned and nodded toward one of his men standing guard by the rooftop entrance. Suma and the chieftains watched in silence as the guard disappeared down a stairwell that connected the rooftop to the floor below. A few minutes later, he returned, this time holding a young man with thin, Hohalian features onto the rooftop at knife-point. The boy's hands and ankles were bound in thick chains, and he was trembling violently, but his expression stayed firm.

"This young fellow was found wandering lost in the jungle nearby a few nights ago," Morgoratt informed his audience, the chieftains intrigued that the leader had already somehow taken one of the Hohalians prisoner. "It appears he must have forgotten that this place is no longer home to his people. He's a trespasser, and trespassing is a crime that, of course, must be punished."

Suma's heart sank as he realized that Morgoratt's unfortunate captive was the young man from Haven who had failed to return from the raid on the village that Nicholas had informed him of in his note. The boy's limbs quivered in fear as he was led forward to stand at Morgoratt's side.

"My fellow Volcarons," declared Morgoratt haughtily. "As you embark upon this most historic mission, please take note of the type of courtesy that I expect to be extended to any headstrong Hohalians that you may encounter—and, indeed, any men of Volcaron who fail to do what is expected of them."

Before the words had fully registered with the men, Morgoratt strode forward and gripped the startled young Hohalian by the back of his collar. With a feverish growl, the Volcaron leader hauled the boy forward and rushed toward the mansion's battlements. It was with a scream of pure terror that Morgoratt's unfortunate prisoner was sent hurtling off the roof, and his cry lingered in the ears of all present as he fell. Then, there was a crisp, cracking sound that prompted Suma to fight against the urge to throw up. Silence and tension hung in the air, and no one chanced to say a word. Each of the Volcaron chieftains was unwilling to speak until they knew it was safe to do so.

Morgoratt turned to face the assembled party, breathing heavily from his sudden exertion. On his face, the Volcaron leader wore a look of pure malice as his grey eyes glared at his speechless followers.

"Now," rasped Morgoratt. "You know what is expected of you and what the consequences of failure will be."

As the party of chieftains made to skulk silently away, Suma stole a reluctant glance across the edge of the rooftop; the young Hohalian's body lay wickedly contorted, and the paving stone around him was spattered red. Immediately, Suma bowed his head and averted his eyes, his entire sense of his place in the world upended by his shame.

32

An oppressive humidity hung in the air as Suma and two young Volcaron fighters tramped through the thick undergrowth of the jungle. They'd been on the move for three days and had traversed an extensive track of the jungle that spread out from New Volcaron and westward into the highlands. Although he moved with a deliberately cautionary step, Suma had journeyed this direction before. He had purposely influenced the delegation of the search-areas to ensure that it was he who was responsible for combing the portion of the jungle closest to Haven and New Hohala. For some time now, he'd been subtly steering the search away from the Hohalians' settlements, but the enthusiasm of his two companions in this mission ensured that it was proving less than straightforward.

Morgoratt had assigned search parties of three—two younger fighters to one of the Volcaron chieftains. Suma considered himself unlucky enough to have been designated a pair of young Volcaron men with whom he'd had the misfortune of working closely during the construction of the "plantation" prison compound. The older of the pair, Groger, was an oafish clod of around twenty-five years, as strong and brutish as he was dim-witted. However, their trek through the jungle had been unexpectedly fast-paced thanks to the burly Groger's combative swashbuckling through the jungle with his sword.

The second of Suma's companions was Kreb, a watchful, out-spoken young man of about nineteen. Suma disliked and distrusted Kreb especially, and he had cursed under his breath when Morgoratt placed the boy in his charge. Since the outset of their expedition, Kreb had been testing the limits of Suma's patience, making indirect comments about his tense relationship with Morgoratt and the inexplicable faults in the measurements and design of Suma's layout for the plantation. Though he knew that Kreb couldn't possibly have guessed his intentional acts of sabotage, those comments did make him uneasy. It appeared to Suma that Kreb had been purposely shooting subtle barbs at him in order to provoke his temper. However, given the high stakes involved in directing the search away from the Hohalians, Suma was determined to resist the temptation to be drawn into a confrontation with the insufferable young man. Most worryingly, Kreb was intelligent. Since the outset of their jungle expedition, they had been charting their progress using a sketched replica of one of Morgoratt's maps of the landscape, and Kreb had been meticulous in marking off any portions of the jungle already covered. It was becoming more and more difficult for Suma to avoid New Hohala, and, now into the third day of exploration, Kreb's map had become unnervingly accurate. Just that morning the youth had announced that there was still one area that remained unsearched, and—to Suma's dread—it constituted the highland surrounding Haven and New Hohala.

As they ventured onward in the direction of the Hohalian settlements, led by Kreb's enthusiastic directions, Suma's panicked mind scrambled to come up with a way to impede their steady march toward the Hohalians. Around midday, he suggested stopping to eat and assess their progress. As Suma had foreseen, Kreb reacted with impatience, such was his eagerness to receive Morgoratt's praise and favor for being the one to find the exiled Hohalians.

As they drew nearer to New Hohala, Suma resigned himself to the prospect of having to take preventative measures against Kreb. The presence of Groger, however, was a problem. Although he was confident he could take on either of the men if necessary, Suma knew it would be difficult to overpower the pair by himself, not to mention the prospect of trying to explain to Morgoratt how both of his young troops had been killed in the jungle while he alone out of the trio had survived.

"I think we've done well so far," declared Suma as he wiped the sweat off his brow and settled himself down gratefully on a dusty tree trunk. "We've covered the entire western portion of the jungle to where the mountains meet. It's best at this point to regroup and to reassemble with Morgoratt and the other chieftains. The day is hot and draining, and it would be foolish to push ourselves any further when the others may have already rooted out the Hohalians."

"What?" spat Kreb. "You know we've been keeping track of our movements, and there's still an area we haven't searched yet?"

"We've gone deeper into the jungle than we agreed with Morgoratt," replied Suma with feigned calmness. "It's crucial that we're efficient with our search efforts, and that we stay in close communication with the others. We might need to advance on the Hohalians quickly and in strong numbers. It's futile for us to act alone without the force of our army."

"Nonsense!" objected Kreb with a sneer. "You know that I've been the one who has been really leading this search, and now that I've narrowed down where those mongrels could be hiding, *you* want to claim the glory for yourself."

"Shut your mouth, Kreb, before I silence you," retorted Suma, purposely not engaging in eye contact with the indignant younger man. "I've no desire to have Morgoratt pat me on the head like a house pet. Maybe you should be less concerned with simpering and worry more about arriving back to the village without your eager nose being broken."

At that, Suma raised his eyes warningly, to which Kreb turned away and muttered angry swear words under his breath.

"Is there something that you'd like to say to me outright, Kreb?" challenged Suma dangerously. "You seem to forget who's in charge."

"Yeah, at the moment," sneered Kreb with a smirk.

"You want to elaborate on that?" replied Suma, his voice rising in response to what he interpreted as a veiled threat.

Groger, who had been sitting on the ground in self-absorbed silence, interrupted the heightening confrontation.

"Suma's right," he piped up. "We've been searching for three days, and I'm tired and hungry. I think we should regroup with the others."

"Are you serious?" objected Kreb. "We have one last area to search, and you both want to give up? There's something not right about this. You two are plotting something, I know it!"

"Can you give it a rest, you idiot!" replied Suma exasperatedly.

"Nobody's plotting behind your back. Don't fool yourself into thinking you're important enough to be conspired against."

Kreb fell into angry silence. Keen to defuse the younger man's confrontational air, Suma then turned to Groger.

"You know the route back to New Volcaron, right?" he queried, peering warningly at Kreb from the corners of his eyes.

"Yup, I sure do," replied Groger.

"I want you to go back to the village," continued Suma. "Link up with the other search parties, and tell them that we've scoured every part of the western country and have turned up nothing."

Noticing the mistrustful look in Kreb's eyes, he added, "Kreb and I are going to search the final portion of the highlands that he is so adamant we explore. You get back and report our progress to Morgoratt. We'll meet up back in the village as soon as we have satisfied Kreb's curiosity."

And then, Suma turned to the rancorous young man.

"Is that agreeable to *you*, then?" he challenged in a jeering tone.

Kreb did not respond, other than with a look of disdain.

"Sounds good to me," replied Groger with an indifferent shrug of his shoulders. "I've had enough of this damn jungle anyway."

At that, he swatted a mosquito with the palm of his hand and rose to his feet.

As Groger made to leave, Suma called after him, "We'll both be right behind you."

Groger gave no reply. However, for a lingering moment, he stood looking at Suma and Kreb in silence, as if he was wrestling with some conflict in his mind. With a final, curious glance that served to unsettle Suma, Groger turned and disappeared into the jungle without another word.

"If we're not back soon," called Kreb after him, "Tell Morgoratt where we are, and come find us in case we've been outnumbered by the Hohalians!"

"Shut up, you lickspittle," mocked Suma, feigning indifference to Kreb's alarming instruction to Groger which he silently willed the departing young man not to have heard.

Picking himself up from the ground, Suma gestured half-heartedly to the suspicious-looking Kreb.

"Come on," he grunted. "The quicker we get this out of the way, the sooner we can be done with this ridiculous search."

Kreb led the way waspishly, his concentration fixed on the route to where he deduced was the final possible location in which the Hohalians could be sheltered. As he followed Kreb in uneasy silence, Suma fumed at finding himself in this predicament, resentful of having the fate of the Hohalians on his shoulders. He'd wanted neither a part of Morgoratt's barbaric plans nor to have become responsible for the Hohalians. And now, he fumed at the thought that he was currently conceding to the whim of an upstart like Kreb. He questioned to himself whether he should have left Nicholas Stone and his men to fend for themselves all those years ago. He knew little of the Hohalians, other than his dealings with Nicholas and a handful of his followers. And even at that, the men of Haven were little more than acquaintances, people that he traded with when either party was in need of supplies. In the sweltering jungle heat, Suma brooded resentfully as he attempted to convince himself that the safety of the Hohalians was not his burden to carry.

After another hour of wandering, the terrain began to slope more sharply, and Kreb insisted that they hike to the steepest point. A wave of silent dread swept over Suma as he realized disbelievingly that his companion had actually managed to happen upon the hillside that marked the perimeter of the Hohalian settlements.

"This is it," declared Kreb smugly, pointing at his map. "By my markings, this is the last possible place in the western portion of the jungle that they could be hidden.

"No, we've climbed that hill already," replied Suma with feigned passiveness as he pointed out a gnarled, distinctive-looking oak tree. "We've definitely been up there. I searched it myself. I remember passing that big tree."

"No, we *didn't*," Kreb challenged, his tone rising as he pointed to the section of the map where Suma knew Haven and New Hohala lay, open and vulnerable. "I've marked every bloody place we searched on the map. It doesn't matter what you say; we haven't been up here!"

Suma stood over Kreb, trying to appear as intimidating as possible.

"Now listen here, you little weasel," he glowered. "I'm in charge. I'm the one Morgoratt ordered to lead you and Groger, and I say we've been this way already."

Kreb spluttered indignantly as he attempted to respond, but Suma interrupted peevishly, "*I* will go up this hill, once again, to verify that there's nothing there but rocks and underbrush and more damn trees. You will wait here, and when I come back down, we're turning straight around and returning to the village."

"Not a chance! I'm coming with you," fumed Kreb, attempting to shove past him.

Suma glared at the petulant youngster.

"You will stay here," he repeated through gritted teeth. "That's an order. I'm not dragging your lazy carcass up that hill with me. You've already pushed my patience to the limit. Your insubordination will not be forgotten when we get back to New Volcaron..."

Before Suma could utter another word, he felt the sudden impact of something blunt striking the side of his head, and he dropped to the ground in a daze. His head spun as he opened his eyes to see Kreb taking off up the slope at a sprint, a thick lump of branch dangling from his hand. Suma struggled to his feet and began wobbling up the overgrown hillside in pursuit of his assailant. The blow to his head had disorientated him, and it was through blurred vision that he attempted locate the fleeing Kreb. Gritting his teeth, Suma used his arms and legs to stagger to the top of the slope. As he reached the crest of the hill, an assemblage of thatched rooftops and thin smoke spires came into distant view, and his heart sank upon hearing the gleeful cheers of Kreb above him.

"Yes! I found them!" he roared down triumphantly at the struggling Suma. "I *knew* they would be hiding here."

"I hope you're happy with yourself now, you treacherous bastard," growled Suma as he stomped furiously toward Kreb.

"Stay right where you are!" roared the younger man, drawing his knife and pointing it at Suma's chest.

"Put that away!" thundered Suma. "How dare you threaten your superior? I'll have you hung by your feet in chains when we get back to the village."

"You'll be the one hanging!" shouted Kreb manically as he advanced on Suma with the blade quivering in his hand. "But it'll be by the neck, you traitor—that's if I don't kill you right now! Oh, wait till Morgoratt finds out that *you* are the deceiver in his ranks. If I was you, I'd get down on your knees and beg me to end your sorry existence right here and now, because you know the last snake who betrayed Morgoratt had his gut cut open and was thrown alive into the sea for the fish to feast on."

Kreb reached to his side and removed from his belt a short length of chain, the ends of which concluded with a pair of thick, metal wrist cuffs. Cautiously, he extended the meter-long coil in the direction of Suma.

"Put your hands behind your back, and tie these around your wrists," he demanded agitatedly. "Oh, you'll answer to Morgoratt for your treason, you filthy imposter!"

Suma simply stared despondently.

"Back off, and put down the knife, Kreb," he warned. "You don't have to do anything foolish."

Kreb's eyes bulged in their sockets. Already imagining his reward and greater status after returning to Morgoratt with the traitor in tow, his face was flush with excitement.

"Actually, you know what?" he considered, feverishly. "I don't think it's worth dragging your useless hide all the way back to the village. If you found it so easy to forsake your own people, then your bloody carcass can rot up here in this wretched place along with the corpses of all of those Hohalians who you betrayed your own race for."

Before Suma had an opportunity to respond, Kreb launched himself at him, the knife brandished murderously in the air. Instinctively, Suma dropped his shoulder as the blade flashed in front of his face, narrowly missing him. As Kreb's momentum carried him forward, Suma stuck out his knee and sent the boy tumbling face-first to the ground. A blistering rage filled Suma as he advanced on Kreb, who lay groaning face-down on the ground.

"You'd try to murder me, you treacherous rat," he bellowed as he towered over the sprawled youngster. "You couldn't leave well enough alone!"

Suma bent over Kreb's panting form and extended his arm to pull him up from the ground. Without warning, the younger man rolled swiftly onto his back, and the knife blade glinted in the sunlight. A searing pain ran up Suma's left arm, and a spray of blood spattered across his face and upper body. He staggered backward, clutching his forearm, a dark, gaping slash wound running from his elbow to his wrist. Before Suma could inspect his wound, Kreb had leapt to his feet again and was rushing toward him with the knife pointed outward. As Kreb attempted to bring the blade edge down on Suma's chest, the bigger man caught his attacker's wrist. The veins in Suma's forehead pulsated as he squeezed hard until he heard bone crack. Kreb cried out in pain and dropped the knife, just as Suma swung his other fist at his face, knocking him on his back a second time.

"Have you had enough, pup!" Suma roared down at Kreb in fury as he cradled his own blood-spurting forearm.

In reply, the mad-eyed Kreb gathered up the knife with his injured arm. He climbed to his feet, and with a look of wild hysteria in his eyes, he lunged toward Suma a third time.

The discarded branch that Kreb had first used to strike Suma lay on the ground nearby. With a movement that was as swift as it was precise, Suma swept up the branch and swung it once at the oncoming Kreb's head. A sharp crack filled the air of the hilltop as Kreb's body went limp and tumbled to the ground. Suma panted breathlessly as he stood over the motionless body, the right side of the boy's skull dented and bloodied.

Suddenly, Suma became aware of the lonely silence of the countryside, and he winced in exasperation and pain as he clutched his blood-soaked arm. He spat on the ground in fury as the dire reality of the situation registered with him. Groger would soon arrive back at the village to report to Morgoratt, and there would be a severe inquisition when Suma returned without Kreb. Aware that time was of the essence, Suma hoisted up the lifeless Kreb by the collar of his tunic. Indulging in a resentful glance down at the silent rooftops of New Hohala in the distance, Suma cursed loudly before turning and dragging the meddlesome Kreb's body down the hillside.

33

SUMA FIDGETED IN a wooden chair next to the hearth in Lawson's cabin. He felt distracted and ill at ease, while the heat from the fire caused his forehead and neck to perspire. As his eyes surveyed the four drab walls of the royal counselor's home, he contemplated changing his mind and making his way back through the jungle. He tried to convince himself that the wellbeing of the Hohalians was not his responsibility, that it was a burden he had not invited; yet, on each occasion that he wrestled with his conscience on the matter, his inner voice reiterated to him that it was still his moral duty to assist the Hohalians in their hour of need.

Now, after a grim afternoon in the jungle, Suma found himself sitting alone and feeling very out of place in the home of the Hohalian king's chief advisor. If Morgoratt and the Volcarons ever discovered that he had been secretly protecting the very people for whom he had designed a prison, Suma knew that he would be put to death in a most excruciating manner. As a high-ranking Volcaron, he had seen first-hand the barbarity that Morgoratt and some of his closest aides were capable of. Thoughts of those acts of cruelty he had witnessed Morgoratt carry out on ill-disciplined Volcarons or those suspected of treachery caused him to perspire in his seat, and he resolved that it was indeed the right thing to at least warn the Hohalians about the Volcaron army's impending arrival.

Following the fatal skirmish with Kreb, Suma had sat in the sun for a considerable period, agonizing about what best to do in the dire circumstances. Having made up his mind to do what he could to hinder

Morgoratt's plans, he had dragged Kreb's lifeless body into a particularly dense part of the jungle and had then spent well over an hour digging a lonely grave with his bare hands. As he'd lowered the young man's corpse into the roughly excavated hole, he'd been consumed by a troubling feeling that the grim moment was one he would carry with him for the rest of his days. For a man who had not cried since he was a child, he'd been taken aback midway through digging to realize that his own eyes were filled with tears. His senses and emotions overwhelmed, he'd wept profusely as he swept and kicked the soil down upon Kreb's cold, stiff remains. The boy's head and face had been the last part of his body to be consumed by the soil, and the sight of his blank, deathly stare peeking out from beneath the earth had shaken Suma to his core. The stark realization that he now and forever had the young upstart's blood on his hands—even though Suma had acted in self-defense—had weighed heavily on his decision to risk his life in order to bring another warning to the Hohalians. After he had patted down the loose topsoil that marked Kreb's shallow grave, he'd walked slowly toward Haven where he hoped to confide in Hamar for a second time.

Hamar had been once again highly suspicious at the sudden arrival of Suma on his doorstep for a second time, but nonetheless, he'd listened to what the big Volcaron had to say. After Suma had explained the latest developments in Morgoratt's plan, as well as the grim deed of burying one of his own in secret in order to protect the Hohalians from being discovered, Hamar had looked severely concerned. Unwilling to waste any further time, they'd rushed straight to New Hohala so that Suma could give the unsettling information to the king and the princess himself. When they'd reached Lawson's cabin, Hamar's introduction of Suma to the king's advisor had been informal and matter-of-factly. Hamar and the men of Haven had not exactly endeared themselves to the king and his aides during their five years in exile, and it had been Hamar's fear that Lawson might react with anger to the idea of a Volcaron being escorted freely into Hohalian territory. But the counselor, being of pragmatic disposition, had accepted Hamar's insistence that Suma's information was worth being heeded.

And so, it was this sequence of events that had resulted in Suma now finding himself alone inside the cabin of the king's counselor as he waited for the monarch's arrival. Being a considerate host, Lawson had provided Suma with seed cake and a tall tumbler of brandy before he and Hamar left together to find King Benjamin. Normally, Suma was not a drinker, and he had observed with shame the effects of alcohol on his fellow Volcarons. On this occasion, however, he savored the gentle numbness brought on by the potent brew as he waited for the return of the others.

Almost a half hour had gone by when Suma heard the rattle of the latch on the cabin door. A moment later, Lawson's figure appeared in the entrance way, followed by Princess Caralisa and then Hamar, who stood back to the side of the door frame as he gestured silently to King Benjamin to enter. Frail and gaunt-looking, the disheveled king entered the barely lit cabin and nodded courteously in Suma's direction. Suma, unsure of what the appropriate response should be, returned a single nod of his head. Caralisa, having been informed of Suma's identity prior to her arrival, instead afforded the Volcaron a distrusting glare before she took a seat at the far corner of the cabin.

When King Benjamin had been seated, Hamar was the first to speak.

"Your Highness, this is the man I spoke to you of," he announced, gesturing toward Suma. "He is a man of Volcaron, but he is unique among his race in that he has chosen to aid the Hohalians, rather than see Morgoratt enslave our people."

King Benjamin's focus switched to Suma. After a moment of studying the big Volcaron's eyes, the king cleared his throat.

"You must be a very brave man, Master Suma," he remarked. "Very courageous—or foolish, as the case may be."

Suma's lips pursed moodily at the king's suggestion.

"I've come to warn you because my conscience tells me that it's the right thing to do," he replied to the monarch in a resentful tone. "I have no allegiance to Morgoratt, only that I find he is the leader of the people I was born into. Before we Volcarons came to Hohala, our native country was a wasteland. Morgoratt promised young men like me the chance of adventure and riches, and I naively joined his cause."

Suma's voice dropped as he averted his eyes.

"The past five years," he continued after a bitter sigh, "I've had little choice but to follow orders. I'm the only one among my people with the skills to design, build, and repair. For that, I was valuable to Morgoratt, and I've been under his charge for a long time. But it has only been recently—since he revealed his plans to enslave your people—that I decided I needed to do something to prevent such a thing from happening. That was why

I came to Hamar here a few weeks back. Since then, I've tried to disrupt Morgoratt by sabotaging and slowing down his plans, but there's been only so much I could do. Now, his prison is built, and his men are sweeping the jungle and the mountains in order to find you all. If he succeeds, he will brutalize and terrorize your people. For five years, Morgoratt has ravaged your village and plundered the countryside around it."

Suma paused before exhaling and continuing:

"…and I refuse to stand aside and watch him to do the same to your people."

Caralisa and King Benjamin listened, wide-eyed, as Lawson stood in solemn silence.

"This is indeed troubling," reflected the king. "And, might I ask how long you believe it will be before Morgoratt's army comes for us?"

Suma swallowed hard before replying, "One of my men, Groger, has returned to the village, and the other who accompanied me is dead. When Kreb doesn't return, Morgoratt will be suspicious, and I've no doubt he'll send his army this way. It could very likely be only a day or two…maybe even hours."

A smashing noise interrupted the exchange as Caralisa let the tumbler of water that she was holding fall out of her trembling hands.

"Hours?" she exclaimed, ignoring the broken clay and water at her feet. "You mean they could already be on their way?"

Suma gave a solemn nod of his head.

"I expect so," he replied glumly. "I could tell by the way Groger looked at me as he was leaving that he knew something was amiss. That's why I came here immediately. Your people *must* act now."

He looked at every face in the room and in a deathly serious tone pleaded yet again, "Evacuate the two villages or get ready to defend yourselves, but whatever you do, do *not* wait idly for the Volcarons to arrive."

There was a collective pause as all present contemplated Suma's stark warning. Finally, Lawson spoke.

"Your Highness," he interjected, touching the king lightly on the hand. "What do you advise?"

The king sat in silence for a moment before lifting his head and looking each person in the eye.

"Gather the people," he instructed sternly. "We have work to do."

*

For the second time in days, King Benjamin stood atop the wooden platform at the center of New Hohala. The streets were filled with nervous Hohalian men, women, and children who had gathered to hear their ruler's unexpected public address. The sudden call to assemble had unsettled the people, the announcement made by way of Hamar knocking abruptly on each door in the village with the hurried command that every Hohalian was to congregate immediately.

The king's long beard was tousled and blown by a chilling wind that seemed to stir up out of nowhere. In the eastern sky, the sun was obscured by dark, rain-threatening clouds and, despite the early afternoon, the village seemed to have taken on a morose atmosphere. Caralisa, Hamar, and Lawson flanked the monarch on the platform, the trio anxious and more than a little confused. The king, unreadable as ever, had not yet shared his decision on how the Hohalians should counter or avoid the impending arrival of the Volcaron army. When implored that afternoon by Caralisa to reveal his intentions, her father had simply instructed her to hold on to her faith in the Nexus and to lead the people by her example.

In the meantime, Suma—having delivered the foreboding news of a possible Volcaron advancement toward New Hohala—had begun the long trek back to his people in the desperate hope that his absence had not been noticed. Before Suma had left, King Benjamin had placed his hand on his cheek and stared searchingly into the big Volcaron's eyes before assuring him that his good deeds would never be forgotten by the Hohalians. At the time, Suma had offered no response. Instead, he'd nodded his head somberly and exited Lawson's cabin without a further word.

Just over an hour after Suma had taken his leave, the gathered crowd waited, anxious and shivering in the gripping wind, for the king to speak. The speculative voices of the congregation grew silent as King Benjamin concluded a silent prayer, opened his eyes, and stepped forward to the edge of the platform.

"My dear people," he rasped in a tone that was weary, but confident. "My sincere thanks to you all for coming here together at such short notice, which I'm sure has caused some measure of apprehension. I am sorry to say that the information I bring to you today is not positive. In light of this, I will be direct and open with you all about the conspiracy against us."

Fearful whispers spread through the crowd. Some of the younger Hohalians began to sob at the sudden, anxious commotion all around them.

"It is my regret to inform you," continued the king, "That the forces who made it necessary for us to leave our home five years ago have grown restless and hungry for violence, and it is likely that they mean our people harm. No longer is New Hohala safe for our community. As I speak to you now, the Volcaron army is likely to be approaching this way. They will be heavily armed and dangerous; we believe they wish to enslave some of us and cause harm to others."

As the significance of King Benjamin's awful announcement filtered through the crowd, some among them grew more vocal, and agitated pleading cries of despair began to be directed at those standing on the platform.

"We must fight then!" shouted one man.

"We've nowhere to go!" cried out another.

All around, children had begun to weep as the adults in the crowd became frustrated and visibly frightened. On the platform, Caralisa's eyes looked to Lawson for reassurance, but the royal counselor simply returned her helpless stare.

"There will be no fighting!" interjected the king as the crowd grew louder. "You all know that the people of Hohala—going back incalculable generations—have been characterized by our peace and prayerfulness. Under no circumstances will we stand to taint our souls with violence. While what I tell you is indeed frightening to hear, I must urge all Hohalians to retain their faith in the guidance of the Nexus. Since the annals of time began, the Nexus has protected and provided for Hohala. I say that, under no circumstances, shall we abandon our principles now. It is my decree as king that there will be *no* violence."

At this, the dissent among the crowd only intensified, with objections fired at the king from all angles.

"Hohalians! Be silent and heed to my words!" thundered King Benjamin.

Immediately, the throng fell silent, struck by the uncharacteristic vehemence in the king's voice.

"I repeat to you," he continued, his pitch returning to its usual, stately tone. "We will not react with violence in the face of aggression. I am decreeing that all Hohalian families shall leave the village immediately. My daughter, Caralisa, and Lawson will direct the evacuation further into the western mountains until a safe and suitable place is found to rest and regroup. In the meantime, I ask for a handful of volunteers to join me to meet with the Volcarons to propose a peace treaty. We will appeal to the better nature of the invaders, and I believe that a concord can be achieved this way. I will lead this peace effort, so that should our attempts at a treaty fail, then at least the rest of you will have the chance to find sanctuary."

"Father," interrupted Caralisa, jumping forward and latching on to her father's arm. "You can't! We need you. You know those brutes won't listen to you!"

The king's brow became stern and furrowed.

"Caralisa, stand down!" he scolded heatedly without looking at her.

Caralisa's grip on her father's arm loosened, and she began to step away from him, her eyes wide with hurt, shock, and embarrassment. She could feel the stare of the astonished crowd fixed on her and, without a further word, she shuffled back into line with Lawson and Hamar. By now, the crowd had grown significantly less vocal, few, if any, having ever witnessed the king react with such umbrage, especially toward his daughter. After a moment of tense silence, the king resumed his address.

"My dear people, go now and gather only what you can easily carry and will sustain you for the time being. Anything that is not necessary to the survival of your families, you must leave behind. In half an hour, Lawson and your princess will meet with you here, and you will follow them to the seclusion of the mountains beyond."

At this, Lawson reached out and squeezed Caralisa's hand reassuringly while the princess attempted to stifle a sob. Her father had rarely ever spoken to her in such a way—especially in public—and she felt confused and belittled by the king's admonishment.

"In the meantime," continued King Benjamin, "As I have stated, I do require a handful of able men without families to accompany me to meet with the Volcarons."

For a moment, there was little said among the crowd as a number of the men averted their eyes from the king's searching gaze. Not one chose to raise his hand.

"Are there none among you who will stand by your king in our people's greatest hour of need?" questioned the king indignantly.

A moment later, an unexpected voice interrupted from the back of the crowd.

"I will stand with you, Your Highness," declared Hamar, stepping forward. "Because you have prohibited the use of violence, I believe that seeking peace with the Volcarons is the only real choice left to us. I don't know that they will accept your offer of an accord, but I do believe that there is a greater chance of success if we are shown to be united and resolute in our conviction."

Hamar then stepped forward and addressed the villagers with silencing sincerity.

"Myself and the men of Haven, like the rest of you, have grown weary of merely surviving on a mountainside," he declared. "There is *no* future for us here. Therefore, I am prepared to take the risk in the hope that the Volcarons can be brought to sense. If all Hohalians are not willing to unify and take on our enemy, then I believe it is critical that we at least show the same such united front in the seeking of a treaty."

At this, he turned toward the king:

"And, if King Benjamin cannot convince the Volcarons that co-existence is the way forward, then it is still possible that a strong, united showing might be enough to deter them temporarily."

The king nodded in response.

"If Hamar goes, then I shall too," called out a young man of Haven named Merek.

Another hand shot up from the crowd.

"I will join you also, Your Highness!"

One by one, Hohalian hands found the courage to rise in support. Conspicuous among the numbers were around fifteen volunteers that, like Hamar, hailed from Haven.

In all, over forty men raised their arms in support of the monarch's plan. King Benjamin, moved by the show of support, lifted his hands above his head.

"My sincere gratitude to you all," he responded, his face tight with emotion. "Now, before the rest of you prepare to evacuate, let us pray together as one and ask the Nexus for guidance during this trying time."

In unison, the Hohalians lifted their arms to the sky, and the king led them in a final prayer as the early drizzle of an oncoming storm prickled icily down around them.

34

DESPITE IT BEING several hours before sunset, the clouded sky had grown oppressively dark by the time King Benjamin and Hamar had led the band of volunteers to the mountain ridge where they expected to encounter the Volcaron army on approach to New Hohala. A stormy bluster whipped around the heads of the Hohalian volunteers as heavy raindrops assailed them relentlessly. The location where the king, in consultation with Hamar, had chosen to confront the Volcarons was a steep mountain passage, closed in on either side by precipitous, jagged rocks. At the base of the sloping valley lay a lowland river basin that marked the frontier between the western highlands and the jungle. King Benjamin had instructed the men to take up positions on the rocky ledges that stuck out at various points along the steep decline on one side of the valley. As instructed by the monarch, Hamar stationed himself to the rear of the assembled volunteers so that he could orchestrate a retreat if necessary. The king himself, as leader of the Hohalian delegation, had chosen to stand alone at the base of the valley, a determination that Hamar could not decide was courageous, brazen, or simply delusional. However, King Benjamin had been purposeful in his directing of the operation, which had gone some way to convincing Hamar that the king surely knew what he was doing.

With his fading, royal-blue robe and wispy beard billowing in the rising gale, King Benjamin stood unaccompanied at the foot of the valley, his back turned to the on-looking volunteers stationed throughout the slope above him. For over an hour, the king remained rooted to the same spot, his eyes fixed on the fringe of the jungle about a half of a mile ahead of him. Perched along the incline of the valley, the Hohalian volunteers shivered amid the downpour which steadily rose to a merciless torrent.

Sudden flashes of lightning cut angrily across the sky, followed by growls of rolling thunder. As the minutes passed, the tempest appeared to drift ever closer to the trembling Hohalians, and the king's lonely form became silhouetted each time the valley was lit up by the ferocious lightning. After what seemed like an eternity, Hamar—irritated and impatient from exposure to the elements—rose from his crouching position on a rocky ledge to instruct the men to turn back to New Hohala. Dusk was drawing in, and he feared that the squall of wind and icy rain might strike the volunteers down with fever *en masse*.

"Men of Hohala!" he called out, his voice straining to overcome the tumult of the storm. "Gather your things! We've stayed here long enough!"

Some of the men nearest to Hamar turned and looked at him quizzically, his words smothered by the roaring storm.

"I repeat," he hollered. "We should return to the..."

Hamar's words were cut short as a violent flash of lightning threw the landscape ahead into illumination. As the clearing below was lit up, a commotion by the jungle frontier caught his eye. Hamar's heart thumped as he attempted to focus his vision through the driving rain and the twilit gloom. A second clap of lightning illuminated the clearing and, to his silent dread, he could make out a hoard of dark figures lurching slowly toward them from the jungle's edge. There were scores, maybe hundreds, and they appeared to be marching in unison in the direction of the trembling Hohalian volunteers.

"Have mercy on us," Hamar prayed under his breath as the row of slouched Volcarons emerged into the open.

Each Volcaron soldier was armed with a blade-tipped staff that glinted with every subsequent flash of lightning. They were robed in black, and they wore plates of metal body armor across their torsos. As the Volcaron surge came into closer view, Hamar saw that some of them carried flags and black banners etched with some sort of white insignia. After several seconds of straining his vision, he could make out that the markings were of crudely painted skulls, their eyes hollow and mocking. Hamar sighed despondently as he came to the awful realization that the approaching horde had most certainly not come in peace.

By this time, all of the volunteers had spotted the oncoming troop. Alarmed, some of the men stirred from their positions as they observed the terrible sight before them. Hamar, concerned that a flurry of movement might undermine their ability to retreat quickly, rushed out into the open.

"Stay where you are!" he bellowed at a pair of fearful-looking young men who had risen to their feet from behind a boulder pile. The men, startled by the urgency in Hamar's tone, crouched back down.

The Volcaron army had by now spilled into the clearing as they marched ominously toward where King Benjamin stood alone and vulnerable. The king remained fixed to the spot, weaponless and showing no sign of retreating.

"The damn fool!" growled Hamar to himself as he willed the king to run while he still could.

By now, only a few hundred meters lay between King Benjamin and the first line of the approaching mob, and although he fumed at the monarch's bizarre behavior, Hamar could not abandon him to the Volcarons' cruelty. Struggling to remain surefooted on the rocky, rain-sodden surface, he stumbled and slid down the steep slope toward the king. A few of the volunteers called out to him, worried and confused, as he passed their positions, only to be commanded by Hamar to remain where they were. The incessant rain had made the ground slippery and treacherous, and Hamar was fortunate to make it to the foot of the slope without falling. With a pounding heart, he tore across the clearing in the king's direction. Once again, a crash of lightning lit up the area and the pale visages of the Volcaron soldiers flashed into view as they trudged ever closer.

"Your Highness!" cried Hamer as he sprinted closer to the motionless King Benjamin, yet, there was no response from the king to his frantic plea.

"King Benjamin!" Hamar beseeched a second time as he reached the monarch's spot, grabbing a hold of the ruler's arm.

King Benjamin gave no response to Hamar's panicked frustration, his eyes focused on the advancing battalion of Volcarons.

"What are you doing?" begged Hamar as a fork of electricity crashed across the charcoal sky. "We can't stay here; we must retreat!"

Once more, the king remained silent.

"I know you want to appeal to the Volcarons' better nature," growled Hamar through gritted teeth, "But it's obvious that they have *not* come to make peace with us. Look at their weapons! Please, let's withdraw from here while there is still a chance that some of our men might escape alive."

Again, there came no response from the king's tightly pursed lips, his long, grey hair soaked and matted to his face.

"You have no right to sacrifice these young men for your own stubborn beliefs!" shot Hamar fiercely. "Do you really want to have their blood on your hands because of your delusion?"

Hamar shook the king's arm roughly.

"Are you so blind that you cannot see the Nexus has abandoned the Hohalians?" he barked.

All of a sudden, King Benjamin's head turned to meet Hamar's eyes, his features tightened furiously.

"Stand down, you blasphemous fool!" roared the king. "How dare you speak ill of the gods who provide for and protect us! Like all of us, you have a duty of faith to the holy Nexus. Repent your words of sacrilege immediately!"

"Your Highness, please!" pleaded Hamar, his heart racing as the Volcaron army marched nearer, their pikes drawn longingly. "Don't allow yourself to be responsible for the slaughter of those men up there. They have no involvement in any of this and are only here out of loyalty to Hohala and the false hope of an accord."

The king stared coldly into Hamar's face, his eyes shining and resentful.

"I pity you, Hamar," he whispered harshly. "Your lack of faith is a great weakness."

Hamar gazed disbelievingly at he the old man's stubborn countenance, his mind flailing desperately to understand the king's blind recklessness.

"For five years, we've lived as homeless vagrants because of your insistence that the Nexus would eventually help us," Hamer spat vehemently. "Instead, your extreme beliefs have led our people to the brink of extermination. Is that what you want your legacy to be?"

Without warning, the howl of the storm was punctuated by a coarse, booming voice from just up ahead.

"Hohalians!" it rasped hawkishly.

Hamar turned to see that the Volcaron horde had halted their march and were now positioned just a short distance away in an imposing formation that stretched across the entire expanse of the clearing. One man stood several meters ahead of the contingent, his hair long and greasy and his lips curled into a vindictive snarl. A heavy, black robe hung off his sizeable shoulders, and in his clenched left fist he held a hooked, silver knife.

"Men of Hohala!" the dark figure repeated. "I am Morgoratt, leader of Volcaron, and I order you to surrender yourselves to the will of our superior nation. I command you, here and now, to come out from the shadows in which you cower and submit yourselves to your inevitable fate. I offer you one single opportunity to do so without resistance. Kneel before the flag of Volcaron, or we will cut every one of you down at the knees instead."

As the storm rumbled and crashed above them, Hamar turned his attention to the Hohalians stationed on the sloping valley ridge behind him; to his dismay, he saw that a number of them—maybe fifty in all—had left their positions and were moving into a defensive formation toward the spot where he and the king stood, open and vulnerable. Hamar's eyes closed in despair as it dawned on him that he'd helped to lead those innocent, eager young men to their likely doom. As Hamar's eyes frantically searched his surroundings for a path with which the volunteers might escape, he was dismayed to see King Benjamin suddenly began to stride in the direction of the Volcarons.

"Your Highness," hissed Hamar in alarm, grabbing hold of the king's shoulder. "What are you doing?"

"Release your grip," demanded the monarch. "Stay with the men. Ensure that they do not respond with force."

"You do *not* have to do this!" urged Hamar, his tone distressed and pleading. "These men do not all have to die here tonight!"

The king did not reply, instead shaking his arm roughly from Hamar's grip. Then, he paused for a moment before adding, quietly and sadly, "Pray, Hamar. Just pray."

With that, King Benjamin lifted his head high and began to march toward the baying Volcaron army. Hamar, distraught at the king's foolhardy actions, cursed in frustration before turning back hesitantly in the direction of the advancing Hohalian volunteers.

On the opposite side of the clearing, Morgoratt's venomous scowl contorted into a bemused smirk as he watched the weaponless, old king stride toward him, stately and unflinching. With a spiteful chuckle, he marched toward the oncoming King Benjamin. After a few moments, both men halted several meters from each other, the king's eyes fixed on Morgoratt's. After stifling an exhausted cough, King Benjamin spoke, firmly and dispassionately.

"I come to you as leader of the Hohalians to invite you to enter into a truce between our peoples," he declared resolutely. "We wish only to foster lasting peace, and we are willing to forgive your past misdeeds against our nation if there can be an agreement to coexistence. The Hohalians are not a warlike people. We live to worship and give devotion to the blessed Nexus, and we have no desire to enter into conflict."

For a moment, Morgoratt remained stony-faced and silent as the king's words registered in his mind. As King Benjamin steadfastly held his gaze with the Volcaron leader, Morgoratt began to snicker derisively.

"Are you really that much of an old fool to think that the great nation of Volcaron would want to co-exist with such a pitiful, cowardly race as yours?" he guffawed before coarsening his tone into a quiet growl. "You will fall to your knees before me and pledge your servitude."

To this, King Benjamin gave no response, instead closing his eyes and raising his hands above his head.

"Guide and protect us, blessed Nexus," he whispered to the sky.

Suddenly, the king was knocked abruptly to the ground as Morgoratt pounced forward and punched him square in the abdomen. As he hit the hard clearing floor, the monarch wheezed in shock, struggling with all his energy to catch his breath.

"Do not look away from me when I am speaking to you, you decrepit waste of bones," hollered Morgoratt, his fists clenched murderously. "I ordered you to kneel before me; now *kneel!*"

For a few seconds, King Benjamin lay sprawled on the ground, gasping to retrieve his breath. A moment later, he lifted his head to face Morgoratt with determination in his eyes. The king's legs wobbled as he managed to stagger to his feet, and Morgoratt's eyes widened at the king's refusal to submit. The monarch had barely composed himself into a standing position before Morgoratt flew forward a second time and landed a thumping uppercut to the king's chin. A sickening crack sounded as the old man emitted a groan of pain, and his body crumpled into the soaking grass.

At the foot of the valley slope, Hamar and the volunteers looked on in horror as Morgoratt proceeded to deliver several forceful kicks to the king's midriff.

"We can't let this happen," urged one of the men named Terryn. "He's going to kill him."

"They're trying to provoke us into coming out into the open," shot back Hamar through gritted teeth. "If we charge forward they will overcome us. We have to retreat! The king made his decision to do what he did. That was his choice."

"I will not stand by while our king is beaten to death by that animal," argued Terryn vehemently. "I am sick of our inaction, no matter the reason."

Before Hamar could reach out an arm to stop him, the young man unsheathed a dagger from his belt and ran in the direction of the waiting Volcaron brigade.

"Stop!" yelled Hamar at the sight of Terryn charging across the clearing toward Morgoratt, his knife raised. As the young man rounded on the Volcaron leader, who had continued to administer kicks to the ailing King Benjamin's mid-section, he let out a cry of aggression before swinging the knife blade at Morgoratt's face.

From where he stood, Hamar heard a grunt of pain splutter from Terryn's throat as Morgoratt's swift defensive maneuver caught his wrist and, in the same movement, plunged the point of the blade into the boy's chest. Immediately, Terryn slumped to the ground motionless. Still holding the knife in his hand, Morgoratt lifted his eyes darkly and caught Hamar's gaze across the clearing. Expressionless, he raised the blade to the rain-swept air. As a vicious spear of lightning cracked across the sky, the Volcaron leader pointed the blood-soaked dagger in Hamar's direction, and cried out, "Volcarons, advance!"

35

IN THE LIGHT of the breaking morning, a black raven cawed hoarsely as damp dawn mist began to envelop the valley clearing. The bird's raucous croak crowed at Hamar's senses, and he suddenly became conscious of the cold, wet ground under his cheek. The glow of early daylight stung his pupils as he fluttered his eyelids open, and groaned aloud at a sudden ache across his torso and limbs. With a moan of exertion, he rolled himself around until he faced the sky, and he saw that the storm clouds of the past evening had dissipated into thin wisps.

Hamar's breathing was painful and labored, and his chest rattled as he attempted to inhale the deep breaths of fresh air that his body begged for. Raising his hand in front of his face, he saw that it was bloodstained, the skin around the tips of his fingers crusted a deep red. Startled, he felt around his chest and stomach and was alarmed to realize that the skin around his collar bone was moist and stung to touch. His heart beat dully in his chest as he groped in the recesses of his mind for an indication as to why he now found himself lying dazed and injured under the pale unfamiliar sky. Trying his best to ignore the severe pain across his neck and chest, Hamar hoisted himself into a sitting position and rubbed his weary eyes with the back of his hand. His vision was blurred as his eyes struggled to focus through the dawn haze. He blinked several times and could make out that he was still situated in the clearing, the jungle's periphery on one side of him, the steep slope of the rocky valley to the other.

The raven sounded its caw once again somewhere nearby, prompting

Hamar to glance in its direction. The sight that met his eyes filled him with a terrible awe: bodies, prostrate and still, littered the clearing. There were perhaps ten corpses spread across the wide, grassy expanse that marked the edge of the jungle, their distinctive, linen robes indicating that they were all men of Hohala. Hamar spluttered in dismal horror, and recollections of the previous evening flashed before his mind's eye. In the cold morning air, he choked in disbelief as he rose to his feet, and a tormented cry emitted from his throat as the full devastation of the scene became apparent to him. A sudden surge of pain shot up through his left calf, and he realized that he was wounded there too. Limping awkwardly, Hamar staggered in the direction of the closest unmoving body. He recognized the young man as one of the inhabitants of Haven, a teenager by the name of Rowan. A dark slash wound ran the length of his deathly-pale neck, and splotches of blood had stained through his tunic like spilled red wine. Hamar swore under his breath, struggling to comprehend the reality of it all. Shuffling dazedly in no particular direction, he inspected the next body that he encountered; it too was the remains of one of his neighbors in Haven. The material across the front of the young man's robe was torn and the skin beneath it bloodied. Hamar shook his head in utter disbelief as the cadaver's blank, muted eyes gaped up at him. Another man, older, with long, grey hair matted and caked with blood, lay nearby with his face to the sky; he too wore the countenance of a fool who had been duped into volunteering for his own slaughter by an idealist with a death wish.

Hamar stumbled in a circle under the empty sky. All around him, the ravages of violent hands lay scattered across the otherwise beautiful clearing. Overcome by the nightmarish reality of the sight before him, Hamar's legs buckled weakly, and he slumped to the ground, unable to strangle the sob in his throat any longer. For a spell, he just sat on the grass and wept. Memories of the previous evening's events flooded his thoughts. He recalled the cold sting of the rain on his face as he had hollered at the earnest, foolish young volunteers to abandon their posts and retreat to the cover of the uplands. He remembered the hysterical cries of the black-clad Volcaron army as they charged in wild bloodlust toward the defenseless Hohalians. Fragmented images of flashing blades and the sounds of panicked, guttural cries besieged his thoughts, and he winced in agony as the images assailed him. Recollections of the exultant roars of the Volcarons as they stabbed and plunged their razor-tipped pikes into the flesh of their defenseless Hohalian victims caused him to claw at his scalp in anguish. The sight of the devastation around him prompted the white-hot pain of the blade that had slashed his own upper body to once again tingle across his wound, the memory fresh and acute. Overwhelmed, Hamar blinked his tear-filled eyes, and he saw that the grass on which he knelt, saturated by the foggy dew, was also stained blood-red. His fists and teeth clenched, he pounded despairingly at the ground as the Volcaron leader Morgoratt's malicious sneer floated across his mind. Enraged, Hamar tore a rock from the soil and thrust it furiously across the clearing. The stone hit the grass with a dull thud and rolled to a stop beside a dark blue robe that stretched across the sodden grass further along the clearing.

Immediately, Hamar ceased his sobbing as he recognized the robe as the one worn by King Benjamin. Filled with dread, he stumbled to his feet before proceeding to inspect the body of each of the slain Hohalians whose light had been so callously extinguished. After having knelt by the side of each of the lifeless bodies—ten in all—and whispered a prayer of sympathy, Hamar was perplexed to conclude that none of the remains belonged to the king. In sorrowful silence, he glanced up toward the sloping valley on which the Hohalian volunteers had been stationed and saw that there were robes, clubs, and boots scattered across the rocky incline—an indication that some might have managed to flee to safety, he hoped.

At that moment, he was consumed with anger that King Benjamin had led those ten, unsuspecting men to their doom in order to satisfy his own misguided beliefs. Once more, he spat a bitter curse at the thought of the king's folly and the staggering barbarity of the Volcarons. With a deep intake of breath followed by an angry, tearless sob, Hamar turned his back on the grim field of slaughter to begin the trek back to New Hohala. As he limped toward the steep valley slope, the black raven cawed mockingly once more before it wheeled across the pallid, dawn sky.

36

It was with a renewed sense of hope that Nicholas and Augee awoke to begin their journey to New Hohala, forty days since they'd first set up camp in the jungle. They rose earlier than normal, and their final preparations were quick and methodical. Before the sun had fully taken its place in the sky above the treetops, the pair found themselves indulging in a final, affectionate glace around the obscure jungle clearing which had housed them so securely, the place where the bond between them had deepened and thrived.

For Nicholas, it was a bittersweet departure, having grown fond of the secluded hideaway. But the plight of the Hohalians—particularly the life of the woman he loved—had become an immutable and insistent calling.

With his thoughts focused entirely on the mission ahead of them, Nicholas climbed across Augee's back and instructed him to take them home. As Augee took flight, Nicholas marveled to himself at the ease with which his friend could maneuver through the air. His aerial skills had improved immeasurably during the hours upon hours that they'd spent sharpening his abilities. Now, against the pink-tinged backdrop of the early-morning sky, Augee soared with confidence. His movements were subtle and graceful, and despite his enormous form, he swooped through the air like a lithe dancer. Nicholas, for all his preoccupation with the dire situation faced by the Hohalians, allowed himself to indulge in the exhilaration of soaring high amid the deep nothingness of the sky. As they flew, Nicholas felt his thoughts merge with Augee's, and he could sense Augee's contentment as they winged over the mountains toward the uplands that hid New Hohala.

The chill of the breaking dawn had long given way to sultry, mid-morning heat by the time the modest rooftops of Hohala and Haven appeared in the distance. To Nicholas's relief, both villages appeared intact, and he breathed a thankful sigh for that welcome sight, having been plagued by the dreadful fear that he and Augee's return to New Hohala might be too late.

As their destination drew closer, Nicholas's attention was pricked by the sight of movement along a rocky ridgeway leading from the edge of New Hohala into more mountainous terrain. As he strained his eyes, he was startled to make out lines of Hohalians—young, old, and in-between—climbing into the hills in great numbers, all carrying bags and bundles, interspersed with a few loaded carts drawn by gaunt horses and oxen. Nicholas was filled with an acute sense of unease as he recognized the same system of hurried evacuation that had marked the beginning of the Hohalian exile five years before.

Driven by urgency, Nicholas directed Augee to glide closer to the mountainside. As they approached, they hovered over lines of despairing, distressed people toiling up the perilous slope, clinging desperately to whatever provisions they could carry.

As Augee swept over them from above, he cast a formidable shadow across the hillside, prompting the fleeing Hohalians to turn their attention to the sky. All of a sudden, screams filled the air as the people observed Augee's massive form gliding above them. Immediately, the crowd along the narrow mountain ridgeway, began to surge forward in a panicked attempt to get out of the open. Everywhere below, people pointed up and screamed in fear, watching helplessly as Augee swooped down toward them, and Nicholas admonished himself for not realizing how frightening the sudden arrival of such a monstrous winged creature would seem to the Hohalians.

The swell and panic of the crowd dictated that it was too dangerous to touch down along the crooked trail, and, terrified of causing a mass stampede that might cost lives, Nicholas instructed Augee to turn back toward New Hohala instead. In response, Augee tucked his great wings down by his side, and he and Nicholas plummeted through the air in a beautiful, perilous dive before sweeping agilely down toward the thatched rooftops of the village. Augee brought them down softly on an embankment of stubbly grass that ran through the center of the settlement. The village was completely still, and as he clambered down from Augee's back, Nicholas's eyes searched for any signs of life among the deserted-looking homesteads. All of a sudden, his heart leapt in his chest as a child's shriek pierced the silence. A young girl of about ten, who had been lingering by a wooden cabin, had spotted Augee and now ran screaming for somebody to open the door.

"It's okay!" Nicholas called out to the child. "We're not here to harm anyone. We're Hohalians too!"

The girl had no intention of engaging a strange man and his enormous, green monster in pleasantries, and she pounded hysterically on the cabin door to be let inside. After several moments of terrified pleading by the little girl, the door swung open and the king's counselor, Lawson, appeared in the doorway. Such was her distress, the girl opted against stopping to greet Lawson, instead pushing past him and attempting to force the door closed while he stood in the way with an utterly perplexed look on his face.

"Now, what in the name of the gods is going on, girl?" he stammered. "Control yourself and tell me what is..."

Lawson's sentence trailed off, and his eyes widened as he looked up in the direction of Augee. The color drained instantly from his face, and such was the counselor's astonishment at the sight of the bizarre creature, he swore loudly—a rarity for the ever-restrained Lawson—before starting to shut the cabin door in fright.

Lawson!" cried Nicholas as he began to sprint in the direction of the counselor's cabin. "Please, wait! It's me, Nicholas Stone!"

The wooden door halted mid-swing, and a moment later, Lawson's nervous-looking face peered through the remaining gap between the door and the doorframe.

"Nicholas Stone?" came the tentative response.

Lawson nudged the door open another inch.

"You're alive!" he exclaimed, as if he doubted the words himself. "Thank the gods!"

Nicholas smiled in return and raised his fist triumphantly in the air. However, Lawson—clearly frightened by the extraordinary sight of Augee—appeared distrustful and reluctant to step out from the security of the cabin.

"What...whatever in the name of the Nexus is that!" the counselor stammered, unable to peel his stare from the towering creature that was unlike any animal he had encountered in his life.

"It's alright," called out Nicholas with an amused chuckle. "This is

Augee. He's on our side. Please, don't be afraid. Come out and I'll introduce you."

Nicholas stretched his arm out and stroked Augee's snout in the hope that it would dispel Lawson's fear. However, the opportunity for Lawson to personally acquaint himself with the magnificent creature before him was lost as the door swung open, and an excited female voice from inside caused him to stumble out of the entranceway in surprise.

"Nicholas!" cried Caralisa hysterically as she bounded out of the cabin.

"I can't believe it. Thank the Nexus! Thank the gods!" Her voice dropped as she tore in his direction, her eyes wild with disbelief

The mere sound of his beloved's voice was like a balm to Nicholas's weary heart and soul. He had longed for her soft touch so often during his time away, and now he wanted nothing but to hold her body against his and breathe in the fragrant scent of her hair.

"Caralisa!" he called back, but his greeting was immediately smothered by a sudden scream from the princess who had stopped dead in her tracks and stood frozen with a look of absolute terror across her face. Nicholas was momentarily baffled by her reaction, but promptly remembered the looming form of Augee right behind him.

"Nicholas! What is *that*?" she screamed, pointing her trembling finger at Augee.

Behind him, Nicholas could hear Augee emit a confused groan, the reaction of the princess having perplexed and unsettled him. Eager not to add to the frenzy around him, Nicholas turned to Augee with an assuring glance and an assuaging gesture of his arm.

"Relax, Augee," he soothed. "It's okay! It's Caralisa."

In return, Augee nodded his massive head once with a gentle, knowing growl, and he lowered himself to the ground into the most docile, unthreatening position he could manage.

"Nicholas!" yelped Caralisa again as she gaped in panic, confounded by the incredible sight of Augee and the indifference of Nicholas to the enormous beast behind him. "What is it?"

"It's okay, it's okay," he cried out again, attempting to regain some calm. "He won't hurt you. Please, can everybody calm down?"

By now, Lawson had leapt in front of the princess protectively, and both of them stood frozen and open-mouthed, barely able to comprehend the unbelievable scene before them.

"What is the meaning of this, Nicholas?" demanded Lawson fearfully, not daring to take his eyes off of Augee for even a second. "What manner of beast is this?"

"Woah, wait, everybody," pleaded Nicholas, raising his arms in a bid to calm the princess and the king's counselor. "Let's all calm down. He's with me."

"What is *he*, Nicholas?" spluttered Caralisa, almost unable to find the words, her eyes fixed on the immense creature as he luxuriated in the gentle warmth of the sun.

"*He* is Augee," Nicholas informed her, his pride in his announcement breaking through his otherwise preoccupied demeanor. "You have nothing to be afraid of. Augee's a friend to all of us. Please, can we go inside somewhere? We all need to talk."

Caralisa and Lawson stared at him skeptically.

"My cabin is just over here," the counselor proposed after a moment's reflection.

"Thank you, Lawson," Nicholas replied gratefully as he threw a nervous glance in the direction of Caralisa.

The princess continued to stare at Augee, transfixed. Noticing that her wariness showed little sign of abating, Nicholas gestured to her calmly to come closer.

"Trust me, Caralisa," he encouraged. "There's nothing to be afraid of."

At his reassurance, Caralisa stepped cautiously forward, her right arm outstretched in anticipation of touching the colossal monster. Suddenly, she started as Augee lifted himself off the ground and craned his great head in her direction. Tilting his neck welcomingly, Augee emitted a comforting groan that succeeded in alleviating some of the princess's worry. Nicholas watched in satisfaction, pleased that Augee had been mindful enough to be gentle with Caralisa at first. Given that he had shared his feelings for the princess with Augee on numerous occasions during their time in the jungle, he appreciated that Augee now seemed to be actively trying to make a positive first impression on her. Caralisa's shaking hand stroked the smooth, green scales of Augee's domed forehead, and after a few seconds, she giggled in nervous relief as he nuzzled against her benevolently. Nicholas smiled to himself as he watched Caralisa stare in wonder at Augee's brilliant, bright eyes.

A moment later, Caralisa's trance was broken as she once again became aware of Nicholas's presence. Wide-eyed and straight-faced, she ceased stroking Augee's head and turned to him.

"I thought you were dead," she announced with an emptiness in her voice that blindsided him. "I had given up hope of ever seeing you again. And now, after all this time, you're back—just like that."

"Caralisa," began Nicholas gently, sensing the princess's upset. "I didn't intend to worry you. So much has happened, and I'll explain it all, but please realize that my going away was the right decision. I'm convinced that the Nexus led me to Augee here. Wait until you see what he is capable of!"

Caralisa responded only with silence as she searched Nicholas's anxious face. Without speaking, she walked toward him, her eyes fixed on his. For several seconds, she stared at him intently, and without a further word, the princess threw her arms around Nicholas's neck and broke down entirely.

"Damn it, Nicholas!" she coughed through angry tears, her face wrought with emotion. "Where in the name of the gods were you all of this time? After my vision at the Eternal Stream, I didn't know what to do but to let you go. I never imagined you would be gone so long."

She took a step back and looked into his eyes with a hurt and anger that made his heart ache.

"You cannot disappear in and out of someone's life like this, Nicholas—you just can't!" she sobbed impassionedly.

"I'm sorry" Nicholas stammered. "I had to see through the mission that the Nexus chose me for. I was worried about you the whole time I was away, and I prayed every day for your safety and that I would soon…"

However, his flustered explanation was cut short as Caralisa threw her arms around him and kissed him, long and gratefully.

"Thank you, dear Nexus, thank you!" the princess whispered in earnest as she parted from him slightly, her tear-glistening eyes fixed hard on his.

Nicholas, for his part, was rendered speechless by the familiar taste of the princess's lips that he had longed for every night during his time in the wilderness, and beneath his bewildered exterior, his heart also soared with thanks for their miraculous reunion.

"I've missed you so much," Caralisa sobbed as she gripped the collar of his tunic tightly. "You've no idea how much I've prayed and cried for you. I thought I'd never see you again, Nicholas. I believed I'd lost you forever. Oh, thank you, dear Nexus!"

Nicholas returned her embrace by wrapping his arms around her shoulders and placing his forehead gently on hers, reluctant to even break eye contact with her, so grateful was he for another chance at a life with her.

"I never intended to distress you, Caralisa," he replied, his voice shaking from the intensity of the situation. "For that, I'm truly sorry. I did what I thought and felt was right, but I never wanted to cause you pain."

Caralisa said nothing in response, and instead, she pulled Nicholas closer to her and pressed her lips to his once more, savoring the masculine scent of his skin that she'd missed so very much. For a short spell, they remained locked together, lost in the moment and each other. However, when they parted, Nicholas was confused to see that the princess's expression was harrowed and her tears had begun to fall profusely.

"What is it?" stuttered Nicholas, disarmed entirely by the look of tortured grief that now shone in her eyes. "Is something wrong, Caralisa?"

The princess's gaze dropped to the ground, and she placed her hand across her face in anguish.

"They took Father, Nicholas," she wept, gripping him tightly with her free hand. "They came for him, and he just surrendered."

"What!" choked Nicholas, horrified. "Who took King Benjamin?"

"The Volcarons," spat Caralisa through an angry sob, as if to even utter the name of their foreign tormentors caused her intense pain. "They took him away. And they killed others. They murdered them…so horribly!"

"Is this all true?" Nicholas shot at Lawson heatedly.

The counselor nodded morosely.

"King Benjamin wanted to make peace with the Volcarons after learning that they had discovered our whereabouts," replied Lawson as he wiped his own welling eyes. "But they had no desire to do so. Now, we have been forced to evacuate the village before the Volcarons come this way."

Nicholas's mind whirled despairingly as the king's dire circumstances registered with him, and his mind returned to the heart-breaking sight of the Hohalians traversing the dangerous mountain ridge as they fled their homes for a second time. He could not fathom why King Benjamin would have been so foolish and reckless, and, as evidenced by the distraught state of the monarch's daughter and faithful counselor, it seemed clear that there was much that he urgently needed to hear from them.

"Let's get inside somewhere we can talk," he suggested despondently.

"This way," agreed Lawson grimly as he pointed to his cabin.

At that, Nicholas, Caralisa, and Lawson made their way into the gloomy light of the cabin. Augee, absolutely perplexed by the situation, but too large to enter with them, settled himself down on the ground nearby to keep protective watch over Nicholas and his new Hohalian acquaintances.

37

A SHORT TIME later, solemn deliberations were underway on the rickety wooden terrace attached to the back of Lawson's cabin. The counselor's plot of land was modest and rugged, a quarter-acre of rock-strewn land incapable of supporting vegetation other than a few scraggly-looking potatoes and bland mushrooms. The back portion of his humble property was obscured from onlookers by a roughly constructed wooden fence with a double gate that provided access to a narrow side street.

At Nicholas's request, Lawson had not objected to moving their deliberations outdoors so that Augee himself could be present. Now, having managed to stuff himself through the creaking gateway of Lawson's fence, Augee lay curled up in the grass at the edge of the terrace so that his enormous head was at the same level as the others who sat around a roughshod wooden table.

Seated next to Nicholas, Caralisa, and Lawson was an ashen-faced Hamar who brooded in cold silence, his expression as haggard as the mountainside on which the Hohalians had subsisted for five years. Following her and Nicholas's emotional reunion, Caralisa had immediately sent the young son of a neighboring family to Haven to fetch Hamar. When he'd arrived at Lawson's cabin, Hamar had been speechless to see Nicholas standing by the fireplace, and after a brief explanation from Nicholas about his whereabouts for the past number of weeks, the four sat down around the small table on Lawson's porch to listen to Hamar recall the terrible night. Nicholas seethed as Hamar conveyed the details of Suma's abrupt warning about the approach of the Volcarons, the folly of King Benjamin's actions and, most distressingly, how the king and a sizeable number of volunteers had been taken captive by the invaders as they left a slaughter-filled field in their wake. To Nicholas's horror, Hamar then pulled down the neck of his tunic to reveal a long, infected-looking wound that ran from his collarbone down his chest.

"They obviously thought I was dead," lamented Hamar as he wiped a tear from the corner of his eye. "'Mercy' doesn't seem to be a word they're familiar with."

"Ten men?" Nicholas mouthed with a quiet fury. "Those bastards murdered ten, honorable men? Ten young, innocent men?"

Hamar nodded sadly and listed off the name of each of the fallen Hohalians, the number taken captive too numerous to acknowledge individually. By the time he had uttered the last of the Hohalian casualties, Nicholas was moved to tears.

"And King Benjamin, gone without a trace?" Nicholas pressed in disbelief.

"They left nothing of him but his robe," Hamar sighed as he shook his head at the pain of remembering it all.

"And all those innocent lives," Nicholas raged as he slammed his fist down on the table, causing all around him to flinch. "Murdered without a thought! Every one of those wretched Volcaron parasites deserve to be…"

Lawson, who had listened quietly as Hamar recollected the circumstances of that awful night, had grown increasingly unsettled by the rising aggression around the table, and he made a guileful attempt to redirect the conversation to the extraordinary sight of Augee, who was curled in a massive heap in the scraggy grass next to them.

"He really is a fascinating creature, isn't he?" exclaimed Lawson prompting the attentions of all present to turn to Augee. "Can he be trusted? Rather, what I mean is, is he a danger to people who *he* doesn't trust?"

"Trust?" replied Nicholas, taken aback by the counselor's abrupt changing of the subject and still smarting from Hamar's dreadful revelations. "Come on, Lawson. Do you really think that the Nexus would have sent me to find Augee if he wasn't pure of heart? Come here, and I'll introduce you properly."

Caralisa and Hamar watched captivated as Nicholas took Lawson's aged hand in his and directed him across the terrace to where Augee lay on the scrubby grass. Sensing Lawson's reluctance, Nicholas slowly guided the counselor into a sitting position on the ground.

"Augee, this is Lawson," he explained as he wiped away a lingering tear from his eye. "Lawson is a friend and a very wise man."

Augee, who had been busy observing his new surroundings, turned his huge head and fastened his pale, green gaze on Lawson's eyes. The counselor, still considerably wary of Augee's enormity, began to shuffle backward. However, upon observing Augee's intelligent eyes and benevolent expression, he extended his trembling hand and placed it gently on Augee's head.

"Hello, Augee," he began with a quiver in his voice.

Augee twisted his head slightly in response and followed it up with a low, genial purr that hinted at his warmhearted nature. Immediately, Lawson turned to Nicholas with astonishment.

"I could hear him greeting me—in my mind!" he exclaimed. "No, wait. I could *feel* him, similar to how we used to communicate with the animals back in Hohala through the Nexus. Only…"

"Only *more*," interrupted Nicholas in excited agreement.

"Yes!" replied Lawson in wonder.

"It's amazing, really," continued Nicholas. "Since the first day I encountered Augee, we've had this intuitive connection. I can read his thoughts and emotions, and likewise, he communicates with me almost by instinct."

Lawson, Hamar, and Caralisa listened speechlessly as Nicholas recounted the details of his expedition to the canyon, the terrifying ferocity of Augee's mother and sibling, and how he managed to narrowly rescue the infant creature. They were awe-struck by Nicholas's verification that the forbidden land of the old Hohalian myths and folk tales actually existed, as well as the solemn disclosure that Nicholas had discovered the remains of unfortunate travelers—presumably Hohalians of past generations—who had never returned from their venture into the western mountains.

"Incredible," whispered Lawson, astounded, "But I do have to ask—is he really…"

Lawson had begun to pose his question to Nicholas, but he paused thoughtfully for a moment before turning instead to address Augee directly.

"Augee, may I ask, are you really willing to help us to regain our home from the Volcarons?" he inquired. "I mean, are you sure you know how?"

Augee dipped his head once in solemn acknowledgement, to which Nicholas added, "Augee's truly a miracle. I've seen his capabilities. His power is awesome, and a bit terrifying at first, and, really, it can only be comprehended by seeing it. He and I can take on the Volcarons without need for the Hohalians to risk their lives—or the purity of their souls—by acting in violence."

He looked intently at every face at the table.

"The Nexus has led me to believe that defending Hohala is my duty and mission," he revealed. "However, it's important to stress that Augee has decided to help us of his own volition. To fight against the Volcarons is not his responsibility, but his choice, and for that alone we must be grateful."

Lawson nodded appreciatively. By this time, the counselor appeared to be at ease in Augee's presence, but Caralisa, who had been sitting silently until now, interjected warily.

"Can you control him though, Nicholas," she inquired. "If he's as powerful as you say, it won't do any good to drive the Volcarons out of Hohala if there's nothing left of the village afterward. To desecrate our sacred home any further than the Volcarons already have would be an affront to the Nexus, even worse than violence against the invaders."

Nicholas shook his head and placed his hand on hers.

"I don't control Augee," he replied softly. "We're friends and equals. He is almost always the way he is now: kind, gentle, happy, and willing to help. That is, unless he feels the threat of danger; then he transforms from the gentle, friendly fellow you see before you, to a creature whose power and strength are not of this world. He can streak through the sky faster and with more precision than an arrow from the most skilled archer's bow, and he has the ability to breathe fire in any volume or intensity. His power and potential are stunning, and we have prepared long and hard to hone his abilities."

Caralisa paused for a moment before she presented the question that hung on her lips.

She asked him directly, "Nicholas, do you really think that you and Augee can defeat the Volcarons? And rescue my father and the others?"

Nicholas stared into the princess's tear-shimmering eyes.

"I believe that we can, Caralisa," he insisted with a tired sigh and a forced smile. "We *have* to believe we can. I'm convinced that the Nexus guided me to Augee—so that we can defeat the Volcarons without the people of Hohala having to commit violence."

"But you and Augee will be committing violence by doing so," Caralisa contested. "Even if you don't kill anyone directly, they could be crushed by falling debris, or burned by Augee's fire, or harmed as they're running away—and that's assuming they do flee at the sight of Augee. What if they decide to stay and fight?"

"We never expected the Volcarons to give up our beautiful land easily," Nicholas replied, his tone laced with a grim resolve. "But regardless of their response, Augee and I can take them."

Hamar, who had been listening quietly, cleared his throat before interjecting in an assertive tone.

"I and the remaining fighters of Haven will come with you to Hohala," he declared with a nod to Nicholas. "If there's a need to fight, we are willing to do so. I pray that there will be no cause for bloodshed, but rest assured, we are ready to do what we must to ensure the survival of our people. Too long we have remained idle in the face of the aggressors. We are ready to support you, Nicholas, by whatever means is necessary."

Nicholas placed his hand on Hamar's shoulder.

"Thank you, Hamar," he replied. "Augee and I would be very proud to have you and any willing Hohalians stand with us in support."

Nicholas then looked to all present at the table.

"Undoubtedly, time is of the essence and we must act fast; however, our uprising will require careful coordination. We must strike the Volcarons unexpectedly and effectively. If they were to notice us coming, then I fear what they might do to King Benjamin and the Hohalians they took captive."

Caralisa squeezed his hand under the table, tears dripping from her delicate eyelashes.

"I promise you, Caralisa," Nicholas continued, "I'll take no risks that might endanger your father or the Hohalian prisoners. Their safe return is my priority, and I swear I'll do everything I can to bring King Benjamin and the others back unharmed."

"I know," replied Caralisa with an angry sob. "I'm furious with him for surrendering himself to those bastards. He allowed them to take him in order to appease the Nexus, with whom he hasn't connected with properly for five years. He's as stubborn as an old boar, and he's so…"

She paused before coughing out the words, "…so *selfish!*"

Taken aback by the princess's outburst, Nicholas slowly raised himself off his seat and knelt in front of her, his hands clasped with hers.

"You can't be angry with him for his faith, Caralisa. You know that," he reassured her gently. "You know that he has only the best interests of the Hohalians—and of you—at heart. We all know that he has only ever acted out of noble intentions. And I admit that I myself have often been one of the last to recognize that."

As Caralisa surveyed his eyes in thoughtful silence, Nicholas stood up and turned to Lawson, Hamar, and Augee, his expression solemn and determined.

"I propose we strike the Volcarons tomorrow at dawn," he announced determinedly.

Lawson and Hamar listened quietly as the imminence of the planned assault began to register with them.

"We will use the rest of today to assemble and brief those willing to join us in our mission. It must be made clear to all who are willing that they will be risking much by taking part. No Hohalian should be pressured into taking up arms. Tomorrow morning, we will reclaim our future from those who desire to plunder it. Pray to the Nexus that we find the courage and wisdom to do what is necessary. No more inaction. The Volcarons *will* answer for their crimes."

Caralisa, Lawson, and Hamar all nodded in unison, and Augee growled in agreement.

After five years, it was finally time.

38

AT THE HIGHEST point in the hinterland of Haven, the cragged highlands blended into a flat and windswept mountain ridge. Ravaged by a prevailing northern wind, living vegetation was scant, save for the bracken that crunched noisily underfoot. The view to the east took in a wide expanse of the plains of Hohala, the bay, and the old Hohalian village, now dubbed New Volcaron by its foreign occupants. Five years previously, when Nicholas and a small band of similarly disgruntled men of Hohala had distanced themselves from the rest of their society, they had chosen the site for their own settlement based on proximity to this advantageous viewing position. The high-rising ridge, Nicholas had discovered, offered an unparalleled observation point, that allowed easy sight of any oncoming attackers. If a large enemy assault was coming, then the lofty vantage position ensured that the approaching aggressors could be spotted early enough to give ample warning to the people in nearby New Hohala.

At the time that Nicholas, Hamar and the others had declared they were separating from the rest of their people, the consensus among the New Hohalians had been that they were selfishly abandoning their responsibilities to the Nexus and their community. In reality, under the influence of Nicholas, the slope on which the settlement of Haven now stood had been chosen so that the men could keep a protective watch over the village of New Hohala and guard against potential Volcaron assailment from the east. Indeed, even as embittered defectors, the men of Haven had nobly assumed the responsibility of sentinels for as long as the Hohalians were in exile.

Now, half a decade later, Nicholas and the men of Haven stood atop the lofty ridge, ready to address the two hundred-strong band of Hohalians who had volunteered to join the uprising against the Volcarons. They had travelled to the meeting point at short notice and in great numbers following the news of a planned preemptive strike on the Volcarons. The widespread enthusiasm for action among the Hohalians had surprised Caralisa and Lawson, and despite the unfolding events, it was with a measure of pride that they now stood before the band of men and women who were ready to defend the Hohalian nation.

Nicholas had taken up position on a small mound of boulders that elevated him above the assembled congregation. To his left, he was flanked by Hamar and Lawson, and standing closely on his other side was the princess, her fingers discreetly linked in his right hand which rested behind his back. Augee, the unquestionable center of attention among the gathered crowd, stood upright next to the mound of boulders, his demeanor calm and benign.

The crowd was full of anticipation, and it fell into a hush as Nicholas raised his hand to gain their attention. For a moment, he stood in silence as he collected his thoughts, the striking natural beauty of the eastern landscape, with the lights of captured Hohala as its distant centerpiece, providing a solemn backdrop to his address. With a deep breath, he spoke, solemn and unwavering.

"Men and women of Hohala," he saluted. "Thank you for joining us at urgent notice. Your commitment is much appreciated, and our chances of success are strengthened greatly by your support. It is heartening to observe that, even after five years of hardship and exile, the Hohalian spirit is still kindled in the hearts of so many of our people. All else aside, that spirit alone should offer us hope that we will prevail against our enemy."

Sporadic shouts of agreement went up from among the crowd, giving Nicholas a slight boost in confidence in his own message.

"Over the past five years," he continued, "We have all lost much; our dreams and ambitions for the future were stolen from us while our families and our community have been torn apart by resentments and quarrels fostered by the invaders. For far too long now, the Hohalians have suffered from division—our differing beliefs and opinions on how we should respond to provocation by the Volcarons has weakened us, causing the future of our society to look bleak and uncertain."

Nicholas paused as he surveyed the earnest sea of faces before him, mixed expressions of determination and hurt etched across their faces.

"It must be acknowledged that much of the division among our nation has been caused by some of our people's abandonment of the basic tenets of our faith in order to survive—I include myself in that number. Indeed, we in Haven who made the decision to leave the security of the commune, have at times had little choice but to hunt animals for food, and, as a result, shed blood."

The men from Haven among the crowd nodded in agreement, while a handful of the less-informed Hohalians exchanged incredulous glances.

"Many here today have never spilled blood before," Nicholas went on, reading the eyes of the captivated men and women before him as they met his gaze with various degrees of nervousness and determination. "And, not one of you has spilled the blood of a human being."

He didn't include himself in this statement; although he hadn't seriously harmed a human, he had shed Morgoratt's blood on the day Nightshade was killed. Deep down, however, he preferred not to reveal to the Hohalians how far he'd actually fallen from their ways.

"I've always been different from everyone else in Hohala," he resumed soberly. "I never had the inner sense of peace that so many of you have experienced. I always wanted to know what was beyond Hohala's borders."

Nicholas's mouth twisted into a pensive frown.

"It may come as a surprise to some of you, but beyond the land inhabited by the Hohalians, there exists danger and darkness that we are blessed to have been protected from. I don't just refer to the Volcarons, but to places and creatures that you could only imagine in your nightmares."

By this point, the crowd listened in attentive silence, captivated by Nicholas's ominous tone and haunting revelations. However, sensing the ripple of unease among his audience, he stepped down onto a lower-positioned boulder and placed his hand onto the warm skin at the nape of Augee's neck. The eyes of the crowd, which had been collectively examining the peculiar, intimidating-looking monster since their arrival, now gazed in Augee's direction.

"But there are miracles out there, as well," Nicholas declared with a smile. "This is Augee, and he is, without question, a miracle—one which I was guided to by the Nexus. Augee is far wiser than I am."

Augee, sensing the attention on him, nodded his head and emitted an affirming upward groan. Some in the audience chuckled nervously, relieving some of the tension.

"But, as our circumstances have revealed, and which I admit to you all in earnest, Augee and I have one thing in common," Nicholas went on, "We have both been touched by darkness and violence in the past, and because of that, I believe the Nexus has chosen *us* to carry out this mission on behalf of the Hohalians. We alone will fight the Volcarons and take the chance of causing harm and even death. If we take on that responsibility, then the rest of you can continue with unstained souls."

At that, there was a general stir among the crowd, and one of the men of Haven who stood near the front called out, "We're willing to fight!" which was met with general agreement from the congregation.

Caralisa, who had been silent until now, stepped up next to Nicholas.

"We know you are," she assured the man appreciatively. "I speak on behalf of all Hohalians when I say that we are truly grateful for your willingness to risk your spiritual purity to protect our people. My father is adamant that the Hohalians should not engage in violence, especially if we have another choice, but I am reassured to know that there are many among us that will join the fight if the situation calls for it."

Nicholas, standing by the princess's side, touched her back reassuringly before readdressing the crowd.

"Those of you who wish to join us, we will meet at this spot four hours before daybreak. Hamar will then lead you through the jungle to the old village of Hohala. You must be sure to follow his instructions exactly. The Volcarons cannot be aware of our presence before we have an opportunity to strike. Hamar knows the route through the countryside as well as any man. All must trust his judgement completely. If he instructs you to retreat, do so; if he tells you to advance, do not hesitate."

Hamar nodded in agreement as those gathered murmured among each other.

"Augee and I will drive the Volcarons from Hohala," continued Nicholas with determination. "The role of all of you will clear the village after we have done our part. You must make sure all of the Volcarons are gone and any that remain are taken captive. Augee and I will…um…*encourage* them to take to their boats and go back where they came from."

A buoyant chortle went up from the crowd, and it was clear to Nicholas and the others that there was a burgeoning sense of optimism among the assembled Hohalians.

"Once the Volcarons become aware of what Augee is capable of, hopefully they will have the sense to leave for good," resumed Nicholas.

He raised his hands once more to gain the attention of those gathered. He spoke slowly and seriously, hoping that the gravity and severe danger of the situation had not been missed by the enthusiastic men and women. He paused before adding in a solemn tone:

"One final time, I want to impress upon you the perilousness of this mission. There is no expectation of any of you; no duty or duress. Those who are not completely certain of their participation, feel no shame or embarrassment. *Should* you indeed choose to join us tonight, know that you face an enemy that is as merciless as they are uncompromising. If they are able, they will torture you, humiliate you, and break your spirit until you beg for death. Then, if you are unlucky enough to be denied a swift execution, they will enslave you until your body can take no more. My brothers and sisters, this is an enemy without morality or remorse. Do not underestimate the risk that you are entering into."

"We are with you, Nicholas Stone!" cried out a voice from the crowd.

"To the end, we submit our service," shouted another.

"Long live sacred Hohala!" called another.

"Praise the Nexus!" roared a voice from the back.

Nicholas, Caralisa, Lawson, and Hamar stood in quiet surprise as the clamor of excitement grew, and, for the first time in five barren years, there was a discernable passion and renewed patriotism among the Hohalians.

"Thank you, all of you," responded Nicholas emotionally. "Together— with the kind assistance of Augee here—we can achieve the freedom that we have been deprived of for far too long. I see before me a proud band of Hohalians, who despite these unjust circumstances, have not given up their hope for a better future, and who, by their presence here today, have demonstrated their defiance in the face of the forces that conspire against us. At dawn, we reclaim our destiny. Tomorrow night, the sun will set on the age of Volcaron, and the light of Hohala will emerge once more. Praise to the Nexus!"

At this, a resounding cheer went up from the crowd. Nicholas turned to Caralisa with a prideful smile and the princess's eyes shone with sanguine hope.

39

BY SILVER MOONLIGHT, Nicholas studied the expressions of the men and women who had gathered before him. They numbered just shy of two hundred, most of them Hohalians who did not have young families to support. They assembled along the mountain ridge high above Haven, arriving in steady, silent groups until the whole area was filled with shivering volunteers. A harsh night breeze swirled about their heads, making their teeth chatter and accentuating the collective anxiety of the moment. The final organization of the volunteers was carried out quietly and methodically, led by a stern-faced Hamar and assisted by Caralisa and Lawson. The presence of both the king's daughter and his counselor had seemed to Nicholas to have a calming effect on the volunteers. There had been whisperings among some Hohalians that the planned mission amounted to treason against King Benjamin's decree, but the sight of his daughter leading the mission herself appeared to have encouraged the assembled group.

Hamar set about arranging the crowd into bands of varying sizes, instructing them of their respective duties once Nicholas and Augee had completed their task of driving the Volcarons from Hohala. The volunteers were to surround the village in large numbers, taking up discreet positions in the jungle just beyond the frontiers of the village. They were not to enter the settlement until Hamar signaled to do so, and as Nicholas had reiterated to them, restraint against allowing their actions to be dictated by their emotions was critical to the success of the mission. Such was the callousness of the enemy, he'd explained, the situation called for cool heads and total composure at all times.

Off to the side, Nicholas stood in fretful silence, his mind inattentive to Hamar's final words of encouragement to the volunteers. He was confident in Augee's abilities, and he could sense that Augee himself was calm and primed to finally put into action the skills that they had trained so painstakingly to perfection. At his side, the imposing and majestic Augee towered above the heads of those gathered, his wings folded in restful anticipation. Nicholas took a sideways glance at his unusual friend and considered for a moment just how far they had come since the fateful day on which he had rescued the defenseless, infant creature from the depths of the smoke-filled canyon. Sensing Nicholas's eyes on him, Augee returned a knowing look that told Nicholas he was ready.

There were no grand declamations or ceremonious parting words before Nicholas gestured to Augee that it was time for them to embark on their journey. With a roar that caused the crowd to grow still and the soil beneath their feet to quiver, Augee extended his great wingspan. In the moonlit gloom, his eyes began to narrow and glow red; black scales rippled across his soft, green skin, overlapping like plates of armor. His benign countenance became etched with a look of furious determination, and a scent of burning filled the night air as Augee exhaled plumes of ghostly, white smoke.

There were gasps among the crowd as some began to retreat in alarm, but shouts for calm from Lawson and the princess were enough to quickly dispel the volunteers' unease at the sight of Augee's unexpected transformation. With the enthralled eyes of the crowd fixed on them, Augee lowered his body to allow Nicholas to clamber up onto his back. Once he had taken up his familiar position between two notches on Augee's spine, Nicholas turned to the watching crowd.

"Hohalians!" he exclaimed, trying his best to mask the apprehension which threatened to catch in his voice. "The fateful hour is upon us. Each of you know your role. Follow Augee and me to Hohala, and support us from a safe distance. You will be there if we need you, but under no circumstances is any man or woman to engage the enemy without explicit command from Hamar. Let him lead you completely, no matter what may happen. After Augee and I have done our part, you all will sweep through the village and retake our home. You will free the king and any Hohalians that the Volcarons have taken captive."

The crowd murmured in agreement as Augee snapped his wings open and closed, preparing to take flight.

Nicholas concluded determinedly, "Our refusal to submit is our greatest weapon against the invader. Today, Hohala stands up for its right to freedom!"

The volunteers responded with a collective cheer and raised their fists to the air fervidly.

At that, Nicholas stroked Augee lightly along his spine. At his touch, Augee flapped his wings once, and they were thrust high into the air, sending a sharp gust of cold wind sweeping over the heads of the volunteers.

Within seconds, they had disappeared from the sight of the volunteers, consumed by the deep nothingness of the night sky.

"Men and women of Hohala," cried Hamar commandingly. "We move out!"

At his instruction, the two hundred-strong band of volunteers promptly gathered their improvised weapons and began to follow Hamar as he led the way down the slope to begin the long-awaited trek home.

*

Nicholas's body trembled in the freezing wind as he and Augee climbed higher into the night sky. They flew in anxious silence, taking a more circuitous route to Hohala over the sea to the east in the hope that it would prevent detection by the Volcarons on the ground. From high up in the cloudless sky, Nicholas surveyed the terrain below, searching the horizon for the lights that would signify the Volcaron-occupied village. The beauty of the landscape, even subdued as it was by the darkness, was a breathtaking sight, and the thought of being free to reclaim the idyllic countryside for its rightful occupants made Nicholas even more determined for the task ahead.

By the time the flickering specks of lamplight from the ancient village eventually came into view, the approaching sunrise had fused the dark sky with a translucent, pink glow that stretched as far as Nicholas's gaze would afford him. By this point, Hamar, Caralisa, and the Hohalian volunteers were to be assembled at their hiding points by the edge of the village, and there could be no turning back.

Nicholas and Augee drifted over the village, empty and silent in the dawn light. From his vantage point high above, Nicholas was infuriated by the sight that met his eyes. Below him, he saw the ravaged semblance of the homes that the Hohalians had left behind. He'd been to the village on numerous occasions to deal with Suma under the cover of night, but never on the ground had he been unfortunate enough to discover the vast destruction of the once pristinely beautiful village. The lovingly tended allotments and meticulously landscaped gardens were gone, carelessly ripped out or trampled into the dirt. Junk and debris littered the streetscape, and the network of babbling waterways that had once flowed through the village were now stagnant, green, and foul-looking. The walls of the whitewashed cottages were now browned and grimy, their thatched roofs rotted and disheveled from neglect. From what Nicholas could make out through the gloom, the streets were virtually empty as the Volcarons slept, unaware of the army of Hohalian encroachers in their midst.

Having passed over the village, they rounded the bay of Hohala along the cliff-fringed coastline to the south, and Nicholas noticed a lightless, sprawling structure that had been newly constructed on the rocky cliff edge. From the description that Suma had relayed to Hamar, he could tell that this was Morgoratt's plantation, the complex that was built to imprison his Hohalian slaves. It was a dreary and imposing edifice, comprised of an assortment of large, windowless cabins fenced in high on all four sides. As they advanced closer, Nicholas was hit with a dull pang of dread as his eyes met the sight of a figure in typical Hohalian dress lying face-down on the ground along the inside of the perimeter fence. It looked to be a young man, and it was with a surge of anger that Nicholas noticed the dark blotches of blood that stained the white tunic covering the boy's back. The unfortunate youngster's hand clutched what appeared to be a length of rope, and Nicholas deduced bitterly that he'd been slain while attempting to escape.

"Augee!" he cried out vehemently, the raw emotion ringing in his tone. "Let's do what we came to do!"

In response, Augee's eyes blazed, and Nicholas could feel his companion's body vibrating as energy coursed through him; opening his fang-lined jaws as wide as he could, Augee emitted a roar of such ferocity that it echoed throughout the landscape. Within moments, Nicholas noticed a sudden, sporadic flickering of lights below in the village. Across the settlement, windows gradually began to glow all around as the inhabitants rose to inspect the source of the booming noise that had woken them from their slumber. Before Nicholas and Augee's eyes, cottage doors were swung open, and the streets began to fill with bewildered Volcarons searching and pointing at the sky. As if not to disappoint them, Augee gave a second resounding roar and blew out a billowing gust of orange flame. Petrified shouts and screams filled the air as the Volcarons observed Augee's terrifying form hovering in the sky above them.

"Dragon! It's a dragon!" hollered a man below, triggering a commotion among the other onlookers, and from there, the streets began to fill with panic as Volcaron men and women fled for cover.

Instructed by Nicholas, Augee twisted in the air, beat his huge wings twice and folded them against his body. Together, they plummeted toward the village, Augee blowing swirling clouds of crackling flame that skimmed the tops of trees as they rushed overhead. Closing in on a disused-looking farm shed close to the perimeter of the village, Augee projected a bolt of lightning from his mouth. With a resounding crash, the ramshackle outhouse exploded in spectacular fashion, sending wood and stone spraying across the village as a profusion of foul, angry smoke erupted into the air. A racket of shattering glass filled the area as debris from the blast peppered houses and shopfronts in every direction.

Pandemonium broke out in the streets below as the terrified Volcarons stumbled in and out of their houses in confusion. With their minds working as one, Nicholas guided Augee to hover above the village. Augee swooped low and fast before eventually hanging in the air just a short distance above the grounds of King Benjamin's former mansion.

As he attempted to balance himself by gripping the notched spines on Augee's back, Nicholas could feel the mysterious energy continue to pulsate through his friend's body. The unearthly sensation invigorated him, and he too felt imbued with a rare and unfamiliar power.

Filled with ebullient energy, Nicholas opened his mouth to address the fleeing Volcarons; yet, as he spoke, he was taken aback to find that his voice had suddenly become amplified, and his words boomed tempestuously across the entire village.

"Men and women of Volcaron!" he called out thunderously, concentrating with all his might to mask his own shock at his unexpectedly magnified voice. "Five years ago, you trespassed upon a land in which your brutality was not welcome. Since then, you have desecrated, ravaged, and violated a once beautiful and hallowed place. Although you don't deserve it, I am offering you a single opportunity to leave Hohala immediately and return to the land that you came from. I am warning you fairly, and should you fail to heed these words, you will burn alive at my instruction."

At that moment, Augee sounded another ear-shattering roar which was followed by a tongue of serpentine flame that whipped through the dark morning sky and sent white-hot sparks raining down on the panic-stricken Volcarons.

The reaction was instantaneous; terrified groups of Volcarons clambered wildly across each other to escape the confines of the village. Nicholas watched on with a feeling of strange bemusement as, within minutes, the beach was thronged with desperate men, women, and children attempting to reach the sailing boats moored by the water's edge. Some of the boats began to capsize in the water as a crowd of Volcarons frantically hoisted themselves into vessels that quickly reached overcapacity, while others hit the water at a dead run and started swimming for their lives.

Nicholas observed the mayhem for a few satisfying moments, but a sudden commotion in one of the streets below him distracted him. A party of Volcaron men had begun scurrying to an allotment that was partially obscured by the gables of two houses, armed with an assortment of arrows and spears. Determined not to give them the opportunity to launch an attack, Nicholas guided Augee in that direction. Immediately, Augee let out a glowing streak of hissing electricity that struck one of the gables with a violent smack and sent dark plumes of smoke into the air. As the smoke began to clear, Nicholas could see that the structure had been obliterated, a pile of charred and smoldering rubble the only remnant. The small gang of Volcaron men that had been positioned in the allotment began tearing hysterically in the direction of the beach, and they swung their arms wildly above their heads as small leaves of flame danced painfully across their loose-fitting robes. They appeared traumatized and mildly burned, but Nicholas cared little. The pain and fear that he and Augee had just inflicted were insignificant in comparison to the drawn-out suffering endured by the Hohalians over five long years as they scraped together a living burdened by fear and depression. As he inwardly reveled in the chaos that he and Augee had wrought, Nicholas's thoughts then turned to the true architect of Hohala's suffering.

"The king's mansion, Augee," he instructed darkly.

40

WITH A FIERY belch of his nostrils, Augee clenched his wings, and they swooped in the direction of the ornate mansion that was the focal point of the village. In the past, its many windows glowed with cheerful lamplight day and night, but now, Nicholas observed a gloomy and forbidding enemy stronghold. The elaborate, marble exterior, tinged by the hue of the breaking dawn, was badly discolored and cracked across the entire structure. From the air, Nicholas was appalled by the sight of the once abundant gardens that had since been vandalized and allowed to fall into neglect. The landscaped stream that in King Benjamin's time had babbled cheerily from one end of the grounds to the other was now still and brown with weeds and vines that smothered the surface of the water. The formerly majestic fountains and white stone busts that lined the interior wall of the grounds were chipped and cracked, with broken rubble strewn across the courtyard. All around, evidence of the abuse and the pollution of the ancient manor by the Volcarons was painfully visible. As he observed the extent of the invaders' destruction of the royal seat of the Hohalian nation, Nicholas's heart grew cold and bitter and, suddenly, an unfamiliar voice from some remote recess of his mind hissed at him to ferret out the one who had orchestrated such ruination.

Below them, Nicholas and Augee spotted a band of five or six Volcaron men darting in the direction of the main entrance to the mansion from behind the tall hedging that encircled the grounds. As they scurried across the courtyard toward the grand, oak doors, they glanced nervously at the sky in the hope of not being detected by the enormous beast. To their alarm, this was not to be the case, as Augee bellowed at them from above. As they neared the mansion's entrance, the men screamed pleadingly for the doors to be opened. Nicholas, disinclined to grant such ruthless adversaries too much respite, gestured knowingly to Augee in their direction. In response, Augee widened his jaws once more and emitted a rasping noise as he inhaled deeply. Within seconds, a reptilian shriek echoed through the grounds as a spherical burst of flame was expelled from Augee's mouth and was sent hurtling toward the ground. A deafening crash set Nicholas's ears ringing as a cloud of dust and smoke erupted from below, and the sounds of shattering glass and panicked screams filled the air. It was several moments before the dust dispersed, but eventually Nicholas could make out the blackened, demolished remnants of a large statue that, until now, had depicted a figure from Hohalian theology. Among the clouds of smoke and ash, the Volcarons below were attempting to stagger dazedly to their feet in a frantic bid to reach the sanctuary of the mansion. Purposely, Nicholas instructed Augee to hold back and allow the startled Volcarons to make their way inside. As the men proceeded to pound on the mansion door, yelling out fear-stricken pleas to be admitted, the immense double doors swung open. The men shoved and shouldered each other to get through the entrance just as the doors slammed shut seconds later.

Events were unfolding as Nicholas had anticipated. By now, the majority of Volcarons had fled to the sea and, at this point, the few who remained were holed up inside of the king's mansion. Among them, he was sure Morgoratt would be found. Nicholas called out once more, and as before, his voice became amplified, and his words boomed across the mansion grounds.

"Foolish Volcarons!" he bellowed. "You were given the chance to leave this place, yet you chose not to heed my warning. Even though I'm tempted to burn every one of you scoundrels for your sins; that is not the way of the Hohalians. I realize that mercy is a concept beyond the comprehension of your wretched people; however, I am granting you one final opportunity to disappear from Hohala with the understanding that, if you ever return, then you will not leave this land alive."

From the air, Nicholas and Augee's eyes were fixed on the entrance doors of the mansion as they waited in anticipation. Several minutes passed by without any indication that the Volcarons were intent on surrendering.

"It appears that you want to continue down a very foolish path," resumed Nicholas, his amplified voice reverberating against the walls of the mansion. "For the last time, I urge you to reconsider where your loyalties lie. The man who brought you here and promised you so much is a fraud. He has no grand design for your people, no desire to create a sustainable nation. He intends to continue to leech from the land and to enslave those who refuse to react in violence because of their principles. That, Volcarons, is no man; that is a pathetic, coward!"

Once more, Nicholas's words were met with silence as the mansion door remained firmly shut.

"Morgoratt!" he roared, his voice vexed and frustrated. "Have you no spine? Is this an example of the might with which you intended to enslave my people? I warn you now, vacate the king's mansion; a place of royalty and nobility is no rat hole for cowering vermin like you."

Several more minutes went by, and Nicholas concluded that the Volcarons had little intention of heeding his demands. He ground his teeth irritably as he resigned himself to the fact that the Volcarons were an enemy who were as belligerent as they were callous.

"Very well, Augee," he sighed. "Let's run them out of there."

Immediately, Augee glided downward and came to rest on the ground alongside the front wall of the mansion. As he sought his bearings, Augee's eyes flitted searchingly across the wall. Close to the entrance, about twenty meters off the ground, a sizeable window had been shattered by the force of Augee's earlier blast. With a deft bound, Augee used his claws to grip the groove in the wall and crane his neck through the open window. Two Volcaron men who had been crouched by the window as look-outs turned and fled down the narrow corridor at the awful sight of Augee's glowering head at the window frame, his eyes wide and scarlet and his nostrils smoking with every exhalation.

"Run all you want, Volcarons," Nicholas called after them warningly. "Tell that gutless Morgoratt to be a man and come out and face me."

Nicholas turned to Augee and nodded to him solemnly. In response, Augee extended his neck as far as he could through the window before proceeding to inhale deeply and at length. After a few moments, Nicholas could feel Augee's chest begin to deflate slowly beneath him as he breathed out steadily through his nostrils. A thick cloud of grey smoke began to rise through the corridor as Augee exhaled slowly. The interior features became obscured to the on-looking Nicholas as the thick plume from Augee's nostrils swelled and quickly enveloped the corridor. For several minutes, Augee's head rested on the window ledge as he continued to fill the passageway with a smog that caused Nicholas's eyes to water. As he tightly clutched the notches on Augee's back, he could see that the cloud had begun to seep out from windows and openings of the mansion, and it was clear that the smoke had breached all or most of its interior. It was a fascinating spectacle to witness as Augee perched by the open window ledge and his powerful lungs filled the mansion with choking waves of smoke. There, Augee remained patiently exhaling for what seemed an age.

It was of little surprise to Nicholas to hear the wooden doors below them crash open, followed immediately by the panicked sounds of the Volcaron occupants choking and spluttering as they attempted to escape the smothering plumes. A frantic company of men staggered into the daylight, several vomiting violently as they struggled to retain consciousness. Others crawled out on all fours, wheezing and sobbing in fear. Suddenly, as Nicholas watched on from above, he recognized—hunched over behind a marble pillar and coughing painfully—the darkly-clad figure of Morgoratt. An intense loathing surged through Nicholas as he watched the Volcaron leader scan the mansion grounds, searching for the nearest escape route. As the smoke continued to subside, Morgoratt stumbled toward a leaf-obscured gardener's gate, seemingly abandoning his men, the majority of whom still lay on the ground, disorientated and breathless.

"Morgoratt!" hollered Nicholas.

There was no hiding from the booming address this time, as Morgoratt turned, wild-eyed, at hearing his name amplified from above. The Volcaron leader's expression tightened immediately at the sight of the airborne Nicholas sitting imperiously astride the colossal, winged beast. For a moment, Morgoratt stood in fearful awe as he stared up at the magnificent creature above him; however, as he gained his composure, his eyes narrowed and his lips twisted into a poisonous snarl.

"So, this is how you intend to reclaim your home?" he sneered. "Hiding behind some monster."

"Ha," taunted Nicholas sarcastically. "You have the audacity to accuse me of hiding when you cower while your own people flee in terror. You really are a great leader, Morgoratt."

There was no immediate response from Morgoratt beyond his icy, unblinking stare. Without another word, he strode back toward the mansion entrance and, covering his mouth and nose with his cloak, he disappeared back inside.

Morgoratt's subdued reaction to Nicholas's taunts had not been expected, and he was perplexed as to why he would submit himself once again to the choking smoke inside the mansion. Within a few minutes, though, the sound of heavy coughing could be heard as a figure emerged from the rolling smog below. Morgoratt's greasy, long-haired head came into view, his cloak still held tightly against his face. However, this time, it appeared that he had not emerged alone. Propped up against his shoulder was a silver-haired man in a heavily charred white robe. Morgoratt dragged the unconscious figure across the courtyard out of reach of the tumbling smoke. The Volcaron leader turned to face Nicholas, and his heart sank to see that the unfortunate individual held by Morgoratt was none other than King Benjamin. Before Nicholas could react, Morgoratt produced a long, shining dagger from beneath his robe and raised it to the king's throat. Nicholas's mind seared with rage as he noticed a light trickle of blood roll down King Benjamin's collarbone. Morgoratt's eyes gleamed spitefully, and he appeared to be relishing in the fury etched across Nicholas's face.

"How does it feel to lose the upper hand, you stupid fool," jeered Morgoratt, haughtily. "You make a single wrong move, and I'll spill this pathetic old man's bowels on the ground in front of you."

"You filthy mongrel!" roared Nicholas lividly. "If you dare hurt him, I'll make sure that all that's left of your wretched corpse is ash and bones."

"You are not in a position to make threats," retorted Morgoratt. "I suggest you settle down unless you want this decrepit old bastard to meet his end before your eyes."

"Morgoratt, I swear," replied Nicholas through gritted teeth. "If you so much as…"

The remainder of his threat went unuttered as Augee reared up with a sudden howl of pain, and Nicholas was filled with the sensation of falling. He landed hard and painfully on the marble ground below, and unable to catch his breath, he lay winded and disorientated. Some seconds later,

Nicholas was filled with alarm to notice Augee slumped on the ground nearby, groaning and flinching in obvious distress.

"Augee!" he cried out in panic as he stumbled to his feet to come to his friend's aid.

As he looked closer, Nicholas noticed a thin stream of blood percolating from Augee's back. A painful-looking wound had opened in his skin, and, at the center of it, the end of a hefty, wooden spear protruded ominously.

"Augee, are you okay?" Nicholas called frantically.

Augee groaned and nodded his head, his eyes wincing. Their sentient connection told Nicholas that his friend was in pain but not mortally injured. As Augee picked himself off the ground, Nicholas spun around vengefully to confront Morgoratt. To his frustration, the Volcaron leader had disappeared from sight, and the rest of his men had started to escape out of the grounds of the mansion. However, it was with an abrupt well of horror that Nicholas's eyes met with the sight of King Benjamin, bloodied and unmoving in the grass nearby.

"No!" cried Nicholas desperately as he charged toward the king.

A wide, crimson wound stained his robe just below his right ribcage, and, on the marble paving stones off to the right, lay a discarded, bloodied dagger.

"Morgoratt!" thundered Nicholas wildly as he attempted to prop up the king's head, the monarch's aged face growing increasingly pale.

"Nicholas?" called a familiar voice from across the courtyard.

It was Suma, standing breathless and confused.

"Suma, come here!" shouted Nicholas in a trembling voice, unmoved by the unexpected appearance of his clandestine Volcaron acquaintance.

Suma sprinted to where Nicholas knelt with the ailing King Benjamin in his arms. "What…what happened?" he stammered, flustered.

"Not now," replied Nicholas, tight-jawed. "Stay with him. Cover the wound and keep pressure on it."

"Don't worry," assured Suma as he lifted the folds of the robe to inspect the king's injury. "It's just a surface wound. He'll need to have it stitched up, but the blade didn't penetrate too deeply."

Nicholas released a long, deep sigh of relief, but his fury still simmered violently within him. Two of those closest to him had been hurt by the hand of Morgoratt and his men. There was no chance that he was willing to allow them to escape after this. Nicholas rose to his feet, his fists clenched and his nerves pulsating with anger.

"Augee," he called out. "Can you fly?"

Augee growled affirmatively in response.

"Let's find that bastard," whispered Nicholas venomously.

Without further hesitation, he hoisted himself hastily onto Augee's back, and he indulged in a final, worried glance at the unfortunate King Benjamin before they took off into the air.

41

THE SKIN ON Nicholas's knuckles had turned white from how tightly he gripped the notches on Augee's back. Such was the speed and urgency with which they flew, he had to compose himself to ensure that he was not unbalanced by Augee's abrupt and rapid movements. They winged high along the fringe of the bay, scanning for any sign of Morgoratt and his retreating chieftains. By now, the bay of Hohala teemed with boats and rafts carrying Volcaron men, women, and children as they fled the wrath of the beast that had terrorized them out of their ill-gotten homes. Others swam, many flailing wildly as they begged to be pulled onboard one of the packed vessels. Shrieks of anger and fear could be heard coming from every direction, and, at one point, Nicholas looked down to witness a young man aboard one of the boats pick up a heavy oar and viciously strike the skull of a much older Volcaron who had been trying desperately to hoist himself up onto the vessel. He watched in disgust as the unfortunate elderly man went still and then sank limply beneath the surface of the water, the sea around him turning a hazy red from the gaping wound in his head. As they flew onward, Nicholas shook his head in abhorrence, and he was filled with even stronger determination to expel the Volcarons from Hohala permanently.

After a short time, Nicholas's heart leapt as he spotted Morgoratt and three of his men attempting to maneuver a rowing boat out of the shallower water. They stood among the rolling waves, submerged to their waists as they attempted to heave the weighty vessel off the sea floor.

"You know what to do, Augee," instructed Nicholas coldly.

Augee shifted the angle of his wings, and they glided downward in the direction of the Volcaron leader's boat. Seconds later, Morgoratt and the men spun around wide-eyed as Augee sounded a deep roar that caused the water around them to tremble.

"Push, you fools! Go! Go!" Nicholas could hear Morgoratt bellowing to his men in panic.

With an almighty, collective shove, the Volcarons managed to dislodge the rudder of the boat. As the vessel rocked dangerously, each of the men—except for Morgoratt—took up an oar and began rowing furiously. Morgoratt, visibly enraged that Nicholas—astride his enormous beast—had managed to locate them, stood up and roared out venomous obscenities that seemed to cause a stir even among the frantically rowing men.

Watching from above, Nicholas could not help but feel satisfaction at the acute distress of his enemies as they flailed their oars through the water. A great, foreboding shadow enveloped the boat as Augee swooped over them. The men cried out in terror at the sight, one of them taking the compulsive decision to dive overboard to escape.

"Augee," called out Nicholas. "Blast them into the water."

Augee growled in response as he flexed his powerful neck muscles and thrust his head forward, his fanged jaws gaping terrifyingly. With a tremendous howl, a long, serpentine torrent of flame billowed forcefully from Augee's throat; the blaze whipped and snapped wildly through the air at unpredictable angles as it hurtled directly toward Morgoratt's boat. With a resounding crash that caused Nicholas to wince, Augee's fiery projectile smashed into the vessel. Splintered wood and fire erupted into the air as the boat was blown to pieces, and its occupants were thrown helplessly into the sea. All around, the force of the blast had caused the water to swirl and foam ferociously, and the Volcarons screamed out for help as they struggled to keep their heads above the raging waves. Then, Nicholas spotted Morgoratt and two of his men who had managed to latch onto wooden debris and were clinging on, helpless, defenseless and beaten.

"You don't have an ounce of decency in you, Morgoratt, you shameless swine," hollered Nicholas as he and Augee hovered above, casting an imposing shadow over the Volcaron leader. "I offered you mercy. I gave you the chance to leave this place alive, even though it was never yours to thieve in the first place. And, in return, you try to murder an old man who chose not to raise a sword to you, even though he'd have been well-justified to cut you down."

Morgoratt had little to respond with, other than a venomous glare and some roared obscenities which Nicholas couldn't make out over the tempestuous din of the foaming water that had been disturbed by the explosion.

Without warning, Nicholas's concentration on Morgoratt was broken as something struck him squarely on the right side of his head. The violent smack caused his vision to blur, and his head throbbed painfully. Disorientated, he clutched his head with one hand as he attempted to remain balanced on Augee's back. Augee, who, at the last minute, had seen the rock soaring through the air just before it struck Nicholas, rapidly shifted angles and carried his dazed passenger higher into the sky out of the range of any further missiles from below. A sharp ringing filled Nicholas's ears, and he growled in vexation as he observed an approaching boat of Volcarons attempting to come to Morgoratt's aid. One man onboard held a lump of rock in his fist, preparing to launch another assault on Nicholas and Augee. By now, Morgoratt had managed to flounder his way to the rescue vessel where the occupants had managed to pull him aboard.

Nicholas removed his hand from the side of his head. Holding it up to his eyes, he saw his fingers soaked with blood, and he could feel that the side of his face was warm and moist.

"That's it, Augee; I'm done with those scoundrels," Nicholas rasped. "They can't be trusted to leave peacefully. Let's do as we should've done in the first place."

Augee huffed through his nose in solemn acknowledgement. Twisting in the air, he spread his wings and let out a roar that caused the waves to rock the Volcaron boat menacingly.

"Faster, you useless dogs! Move!" Morgoratt could be heard screaming from below as he stared upward with a frenzied glare.

The Volcarons, swung their oars wildly through the waves, struggling hysterically to escape the range of Augee's fire. However, the realization that escape was futile became etched on the Volcarons' terrified faces as, once more, Augee craned his neck backward and inhaled deeply. His eyes pulsated and burned like ghostly embers, and the scales all across his body hardened and darkened further. The fearful occupants of the boat below cried out in horrified anticipation as they raised their arms across their faces. The wind seemed to die down, and for several seconds the scene was a vacuum of silence. All was calm, and the Volcarons stared at Augee in silent dread. Such was the power of the blast that followed, it created a kick-back that almost knocked Nicholas from his perch. Out of Augee's gaping jaws, a spinning, cyclonic inferno gushed forth in a furious torrent that rained down ruthlessly among the Volcarons; hysterical, blood-chilling screams and the splashing of water filled the air as waves of flame tumbled and slithered all around them until the boat was engulfed by the blaze. Like a skeletal carcass, remnants of the vessel remained afloat as the wood crackled and burned, and the very surface of the water itself appeared to be on fire.

Stunned at the awful power of Augee's blast, Nicholas scanned the water for any sign of movement from the Volcarons. Black pyres of smoke converged to consume the entire area, obscuring visibility. As the plumes began to attack his breathing, Nicholas spluttered instructions for Augee to fly higher. They rose above the billowing cloud, and both gladly inhaled the crisp, sharp air. After a short time, the smoke cleared slightly, and the flicker of distant splashing far across the bay caught his eye. Soaked, disheveled and weary, a small cohort of Volcarons swam madly through the water in the direction of the flotilla of boats and rafts that were already on course to leave the Bay of Hohala. Propped up by the scruff of his neck, an unconscious Morgoratt was being hauled by the other men who struggled to keep his head above the water. From what Nicholas could make out, the Volcaron leader's face was cut and badly bloodied, and his body dragged limply as he was lugged through the water.

As Nicholas was contemplating their next move, Augee swung his head around and shot him a questioning glance. For several moments, Nicholas pondered the prospect of a follow-up assault on the absconding Volcarons. They were immobilized and vulnerable, entirely at his and Augee's mercy. Nicholas's mind wrestled with the temptation to direct Augee to carry out one final strike that would permanently eradicate the blight of Morgoratt's influence from the world. Just one final burst of flame, and any threat posed by the insidious Volcaron leader would be extinguished for good. Yet, despite the fact that his head screamed at him to instruct Augee to finish off the fleeing Volcarons, another voice deep within his subconscious prevented him from uttering that decisive command. As Nicholas's mind raced, Augee patiently kept them hovering in the air, his gaze fixed on

Nicholas's fretful countenance. Nicholas swore in frustration as his conscience and Hohalian instincts induced him to—very reluctantly—resist commanding the execution of Morgoratt. As he watched the Volcaron leader and his accomplices reach the waiting flotilla, Nicholas breathed a sigh of resignation and attempted to convince himself that Morgoratt and his people had been sufficiently deterred from ever returning to Hohala. For a short spell, he and Augee hung in the sky and watched their enemies' vessels disappear beyond the horizon. Fire and smoke continued to smolder from the wreckage strewn about the water's surface, a grim reminder of the violent measures that Nicholas had been forced to take in order to ensure the preservation of the Hohalian people. With the Volcarons gone from his sight, his thoughts turned to the welfare of King Benjamin. With a renewed sense of urgency, Nicholas gestured to Augee in the direction of the village, and they turned around to seek out Hamar, Caralisa, and the rest of the Hohalian volunteers.

42

By the forest's edge, Hamar and Princess Caralisa were crouched in the underbrush, their minds alert and their weapons of makeshift clubs and pointed staffs at the ready. Crashing explosions and tortured screams had echoed within the confines of the village for some time as the concealed Hohalian volunteers—positioned just a short way back from where the jungle met the village outskirts—listened, unsettled and fearful.

Hamar, careful to maintain his composure despite his own unease, kept an assuring hand on the shoulder of the restless Caralisa, who started anxiously at every cry and explosive rumble that emanated from the village. On more than one occasion, Hamar had to whisper a reminder to the princess that it was the duty of every volunteer to remain level-headed at this most critical point in their plan. As Hamar had emphasized, laying siege to the village in a reactionary manner would result in a mass confrontation with the Volcarons and would certainly end with Hohalian casualties. Caralisa, overcome with worry for both her father and Nicholas, begrudgingly promised Hamar to remain hidden until the right time, though neither knew when that moment would be.

In the distance, the calamitous din brought about by one of Augee's blasts resounded ominously, and through the gaps in the trees, the Hohalians could make out a massive spire of black smog unfurling on the horizon. As Hamar watched the dark, rolling plume extend high into the cloudless sky, he caught a glimpse of activity along the perimeter of the village. He felt Caralisa stir in reaction to the movement, though the source was largely obscured by the mesh of vines and leaves that marked the edge of the jungle. Hamar held on to the princess's shoulder tightly, for fear she would give away their position. From what he could make out through the thick foliage, there were two figures, both male, with one appearing to be propping the other up by the shoulder. The more able-bodied looking of the two seemed to be guiding the other man toward a lonely hut by the forest's edge. Hamar's free hand slid silently to the handle of the dagger that hung from his belt, and he held his breath as he prepared himself for possible engagement.

"Father!" came Caralisa's unexpected cry.

Hamar's heart skipped a beat and he stumbled backward in surprise. Before he could stop her, the princess tore through the vegetation toward the mysterious pair. Swearing in surprise and exasperation, Hamar leapt to his feet in pursuit of Caralisa, ripping his way past the briars and vines before emerging into the daylight of the village precincts. A little off to his right, Hamar spotted two club-wielding Hohalian volunteers peeking their heads out of their hiding spot among the foliage.

"Stay where you are!" he hissed at them as he cautiously followed after Caralisa. She called out her father's name loudly a second time, and, with the princess having given away their position, Hamar readied himself for the possibility of a Volcaron onslaught. By this point, Caralisa had caught up with the two men up ahead and had flung her arms around the elder of the pair who hung uncomfortably from the shoulders of his companion.

"Father, what in the name of Nexus did they do to you?" cried the princess upon noticing the seeping wound that had stained the upper part of King Benjamin's robe. "You're bleeding!"

The king's face was grey and strained, but his eyes flickered open drowsily at the sound of his daughter's voice.

"My sweet Caralisa," he replied dazedly, raising his hand to her cheek. "What are you doing here? This is no place for you. You must go to safety before it's too late."

"I don't care!" blurted the princess, her teary eyes narrowing as she scrambled to come up with a next step. "We need to get you help, now!"

Suma, who had been propping up the flagging monarch, cleared his throat self-consciously.

"It's just a flesh wound," he mumbled gruffly. "It looks worse than it is.

But he needs to have it cleaned and stitched up properly, which was what I was taking him to do before you turned up."

Caralisa's eyes shone with relief, and she bent to wipe flakes of smoky ash from her father's matted grey beard. As she looked up, she took her first meaningful glance at the enormous individual who held her father upright. Her eyes widened as she surveyed the man's clothing and facial features for the first time, and, suddenly, his identity dawned on her.

"It's you!" she stammered recognizing Suma as the Volcaron who had visited New Hohala with the warning that had prompted her father's reckless confrontation with Morgoratt. "This is your fault! You caused my father to submit himself to the Volcarons!"

Suma looked dumbfounded by the princess's fierce accusation, and he shot an incredulous look at Hamar who was sprinting toward them with exasperation etched across his face. Before Hamar had a chance to intervene, Caralisa sprang forward in an attempt to wrestle Suma's grip from King Benjamin.

"Get your disgusting Volcaron hands off my father," she raged as she tugged at her father's robe with one arm and began thumping Suma's barrel-like chest with the other. Suma, somewhat perplexed as to what he'd done to provoke the petite Hohalian woman's ire, raised his arm to hold her back.

"Princess, *stop!*" interrupted Hamar, grabbing her shoulders from behind. "This man is on our side; he's trying to help us!"

"He's one of them," retorted Caralisa, shrugging him away. "They're all the same."

"Believe me," interjected Suma heatedly. "I would very much like to wash my hands of you and your people. You have no damn idea what I've had to do to help you...the *risks* I've taken!"

"Well isn't it quite the coincidence that we catch you here carrying my injured father. I swear, if you've harmed an inch of his body..." pronounced Caralisa, unconvinced by Suma's defense of his motives.

"Give it a rest," he shot back irritably. "Your friend, Nicholas, instructed me to bring your king to shelter and tend to his wounds. Now, if you have something to say about that, then I've no problem leaving him here on the ground for you to look after. I try to do the right thing, only to be..."

"Wait! You've spoken to Nicholas?" Hamar cut across. "Is he okay?"

"I hope so," replied Suma moodily. "He and the dragon flew off after Morgoratt and his chieftains a little while ago. I haven't seen him since, but I've heard explosions and seen a lot of smoke over the bay. Whatever's happened, that creature of his has caused some mayhem, that's for sure."

Caralisa bit her lip in worry as she looked to the sky.

"Who did this to King Benjamin?" inquired Hamar darkly.

"Who do you think?" answered Suma, a hint of bitterness in his tone. "You see now how ruthless that fiend is? Your king is incredibly fortunate that the knife just missed his heart. Morgoratt is one dangerous bastard, and I've had a dagger hanging over me since I promised I would slow down his plans."

Hamar placed his hand on Suma's shoulder.

"Your efforts will not be forgotten by any Hohalian when all of this is over," he reassured. "But, for now, we must remain concentrated on the task at hand. Please, take King Benjamin to your cabin and look after his injuries. He's old and has lost quite a lot of blood."

Suma gave a solemn nod in agreement. As he firmly grasped the semi-conscious King Benjamin's upper body, he threw Caralisa a wounded glance. The princess dropped her eyes in embarrassment at her previous naïve outburst, and she watched Suma patiently shoulder her father's weight as they made their way to the cabin.

By this time, several of the more inquisitive Hohalian volunteers who'd heard Caralisa's vehement remonstrations had emerged tentatively from the jungle.

"It's okay," called Hamar, resigned to the fact that the volunteers were unlikely to stay put for much longer. "You may come out of your places."

From the woodland, the multitude of Hohalians emerged in pairs and small groups, their demeanors vigilant and their weapons drawn as they had been instructed by Hamar. Their caution was pleasing to Hamar, and he felt proud in the knowledge that he had assembled a disciplined and dedicated band of soldiers in such a short period.

The Hohalians congregated in the open space by Suma's cabin that marked part of the village frontier. More than one hundred pairs of eyes scanned the air for a sign of Nicholas and Augee. In the distance, slowly rising smoke stained the cloudless blue sky, and the volunteers discussed in anxious whispers whether or not it was a sign that Nicholas had indeed been successful.

She was not sure exactly how much time had passed, but Caralisa's heart skipped a beat at the sound of one of the volunteer's excited exclamation.

"There! To the east!" shouted the man, pointing to the sky.

As those gathered turned their eyes in the direction of the man's gesture, a rapidly approaching blotch was visible on the horizon. Seconds later, a chorus of passionate cheers erupted as Augee's winged silhouette came into focus. Before long, the volunteers could discern the outline of Nicholas astride Augee's back, his fist raised triumphantly. The crowd, overjoyed by the indication that their heroes had achieved victory, cheered and embraced each other. Standing next to Caralisa, Hamar glanced discreetly in her direction, and he could see that the princess's eyes were lined with tears, and her lips were pursed into an exhausted smile.

The crowd whooped in delight as Augee glided downward and touched down gently on the soft grass that separated the jungle and the village perimeter. As Nicholas attempted to compose himself upon landing, the Hohalians surged forward and circled Augee who remained good-naturedly calm in the midst of all of the excitement and his own fatigue.

Nicholas, despite still bleeding from the wound on his throbbing head, allowed himself a moment to appreciate the momentousness of the scene. Having succeeded in his mission, his fellow Hohalians—from whom he'd been exiled for over five years—now surrounded him, chanting his name and demonstrating their gratitude for having vanquished their enemies and finally delivering the Hohalians from their purgatory.

Then, from the periphery of the throng, he spotted Hamar and Caralisa; the former raised his fist in a victorious gesture, which Nicholas acknowledged with a nod of his head. Caralisa however, overcome with relief, stared at Nicholas with beaming, tear-stained eyes. He grinned knowingly in return, and his heart suddenly ached to be alone with the beautiful princess whose joyful smile at their victory made the entire struggle seem worthwhile.

Sensing that the crowd's excitement was unlikely to abate any time soon, Nicholas thought it best to address them with a few brief words. He raised his hand to quiet the chatter, and the volunteers hushed one another in anticipation of his words.

"People of Hohala," he boomed, his voice still mysteriously amplified while he was perched on Augee's back. "I have the privilege of confirming to you that, after five long years, the Volcarons have at last been expelled from our land."

A thunderous cheer went up from the crowd who had been collectively taken aback by the magnification of Nicholas's voice. Men and women hugged each other gratefully, and the excitement among them was simply electrifying.

"As I speak to you," continued Nicholas, a triumphant smile lining his face, "The tide is carrying the Volcarons away from our shores. Now they know the terrible fate that awaits them should they ever trespass upon our lands again."

Nicholas gestured toward Augee, his friend's great, green eyes shimmering spectacularly in the sunlight.

"The recognition for this success must go primarily to Augee," Nicholas declared proudly. "Without his bravery and power, we would never have been able to achieve our victory today. So, Augee, on behalf of the Hohalians, I offer you our eternal gratitude and friendship."

At that, the volunteers burst into a vigorous chanting of Augee's name, and those near the front of the crowd surged forward to pat him appreciatively.

"Thanks to Augee," continued Nicholas, "We defeated our enemies and—more importantly for the principals of non-violence that our people hold so dearly—I can gladly tell you that, although many of the Volcarons have been left bloodied and beaten, not one life was lost at our hands during the attack, in keeping with the wishes of the Nexus."

The crowd cheered in approval, and Nicholas raised his fist to the air once again.

"Long live sacred Hohala!" he cried victoriously. "Praise to the Nexus!"

As the volunteers chanted his words enthusiastically in response, Nicholas lowered himself onto the ground. As he was dusting off the front of his tunic, Caralisa appeared from among the throng and threw her arms around his neck. Nicholas was taken aback by the vigor of her embrace as she pressed her lips against his. As they stood, their arms wrapped tight around each other, some within the crowd cheered teasingly at the scene and quipped good-naturedly about what a lucky fellow Nicholas was.

As they parted, Nicholas smiled at the princess's delighted expression. Her twinkling eyes reassured him and made his soul thankful. He squeezed her delicate hands in his and realized that all that he had hoped and persevered for had finally come to pass. After reveling for a moment in the ecstasy of it all, Nicholas spotted Suma standing aloof and unsmiling outside of his cabin. His thoughts instantly turned to King Benjamin, who he had last seen being tended to by the big Volcaron back in the grounds of the royal mansion.

"Where is your father?" Nicholas inquired of Caralisa, talking close to her ear over the din of the celebrating volunteers.

"He's in there," shouted the princess, as she pointed to Suma's cabin. "He's wounded, but he's going to be okay!"

Nicholas sighed in relief.

"Let's go see him," he smiled as he wound his fingers around hers.

As he walked hand-in-hand with Caralisa in the direction of the cabin, Nicholas noticed the grim-faced Suma approaching them from the fringes of the crowd.

"Suma?" he called out, his voice lilting with curiosity as to why the man's expression seemed so dour. Suma, for his part, did not respond in kind.

"You didn't kill him?" he spoke brusquely, his lips pursed and his features rigid.

"Kill? Kill who?" responded Nicholas confusedly.

"Who do you bloody think?" shot back Suma through gritted teeth. "You're seriously telling me that you had the chance to finish him off and didn't take it?"

"You mean Morgoratt?" Nicholas replied. "Morgoratt is gone, Suma. Augee roughed him up so much that there is no chance he'll ever venture this way again if he's smart."

"You don't *know* him," urged Suma, grabbing Nicholas's shoulder. "You should have killed him and removed his poison from the world for good."

Nicholas stared at the big Volcaron for a moment before adding, "Suma, I promise you; if you'd seen the fear on Morgoratt and the others' faces, then you'd be left in no doubt that we've seen the last of them. Please, rest assured that the will of the Nexus has been done, and that this land has been cleansed of Morgoratt's wickedness for good."

Suma offered no response, other than a troubled, uncertain sigh to which Nicholas simply slapped the big man encouragingly on the back.

"Come on," he entreated him. "Let's go and see King Benjamin and let him know that he's going to have to get re-accustomed to grander sur-roundings than his hut by the Eternal Steam. *You*, for one, are going to be in very good favor with the king for your bravery and generosity to our people—if there's a particular house you like in the village, then I reckon now would be a good time to ask!"

Nicholas chuckled as Caralisa led him off by the hand to see the king. Suma, however, remained behind, his expression morose and distracted as he watched the newly carefree Nicholas and his princess enter the dim cabin.

43

THE HOHOLIANS SPENT the remaining daylight hours journeying back to their settlements at Haven and New Hohala. Fatigue had set in among the volunteers, but the spirit of optimism and anticipation was palpable as they trekked light-heartedly through the jungle. Led by Hamar, they chattered merrily about the extensive reconstruction that would soon be at hand and of their renewed hopes for the future. Prayers and hymns of praise were sung during the course of the journey—a stark contrast to the tense expedition that they had undertaken under the cover of darkness only hours before.

King Benjamin's recovery, thanks to Suma's treatment of his injuries, had been remarkably swift. With Nicholas in attendance and Princess Caralisa holding the king's hand in hers, Suma had expertly stitched-up the blade wound under his collarbone. Sore, stiff, and slightly groggy, the king had beamed as Nicholas and Caralisa regaled him with their exuberant versions of the Hohalian victory over the Volcarons. His eyes had watered proudly as he listened to Nicholas's account of how he and Augee dispelled the Volcarons purposefully but, importantly, without fatalities on either side. The revelation that not a soul had been mortally injured during the confrontation appeared to invigorate the king, and his frail arms had embraced Nicholas affectionately in response.

Suma, who had remained quiet throughout the high-spirited reunion of Caralisa and her father, had also been received warmly by the monarch. Having been informed by Caralisa of the courageous foreigner's exploits in glowing terms, Suma received a heartfelt expression of gratitude from the king and was assured of his place in a rejuvenated Hohalian nation. To his satisfaction, Nicholas had noticed the self-conscious smile that had cracked across the big Volcaron's face upon being promised the freedom of Hohala. It was only in the aftermath of victory that Nicholas had the opportunity to reflect on the enormous risk Suma had taken in order to hamper Morgoratt's intended onslaught on New Hohala. So very different from others of his race, he had acted according to his conscience. He had been the *imperfect* Volcaron—righteous, committed, courageous, and kind-natured—the very qualities that marked a good Hohalian, and the antithesis of those valued most by Morgoratt.

Now, as the volunteers journeyed back to Haven and New Hohala to gather their families and possessions before returning to their rightful home, Suma had agreed to stay behind to begin planning for the long rebuilding process that was to come. In an attempt to make official his welcome to Suma, King Benjamin had requested that he take charge of a band of volunteers to stand guard around the village while the rest of the Hohalians travelled back to New Hohala. While Suma and the fighters secured the village perimeter, Caralisa and Lawson remained with King Benjamin who was not fit to undergo the arduous journey back to the mountain village.

Meanwhile, as the volunteers tramped along the jungle route to Haven and New Hohala, and Caralisa and Lawson cared for the king, Nicholas and Augee patrolled the coastline and the Bay of Hohala. By mid-afternoon, the sun had bathed the landscape in a lustrous blanket of light that caused the blue-green water of the bay to sparkle and cast the lush, summer vegetation of the countryside into a vivid patchwork of color. From the air, it was a magnificent tableau, a reminder of the beauty and splendor that the Hohalians had been deprived of during their half-decade of exile in the western highlands.

As they soared across the fathomless sky, Nicholas could not help but be struck by the aching sublimity of the Hohalian lands, and he felt a twinge of melancholy at the thought that his people had been disconnected from their home for so long. After years of yearning for adventure, Nicholas finally saw the blessings of his homeland. He felt the guiding spirit of the Nexus in the air, not as a confining force, but a generous patron. Sweeping across the unrivaled medley of dense jungle, obtrusive highlands, and sparkling waterways, Nicholas pledged to himself that he would never again pine for the unknown that lay beyond the land where the Nexus spread its loving influence—he had no need to, with all of the blessings that he now knew were his. Astride Augee—the friend he was certain the Nexus had guided him to—Nicholas felt weightless, unburdened, and, for the first time in his life, that his soul was no longer isolated from his people and their spiritual bond with the Nexus.

As they moved south along the coast in order to scout the mouth of the bay, they passed over the dismal structure that was Morgoratt's plantation. An inhospitable sea wind whistled and whipped about his head as Nicholas gave Augee the instruction to touch down inside the perimeter of the complex. Coming in to land, the dreary, wooden structures within the enclosure came into closer focus. The abandoned corpse of the young man they had previously seen from the air remained slumped by the exterior fence, the rain having turned his white, blood-splattered robe a pink hue.

The plantation, situated at the highest cliff point for miles, was miserably assailed by a constant, icy maritime rain as biting as it was dispiriting. An unsettling silence pervaded the interior of the complex as Augee came to rest on the damp scrub that grew in tufts within the perimeter fence. The resplendence of the summer countryside that Nicholas had earlier breathed in so eagerly was replaced by a funereal gloom, as mist and misery converged to create a haunting, hopeless atmosphere. The five windowless cabins were spread in lonely formation across the grounds, creaking and groaning as the harsh coastal elements laid siege. After alighting from Augee's back, Nicholas moved cautiously toward the largest of the cabins, the entrance to which was secured by a weighty coil of rusting chains. Glancing around warily, he knocked on the thick, timber door before pressing one of his ears against the wood. Suddenly, Nicholas stumbled backward in shock as the sound of muffled cries met his ears. His heart pounded intensely as stifled voices percolated from inside the structure.

"Augee!" called out Nicholas through the swirling downpour. "There's somebody inside this one!"

Augee, who had been mournfully investigating the discarded remains of the young man that they had seen from the air, turned and bounded to where Nicholas stood by the door of the largest cabin.

"There's someone inside," repeated Nicholas, shouting across the tumult of wind and rain. "I can hear voices."

In response, Augee gave a soft groan of curiosity and craned his great neck toward the heavily chained door. For a moment, he inspected the latch thoughtfully before, all of a sudden, he bared his razor-like teeth and bit down hard on the chain. With a neat crack, the thick coils snapped, and the chains dropped onto the sodden cabin doorstep. As the heavy metal clunked onto the wooden steps, the dull commotion within the cabin ceased, leaving the bluster of the gale the only sound. Nicholas gave Augee a nervous glance before extending his trembling hand toward the door latch. With a coarse rasp of its heavily burdened hinges, the door creaked slowly open to reveal an unlit interior. Inside, the cabin was pitch dark, and the air was damp and foul-smelling. With his right hand fixed firmly to the handle of the blade that hung from his belt, Nicholas stepped across the threshold. Immediately, his blood ran cold as the sounds of frantic whisperings sounded from deep within the shadows.

"Hello?" called Nicholas anxiously. "Who's there? Show yourself!"

As imposing as he attempted to come across, his half-hearted assertiveness was met with silence. Once more, he called out:

"Whoever's in here, make yourself known; I won't hesitate to use force if I need to."

A second time, Nicholas's inquiry went unanswered. As his eyes strained to refocus to the darkness, he noticed a copper wall fixture next to the door frame of the entrance. Attached were the remains of a nearly spent wax candle, the wick of which was thin and charred. With his eyes and ears alert for movement, Nicholas cautiously pried what remained of the candle from the rest of the wall fixture. Stepping back out into the daylight, he held the waxy nub to Augee's snout. Understanding Nicholas's intentions immediately, Augee took a shallow breath and let out a gruff snort. A curl of orange flame rolled out of his flared nostrils and caught the wick of the candle with a sharp fizzle of smoke. The weak illumination from the candle threw an eerie glow across the entranceway, casting dim shadows that appeared to shimmer and dance along the timber-framed walls. The floorboards groaned noisily as he ventured further into the darkness of the cabin, and his eyes flitted in every direction in an attempt to identify the source of the earlier commotion. After a moment, the burning candle highlighted one of the far corners of the cabin, and Nicholas's weary eyes met with a most chilling sight. Lined against the damp timber wall, there were hunched around a dozen pale, barely clothed figures, their sunken eye sockets returning Nicholas's aghast stare. They appeared to be mostly men, some of whom were wrapped in pale-colored cloaks similar to the one which was draped around the bloodstained body of the young Hohalian outside. By the glow of the candlelight, it was clear that the men were famished and filthy, and Nicholas's head now swam from the stench that filled the air. Forcing back a wave of nausea, he fixed the light on the faces that returned his startled gaze, only for the men to groan and shield their eyes from the sudden brightness.

"I am Nicholas Stone of Hohala," he stuttered. "The Volcarons are gone and no longer hold control over these shores."

"Nicholas?" called a quivering voice from the shadows. "Nicholas Stone?"

A young man named Merek, who Nicholas recognized as a neighbor back in Haven, rose from his hunkered position on the floor and shuffled forward cautiously. His face was thin and ghostly pale, with a scraggly, unkempt beard.

"Merek!" Nicholas exclaimed as he fought the urge to embrace the young man for fear of alarming him. "Thank the gods we found you! It's okay now—you're safe."

Merek gave no audible response; instead, Nicholas noticed that the young man's eyes shone with tears. Some of the other men had begun to rise to their feet and, within a minute, Nicholas was surrounded by gaunt visages that searched his eyes imploringly. In the feeble light, he saw that each of the faces was of distinct Hohalian bone structure, and his anger rose at the thought of their ordeal. Nicholas noticed that the arms, faces, and torsos of the men were bruised and badly scarred, as if they had been beaten and cut. Deep, crimson slash marks, the result of some bladed implement, crisscrossed each man's skin, and some displayed wounds that were badly infected. Nicholas stood in silence for a moment, attempting to comprehend the inhumanity of it all.

"Why did they do this to you?" he gasped.

Merek simply stared back at him, his expression deadpan and his eyes lightless.

"To set an example," he replied colorlessly. "To make a point as to what would happen if our people refused to submit to the Volcarons' plans to enslave us."

"None of you have to worry about that anymore," returned Nicholas through gritted teeth. "The Volcarons are gone. They have been driven out to sea and won't be back. All of you are leaving here, right now."

After a poignant silence, there was a flurry of whispered, joyful animation among the men as the reality of their liberation set in, and they began picking up their ragged belongings. Just as they made to leave the cabin, Nicholas informed the men of Augee's presence and urged them not to be startled by his size or appearance. Nervously, each man stumbled into the stormy daylight, squinting as they held their hands across their eyes.

The last to exit the cabin was Merek who had stayed behind with Nicholas.

"There are more prisoners," he revealed. "In the other cabins. When they ambushed us weeks ago, the one called Morgoratt took the king, and we were marched all the way here—at least, those of us who were spared. There were around thirty of us brought here."

"Well, the Volcarons are no longer a threat to you or any Hohalian," spat Nicholas indignantly. "You've nothing more to worry about."

As Nicholas made to leave, Merek stuck out his arm to block him.

"You do know he won't stop, don't you?" whispered the young man. "He's not going to give up."

For a moment, Nicholas just stared at Merek in return, searching his eyes somberly. Then, upon hearing the anxious voices of the rest of the men outside as they set eyes for the first time on the colossal Augee, Nicholas placed his hand on the young man's shoulder in feigned reassurance.

"Come on," he sighed. "Let's free the others."

44

AN EBULLIENT CELEBRATION had gotten underway by the time the last of the Hohalians finished their final journey from New Hohala to retake their spiritual home. It had been a gruelling effort, with every adult and child participating in the relocation from their mountainside place of exile to the sacred settlement that had been the cradle of the Hohalian race for uncountable generations. As the people had tramped and heaved through the sweltering jungle humidity, there had been a genuine sense of homecoming pride in the resilience that saw them endure five years of toil and the constant fear of persecution. Along the harsh, overgrown jungle route home, they'd sang songs of thanks to the Nexus and conversed excitedly among each other about their hopes for the future. And while the overall mood had been one of joy, the Hohalians had been mindful not to lose sight of the sacrifice of those that had been lost during the recent confrontation with the Volcarons. In the groups of ten or fifteen in which they had carried their possessions from Haven and New Hohala to the ancient village, they had chanted prayers of commemoration; in the instances where a relative of one of the slain was present, the others in the group had been careful to temper their buoyancy at their impending arrival home.

With evening descending, amid the rubble strewn across the grounds of the royal mansion, King Benjamin stood grateful and proud as he prepared to address his subjects for the first time since their return to their homeland. His public address had been scheduled for dusk to allow the weary travellers time to recuperate a little. It seemed, however, that few of the Hohalians had availed of the opportunity to rest, and a dense crowd had assembled in the square by the king's palace to drink wine, dance, and celebrate their new freedom. A steady trickle of people had begun to flow through the welcoming gates of the mansion by the time Augee touched down on the central lawn with Caralisa and Nicholas astride his back.

Some of the younger Hohalian children gasped and shrieked at the sight of Augee's enormous form, his great shadow eclipsing the light of sinking sun as he swooped down from the purpling sky. By now, however, the news of Augee's incredible feats had spread among the people, and the crowd cheered and whooped as he flew overhead. Despite Nicholas's eagerness to avoid his new hero status, King Benjamin had been insistent that the Hohalians' liberators be presented to the grateful citizens. Reluctantly, and after the encouragement of an overjoyed Caralisa, Nicholas had agreed to join the princess and her father during the king's momentous speech. Suma wasn't spared the ordeal of the public spotlight either, as King Benjamin had been resolute in his insistence that the big man be present during the public ceremony. As the crowd began to swell inside the mansion grounds, Suma self-consciously took his position next to Caralisa, Nicholas, and Lawson on the topmost step of the palace entrance. To the surprise of all four, Hamar was nowhere to be seen, and Nicholas wondered to himself if his trusted former neighbor had decided to opt out of the festivities because of the barely healed wound to his chest.

Twilight had engulfed the village, and a cheerful congregation of Hohalians—some more tipsy than others—had gathered by the time King Benjamin raised his arms, smiling, to gain their attention. The traditional reverential silence to the king's presence was, on this occasion, replaced with cheers of joy from the mirth-intoxicated crowd. Taken aback by his people's uncharacteristic display of informality, King Benjamin could not help but crack a wide smile which caused those gathered to cheer with even more vigor. Beside him, Nicholas could feel Caralisa attempt to stifle an outburst of laughter as her father shuffled his feet. She turned to Nicholas with a smile and squeezed his fingers lovingly, to which he responded by clasping her hand tightly in his. A second time, the king attempted to hush the crowd by raising his hand sagely, at which they fell respectfully silent. Clearing his throat, he broke into a jovial tone.

"My dear people," he began. "I am very pleased to see you all here tonight in such high spirits. I realize that this day has been five long, difficult years in the making, and that our faith and spirits have been tested greatly. I do say this, however, with no hesitation: our people have shown an unprecedented resilience and bravery. No previous generation of Hohalians have ever had to endure detachment from this land, the spirit of which our souls are so intrinsically connected to. As we have seen this past half-decade, separation from our motherland caused us to wilt as a people, and, as is clear from the ruin you see around you, the land itself has suffered greatly. There is no doubt in my mind that the spirits of our home and our people are interwoven—one cannot survive without the other, and it is our exile from Hohala that caused that truth to become so deeply evident. From today, we go forward with renewed appreciation for the beauty and bounty of this land, and we will curate it with the love that it deserves."

A raucous cheer erupted from the buoyant crowd.

"Yes, my dear Hohalians," continued the king. "We will never take for granted the second chance that we have been gifted. We must pray and reflect and appreciate this new beginning and build a better Hohala in which to realize a greater future."

Once more, the crowd roared out in united enthusiasm, some embracing and kissing each other as if the reality of their liberation was still unregistered in their minds. The king smiled contently at the scenes of happiness that until that day had seemed beyond impossible.

"Indeed, there are some to whom we owe a great debt of gratitude," he continued as the crowd grew settled once again. "Firstly, to my daughter and your princess, Caralisa, without whose resilience, good judgement, and powers of organization we may not have coordinated the mass migration of our people back to this beautiful land. Please, show her the appreciation that she deserves. It is already clear that she will make a most excellent queen one day."

Caralisa averted her gaze and blushed shyly as the crowd erupted into applause. After a moment, the king gestured with his hand toward Suma, who appeared equally self-conscious.

"The man you see before you...," resumed King Benjamin, "...is not of our shores. Indeed, it is important that we are transparent as to how and why he stands by my side tonight. For those of you unacquainted with him, his name is Suma, a man of Volcaron."

Startled gasps emitted from within the crowd and, inside, Suma quivered with frustration at what he considered a terrible lack of diplomacy on the king's part. The revelation of his identity—of the nationality of which he was so deeply ashamed—he thought wholly unnecessary and now put him in fear of ostracization from the only community that he now knew.

"I ask you to listen carefully to my words," continued the king, his voice rising and his tone growing sterner. "This man stands as an example to us all. He was not born a Hohalian, but he has risked a great deal in order to protect us from the sinister intentions of the invaders. He had nothing to gain from his actions; yet he chose, out of good conscience, to secretly work against the plans of the Volcaron leader, Morgoratt, and his ilk to bring us warning—twice—of the impending attack on New Hohala."

As a perplexed murmur rippled through the crowd, King Benjamin turned to Suma and grasped him tightly by the hand.

"Suma," he addressed the big Volcaron with a smile. "Tonight, we honor your courage and empathy, and we humbly request that you join us by accepting the freedom of Hohala. We invite you to be part of our future and help us to rebuild our society as a member of the Hohalian nation."

Suma's cheeks grew crimson and sweat dripped from his forehead as he felt the stare of the multitude on him. Feeling obliged to give a response, he waved bashfully at the bemused crowd who, to his enormous relief, responded with a round of fervent applause and shouts of "Welcome, Suma!" He was grateful when he felt Lawson's hand slap him on the back appreciatively, slightly deflecting attention from him.

Once more, King Benjamin raised his hands to subdue the crowd.

"There are two more who deserve our deep appreciation," declared the king, before he inserted a hint of joviality into his tone and gestured in the direction of Augee, whose hulking body took up a substantial part of the set of wide marble steps. "I suppose you have all been informed as to who this charming fellow is."

The biggest cheer of the evening so far burst from the crowd, and Augee stirred from his state of restful drowsiness as he realized that he was the focus of the attention.

"Yes, my dear people," the king went on. "This is Augee, the miracle to whom we are so indebted. Like our new friend, Suma, he is not of our people or of our world; yet, like Suma, he selflessly assisted us in our time of need, and it is true that Augee has shown us that miracles do occur."

At that moment, King Benjamin turned and approached Augee, and the crowd gasped in disbelief as the king lowered his head and planted an appreciative kiss on Augee's domed forehead. Taken by surprise, Augee responded with a confused, benevolent growl, and the congregation burst into congenial laughter.

Returning to his central position above the crowd, King Benjamin cleared his throat again and ushered to Nicholas to join his side.

The monarch spoke, softly and assertively:

"My friends, when we speak of the characteristics that best define the Hohalian spirit, we think of words such as bravery, generosity, virtue, intelligence, creativity, perseverance, and above all, faith. These are the traits that we all strive to achieve, and they are attributes that set our race apart from peoples such as the Volcarons who wrought such misery and destruction. But I tell you now, if there has ever existed a man of Hohala that embodied all of these precious qualities, it is the man that I present to you now. Nicholas Stone has endured the most testing of ordeals and battled through trials of both the body and the mind in order to protect and provide for our people. His deeds are too numerous and too fantastic for this old man to do justice to this evening. But let me tell you now, Nicholas is a hero, a martyr, and is, indeed, the consummate Hohalian. He is a living legend and a man who will be immortalized in the annals of our people."

Nicholas listened, wide-eyed, at the king's profuse tribute, and he smiled nervously as the ruler reached out and lifted his arm.

"The heroic deeds of Nicholas Stone will be told many a time this night and by Hohalian firesides for many years to come. Please, all of you, take this moment to show your appreciation for the immense efforts that he has made in our name."

At this, there was a deafening din as an almighty clamour broke out among the crowd. Some applauded, some roared in elation, and all smiled gratefully in the direction of the man who had, for so many years of his life, considered himself an outcast and unworthy of his place among his own people. Although Nicholas had never really been of a sentimental disposition, he was surprised to find himself overtaken by the emotion of the moment, and he dropped his forehead as he felt a tear creep from beneath his eyelid. As he turned his head to avoid the gaze of the euphoric crowd, he saw Caralisa smiling at him with joyful tears of her own streaming down her cheeks. Feeling a sense of obligation, he took Suma's lead and simply waved at the crowd before mouthing a silent "Thank you" and stepping back in line with Caralisa and the others.

"There is one more offering of thanks that we must give before the celebrations continue," interrupted the king. The crowd hushed in wonderment as to who the king referred. "For five years, I implored you, my friends, to retain your faith in the blessed Nexus and to believe—to *really* believe, as I did—that the gods were directing us in unknown and mysterious ways, and that we would soon be released from our time of trial. Our faith in the Nexus has been rewarded at last. The gods have delivered us safely from exile and shown us that we were justified in remaining patient while their mysterious will was done. Tonight, we realized that all this time—despite the challenges that we faced over those five years—we were being lovingly guided and protected by the benevolent Nexus. Let us now pray together in gratitude."

The king then lifted his hands to the sky and closed his eyes. However, as he opened his mouth to speak, a voice of dissent rose unexpectedly from the front of the crowd.

"The Nexus is a fraud," shouted Hamar, his neck still bandaged over the wound he'd received during the king's disastrous attempt at a truce with the Volcarons.

Commotion stirred among the Hohalians at the heated outburst, and looks of incredulity were exchanged between Nicholas, Caralisa, and Lawson.

"What?" snapped King Benjamin, stunned at the interruption.

"The Nexus abandoned us in our time of need," denounced Hamar at an angry shout. "Where was that divine protection when the Volcarons were slaughtering the innocent men of Haven? Ten lives were lost that evening. Thirty more were taken captive by the enemy and imprisoned in the cruellest conditions. One of those prisoners was also beaten and stabbed to death at Morgoratt's command. All because of *your* stubborn obsession with a divine power that abandoned us long ago."

Hamar then turned to face the rest of the silenced crowd.

"You can choose to be led like foolish sheep," he declared passionately. "But before you blindly follow the misguided nonsense that we have heard from our king tonight, remember the faces of those eleven innocents that were guided to their doom by a lie."

Hamar folded his arms defiantly as he spoke the last scathing words of his accusation. A tense silence filled grounds of the palace as the Hohalians waited with bated breath for the king's response. The monarch, frozen in disbelief at the obtrusive interruption, glared furiously at Hamar, the mood of the evening irrevocably altered.

45

CARALISA GENTLY SQUEEZED the tips of Nicholas's fingers. She had a knowing, mischievous glint in her eye that caused his heart to flutter. A heated public exchange had gotten underway as King Benjamin and Hamar deliberated as to whether or not the former's outspoken comments constituted blasphemy and disloyalty. While the gathered Hohalians had been stunned initially by Hamar's outburst, after a quarter of an hour of vociferous debate on dogma and scripture between the pair, the mirth-seeking crowd had begun to slowly trickle out of the grounds of the royal mansion in search of further revelry—an anti-climactic conclusion to the king's momentous address.

Nicholas looked to his left to see Suma crouched by Augee's side, having by this stage detached himself from the king and Hamar's increasingly tiresome discussion. Captivated by the sheer otherworldliness of Augee, the inquisitive Volcaron was absorbed in a one-way conversation about Augee's origins, the main points to which Augee responded to by nodding his head or growling in affirmative response. With the attentions of everyone around them preoccupied, it was the perfect opportunity for a discreet exit. Catching Caralisa's impish insinuation, Nicholas pressed gently against the skin on her palms before approaching Suma discreetly. After a few brief words in his ear, Suma gave Nicholas a nod of his head and patted Augee on the back.

The princess glanced at Nicholas coyly, and her cheeks flushed slightly as she smiled. Taking a moment to throw a furtive glimpse around him, Nicholas grabbed Caralisa's hand, and the two slipped around to the back of the mansion. As they turned the corner that led to what once was the royal family's private garden, Nicholas reached his arm around the princess's bare, delicate shoulders, to which she responded by resting her head softly on his shoulder. Together, they walked quietly through the garden in the dusk light amid the peaceful chirp of crickets and the lightly perfumed air. The discreetly positioned gateway that led from the palace grounds to a beach trail was obscured by out-buildings and overgrown foliage, and the balmy, evening breeze made for a most pleasant meander along the path that they'd walked together often in their youth. Silence hung in the air between the two, and while they spoke little as they traipsed along the sandy path in a tight embrace, there was no awkwardness or discomfort between them. The chasm of separation that had intruded on their relationship for five years seemed to have been dispelled along with the Volcarons, and, in the honey-suckled night air, it felt as if they had seamlessly picked up from where they'd left off. The connection they felt in that moment went beyond spoken words, transcending casual talk.

As they turned the corner around the ruined shell of a stone farmhouse, the path widened to greet the sweeping coastline. The beach was bathed in a honey-tinged light, and the whisper of the silver waves drifted on the breeze. Softly rounded sand dunes sloped nearby to the secluded entrance to the seafront, and removing their sandals, Nicholas and Caralisa tiptoed barefoot across the silky beach. Upon reaching one of the more obscured sand embankments, Nicholas removed the linen robe that covered his shoulders and spread it across the sand. Caralisa smiled at him shyly as he made an exaggerated, chivalrous gesture with his hand, and the princess lowered herself comfortably onto the makeshift blanket. Reaching his arm around her once again, Nicholas sat next to her and breathed in the ocean sunset.

"Looks like we made it," smiled Nicholas warmly, his eyes fixed on the glimmering Bay of Hohala. "Today seemed very far off not too long ago."

"Yeah," agreed Caralisa thoughtfully, nuzzling her head closer to his neck, but after a pause, he felt her eyes look up at him. "For a long time, I thought you'd given up...on us."

Nicholas drew back slightly and locked eyes with her. His smile hardened, and he felt a strange pang in his chest that he struggled to decipher. Sliding his hand down the smooth skin of her arm, he looked at her intently and tangled his fingers in hers.

"I never gave up, Caralisa," he told her tenderly, but firmly. "Our circumstances, your father's insistence on surrendering our home, the harshness of life in the mountains—all of these things that were beyond our control—were what separated us. During those five years, there wasn't a single day that I didn't close my eyes and remember the days we walked together on this beach. The day we came down here with Nightshade and you kissed me in the sand…you have no idea how many times I lay awake in that cold, dark cabin and felt comforted by that thought."

Caralisa's eyes searched his face in reply as he went on.

"In those five years," continued Nicholas in a subdued tone, "I felt completely detached from the rest of the people. I felt ashamed, believing that I was a sinner, unworthy to be part of Hohala. Numerous times I seriously wondered to myself if it would be best if I was to just leave these shores for good in the hope of finding somewhere else in the world that I might belong. On several occasions I really was close to doing so. But…"

Nicholas paused momentarily.

"What?" urged Caralisa.

Nicholas raised his eyes to hers once more.

"I settled in Haven so that I could be near you; I stayed there so that I could be sure you were safe and had what you needed to survive. I watched you from the hilltop every morning as you walked the path down to the Eternal Stream with food for your father."

Once more, he paused before continuing.

"I stayed there for five years in the slight hope that, maybe, one day we might be able to continue from where we left off…"

She stared at him in surprise, for the first time realizing that their separation had been to their mutual heartbreak. And in that moment, Caralisa once again saw the face of the younger, more innocent Nicholas she'd once fallen in love with behind the hardened visage before her. She cleared her throat to stifle the fact that her eyes had begun to water at the corners.

"I…felt the same," she stuttered. "It just seemed so impossible, because of my father's insistences you couldn't live in our company…in my company."

Nicholas looked thoroughly at Caralisa, her eyes shining with honesty. His mind raced at the thought of the wasted years he had spent pining for the princess from afar while all the time she had felt just as frustrated.

Eventually, he sighed and then planted a tender kiss on Caralisa's forehead. He cracked a smile, attempting to break the tension that hung in the air.

"Seems like we need to work on our communication," Nicholas chuckled.

Caralisa grinned as she rested her head against his. For a brief spell, they sat in thoughtful silence, each mulling the revelation that they had just shared against the context of the newfound liberation of their people. To both, the path ahead seemed open and unrestricted and the notion of their future together was an unspoken but mutually understood ambition.

"Do you think the Volcarons are really gone for good?" Caralisa asked all of a sudden.

Nicholas bristled at the unexpected question.

"Are you worried that they'll return?" he replied, drawing back to look at her.

"I mean, I know that you said that you and Augee drove them away," she stammered, as if she had been holding back on sharing her fears with him until now. "But I just can't help wondering if Morgoratt might regroup and come back to Hohala. You know how ruthless he is and how inept the Volcarons are at providing for themselves. As Suma told us, Morgoratt promised the Volcarons that their future would be secured by enslaving us. They believed him, and now that they've been banished from the place they called home for five years, he might have no choice but to come back for revenge. There are going to be a lot of angry, disillusioned Volcarons right now. As I said, I'm just really afraid that…"

"Caralisa," interrupted Nicholas, placing his hand softly on her shoulder. "I promise you, Augee and I will do our best to ensure that never happens. I told you how easily we drove them away. They fled with their tails between their legs. The poor bastards had no idea what was happening to them. I doubt very much if Morgoratt would be foolish enough to come back this way."

"I know," Caralisa frowned. "I'm just so afraid that we mightn't have seen the last of them."

"As I said," replied Nicholas. "Augee and I will make it our job to protect Hohala. We'll do daily checks across the bay, and if there was even a *hint* that the Volcarons were coming back this way, we'd quickly put that idea out of their heads."

Caralisa pursed her lips in reluctant acceptance and wove her fingers into his once more.

"You know," she quipped, switching the subject in a mischievous tone. "My father has mentioned, now that we're finally home, he'd like me to find a suitor sooner rather than later. He's never spoken to me about that subject before, and then all of a sudden you come along and save the day…"

She nudged him playfully as she made her less-than-veiled insinuation.

"Well," responded Nicholas with feigned coolness. "You know I'd be happy to take on that *burden*, but we'd have to ask Augee's permission, of course…"

Caralisa slapped him gently on the top of the head.

"I think I can get along okay with Augee," she smiled affectionately, her eyes locked on his.

"Sounds like a plan," whispered Nicholas with a grin that caused the princess's pulse to race.

With that, Nicholas lifted his hand to Caralisa's chin and brought his lips softly toward hers. They embraced longingly, the princess reaching her hand around the back of his head and passionately pressing his face closer to hers. Wrapping his arms around her shoulders, Nicholas drew her body closer, and they collapsed on the soft sand in loving, grateful unison.

46

THE DEAD SILENCE of the barren shore, strewn with the skeletal remains of both flora and fauna, was broken by the sound of anguished cries and exhausted coughing. In the evening light, the battered rowboats and rough-shod rafts were tossed uncaringly toward land, their occupants soaked and hysterical. Clambering across one another, the Volcarons tore in fearful panic through the freezing water and onto the beach. The tide was coming in, and the spiteful waves carried them right up to the backshore where men and women collapsed and broke down in distress. A small handful of men assisted some of the women and their sobbing children ashore, while most—concerned with self-preservation—jostled each other out of the way in order to reach the respite of the land. By the arid dunes along the upper reaches of the beach, they lay strewn about the sand, some arguing while the rest attempted to take stock of the dramatic turn of events that had so abruptly led to their expulsion from Hohala.

They had drifted east for days before finally reaching the only other place that they had known as home, and, in the grey twilight, it seemed little had changed in the five years since they had left. The scent of stale wood and rotting matter drifted on the biting wind—a pungent, familiar odor that already clung to skin, hair, and saturated clothing. The coastline, rugged and lightless, appeared to be absent of all life and was cloaked in a dispiriting ambience that was nightmarish in its familiarity.

With darkness setting in across the island of Volcaron, chaotic attempts were made by its returning natives to locate family members separated during the tumultuous sea journey. Wails of mothers searching desperately for their children coalesced with the oceanic roar to create a maelstrom that distorted the senses and laid further siege to struggle-weary bodies.

In the middle of the anarchy, Morgoratt crouched silently in the sand. Saturated and seething, he knelt forward with his forehead on the ground, and pressed his fists into the sludge. His teeth churned against each other, and murderous thoughts tore violently through his head. During the course of the torturous sea journey, his mind had smoldered over his people's punishing eviction from Hohala. His body was aching and injured; his pride and dignity even more so.

With his legs quivering under the weight of his body, he staggered wearily into a standing position. The screams for help directed at him from all sides by pleading Volcarons met his ears as muffled, inconsequential humdrum. As he attempted to steady himself, one middle-aged woman, bawling and distraught, confronted him in a hysterical state. Without warning, a slick crack sounded as Morgoratt's fist struck her hard under her jaw. The woman's body was propelled backward, and she hit the ground with an impact that caused her to bounce once before slumping onto the wet sand.

As the other men and women in the vicinity looked on in stunned silence, Morgoratt lifted his fist to his face to see the blood gathering around his knuckles. For the first time, he was taken aback to notice a seeping wound running the length of his right arm. A barbed tangle of pinkish coral had tangled itself around his forearm, and the skin around the injury was tinged a dangerous shade of purple. With a single twisting motion, Morgoratt used his left hand to wrench the embedded tubers from his skin, sending a violent spray of blood across the sand. He emitted no whimper or groan of pain, such was the Volcaron leader's vexation. With the spiked coral hanging from his blood-drenched fist, Morgoratt strode across the beach in the direction of the tumbledown village where his modest, former home was located. A thousand Volcaron eyes watched his sullen form skulk into the darkness beyond the beach, none daring to approach him or draw his attention.

Even in the dusk light, Morgoratt easily recalled the winding pathway to where his old cottage stood. The once visible trail was thickly overgrown from five years of disuse, but he navigated the treacherous path instinctively. His wounded arm throbbed and bled, but the severe pain barely registered in his consciousness. Purpose and vengeance were his sole emotions; pain and consequence were but wasteful distractions.

Within a grove of gnarled, deciduous trees—deformed at unnatural angles from scarcity of sunlight—the village stood in lonely disrepair. The grey stone huts were moss-covered, and the once thatched roofs were now sunken in and rotten. Several feet of dense grass and weeds carpeted the ground, undisturbed by the feet of man in a half decade. The air was still, and the place deathly quiet, save for the intermittent screams of Morgoratt's traumatized countrymen and women in the distance. He moved silently and intently to where a larger, somewhat more elaborate stone cottage was situated. For a moment, he stood quietly and surveyed the corroded ruins of the building where he had grown up. It had been the homestead of his family and their ancestors before them. As an adult, Morgoratt had assumed ownership, and it was there that he had spent the years dreaming and speculating to himself about the great things that he would achieve. The modesty of the place had acted as a foil to his ambitions—its humble size serving to fuel his thirst for grandeur.

As he surveyed the front façade of the oblong hut, ghosts of the past filled his mind—in particular, recollections of his embittered, old grandfather who had filled his young mind with fantastic tales of their familial ancestors' exploits—in particular, those of Morgoratt's great-great-grandfather—on the high seas. He remembered vividly the decrepit old man's rasping voice as he whispered hateful, poisonous ideas of conquest and supremacy in the young Morgoratt's ear. He'd told of how his great-great-grandfather had ravaged countless foreign settlements, and how he had forced "weaker" races to submit to his will. As he'd grown into adolescence, and the old man had become ever more raving with age, Morgoratt became obsessed with the idea of emulating his great-great-grandfather's exploits. When, as a sixteen-year-old, he'd stood by his grandfather's deathbed, Morgoratt had listened, fixated, as the ailing patriarch gripped his hand and whispered to him about the existence of a land of tremendous bounty far across the western ocean. His final words to Morgoratt had been an insistence that the youngster seek out that fabled country and restore the imperial pride of the Volcaron nation. As Morgoratt had nodded his head in solemn agreement, his grand-father had pointed in the direction of an unassuming wooden crate that had served as a footrest for as long as Morgoratt could remember. With that, the old man closed his hate-filled eyes and breathed his last. Yet, while his aged body had given out, his vindictive spirit remained, entrenched deeply in the impressionable mind of his grandson. Morgoratt had used a rock to smash open the wooden crate, inside of which he'd uncovered the rolls of ancient parchment that sketched a sea path toward a land called Hohala. From that moment, the notion of leading his people to untold wealth in a far-off land became an immutable calling that haunted him night and day.

Now, in the gloom of the place of that childhood, he seethed at the thought of his own failure to establish a permanent, dominant order in Hohala. To have been caught unguarded infuriated him; that the balance of power had been tipped the way of his adversaries by a flying beast of such power caused his mind to fume. Ultimately, however, it was the knowledge that one of his own had betrayed him that now ignited a desire to unleash the brutal weight of his vengeance upon the world.

"Sir!" came an eager salute from behind him.

Morgoratt turned with disinterest, his eyes bloodshot and glazed and his mouth expressionless.

"What's going on, sir?" asserted the youthful voice a second time.

Morgoratt's eyes strained in the paltry moonlight, and he saw that the voice belonged to Groger, the young man who had previously alerted him to the whereabouts of the Hohalians' in the western highlands. He found the boy to be a slothful buffoon but had praised him highly in public, and since then, Groger had done his utmost to endear himself to the Volcaron leader.

"Sir!" attempted the insistent youth again. "The others are fighting among themselves. There's been a few that have been badly injured. One of the chieftain's head was split open and…"

"Quiet," hissed Morgoratt.

Groger stood in awkward silence, his limited intelligence failing to ascertain the appropriate reply. A stifled scream sounded from the direction of the beach, causing the younger man to turn instinctively in its direction.

"Anarchy has infected our people once again, it would seem," mused Morgoratt in a flighty tone that made Groger feel uneasy. "Not for the first time, the Volcaron race degenerates into chaos and mindless disorder."

Groger stared blankly and gave no response.

"We were so close, Groger," continued Morgoratt, staring absently at the starless, black sky. "Had it not been for that accursed, winged monster, we'd have ensured the dominance of our people for generations."

"We can do it again!" simpered the young man, desperate to please. "We have to find a way to kill the beast; then we can enslave the Hohalians and take back country. We just need someone who can build a weapon powerful enough to take it out of the sky. If only Suma was still here—*he'd* know how to build something like that."

Morgoratt's attention was suddenly grasped by the boy's words.

"Suma is not here?" he demanded sharply, spinning around to face Groger with a baleful scowl.

"No," replied the young man. "We lost him when the dragon attacked us back at the king's mansion—I mean, *your* mansion. When we all ran for the beach, Suma stayed behind. I thought it was weird at the time that he didn't run for cover like the rest of us, but I just figured he knew something about dragons that we didn't. He's very smart, you know."

Morgoratt deliberated on Groger's words in silence for a few moments. His mind raced back to the afternoon of the attack by the beast, and, for the first time, it dawned on him that he had indeed not seen Suma since then. Not once had he noted the engineer's presence in the days that the Volcaron flotilla had spent drifting across the sea. A sobering realization smoldered in Morgoratt's mind, and his angry disenchantment gave way to vengeful bloodlust.

After about a minute of murderous ruminating, Morgoratt became aware once more of the presence of Groger who had watched his leader's face contort as he spoke about Suma's disappearance. Composing himself, Morgoratt forced a thin smirk and turned his stare to the young man.

"I think you're right, Groger," he declared with feigned enthusiasm. "I think it has been a travesty to discover that we may have left one of our most skilled and talented men to the mercy of our enemy."

Groger eyed Morgoratt skeptically but nodded his head obediently.

"Yes, I do think that it is our responsibility as loyal Volcarons to ensure none of our people are left behind," Morgoratt went on. "Suma needs our help, so let's find him and show him that his important role in all of this has not gone unnoticed."

"That sounds good to me," responded Groger unassumingly. "I'm sure he'd be shocked to see us come all the way back there to find him, though."

"Indeed," mumbled Morgoratt to himself before returning his attention to the youth. "Go back now to the beach and build a fire. Get the people warm and see if you can find some source of food. There will be much work to do soon."

"Yes, sir!" replied Groger eagerly before bowing and jogging back toward the jungle trail.

Alone with his thoughts, Morgoratt strolled around to the back of his old family home where there lay a small allotment of grassy land, marginally less overgrown than the rest of the copse. Dotted throughout the small plot were around a dozen headstones that had been chiseled carelessly into shape. In the settled darkness, Morgoratt slouched toward one of the furthermost headstones that stood half-smothered by a contortion of briars. Stopping in front of the grave marker, Morgoratt thought of his old grandfather lying ignorant and indifferent beneath the stony, grey Volcaron soil.

"I wish I had you here now," he murmured under his breath.

For a moment, Morgoratt stood in thoughtful silence before suddenly shifting his weight and delivering a thumping kick to the decayed headstone, causing it to split and break into two chunks. Before turning away, Morgoratt spat on the crumbling remnants of his grandfather's gravestone and wished ill-rest upon his departed soul.

47

"CARALISA!" WHISPERED NICHOLAS as he shook the sleeping princess gently by her shoulder.

Her hair tousled about her head, Caralisa murmured sheepishly in response to Nicholas's light finger strokes, her mind still engulfed in the dream that was causing her to whimper in her sleep.

"Caralisa," he breathed a second time as he watched his lover wince again, her thoughts clearly unsettled. He squeezed her arm and the princess finally responded with a start. Amid the shadows of Caralisa's refurbished sleeping chamber at the royal mansion, she jerked her head from one side to the other, clearly disconcerted by the nature of her dream.

"Huh?" she mumbled in a worried tone, to which Nicholas responded by placing his broad arms around her.

"Sssh –it's okay," he soothed, stroking the princess's flushed cheek. "You've just had nightmare."

Suddenly, Nicholas felt her fingernails dig into the skin on his arm as she struggled to make sense of her abrupt wakening. By the moonlight that had exploited a crack in the curtains, he could see that she was wide-eyed and pale, and, despite the balmy night, her shoulders had begun to tremble. He held her closer and stroked her cheek reassuringly, feeling the moist tears that had seeped silently down her face.

"I can feel them," Caralisa trembled, causing Nicholas's ears to prick. "They're moving closer."

"Who?" questioned Nicholas, perplexed and eager to probe her further while her words were fresh. "Who's moving closer?"

Caralisa finally comprehended the reality of her surroundings, her eyes refocusing on Nicholas's concerned face and the frightened rigidness loosening from her body.

"Nicholas?" she gasped.

"Yes, it's just me," he soothed. "No one else is here."

"Oh, Nicholas," she sobbed, her exclamation followed by a deep sigh of relief as she allowed her limbs to relax. "I'm so glad you're here."

"Of course I am," he assuaged in a low tone. "I'm not going anywhere. There's nothing that can harm you anymore."

"I saw them," the princess quivered. "I saw them in the jungle; I heard them moving through the dark. They had malice in their hearts, and their words were full of hate."

"Who?" interrogated Nicholas, his worry and confusion manifesting as mild irritation in his voice. "Who did you see? You mean the Volcarons?"

Caralisa bit her lower lip, and she looked him in the eye and gave a solemn nod. "It was him –Morgoratt—and others. They were on their way back to Hohala."

"Caralisa," sighed Nicholas, attempting to stifle the exasperation in his tone. "You know that the Volcarons are gone for good. There's no way they would be stupid enough to come back. And in any case, Augee and I have been circling the bay every day for weeks now, and there's been no sign of them at all. Please, don't be worried. We're safe now."

"But you and Augee only scout the bay in the mornings and the evenings," she persisted, her eyes wild as a frightened bird's. "In my dream it was dark, and I saw them moving across the land, not the sea."

"Okay then," responded Nicholas. "If it makes you feel better, from now on we'll do a fly-over of the coastline and the village every night. In that way, we can be absolutely sure that there's no possibility of the Volcarons creeping up on us. Would that help to convince you that we're secure?"

The princess offered no response, and the fear in her expression showed no signs of abating.

"Caralisa?" persisted Nicholas with a sigh. "It was a nightmare. That's all. After what we've been through, it's natural to have bad dreams, to see things that bring the unwelcome memories back. I've had unpleasant dreams for five years, and I've seen things in my sleep that I wished that I could just forget."

"I didn't just see them, Nicholas," she shot back. "I *felt* them."

"Felt them, how?"

"I don't know how to explain it," she stuttered. "It was as if I could feel their—*his*—anger and hate. I could feel his eyes on me, and it was as if he was looking at me like he wanted to hurt me—like he wanted everything to burn."

"Caralisa…" Nicholas began. "Morgoratt's gone. Chances are he's been killed by one of his own for what happened to the Volcarons. He could very likely have drowned at sea. Who knows? But the idea that he is still alive—*and* has returned here without us knowing—really does sound…"

"What? Sounds what?" she rounded on him heatedly, shifting her weight to look directly at him. "Sounds crazy?"

"No, I didn't mean…" Nicholas began backtracking.

"Nicholas, I know what I felt, even if it was a dream," she vowed. "My heart told me that the Nexus is disturbed. I *did* feel something."

"Okay," he conceded. "Tomorrow, Augee and I will sweep the sky over the village, the bay and the mountains. We'll make sure there is not even a hint of the Volcarons anywhere to be seen."

"What about the jungle?" Caralisa pushed further. "You can't possibly inspect all the land that it covers from the air…"

"Then we'll send some of the men to scout the forests, if that makes you feel better," he interjected, his tiredness and impatience growing. "I'll have to speak to Suma about pulling a team of workers away from the restoration work for the day, but if it'll reassure you, then it's worth it."

Caralisa said nothing in response, her thoughts still lingering on the chilling content of her dream and her annoyance at Nicholas's scepticism.

"Hey," he persisted, his tone growing softer. "You shouldn't be worrying about things like this. It is mine and Augee's job, along with Hamar and the rest of the volunteers, to safeguard our home. We haven't let our guard down and there's been absolutely no indication that the Volcarons could return. Please, just trust me to do my job, and know that we're safe."

Nicholas paused for a moment before adding with a playful nudge to her shoulder, "Besides, you have plenty to be occupying your mind with besides Morgoratt and his sorry race. The whole of Hohala is full of excitement about the wedding. It's all they talk about these days, and what a great celebration it's going to be—not just for us—but for all of the people. It's no small thing for their beloved princess to tie the knot, as they say."

He winked at her before lightly planting a kiss on her hair-strewn forehead. Caralisa responded with a self-conscious grin and a kittenish glint in her eyes which gave Nicholas the confidence to lean back and draw her closer to him until she lay with her head on his chest.

"You know, my father has told me how proud he'll be to hand over his crown to you, eventually." Caralisa spoke up, changing the trajectory of the conversation. "He says that he sees a lot of his younger self in you."

"Really?" responded Nicholas in genuine surprise, given that his own wavering faith in the past had stood in stark contrast to the king's steadfast beliefs. "I mean, I knew King Benjamin was supportive of us getting married, but I didn't think that he would have so openly say such a thing, especially since things—for us all—are still, you know…*raw*."

Caralisa's eyes smiled up at him.

"He really did say that to me," she assured him. "He told me that he'd be proud to have you as his son and heir."

"Wow," replied Nicholas, exhaling silently and at length.

"Now, don't get too over-confident," the princess teased, turning her head and kissing him gently from his neck to his chin and then to his lips. "I'd be worried that your head might swell *too* big, and then our marriage portrait would be ruined."

Nicholas squeezed her warm shoulders affectionately as he chuckled good-humoredly.

"Speaking of," he remembered. "I was actually thinking of asking Suma if he would paint it, if you had no objection. You know how talented and artistic he is; I think he'd do a fine job. And, besides, it would be a great way of making him feel more like he belonged. It's a great honor, and there are few prouder legacies for an artist than to have their work preserved in the royal palace into the future. I'm sure Suma would be happy to do it."

"I like that idea," replied Caralisa, nuzzling her head closer to his. "I've gotten the impression sometimes that Suma has found it difficult to fully integrate into the community. I think he finds it difficult to consider himself anything but different to the Hohalians, even though everyone has been so welcoming to him. Maybe being commissioned to create something as important as the royal wedding portrait will help him feel more at home here."

"I hope so," agreed Nicholas. "If Suma, out of all of us, can move on from the trauma of the past five years, then it looks like we can all share a beautiful future."

As Caralisa's arms tighten around him, Nicholas's eyes hungrily ran the length of her curved form.

"Speaking of beautiful…" he declared after a moment's pause, his tone dropping to a mischievous whisper as he brought his hand slowly to rest on her hip.

Sensing the meaning in his touch, the princess caught his eye with a flirtatious glance before raising her lips tantalizingly toward his.

48

THE CLEAR SEA water, cool and soothing on his skin, sparkled in the bright afternoon light as Suma drifted limply on the current. The day was heavy and humid, and he had daydreamed since early morning about immersing himself in the invigorating waters of the bay. After a taxing morning of directing various rebuilding and restoration projects in the village, he was weary of trivial talk and longed for the solitude of the obscured cove where he could be alone with his thoughts.

Suma had been welcomed wholeheartedly by the Hohalians who were at pains to demonstrate their sincere gratitude to him. For two weeks now, he had been showered with gestures of goodwill in the form of food, social invitations and general well-wishes. A comfortable cottage with an attached work shed, located on the outskirts of the village, had been gifted to him by King Benjamin, and he was visited daily by local women who offered to do chores from cooking and cleaning to washing and gardening. In the evenings, some of the Hohalian men would even call to his door with offers to play sports or join them in drinking sessions. The hospitality that he had received since the expulsion of the Volcarons had been indeed wonderful.

And yet, Suma was by nature a deeply private person, and it was with more than a hint of melancholy that, despite the warmth and generosity of the Hohalians, he acknowledged that, ultimately, he was not one of them. He felt distance from their celebrations; their religion—such a fundamental aspect of their lives and community—did not speak to him, and having been brought up in a society that placed little emphasis on spirituality, he struggled to relate to many of their philosophies. And finally, while the Hohalians had done their utmost to make him feel included in their society, he felt the sense of a tight community to be smothering. That afternoon, however, alone in the comfortable solitude of the lagoon, Suma felt a rare sense of contentment. Bathed in the soothing warmth of the sun and surrounded by the pleasant coolness of the water, he closed his eyes and allowed sleep to overtake his senses.

A sudden, violent grip seized Suma by the neck, and he was wrenched aggressively from his slumber. To his panic, he found himself unable to breath, and he realized he was being held under the water. Suma trashed his arms wildly in an attempt to break free, and his cries of alarm met his ears as muffled growls. Through the blur of the water, he looked up to see the outline of a sizeable figure in black. He tried frantically to punch and kick out at his assailant, but the powerful grip around his neck prevented him from making contact. For what seemed to him like an age, Suma remained submerged and, eventually, he found himself reconciling with the prospect that his time was at an end. However, just as his vision began to darken over, he felt himself being hauled upward by the hair. As his head emerged from beneath the surface, he gasped and choked in panic to catch his breath. His lungs continued to heave as he felt the impact of punches to his face and chest, and he began to drift helplessly into unconsciousness.

When he woke, Suma found himself lying on dry ground. His upper body throbbed painfully all over, and he found it difficult to open his right eye. As he coughed to regain his breath, he became aware of the presence of others around him. Wincing in pain, he managed to widen his left eye, and he could make out the blurred outlines of several figures standing over him.

"Hello, Suma," rasped a familiar, mocking voice that caused his blood to run cold.

As his vision refocused, Suma recognized Morgoratt's burly form towering over him. He cursed in rage and attempted to spring to his feet, but he was thrust immediately to the ground by the oppressive sole of the Volcaron leader's boot.

"Lie down, you filthy rat," hissed Morgoratt venomously.

Powerless to move, Suma's eyes flitted all around him, and he observed Groger along with two of Morgoratt's chieftains and a number of younger

Volcaron men standing shoulder to shoulder with malicious, jeering expressions on their faces.

"How was the water?" queried Morgoratt spitefully, before administering a kick to Suma's groin that caused him to gasp out in pain.

"Get this traitor up," he snarled at the others.

A flurry of hands seized Suma by his bare arms and hoisted him to his knees. As his mind struggled to comprehend the situation, he spat blood from his mouth and realized that his front teeth were jagged and broken. With his hulking upper body obscuring the light from the afternoon sun, Morgoratt stared down hatefully at Suma, his mouth and nose twisted into a sneer that would normally be reserved for some repugnant odour.

"So, this is what a man of treachery looks like," he snarled. "*This* is the face of a rodent who would deceive and forsake his own race; the face of a fool who will very soon understand the consequences of his treason."

Suma offered no response, other than to return Morgoratt's hateful glare.

"Did you think that your betrayal would go without consequences?" Morgoratt resumed icily. "I had always thought of you as an intelligent man, Suma. How wrong I was."

"Don't waste your breath," scoffed Suma defiantly, and tilting his head to expose his neck, he challenged, "Go on. You want to cut my throat? Then do it, and spare us all your bluster."

Morgoratt's lips pursed into a thin smirk as his ash-grey pupils burned into Suma.

"Don't be so naïve to think that I'd grant you the respite of a quick death," he spat contemptuously before stamping the heel of his boot down on Suma's hand that lay open. The big man yelled out in agony as he felt one of his middle fingers crack at the knuckle.

"That's only the start of it if you persist with your insubordination," he continued threateningly. "Now, get to your feet and walk as you're told."

"You're a rotten bastard!" growled Suma, resigning himself to meeting his end. "I'm going nowhere with you. You're going to kill me anyway, so why would I bother to follow you anywhere?"

Morgoratt gave a brief, malevolent chuckle.

"Oh, filthy deceiver," he laughed. "That dexterous mind of yours is what is sparing you temporarily from a most excruciating death. And that will come, I promise you; but for now, I have a use for you. Our people have lost their home because of you, and now you are going to ensure that it's returned to us."

Suma snorted in scornful defiance.

"Are you really that deluded that you think I'm going to help you in any way?" he retorted. "I'd rather a slow, painful death than to know I helped you further. My soul is already blackened by my participation in your foul plans; there's nothing you can do to me that will make me cooperate."

Morgoratt stared at him in thoughtful silence before responding in a low tone.

"I thought as much," he muttered coldly.

Before Suma could respond, the Volcaron leader drew a dagger from beneath his cloak, and with a movement that would be lost in the blink of an eye, he turned and swiped the blade through the air. Suma's eyes widened in horror as a torrent of blood sprayed from a gaping wound in the neck of one of the young Volcarons standing around the tense scene. Spluttering and grasping at his throat, the boy fell to his knees in anguish before dropping lifelessly to the ground.

Suma stared in disbelief, the words of contempt that he wished to hurl at Morgoratt strangled in his throat.

"Is this what you want!" thundered Morgoratt, grabbing a second boy from the group of young soldiers, who all stood watching with pale, terrified faces. "Do you want more blood on your hands? Is that what it will take for you to submit?"

At that, the Volcaron leader raised the blade to the whimpering youth's throat, and drew in his breath in lustful anticipation.

"No, wait!" bellowed Suma desperately.

A heinous, triumphant smile crept across Morgoratt's face.

"I figured as much," he sneered. "Now get to your feet, and move as you're told. Your homecoming to Volcaron is much anticipated."

As he was dragged to his feet, Suma dropped his head defeatedly, dejected at his own helplessness. As one of the Volcaron fighters shoved him roughly in the direction of the jungle, Suma took a final, devastated look at the slumped corpse of the young soldier, the amber sand around him stained deep and red.

49

A RISING GLOW that penetrated through a ceiling crack in the dank, subterranean holding cell told Suma that his incarceration had lingered into a fourth day. He was weak and undernourished, and the severe dampness in the air seeped through his pores, causing his chest to wheeze and his muscles to tighten painfully. In the dark recesses of the chamber, he heard the incessant scurry of rodents, and he fought constantly against the temptation of sleep for fear the hungry vermin might take advantage of his lowered guard. He was exhausted, having not slept in days, and was growing delirious from starvation and lack of sunlight. The putrid stench of death wafted throughout the cell as the slain remains of three more unfortunate, young Volcarons lay around him in the early stages of decomposition, and he listened in repulsion and anguish to the sporadic feeding frenzies undertaken by the voracious rat pack.

His senses dulled and his body weakened, Suma's emotions simmered in the darkness; hopelessness, helplessness, guilt, fear, and fury all melded together in a tempest of mental torment that caused the naturally dispassionate engineer to weep bitterly. However, the emotion that gnawed most at his ravaged disposition was that of hatred, cold and profuse. His heart had never before known such raw and uncompromising loathing as that which accompanied him in his dark and lonely prison.

Early on each of the three previous mornings since he'd been incarcerated, Suma had been visited by Morgoratt. On each occasion, the Volcaron leader had been accompanied by a different unfortunate, young man who had wept fearfully as the interrogation of Suma took place. On each occasion, Suma had remained steadfast and refused to cooperate with Morgoratt's plans. On each occasion, the throat of an unwitting young man had been slit by the Volcaron leader as retribution for Suma's silence. And on each occasion, the beating and torture that followed his observation of yet another brutal murder had led Suma's resilience to diminish further. The unfathomable cruelty that he had witnessed in recent days shook him to the core of his being, and, if not for the fact that his spirit held steadfastly to some shred of defiance in the face of Morgoratt's abominable conduct, he would have welcomed the soothing release of death long before now.

As with the mornings gone by, Suma reclined painfully against the damp dungeon wall as he waited in dreadful anticipation for the purposeful, ominous boot steps to descend the stone staircase that led to the underground chamber. Suma looked down in frustration, and through the gloom he could just about discern the outline of the thick cuffs that were connected to a length of weighty chain, which itself was attached to the opposite chamber wall. Since the first day of his incarceration, his engineer's mind had tried to identify a weak point in the shackles, and by now, his hands had struggled with such desperation that his wrists had become raw and bleeding from the abrasive edges of the cuffs. All over his body, slash wounds and bruises inflicted by his former comrades had become infected from exposure to the filth of the cell, and by the fourth morning of his imprisonment, both his body and mind screamed out in agony.

It wasn't long before the rusty creak of the trapdoor could be heard, followed seconds later by the crisp stomp of heavy boot soles on the cold, stone steps. Suma's limbs went rigid with foreboding, and his breath quickened as the heavy, wooden door was thrown open. Familiar lantern light filled the chamber, casting wicked shadows across the walls and sending the feasting rats scurrying into the unilluminated corners. In the dim light, Morgoratt's pale, bony visage and long, dishevelled hair ghosted into view, his eyes full of malice and spite. Suma watched in defiant silence as his captor produced a glinting dagger from underneath his cloak and proceeded to scrape the blade along the stone wall, the memory of its excruciating edge still fresh from the day before. As trepidation consumed him, his heartbeat increased, and he found himself praying to no one in particular to be relinquished from his torment.

"Another day, Suma," came the hushed, sneering voice in the dark. "I imagine you've gotten quite accustomed to your new surroundings by now."

Suma gave no reply, yet he hoped that his abhorring glare could be seen through the murkiness.

"I do say, my friend," continued Morgoratt as he prodded the bloodied remains of one of the young victims with his foot. "There's a fierce stench growing in here. I don't know how you stomach it all day and night."

Again, Suma said nothing as the sound of the Volcaron leader's footsteps moved closer toward him. Robed in black, he could see little of Morgoratt's frame, and it appeared as if his ghostly countenance was suspended before his eyes. As the face drew closer, Suma was filled with seething venom, the blemishes and imperfections on Morgoratt's skin appearing even more grotesque than he'd remembered.

"Have you given my proposal any further thought since yesterday?" inquired Morgoratt, his measured tone filled with jeering, feigned concern. "I do pity you, Suma, for putting yourself through such unnecessary pain just to protect those who are not of your kind and, if you're honest with yourself, who really don't care a damn for your wellbeing."

Suma swore belligerently in response, his voice lowered to an emphatic growl.

"You risked so much for so little," continued Morgoratt, the mock sincerity of his tone betrayed by the dark glint of derision in his eyes. "You really were a fool to think that you could forsake your own to protect such weak, feeble cowards from their inevitable fate."

"You're a sick, deluded bastard!" shot back Suma with as much vehemence as his fragile state would allow him to muster. "The Hohalians have more decency and strength than your sadistic mind could ever comprehend."

Morgoratt paused contemplatively for a moment, and even in the darkness, Suma could sense his demeanour shift away from his faux cordiality.

"Your words are those of an errant fool," Morgoratt hissed. "You know nothing of the laws of nature, of survival—of supremacy! You think that those craven weeds who seduced your impressionable mind are deserving of the riches and bounty that have been taken from us so unjustly? You think they have *earned* their wealth and comfort? And all the while, our race should simply accept the squalor that we've festered in for generations? Where is the justice in that? Why should the circumstances of our birth prohibit us from the riches of the world? No, Suma; *life* is unjust, and only those who are superior can rise above all others and achieve their rightful destiny."

"You're insane," choked Suma. "You think the Hohalians are weak, but they are the ones who survived on the side of a mountain for five years. They're the ones who had their homes stolen from them. And through all of that, they had the dignity not to react with cruelty or cowardly violence. They built Hohala and cultivated the land with hard work. Their prosperity is their reward. *You*, however, chose to plunder their wealth like a common thief. You show up on their shores with barbarians and brutes of your own making—idiot boys like Kreb and Groger—armed with knives and delusion, and you call that an achievement. No, Morgoratt, neither I nor the Hohalians are fools—the fools I see are you and your blind followers."

A solid crack filled the chamber as Morgoratt's boot caught Suma square in the stomach, and the big man rolled onto his side as he clutched his winded belly.

"You dare to speak to me in such a way!" Morgoratt roared in vexation, the spittle from his mouth spraying the wincing prisoner. "You treacherous ant! Let me tell you now that every fiber of my being is pleading my hand to slice you open alive and leave you down here for the vermin and parasites to feast on. If I had my wish, I'd ensure that you rotted down here in agony until the rats gnawed your worthless heart from your chest. And you know what? You'd be missed by no man or woman or child. Poor orphan Suma—whose legacy will be a sorry mound of bones that no person thought enough of to even shed a tear."

"Kill me then," retorted Suma defiantly. "Do it now. Listening to you spewing your hatred and stupidity day after day is as painful as any torture that you could inflict on me. Quit your pathetic posturing, and put me out of my misery."

Although he couldn't see his expression, Suma could tell from Morgoratt's heavy breathing that he had struck a nerve. He knew the retribution would be hard and painful, but he didn't care. He clutched his midriff defensively and waited for the inevitable knife stab or kick to the head. To his surprise, however, the blow never came, and he was unnerved to observe the chamber door swing open before Morgoratt's silhouette, standing at the bottom of the stairs, made a summoning gesture to a person above.

Moments later, the clunking of heavy chains met Suma's ears, and, for the fourth day, he felt a familiar sinking sensation.

"Please!" cried a terrified male voice from the passageway, the source still not visible from Suma's prostrate position on the dungeon floor. "I haven't done anything! Please, sir, no!"

"Shut your hole!" followed a gruff, uncompromising growl from above.

All of a sudden, a pained howl filled the chamber, immediately followed by the clatter of a person falling down the curving, stone staircase. A thin figure tumbled awkwardly into view, coming to a stop by the waiting Morgoratt's feet. The unfortunate individual—clearly yet another young male as far as Suma could make out from the boyish whimpering—was given little opportunity to gather himself up as the Volcaron leader gripped him by his hair and dragged him into a standing position.

"You remember this fellow, Suma?" queried Morgoratt.

Suma strained his eyes in silent dread, and to his despair, recognized the face of Quinn, one of the youths that had assisted him from time to time at his workshop back in Hohala.

"Tell him, Suma," mused Morgoratt, "About the fate of his three comrades who reside with you here in this wretched tomb."

Before Suma could even consider a response, Morgoratt raised his free arm aloft until the lantern light spread across the chamber and cast a dim blanket of light across the ravaged, bloodstained bodies that littered the ground.

"Please! Oh, please no!" screamed the boy terror-stricken. "I swear, I'll do anything. I'm begging you, don't hurt me."

"It's not my decision, boy" sighed Morgoratt disingenuously. "I am only doing what is necessary and best for our people. It's Suma here who is choosing the welfare of a foreign race over yours. It is his stubbornness, I am sorry to say, that has you in this very unfortunate situation. Only he can spare you from joining these three fellows you see before you."

"You're out of your mind!" roared Suma despairingly, hot, anger-filled tears welling in his eyes. "Just kill me; I'm not helping you. I'm not going to play any further part in your savagery. Let the boy go, and just cut my throat here and now."

"That's too easy," snickered Morgoratt devilishly.

Without a further word he set down the lantern, and to Suma's horror, he pulled the howling youngster by the hair and brought the knife down rapidly onto the boy's right hand. Quinn emitted a scream of agony that stabbed at Suma's soul as Morgoratt threw him to the ground, the youth's bloody, severed finger in his fist. His stare then turned to Suma, and a callous smirk crept across his face in the lamplight.

"Nine more to go," he smiled evilly. "Then we'll start on the toes. Which finger shall we go for next, Suma? I fancy a thumb this time."

Before Suma could respond, a sickening snap punctuated the darkness, followed by a second tortured squeal from the dungeon floor.

"Will we go for a third, Suma?" queried Morgoratt demonically, the knife primed for further blood. Once again, Suma was nauseated by the familiar chorus of snapping bone and pleading, agonized cries.

"Stop!" bellowed Suma frantically as he jostled wildly in vain to break free of his chains. "Please, he doesn't deserve this!"

"It's your decision, Suma," continued Morgoratt matter-of-factly as he prepared to sever a fourth finger from the hysterical youngster's hand.

"Enough!" roared Suma with a devastated sob in his throat. "I'll do it! I'll do whatever you bloody want!"

At that, the big man placed his face in his shackled hands and wept profuse, devastated tears. The knife clattered noisily to the ground as Morgoratt relinquished his grip, and the chamber was quiet, save for the anguished cries of the young, disfigured Quinn.

"I always said you were an intelligent man, Suma," mocked Morgoratt with poorly smothered glee. "It's so heartening to know that your talents won't go to waste after all."

Suma had no response.

"I'm going to give you a little more time to think things over," the Volcaron leader went on coldly. "And soon, we'll set you to the work that you are so uniquely expert at."

He paused for a moment before gesturing at the writhing form of Quinn at his feet:

"I'll leave him here to keep you company, and to remind you that there's plenty more of him that can be harvested for rat food, should you have a change of heart."

At that, Morgoratt flung his hand through the air, and something warm and moist smacked against Suma's face. Without another word, the

Volcaron leader turned on his heel and swept out of the chamber, slamming the wooden door dully behind him. Suma picked up the object that had struck him, and the sight of Quinn's dripping, severed thumb caused the blood to drain from his face. With the boy's relentless moans searing in his brain and Morgoratt's departing footsteps echoing in the distance, Suma closed his eyes and prayed hopelessly once more to a god that he felt no reason to believe in.

50

"ARE YOU FEELING alright, love?" asked Caralisa thoughtfully. "You've been quiet all evening. Is it nerves? Or are you having doubts?"

Nicholas sat in the corner of one of the master sleeping chambers in the royal mansion, plucking absent-mindedly at white specks of fluff that had accumulated on the violet-colored robe he was to wear the following day. It was the garment that the king himself had donned on the day he had taken Caralisa's mother as his wife and queen. She had been a beautiful bride, and the king was remembered as being as handsome as any Hohalian of his day. The unification of the young Prince Benjamin and his betrothed had been a celebration that stretched for five days and five nights and was talked about even to the present day. Caralisa had never known her mother, the young queen having passed away during a complicated childbirth; yet, the princess marvelled at her parents' exquisite wedding portrait which hung with pride in the mansion's atrium alongside the renderings of other royal couples from generations past. Tomorrow, she would dress herself in the elegant, golden dress robe and delicate veil, both of which her courtly-looking mother had adorned on the occasion of her wedding. Caralisa was excited, yet her anticipation on the eve of her own big occasion was tempered slightly by Nicholas's uncharacteristic silence throughout the previous day or two.

Shaken from the quietude of his thoughts by the princess's inquiry, Nicholas looked up at her and smiled, his eyes unable to disguise the faint melancholy in his expression. Her fingers rested supportively on his shoulder, and he reached back to squeeze them in warm reassurance.

"Yes, I'm fine," he replied quietly. "It's nothing important."

"There's something bothering you," Caralisa continued. "You've been reserved for most of the day. Everything is ready. Most of the preparations are done, and all that is required of us is to enjoy ourselves tomorrow and savor the occasion."

Nicholas smiled at her once more in return.

"I know," he sighed. "I'm really looking forward to tomorrow. It's just…"

"Just what?" she probed further, her tone becoming marginally irritated by the obscureness of his responses. "I wish you'd tell me what's on your mind. Is it something I've done? Is there something that you're not telling me?"

"Not at all," Nicholas replied, coiling his fingers tightly through hers. "I'm the happiest, luckiest man in Hohala, and the thought of marrying you tomorrow is like a dream about to come true."

Caralisa's hand returned his squeeze, but her expression was still one of frustration.

"But there's still something," she persisted in a flat tone.

Nicholas sighed.

"It's Suma," he admitted finally, his gaze averted to the floor.

"Oh, for the heavens' sake, Nicholas," replied Caralisa exasperatedly, releasing herself from his grip and throwing her arms into the air.

"Do you really have to dwell on this, still? Suma's been gone for over a month. *He* made the decision to disappear without telling anybody, and there's nothing we could've done to prevent it. You know he wasn't ever really at home here. We did everything we could to make him feel welcome and part of the community. Dear Nexus! My father even made him a citizen of Hohala. And then, for him to vanish off into the wilderness without informing anybody, well, it suggests to me that he never really wanted to belong in the first place."

Nicholas shook his head in quiet objection.

"I know the man," he sighed. "I simply can't understand why he would just disappear. Even after we asked him to paint the wedding portrait, which you know he told me he had begun the preparations for. It's not his way to abandon people or to let them down. I'm just…mystified."

"Nicholas," spoke Caralisa, her voice steely and firm with purpose. "For the last time; Suma is gone. He left without telling anybody. He clearly did not consider himself to be a big enough part of our community to stay. After all, he wasn't one of us. He's a Volcaron, and no matter how good a person is deep down, or how righteous their actions may seem, upbringing and blood do ultimately matter sometimes. Our ways are not his, and to be honest, I kind of understand his reasons for leaving."

Nicholas shook his head once more, convinced that Suma's sudden disappearance was due to more than the big man's awkwardness or lack of identification with the Hohalians. Tonight, however, as his bride-to-be stood before him, her hair combed beautifully in preparation for the following day, he decided that the time was not appropriate for extensive questioning about Suma's whereabouts.

"Maybe you're right," he conceded, eager to abandon his fretting and concentrate on sharing in the princess's bubbling anticipation for the big day ahead. He winked at Caralisa mischievously, eager to change the subject before she became further agitated. "I meant to tell you. One of your father's valets informed me that the bridal suite is looking very, very impressive. Apparently, it's been lavishly redecorated under the king's instruction… kind of a surprise. I reckon it's going to be difficult to hold back on paying it a visit before we're supposed to."

"You behave yourself until after tomorrow," she replied with a sheepish grin, nudging him gently with her elbow. "I do think it's going to be an unforgettable day, from beginning to end. I'm nervous, but looking forward to it. My father's so excited. He told me that our marriage will be his proudest moment as king, and he feels now that he can happily grow old knowing that we are worthy, responsible heirs to his throne."

Nicholas failed to hide the look of pride that glinted across his face. In the past—even during the early days of his courtship of Caralisa—he'd never genuinely fathomed the idea that that he might one day become king of Hohala. Needless to say, however, it was a daunting prospect, one that had caused him on numerous occasions to lie awake at night and fret to himself. It meant a lot to him to know that the king so keenly endorsed his betrothal to the princess, and, privately, he had made a solemn pledge to uphold all the responsibilities and values that came with that honor.

For the most part, his life to this point had been one marked by confusion, loneliness and, ironically, a hesitant sense of belonging to the community to whom he would eventually become monarch. It was a daunting prospect, and, still, he worried often about his own connection to the Nexus which he considered to be flimsy in comparison to the resolute devoutness of King Benjamin. Since the expulsion of the Volcarons from their shores, events had moved more quickly than he had anticipated, and, coupled with Suma's bizarre disappearance from the village, he found himself anxious, not that he shared those unsettled thoughts with Caralisa. Since the reclamation of Hohala, the princess had seemed so content and happy that to burden her with the uncertainty of his thoughts would be to cast a shadow over the sunny disposition that he loved and had found encouragement in during his times of unease.

Now, on the eve of his wedding, the most pressured moment of his young life, Nicholas took solace in the pearly smile of his wife-to-be and resolved to expel his worries until after the wedding celebrations. In Caralisa's eyes, he saw everything that he had ever wanted in his life—a beautiful woman, a kindred soul and a devoted friend. And in that moment, his thoughts turned to the only other true friend that he counted in his life.

"While you're finishing your preparations for tomorrow, I think I'll pay Augee a visit before he turns in for the night," Nicholas announced. "I've hardly seen him since this morning and I just want to make sure he feels as involved and important as he should."

"I think that's a great idea," replied the princess, kissing him lightly on the crown of his head. "Give him my love and tell him that we're all very excited to have him taking part in the ceremony."

"I will," agreed Nicholas, squeezing her arm. "I also want to do one final fly over the bay before the sun goes down, seeing as we won't have time to do so tomorrow before the ceremony and celebrations."

A fleeting glint of concern flashed across Caralisa's face. Nicholas, anticipating her reaction, immediately sought to alleviate her concerns.

"Please, Caralisa, don't worry," he assured. "It's just precautionary. It's been months since they left, and there's been no sight of them in all that time. The Volcarons have moved on. It just does no harm to survey the bay from time to time."

He paused for a moment before shooting her a grin and a wink.

"In any case, I also want to have a good look at that sunset, just so we can be sure the weather will be fine on the big day."

"Well, that *is* important," she laughed. "Sounds good to me. Just try not to be too long. My father really wants us to join him and Lawson for dinner and final prayers this evening. It would mean a lot to him."

"I'll be back shortly," promised Nicholas as he rose from the chair and kissed her a brief farewell.

*

Augee came in to land on the meticulously manicured lawn of the royal mansion. The grass was dew-covered and cool to his feet, and the abundance of floral decorations that had been lavishly festooned across the grounds had infused the twilit air with a most opulent aroma. An enormous bandstand and a vast reception area had been erected to accommodate the throng of excited Hohalians who would occupy the mansion grounds from early the next morning and through several days of festivities. The king's mansion itself had received extensive refurbishment and repair; the marble steps that led to the palace entrance were polished to perfection, and the gold-plated fixtures that adorned the roof and façade of the mansion seemed to take on the appearance of flames as they reflected the evening light. To Nicholas, the scene appeared as if it was holding its breath in expectation of a unique and dramatic event. With a deep intake of breath, he lowered himself down from Augee's back and took a moment to drink in his magnificently decorated surroundings. After a moment of quiet reflection upon past and present, he turned to Augee and beamed thankfully.

"We made it, Augee," he smiled. "We did it."

Augee, whose towering form cast an immense shadow over the land-scaped garden, gave an affirmative growl and nodded his head in agreement.

"You know how grateful we all are to you, don't you, Augee?" Nicholas went on. "Caralisa, King Benjamin, and I—all of the Hohalians—owe you more than we can ever hope to repay you."

Again, Augee nodded, his eyes averted humbly.

"I want to make you a promise," resumed Nicholas intently. "You have shown me and my people nothing but friendship, loyalty, and selflessness, and, seeing as tomorrow I am going to make a life commitment to Caralisa, I also want to make a commitment to you."

Augee's growl lowered to something resembling a purr as he listened curiously. Gripping one digit of his friend's enormous right claw in his fist, Nicholas raised his eyes to the sky and began to pray.

"As we stand here tonight, dear Nexus, I wish to offer sincere thanks to you for leading me to my great friend, Augee, and for bringing us and the Hohalians to salvation. Accept my words as a sign of my devotion and faith in your guidance. On the eve of my unification with the Hohalian princess, Caralisa, I ask you also to safeguard the bond that I share with my dear friend, Augee. You brought us together to fulfil your will and deliver the Hohalians from exile. Now, in better times, I implore you to grant us the gift of that bond of friendship into the future, and to tie our souls together as part of the divine Nexus. We—both Augee and I—entreat you, humbly and in earnest…"

At the conclusion of the prayer, Augee gave another low groan; this time, however, his tone sounded thoughtful, as if to concur with Nicholas's solemn petition. And, without warning, to their mutual surprise, the waking moon appeared suddenly from behind a wisp of clouds and the gardens became bathed in soft, silver light. Whether it was the moment of closeness that he'd just shared with Augee, or excitement for the coming day, or even the residue of exhilaration from the flight they'd just undertaken, Nicholas was not sure, but all of a sudden, he felt surrounded by the aurora of something special, intangible, and unexpected. As they stood together in the splendid, lunar light, Nicholas and Augee exchanged a knowing look that caused both of their hearts to smile, assured, as ever, of the unbreakable fortitude of their friendship.

51

AND SO, THE Volcarons rose up once more in weary unison, mocked by the dark expanse of ocean that for their haggard nation represented the divide between wealth and squalor; of pride and disgrace. In the breaking light of a harsh, new reality, their vengeful spirits were tantalized by the prospect of retribution and rampage.

Reinvigorated by a vindictive purpose—with the wound to their pride still stinging deeply—the Volcarons had planned heavily in order to cast off the uncertainty of chance. Galvanized by hate, loss, and experience, they were meticulous in their preparations. Across several months, their desperation and humiliation drove them—every man, woman, and child of work-able age—to forgo rest and to submit themselves entirely to their common cause of revenge. Under uncompromising surveillance, the weary people of Volcaron felled trees in the hundreds and forged tools and weapons from the remaining resources of the earth that they had not already laid waste to in the past. A fleet of sturdy boats were assembled, and the surrounding ocean—replenished of its fish stocks throughout five years of reprieve—was once more plundered voraciously to fuel the frenzied effort. Together, they labored like wild-eyed Trojans, uncharacteristically united in their imperious goal of reclaiming the ill-gotten bounty to which they'd grown accustomed over a half decade. For those few who complained or shirked their share of the toil, punishment was severe and public, justified under the premise of "the common good."

At the heart of it all was Morgoratt. His vitriol in the aftermath of their expulsion from Hohala had been fearsome and uncompromising—his zeal for revenge and reclamation so terrible that his disillusioned and devastated people felt they had little other option than to submit to his unbending decrees. It was heralded by Morgoratt as the true second coming of their nation—a moment of renewal and retaliation—and to his exhausted subjects, he quoted often the lines of verse, discovered among the yellowing parchments of his great-great-grandfather, that in his own youth had nourished the seed of unyielding ambition within him.

"Undaunted by the foes we face,
The superiority of our race
Ensures our noble history
Is marked by fearless victory.
Oppose us, and await a flood,
An ocean-deep of tears and blood.
All hail upon the rising dawn
The fatherland of Volcaron."

Daily, the fatigued hordes were coerced into delirious, unified renditions of the chant which Morgoratt was convinced would drive the work effort forward. As hard and uncompromising as a northern tundra, he pushed, threatened, and harried the people to work to the limits of their crippled spirits and famished bodies. There were almost daily deaths from exhaustion or accidents, while the ill-advised few who raised their voices in weary objection, more often than not, were not seen again the following day.

The one man who wished he could be counted among that ill-fated number released by death was Suma. His body decimated by torture and his soul ravaged by regret, he'd adhered under duress to the maniacal demands of the Volcaron leader by sharing his expertise in design and construction—a circumstance that had sharpened his bitter resentment. His sense of guilt, following the deaths of four innocent, young men and the savage mutilation of another as a result of his initial refusal to yield to Morgoratt's will had weakened his resolve and, despite his revulsion toward the leader's ultimate goal, he'd relented and undertaken the multitude of tasks that he'd been assigned. Outside of drawing up plans and directions for the building of boats, battle-axes, and daggers, Suma had been charged with the design of a unique and complex weapon that, as demanded by Morgoratt, would ensure their people of their triumph.

"The beast," as Morgoratt termed the infuriating creature, was deemed by the Volcaron leader to be the sole obstacle in the path to glory. Over the course of several months, haunted by a remorse that cleaved at his conscience like a blade, Suma invented a complex apparatus that he believed had the capability to eliminate the beast's aerial threat. The mechanism was elaborate and imposing, it's primary function to launch a torrent of boulders at rapid speed and then repeat the same strike in quick succession. The design incorporated two eighteen-foot-long tapered wooden whips, which were four inches in diameter and made from a particular species of tree that was distinctly flexible and durable. The fruit of Suma's unwilling labors was an armory of twelve painstakingly constructed catapults. They were towering contraptions, anchored to the ground by weighty and wide-set wooden bases with great wheels that trundled and grinded oppressively across the earth. On the end of an extensive hinge, along which the wooden whips were attached, a net of thick and sturdy rubber webbing that resembled a vast basket crowned each remarkable machine. With a series of pulleys and straps, teams of men could easily bend the strong, flexible whips down to the ground. Upon loading the boulders into the webbing, the whips could be released, and projectiles launched with devastating accuracy. And while the power of the machines' strikes was indeed ferocious, it was the rapidity and flexibility with which the devices could be reloaded, angled, and transported that demonstrated the extent of Suma's engineering genius.

Upon completion of the newly built jewels in the Volcarons' arsenal, Morgoratt's obsessive focus switched to ensuring that his soldiers were proficient in the operation of the catapults. Extensive training was provided for those men most physically capable of maneuvering the immense levers and muscle-wrenching hinges. Long days that stretched to weeks were given over to ensuring that there was no possible ambiguity as to the most effective methods of delivering lethally-accurate strikes to counter the agility of the Hohalians' winged protector. Overall, Morgoratt's preparations—from the retraining of his fighters in combat and arson to the instructing of his charges in methods of interrogation and torture—were meticulous and marked by a determination to leave nothing to chance. His patience was cool and measured, the necessity for calculated planning winning out over his festering lust for fire and blood.

It was not, however, the timeframe for training and preparations that dictated Morgoratt's ultimate determination as to the date they would make the voyage back to Hohala. To the Volcaron leader, a mere siege of the village was insufficient. So deeply ran the wound to his hubris, that he could not be consoled by the idea of bringing forth the hand of destruction alone; Morgoratt yearned for terror and misery—for tragedy in its most searing guise. Through the brutal torment of Suma's body and spirit, he'd eventually extracted the information that made the embers of his black heart flicker malignantly. The marriage of the Hohalian princess to the man that had caused him such grievous humiliation was the type of fateful occasion that his vindictive mind had thirsted for in the dark and solitary nighttime. On one unfortunate evening, a dazed and harrowed Suma—barely-lucid from the latest sadistic beating he'd endured—had mumbled under duress the date of the impending Hohalian wedding celebration through swollen, punctured lips. With his battered body barely clinging to consciousness, he'd divulged the details of the royal couple's nuptials, and Morgoratt had been practically ecstatic at the revelation.

On the night before his army's much-anticipated departure, as the riot-hungry Volcaron legion loitered along the coastline, and as a devastated Suma wept in dreadful expectation from his vermin-infested cell, Morgoratt sat in the darkness of his sleeping quarters—a dram of harsh moonshine in his fist—and visualized the hypnotic spectacle of a Hohala in flames. Drunkenly, he sneered to himself as his eyes wandered across the gold-tinged tumbler, the brooding glow of the fireplace glinting along its transparent edges. As his blood stirred with suspense and intoxication, overcome by the surge of violence in his veins, the Volcaron leader drank in deeply the remaining contents of the glass before flinging the container at the crackling hearth. A course shattering filled the glum silence of the cottage, and as the wayward droplets of the liquor hissed angrily among the coals, the remaining cinders were extinguished, and the firelight was overtaken by darkness.

52

ALONG THE NARROW pathway that wound through the village, from its outskirts to the royal palace, the jubilant wedding parade meandered along the lavishly decorated streets of Hohala. It was a tremendous spectacle, with elegant carriages and carts adorned in fine purple silk and gold decorative fixtures that winked merrily in the sunlight. The citizens of Hohala, dressed all in their finery, cheered and applauded as the procession moved slowly toward its final destination at the royal mansion. Alongside them, pipers and dancers entertained and burnished the scene with a carnival mood that gladdened the hearts of everyone present. To all, it felt like a true homecoming for the Hohalians—a day they believed would be talked of and remembered long into the future.

At the front of the parade, the royal carriage transported the handsomely-dressed King Benjamin, Lawson, Nicholas Stone, and—the unsurprising focus of the sea of eyes—a ravishingly beautiful Princess Caralisa. In the ceremonial, autumnal colors of her elegant, figure-embracing gown, the princess was a spectacle unto herself. The Hohalians spoke in hushed whispers about how they believed there had never before been a more radiant princess or queen, and among the menfolk, there was mischievous, laddish gossip as they speculated enviously as to what a lucky fellow Nicholas Stone was. Nicholas—not unhandsome himself in his regalia of striking, violet tones—smiled widely as he gazed upon the supportive throng of his fellow countrymen and women, and whenever his eyes met the breath-taking sight of his beautiful bride, he wondered to himself if the despondency and hardships of recent times had been just some distant nightmare.

Later that day, as the sun nestled the village in a serene glow that many took as a wedding gift from the heavens, the bulging crowd of Hohalians scrambled to take up standing space across the wide expanse of the king's refurbished lawns. All around, there were newly carved, marble water features, meticulously sculpted rose bushes, and elaborate ribbons of regal colours carefully woven around grandiose shrubbery across the entirety of the king's palatial grounds. The centrepiece of the scene, situated at the front of the impressively renovated royal mansion, was an immense podium at the center of a pavilion of shimmering purple and gold silk.

King Benjamin proudly as an owl, strode to the forefront of the platform, his silver beard lightly plaited and glinting in the sunlight. His face was cemented with a smile that caused his many wrinkles to bunch together around his eyes, yet his true age was disguised by the youthful radiance in his eyes. Behind him, an ornate wooden alter—the four-pillar frame magnificently carved with detailed replicas of figures from Hohalian theology—waited expectantly for the much-anticipated arrival of the princess and her betrothed. By the king's side, as ever, stood Lawson, his blue ceremonial robe immaculately preened as he waited to perform the ancient ritual that would see Princess Caralisa and Nicholas become one in the eyes of the Nexus.

Finally, the moment that the patient crowd had anticipated came upon them as the royal trumpeters launched into the boisterous, ceremonial air that announced the imminent arrival of the new royal couple.

Across the excited chatter of the crowd, Lawson called out spiritedly, "Citizens of Hohala! On this most joyous and hope-filled day, please welcome your princess, Her Excellence, Caralisa and your new future king, Master Nicholas Stone!"

To the surprise of the crowd, Lawson pointed to the sky, and the eyes of thousands of Hohalians looked up excitedly. A boisterous cheer went up as, in the distance, Augee's winged silhouette appeared just above the mountainous western horizon, and, as he flew nearer, the attendees became increasingly animated to see Nicholas astride a brilliant red and gold saddle with the princess clutching him tightly from behind. Swooping into closer view, Augee let out a dramatic burst of flame that incited another thrilled roar from the crowd. Beaming from ear to ear, Nicholas and Caralisa waved appreciatively in response, and Augee indulged in a second spectacular belch of fire, one that whirled into the heavens like a blazing typhoon.

Indeed, while the gathered Hohalians continued to marvel at the elegance of the royal couple—dressed so exquisitely that some joked they had been groomed and apparelled by the gods themselves—all present were astounded by the magnificent sight of Augee, bedecked for the occasion with princely purple and gold ribbons that were offset brilliantly by the mesmerising emerald tones of his skin. As his great wings threw billowing gusts across the crowd, Augee set down at the front of the podium where the king and Lawson both waited with glowing smiles. With a bound that betrayed his spirited demeanour, Nicholas hopped to the ground before extending his hand chivalrously to assist the princess. Inching herself down on the soft grass, the princess stopped momentarily to face Augee, and gripping him gently around the trunk of his enormous neck, she extended her lips to kiss his bowed forehead. Caralisa and Nicholas grinned to each other as the crowd whooped and crowed buoyantly in response, and hand-in-hand, they stepped lightly up the wooden podium stair to the waiting Lawson.

As they passed the beaming King Benjamin, the monarch directed a rare and playful wink toward Nicholas, which caused his son-in-law-to-be's cheeks to burn giddily, if self-consciously. At last, the moment for which Nicholas had long yearned for was upon him, and despite the fact that a combination of nerves and adrenaline was causing his heart to drum intensely, the king's calm body language served to ease his mind.

Taking up their positions facing each other—the crowd in front of them and a smiling Lawson standing behind—Nicholas and Caralisa intertwined their hands and locked eyes with affection and anticipation. Lawson, visibly excited himself to be conducting the auspicious ritual, turned discreetly to the king for his prompt. Ordinarily strong-jawed at all times, it appeared that King Benjamin too had been struck by the emotion of the moment, and it was with glistening, smiling eyes that he gave a subtle nod to his counselor, thus entrusting his treasured daughter's hand to the young man he'd grown to love as a son of his own. Stretching his arms to the sky in prayerful concentration, Lawson addressed the heavens.

"Look down favorably upon us today, great spirits of the Nexus," he began, his tone authoritative and pious. "As we gather in this hallowed place to ask that you grant unto us your celestial blessings and tie with you in eternal unity the souls of these two humble subjects before us."

At Lawson's words, the atmosphere turned quiet and reverential as all gathered bowed their heads and opened their minds to the faintly tangible touch of the Hohalian gods upon their collective spirit. Nicholas and Caralisa remained facing each other with their hands joined and their eyes locked firmly on each other, their shared anticipation kept subdued by the solemnity of the moment.

"As it has been across countless generations," continued the counselor, "We beseech you to reach forth and extend your protection upon the true love of this woman and man before you, and, according to your divine will, let the fate of that love be forever tied to your omniscient design."

For a moment, a feeling of unfamiliar, unidentifiable serenity began to awaken in Nicholas, and he could see from the intent that stirred within Caralisa's gaze, that she too shared in the sudden, unearthly sensation. Only seconds passed, yet it felt to Nicholas as if he'd been rooted to that spot for an age, bathed in a warm and serene tranquility. The presence of the crowd was now muted and incidental, and he felt as if he and Caralisa were alone together, detached completely from the physical world around them. Embraced by a caressing glow that caused both of their hearts to ache and yearn for one another, the couple shared a longing gaze of comfort and trust, and as unseen hands drew their spirits together, they felt the seed of their love blaze with an intensity that was at once startling and blissful.

It was over too soon.

Wide-eyed and breathless, the couple's senses awakened to observe the jubilant roar of the watching crowd, as King Benjamin and Lawson stood in emotional applause next to them. Hugs and embraces were exchanged between all on the podium and then, from the rooftop of the mansion, a riot of noise broke out across the grounds. From throughout the cheering sea of Hohalians, a host of purple and gold flags were thrust up to the flawlessly blue sky. There they twirled and waved in unison, heralding the coming of age of the princess and welcoming the new male heir to the Hohalian throne. As if to consummate the joyous drama of the moment, a blushing Caralisa and Nicholas exchanged bashful, tear-filled smiles, before embracing each other in a kiss that caused the electrified crowd to erupt into cheerful bedlam.

As the blaze of euphoria surged throughout the grounds of the royal mansion and out into the packed streets of the village, it at last appeared as if the days of tribulation were at an end for the Hohalians, and all believed that they stood at the edge of a great and promising future.

53

AFTER MONTHS OF anguish, abuse, and self-loathing, the day that Suma had dreaded arrived, and he found himself, shivering and disconcerted, aboard the flagship vessel tasked with leading the Volcaron fleet on its latest ocean voyage. He sat in a weary silence as the frigid spray and foam of the waves spat in torrents across his saturated clothing and hair. Too feeble to row, he had been ordered by Morgoratt to travel in the leading warship where he could be on-hand in the event that his technical expertise was required. Huddled among the throng of fellow seafarers, with a flea-ridden cloak draped across his trembling shoulders, a despairing Suma gazed around the massive vessel that he'd been forced to design.

It was an imposing craft with a hull that extended almost one-hundred feet toward its stern, and along its edges were rows of narrow benches for rowers to man the formidable oars. At the center of the ship, a platform towered above the heads of those unfortunate enough to be charged with propelling the vessel through the uncompromising ocean waves, and attached to it was one of the tremendous catapult devices to which Morgoratt's hopes were so strongly pinned. A vast quantity of boulders, rocks, and assorted shrapnel left over from the construction of the new convoy was dispersed throughout the flotilla, stored in great, wooden barrels ready to be deployed. The Volcarons themselves, apparelled in rough-shod body armour and hostile grimaces, were armed with sharply honed daggers and pikes topped with grotesque, serrated hooks. Throughout the lengthy journey toward the Bay of Hohala, there was little frivolity among the rancorous horde, radicalized as they were by Morgoratt's dark gospel. Among the rowing Volcarons, there was only sullen quietude against the tumult of the elements; a hanging tension that, for Suma, made the journey drag on interminably.

At long last, the familiar horizon of Hohala came into view, and the collective mood of the Volcaron legion grew agitated and thirsty for violence. The dimming veil of early evening had already begun to descend, and an uncharacteristic chill clung to the usually balmy air of the bay. Resignation brought Suma's spirits to their lowest point as he scanned the purpling sky for sight of Augee's silhouette. As he'd feared, there was no sign of the Hohalians' winged savior, and, with no remaining hope left to him, he whispered a clumsy, beseeching prayer to any unlikely deity that might happen to take pity on his desperate petition.

Without warning, the ears of all present were assailed by the caustic rasp of Morgoratt's roar against the tumult of the ocean wind.

"Warriors of Volcaron!" he boomed with such force that the ligaments in his neck stood out visibly. "Hohala lies open and vulnerable before you. Go forth now and write your legacy in the blood of the meek; take for good all that you deserve and desire, and leave no blade of grass unscorched or grain of earth untrodden by your boots. Today, we retake the land undeserved by cowards and weaklings, and from the ashes of our conquest, we will rebuild an empire in our true likeness. All hail mighty Volcaron!"

A roar of malevolent triumph went up among the soldiers, and, like a chain reaction, the clamour rose up throughout the fleet of surrounding vessels. In the manner of rabid primates, the Volcarons thumped their fists and stabbed the air with their daggers, and as the emboldened chorus rained down upon Suma's ears, his tortured psyche was moved to conclude that they were indeed the shrieks of demons.

*

"Well, when the annals of our generation are written up," chortled a drunkenly merry reveller, "I reckon it'll be the after-party, not the marriage that will go down in history!"

All within listening distance laughed heartily in agreement as the man hiccupped and slapped the new Prince Nicholas on the back boisterously.

Nicholas simply smiled good-naturedly and lowered his eyes to Caralisa with a knowing smile.

"Yes, I've no doubt about it, sir," he replied patiently, before shaking the man's hand and moving onward to dutifully mingle with more of the army of guests. Hand in hand, Nicholas and Caralisa navigated the crowded gardens of the royal mansion which had been lavishly set up to accommodate as many Hohalians as could possibly squeeze through its gates. Outside the grounds, the festivities had spilled into the streets of the village, and a carnival was under way, the likes of which had never been experienced by any living Hohalian. There were performers and musicians of every classification, and an enchanting miscellany of musical strains infused the balmy evening. Fine food and exquisite libations had been laid out generously by the king who had stipulated that no expense be spared for what he'd considered to be the proudest moment of his reign. In a pocket of the immense canopy that spread out across part of the gardens, Caralisa spied her father as he regaled a group of bemused-looking guests with some animated anecdote. In that moment, it seemed to her as if the faith-shaking burden that had characterized her father for five years had finally been lifted, and, watching him joke and banter with his guests, it struck her that he had returned to the reassuringly self-possessed man who had raised her. As she and Nicholas traversed the grounds, all around them there were people making merry and letting go of the trauma of recent times. Yet, as they squeezed their way apologetically through the crowd—showered with the praises and well wishes of all who they passed—they noticed that one person sat alone on the fringes of the revelry. Perched on a small stool with an overflowing goblet of brandy in his hand, was Hamar, his demeanour at odds with the gleeful mood around him. Concerned for his doleful-looking companion, Nicholas squeezed Caralisa's hand and gestured discreetly to her to move in Hamar's direction. The big man who rose unsteadily to greet them with a forced smile as Nicholas and Caralisa exchanged furtive glances with each other.

"Nicholas!" he slurred, drunkenly throwing open his arms. "My very best congratulations, my friend! And, dear Princess Caralisa, you look more stunning than one could have imagined!"

"Thank you so much," smiled Caralisa returning his hug. "We're both really happy, at last."

Nicholas peered at Hamar questioningly as he shook his hand.

"Is something the matter?" he asked gently, eager not to make it too obvious that his own curiosity was what had drawn him in that direction. "You look a bit subdued over here. I thought you'd be making the most of all the fine food and drink that we fantasized about for so long back in Haven!"

Nicholas added a chuckle to lighten the awkwardness of his question, yet the grin faded from his expression as he noticed the tears that had appeared in the corner of Hamar's eyes.

"Hamar? What's the matter?" questioned Caralisa, her voice laden with concern.

"Sorry. I'm sorry," Hamar replied, clearing his throat in an attempt to regain his composure. "I blame this excellent booze. Don't mind me; this is a wonderful celebration."

"Clearly, something is wrong," asked Nicholas gently. "Whatever it is, you can say."

Hamar bowed his head self-consciously, and when he spoke, his voice was low and emotional.

"It's just the thought of the men those despicable Volcarons took from us that day in the valley near Haven," he growled angrily. "It's just sad that they aren't here to share in this happy day. I know that everybody needs to move on from that terrible time, but I just have this feeling that something isn't right...it's as if that darkness hasn't been banished...I can't explain it, but...."

Hamar sniffed and rubbed his eyes in embarrassment as Nicholas and Caralisa stared at him sympathetically.

"Don't mind me," he repeated, forcing a less wavering tone. "As I said, it's probably just your father's magnificent brandy. This is a fantastic party. I'm sure you're both so happy, and you deserve every blessing in the future."

"Thank you, Hamar," replied Nicholas, still unconvinced of the source of his friend's mournfulness. "Come on—why don't you join us. We're going to check on Augee before we do any more mingling."

Hamar laughed as he glanced across the garden in the direction of the enormous Augee, who at this point was entertaining a group of delighted teenagers with impressively controlled fire blasts that swirled and twisted in the air.

"I think Augee has stolen the spotlight from both of you, by the looks of it," he grinned. "He's certainly become part of the community, hasn't he?"

"Definitely," agreed Nicholas with a smile as the three of them turned in the direction of their winged guardian. "He really *is* a miracle."

54

IT WAS WELL past midnight, and a great dance had gotten underway as the Hohalian celebrations showed little sign of abating. All laughed and revelled in the pure exaltation of the occasion, and every citizen—young and old—danced and sang with carefree abandon.

Sweating as he tried to keep up, Nicholas excused himself from the exuberant elderly lady who had pulled him out to dance. Lowering himself onto one of the marble steps that led to the entrance of the mansion, he indulged in a generous swig of ale and took a moment to gaze at his beautiful new wife as she waltzed gracefully in the arms of her father, the king himself beaming as proud as a lion. Nearby, Augee was revelling in the attention of a group of tipsy young ladies who giggled as he snorted clouds of steam at them playfully. Nicholas smiled to himself, and at that moment, he felt finally content, as if the insecurity, the doubts and the hardship of his youth had finally been consigned to the past. As he considered all that he had been through—all of the burdens and sorrows that he'd borne—he was filled with gratitude and felt at last that he could accept his happiness.

Not seconds later, Nicholas sprang to his feet as a sudden, thunderous crash ripped through the gaiety of the party, obliterating the jaunty music and dousing the carefree chatter. Screams of panic filled the air as flaming debris and masonry rained down violently on the lawn, and the revellers tripped and fell over each other in terrified confusion. A billow of choking smoke began to spread rapidly, and the sinister scent of fire invaded the nostrils of all.

Shielding his eyes, Nicholas looked up in astonishment to see that a sizable portion of the royal mansion was now caved in and in flames. A devastatingly familiar stab of dread crashed down upon his short-lived bliss, and his mind struggled desperately to comprehend the sudden assault on the joyous atmosphere.

Without warning, a hail of flaming projectiles slashed across the night sky, and the Hohalians screamed out in terror as more rock and shrapnel cascaded around them. Petrified wails and weeping rose up everywhere across the gardens and beyond, and there was utter bedlam all around as people scrambled for cover and clarity.

Nicholas's eyes scanned desperately for Caralisa, but the unfurling cloud of smog obscured his view in every direction. At every angle, he saw bodies and blood, some still and afflicted with grotesque injuries, others maimed and hysterical as they attempted to claw themselves out of the open.

"Caralisa!" roared Nicholas, his thoughts disconcerted; again, there was no sign of the princess.

His mind turned to Augee, and Nicholas called out wildly for his friend. This time, his heart leapt to see Augee standing in dazed bewilderment by the obliterated remains of a large, marble fountain, his skin charred and bleeding from several evil-looking puncture wounds.

"Augee!" he bellowed again.

This time, Augee turned in his direction, and his frightened, green eyes implored Nicholas for help or direction. A third eruption and subsequent storm of falling rock and fire assailed the fleeing Hohalians, with more wounded falling to the ground, panicked or unconscious. Using all of his willpower to block out the pain from a scatter of red-hot embers that clung angrily to his tunic, Nicholas tore across the grass toward Augee, as desperate, injured Hohalians moaned at him and tried to grab at his feet. Augee, visibly relieved to see Nicholas, regained some slight composure, and lowered his back in anticipation of Nicholas's intentions.

Leaping with all of the strength he could muster, Nicholas flung himself onto one of the notches along Augee's spine and roared out for him to take to the sky. Without hesitation, Augee sprung into the air, and within seconds, Nicholas could see the true scale of the devastation. From his vantage point in the murky sky, through pockets in the dense smoke, his very soul was shaken to see the entire village of Hohala ravaged by flames, its streets filled with the bedlam of its fleeing citizens. Swooping down lower, beyond the widest expanse of the rolling, black cloud, Nicholas's panic turned to fury as his disbelieving eyes observed the slow and gloating march of none other than the Volcaron army entering the village from every major entrance around its perimeter, their identity unmistakable from their hunched and slouching forms.

"Damn it, no!" Nicholas cursed in horror at the sight of the ravaging horde as they descended eagerly on the settlement, each Volcaron soldier brandishing a bladed weapon or some fire-spreading implement of destruction.

Gesturing to Augee to remain hanging in the air, Nicholas's eyes skirted across the devastated scene, and as they followed the teeming trail of oncoming Volcarons beyond the village, his heart sank at the sight of the source of the fiery devastation. Twisting and winding rapidly at grotesquely sharp angles was a towering, catapult-like machine positioned along the beach. Beside it rested an immense armada of familiar vessels, now enhanced and repaired and from which more Volcaron soldiers clamoured in frenzied excitement.

Through the smog, Nicholas could make out that a team of lumbering soldiers manned the enormous contraption which they launched and reloaded with flaming debris with systematic precision and speed. His mind torn between his desperation to find Caralisa and the obvious urgent need to disable the catapult, Nicholas strained to find the princess among the chaos. Signalling to Augee, the pair swept down lower through the smog to scan the ruined grounds of the mansion as Nicholas growled a hurried, pleading prayer for her safety. The streets immediately surrounding the mansion were filled with screams and bloodshed as the approaching Volcarons swept through the village with indiscriminate brutality. Trampled, bleeding corpses littered the winding lanes, and the roofs of thatched cottages crackled and groaned under the oppression of vindictive, dancing blazes. Nicholas's horrified pleas to the Nexus were strangled in his throat at the wholly cataclysmic scene, and he found himself questioning in paralysed silence if, in reality, there did exist a divine power beyond the influence of demons.

Nicholas's desolate thoughts were interrupted abruptly as they passed over the king's mansion. Sheer devastation met his eyes at every angle; lifeless bodies and the tortured, screeching silhouettes of desperate men and women littered the now-ravaged gardens as cackling flames consumed the decadent wedding decorations in all directions and caused the once-opulent flower blossoms to shrink and contort hideously. And all the while, the fiery Volcaron deluge continued to rain down inexorably on the helpless Hohalians who had sought shelter within the grounds of the ravaged royal mansion.

A choking horror overcame Nicholas as he suddenly spotted King Benjamin himself lying bloodied and broken on the lawn, his ever-faithful counselor, Lawson, kneeling vulnerably by his side. Horrified by the agonizing sight of his injured father-in-law, Nicholas's eyes scanned pleadingly across the gardens for a glimpse of Caralisa, and despite his subconscious awareness that his voice would be smothered by the chaos below, he cried out in the hope that the princess might hear him.

Amid the tumult of screams and crashing rubble, relentless torrents from the Volcaron catapults continued unabated, the flaming projectiles whistling through the air at unpredictable heights and in every direction. At one point, Nicholas's heart dipped in his chest as Augee flinched his body dramatically to avoid impact with an oncoming boulder, and he was forced to grasp blindly at the closest notch on Augee's back to prevent himself from falling into the night sky. Composing himself after a brief, panicked moment, Augee spat out a shrill howl of rage, and Nicholas noticed that the scarlet light behind his eyes had deepened to a sanguine, blood-red, leaving little doubt as to his friend's vexation. Augee's head darted urgently as his concentration piqued, and he surveyed the scene below him strategically. Furls of smoke began to roll from his flared nostrils as he took note of the clamoring droves of Volcaron troops progressing through the main arteries that led into the village from Morgoratt's harbored fleet in the bay.

With a tone of trembling wrath in tune with the fury that pulsated from Augee's eyes, Nicholas pointed toward the bay and roared out vehemently:

"Enough of this, Augee! Burn them! Burn them where they stand!"

With a screech that pierced through the night air, Augee swooped low and at full speed, coming down across the village as it brimmed with fire and terror. The catapult-manning Volcarons, having spotted their winged nemesis descending from the sky, sent a barrage of assorted burning missiles through the air. His mind full of vengeance and purpose, Augee twisted in the air agilely, avoiding the onslaught and continuing his low advance toward the bay. As the projectiles swooshed narrowly passed his own ducked head and tightly tucked limbs, Nicholas peered down in loathing silence as the monstrous hordes continued to lay waste to the Hohalians' beloved home. Spotting a troop of hunched Volcarons assembled in a narrow cul-de-sac, Nicholas instructed Augee to dive in that direction. At hurtling speed, they swooped toward the animated gang who appeared to be making rapid stabbing motions with their clubs and the handles of their pikes. Skillfully avoiding yet another oncoming boulder from above them, Augee widened his jaws in familiar fashion and Nicholas could feel the fire begin to stir tempestuously in his friend's belly. At that moment, to his alarm, Nicholas spotted the source of the Volcaron gang's excitement and realized that Augee was about to incinerate the pair of young Hohalian men sprawled on the ground to which the blood-lusting brutes were administering a relentless beating.

Nicholas's roared warning to hold fire came seconds too late for Augee to prevent it completely; just as the ball of fire was dispelled from his throat, Augee whipped his neck to the side awkwardly, and the shot swirled through the air as a frenetic tongue of orange flame. Leaves of white-hot embers cascaded down like glistening hail on all in the vicinity of the cul-de-sac, and the clothes and skin of the Volcarons and their bloodied Hohalian victims began to blister and smoke on contact. Pained hollering filled the air as they all thrashed and scrambled haphazardly. To his relief however, amid the pandemonium Nicholas could see that the young men had managed to stumble out of the sight of their persecutors and had taken refuge in the undergrowth leading to the jungle's edge.

"Right, Augee," called Nicholas determinedly as he pointed toward a crowd of Volcarons that had just breached another section of the village's northern perimeter. "Torch them all!"

Without further delay, Nicholas felt Augee's belly rumble once more beneath him, and he was forced to hold on with all of his strength as Augee reared up. A great effusion of fire rolled like a lumbering inferno down on the oncoming Volcaron legion before spreading relentlessly across the abandoned village outskirts. Nicholas watched in silent awe as the wide-eyed Volcaron soldiers, rooted to the spot in pure terror, were consumed voraciously by the blaze, their high-pitched, anguished screams lingering briefly on the air behind them. Beyond the village, all across the sandy margin of the bay, the next advancing wave of Volcaron ground troops stopped in their tracks at the ghastly fate of their compatriots and began to retreat in panic back toward the water's edge.

"Drive them back, Augee!" cried Nicholas, his voice quivering as he became increasingly encouraged by the sight of the fleeing horde.

Without hesitation Augee began to spray the beach with fizzing crackles of lightning and slashing blades of flame while Nicholas looked on from above. In the distance, he could see that the catapults had already been rolled back into position onto the most immense of the vessels, and a number of boats had begun to retreat to the sanctuary of the outer bay. Nicholas directed Augee to bring them higher, and as they rose to greater altitude, his eyes scanned the beach and the ships for a sign of Morgoratt. A warning burst of flame accompanied a deafening roar from Augee as he observed a slouching cohort of Volcarons attempting to hoist themselves up onto one of the catapult platforms in a seeming attempt to launch another airborne attack. Nicholas cursed in frustration as he realized that he could only distract the Volcarons by the water for a short period for fear that those already rampaging throughout the village might find Caralisa, if they had not done so already. It was obvious that the catapults were too large and too numerous to destroy all of them in time to rescue the princess and what remained of the village. After motioning to Augee to launch one last wide scale attack, Nicholas directed him to fly back toward the king's mansion. With a great, reptilian shriek, Augee spat a twisting swirl of fire across the beach, once again sending numerous Volcarons diving for cover, before tongues of flame licked up along a small number of the marooned boats, setting them alight in a deafening, almost instantaneous eruption. To Nicholas's satisfaction, the brisk ocean wind began to quickly toss the clawing flames higher and higher, and to the audible distress of those on board, caused one of the larger catapult-laden ships to go up in fire as well.

By now, Nicholas felt that they'd wrought sufficient chaos that might distract the Volcarons by the bay long enough for him to locate Caralisa and neutralize the enemy soldiers that remained inside the village. Together, he and Augee sped through the sky back toward the royal mansion which was becoming unrecognizable from within the engulfment of smoke and the devouring blaze. The grounds by now appeared almost entirely charred black and were littered with rubble and masonry, and Nicholas was dismayed to observe that the number of motionless bodies strewn across the lawn had noticeably increased since they had flown overhead a short time before. Then, he spotted among them, in the same, unchanged position, the motionless form of King Benjamin with an agitated Lawson still crouched faithfully by his side. The counselor, disregarding his own safety, knelt by the monarch, rubbing soot from his face and shielding him from shards of hissing ash that spat into the air from out of the piles of burning debris surrounding them.

Without waiting for instruction from Nicholas, Augee came in to land close to where the king was sprawled. Before Augee had fully touched down, Nicholas had already thrown himself to the ground; picking himself up painfully, he tore toward the motionless king just as the monarch's head was narrowly missed by a falling piece of rubble that smashed into the earth from the mansion roof above. Flinging himself at a stunned Lawson, Nicholas knocked him to the ground and covered both his and King Benjamin's heads as more of the flaming roof structure crashed noisily around them. After several moments that seemed to them an age, Nicholas shook himself to his senses and turned fiercely to his ailing father-in-law and the counselor.

"Your Highness!" he roared seconds later at King Benjamin who lay looking up at him in confusion. "We can't stay here! We have to go now!"

"Do not fear, Nicholas," rasped the monarch. "The Nexus will protect our people. We must have faith."

"Damn it!" cursed Nicholas, throwing up his arms in frustration, just as another lump of burning masonry dropped from above and shattered the marble bust of a former Hohalian king to their left. "Lawson! Please tell me that you can see the truth! The Nexus is not going to save us. We have to go, now!

Lawson, torn between common sense and loyalty to the king simply returned Nicholas's stare as tears of hopelessness welled in his eyes.

"I'm sorry, Nicholas," he sobbed forlornly. "I must stay with His Highness until the end. It is my duty above all else."

"Where is Caralisa?" growled Nicholas in frustration, his eyes flitting around him for his wife and for Augee who sat flinching beneath a large, smoking tree a few paces off.

"She's safe...I think!" stammered Lawson above the relentless din and choking smoke of the inferno. "I'm sure she's okay! She was helping some of the wounded, and I think they made it out of the mansion grounds along the southern perimeter and into the jungle. She told me to tell you to find her…that she'd be waiting for us all in the hills."

Nicholas whispered a brief, uncertain prayer of thanks and, overcome by relief, closed his tear-filled eyes briefly in gratitude.

"But Nicholas…" interjected Lawson, struggling to be heard over the din.

The counselor's voice was faint and quivering, and a stream of tears fell profusely from each of his soot-lined eyes.

"The king," he sobbed. "I fear he won't be with us for much longer."

"Stop!" shot back Nicholas heatedly as, to their mutual horror, a torrent of fiery projectiles whistled through the air above them, smashing with blistering speed into the crumbling mansion wall and spraying the area with a vast torrent of rock and metal across the ground, an indication that the Volcarons had deemed it safe to resume their devastating, catapult-led assault.

"Lawson," Nicholas resumed at a vehement roar. "We're not giving up. We're getting out of here. We can get the king to the mountains where one of the Hohalian healer women can maybe…"

Suddenly, to his surprise, Nicholas felt King Benjamin grasp roughly at his arm. He dropped his eyes to see the monarch staring up at him, a glare of resolute defiance in his eyes.

"No, Nicholas," he interrupted sternly. "I do not have much time left. I…"

"Your Highness!" Nicholas cut across disobediently. "We *can* still help…"

"Listen to me, I say!" came the king's reply, the anger and determination in his tone taking both Nicholas and Lawson by surprise.

"I want to be taken to the Eternal Stream," continued the monarch doggedly. "My will in this regard must be done. Do not deny a dying man his final wish."

"Please, Your Highness," attempted Nicholas for a final time. "There's still hope. Everybody's evacuating. We must too!"

Suddenly, an ear-splitting boom in the near distance punctuated their dire exchange, sending a cloud of dust and rubble spraying across the grounds, and the insidious roars of triumph that followed told them that the Volcarons—armed and with the taste of violence on their lips—had breached the eastern gates of the estate.

"Nicholas, listen to me!" King Benjamin wheezed as the triumphant cheers of the Volcarons cackled steadily in their direction. "*You* are the last hope. Now, please. My time is short. Do as I ask of you."

Nicholas stared into the king's sullen face for a moment before raising his gaze and exchanging a confounded glance with Lawson. The counselor, resigned to his master's wishes, simply returned a subtle nod.

With a deep sigh, Nicholas leapt to his feet.

"Augee!" he hollered.

Augee, who had stood nearby nervously anticipating an exchange of fire with the newly arrived Volcaron soldiers, turned toward his companions and lowered his great body as closely to the ground as he could manage.

With the help of Lawson, Nicholas heaved his injured father-in-law's body across Augee's back before throwing himself aboard and hoisting the counselor up behind him hurriedly. In an instant, Augee took to the air once more and rose high above the burning manor as the baying Volcaron soldiers shook their weapons in frustration and spat spiteful curses up at them.

55

ACROSS THE SULLEN, moonless sky they glided in silence. The countryside below them was obscured by ink-like darkness, and the outlines of the mountains, the forests, and even the Great Bay of Hohala were barely visible to the eye. As the frigid night air whipped harshly at the exposed skin of their faces and arms, the world around them appeared as a chasm of bleak and uncertain nothingness into which they had been thrust without warning.

Positioned at a limp angle, King Benjamin lay astride Augee's back with his pallid visage staring despondently into the starless night. His breathing had grown progressively labored, and Nicholas could feel the pulse in his father-in-law's arm becoming fainter as he gripped the monarch tightly out of fear that his body might become unbalanced. Tears of hopelessness and fear welled up in the corner of Nicholas's eyes as he reflected in disbelief on the sudden and devastating events that had just befallen them. A state of pure happiness, a bliss to which he'd been hitherto unaccustomed, and a future filled with abundant promise had been wrenched callously from his grasp; and while he mourned the loss of his own false destiny, the grief in his heart gnawed at him even more deeply at the thought of the innocent Hohalians that had just been so brutally cut down, as well as the survivors who now had nothing in their futures except for the uncertainty and hardship of renewed exile. As the faint outline of the western mountains began to reveal itself, Nicholas indulged in a rueful glance across his shoulder, and far behind them in the darkness, the flame-engulfed village of Hohala appeared like the dying ember of a spent hearth.

The exact length of the journey to the Valley of the Eternal Stream didn't register in Nicholas's consciousness. His concentration lay in ensuring that the ailing King Benjamin remained secure astride Augee's back and that neither he nor Lawson became unbalanced by the disconcerting blackness of the night. After what seemed an age, Augee began to glide at a soft downward angle, and the rough outline of mountain treetops came into view. Their landing was steady, undoubtedly an effort by Augee to ensure that the suffering of the declining king was not accentuated further. Without speaking, Nicholas lowered himself onto the grassy forest floor, and he felt the warmth of premature morning dew sooth his feet through the broken soles of his boots. Together, he and Lawson hoisted King Benjamin carefully off of Augee's back and carried him slowly by the shoulders in the direction of the tinkling sound of water. Behind them, Augee followed quietly, his mind alert for any unexpected movement from within the dense forest. As they rounded a copse of mountain conifers, the glimmer of the Eternal Stream's pristine waterfall came into view and offered respite from the fathomless darkness that seemed to Nicholas to have engulfed the entire universe.

As they reached the edge of the perfectly-still pond, the surface of which was tinged with a shimmering light whose source could not be discerned, King Benjamin suddenly regained consciousness and began to rasp frantically at them to set him down on the grass. Nicholas and Lawson, though unsure of the correct course of action, offered no objection, and they lowered the king onto his back by the water's edge. Before he could raise himself back into a standing position, Nicholas felt the king grasp his right hand, and by way of the glow from the pond's surface, he could make out that his father-in-law's eyes were fixed intently on him.

"Listen closely to me, Nicholas," instructed the king, his voice lowered to an exhausted croak. "Your part in all of this is only just beginning."

"Your Highness…" began Nicholas, his tone disconsolate and weary.

"No, my boy!" the monarch cut him off irritably. "Stay quiet while I speak…while I'm still able."

Nicholas fell silent. He felt exasperated—his mood inconsolable—and there was part of him that was still angry at what he perceived to be the king's complacency over the previous five years. Yet, at that moment, his heart ached and was filled with sorrow at the realization that the only man who had come close to being a father figure to him was slipping away, and he reasoned that it was only right to heed the final wishes of a dying man.

"I'm sorry, Your Highness," he relented, unable to stifle the sob that accompanied his apology.

In the darkness, Nicholas felt his father-in-law place his hand solidly on the side of his face, and as he spoke, the king's voice became unexpectedly resolute.

"Nicholas, my time is at an end. Listen to my words and swear by them. Very soon, I will go to meet my reward, and at last I will become one with our beloved Nexus. Tonight, I pass my crown to you, and you will preside as king over the Hohalians. You—with my dear Caralisa as your queen—will lead our people, and it will come to pass that Hohala will once again be the beautiful, sacred place, it was meant to be."

King Benjamin paused momentarily, and Nicholas could make out that his eyelids had begun to shine with silver tears.

"Promise me however, Nicholas," he continued. "Promise me that you will always hold onto your faith. Promise me that you will nurture and cultivate the Hohalian faith among our people; no matter how trying the time, how difficult the circumstances, or how long the suffering, never abandon faith."

The king gripped Nicholas's wrist even tighter.

"Because, Nicholas," he added. "Without our faith, we are lost. I ask you now; do you promise me this?"

Nicholas nodded solemnly as his own tears dripped onto King Benjamin's face.

"I promise you, sir," he sniffled. "I will do as you ask."

Nicholas then felt the king's grip loosen as he gestured next for Lawson's attention. The counselor lowered himself to his knees and held the king's limp arm gently in his hand.

"Lawson, my trusted friend and counselor," he wheezed. "I have, by my authority, passed the crown, and leadership of Hohala, to Nicholas Stone. You, Lawson, shall be written into the annals of our people as the witness to this event. You have been instrumental in all matters of Hohalian governance and in my own personal decisions as well. Caralisa and I could not have made it through our most difficult times without you. The occasions that you have been there for us are more numerous than the grains of sand in a barrel. You've been both a brother and a best friend, and my soul will rest peacefully if I know I can count on you to continue to stand by the new King Nicholas as his aide."

Lawson's voice shook as he struggled to compose himself.

"Fulfilling your wishes will be a blessing to my soul, my King and old friend," he sobbed. "I wouldn't have it any other way, and you can count on me until the day that I am called on by the Nexus to sit by your side once more."

"My trusted Lawson," King Benjamin smiled weakly. "Until our paths converge once more beyond this world, I thank you for all that you have done thus far."

The king's tone then changed once again as he addressed both of them together.

"The two of you must perform one final task," he directed softly, "And then your duties to my earthly carnation will be done."

With that, King Benjamin gestured weakly to the still waters of the pond, and Nicholas and Lawson nodded reverently in unison.

The water felt cool and strangely consoling as Nicholas stepped into the pond, the surface quickly reaching to his waist. With the utmost care and concentration, he and Lawson lowered the dying king into the water and released him to the tender embrace of the Eternal Stream. With a sorrow that wrenched at his very soul, Nicholas released his gentle grip and watched as King Benjamin's body drifted, as if by some unseen force, into the center of the pond where it floated serenely for a short time.

All of a sudden, an unearthly glow rose up across the pond, and the water and all of its surroundings were bathed in soft, pinkish light. Nicholas and Lawson watched in awe as the light grew until it consumed the whole area and then danced through the tree tops as if it was being orchestrated by some unseen conductor. At the center of the pond, the light concentrated around the king, and it pulsated brilliantly around his body. In a moment that dispelled all doubt as to the validity of King Benjamin's steadfast faith in that obscure body of water, the lingering darkness of the nighttime was suddenly vanquished by a brilliant pillar of light that shot silently into the sky from the surface of the pond. By the bank of the pond, Nicholas and

Lawson were forced to shield their eyes to avoid being blinded by the sheer brilliance of the glare.

And then, as if consumed by some impetuous vacuum, the brilliant luminosity disappeared, and the clearing was once again bathed in a dim, roseate glow. Rubbing his eyes, Nicholas saw that the waters had become still, and King Benjamin's floating body had vanished from sight. Once more, the place was consumed by silence, and to Nicholas, the world again felt empty and forsaken.

Wearily, Nicholas and Lawson waded the few short feet back to the shore where Augee stood waiting quietly. As he hoisted himself up onto the grassy embankment, Nicholas was surprised to notice that Augee's attention was fixed on the sky. Raising his own gaze, his heart fluttered in his chest, and he whispered to Lawson to look up also. There, at the very center of the dawn-wakening sky, was a single, resplendent star that winked down at them reassuringly with a sparkle that reminded them of the mischievous glint that had so often radiated from King Benjamin's eyes during happier times.

56

NICHOLAS, LAWSON, AND Augee sat in quiet contemplation by the water's edge, the mindsets of all three united by a combination of grief and confoundment at the harrowing turn of events that had befallen them so suddenly. Their home had been destroyed, the Hohalians were uprooted once more, Caralisa's whereabouts were unknown, their beloved king was dead, and the hope of a bright future left in ruin.

For a period, neither Nicholas nor Lawson spoke, and Augee, dumbfounded by the circumstances, remained mournfully silent. About half an hour passed before the morning sun chanced to peak across the tree tops, and the lonely star that had hung above them consolingly faded into the oncoming day. Nicholas was jolted from his dispirited reflections by the gentle pressure of Lawson's hand on his shoulder. The former king's trusted aide, seated next to him on the grass, wore an expression of sympathy and a smile that failed to mask his own deep sorrow; yet, in spite of the heartache etched on his face, Lawson's wisdom shone behind his eyes, and Nicholas felt himself ever so slightly comforted by the counselor's presence.

"We must continue onward now, Nicholas," began Lawson softly.

Nicholas nodded in agreement, his heart torn between the need to confront the aftermath of the previous night's devastation and the strange solace of the Eternal Stream.

"I have to find Caralisa," he replied. "She's no doubt terrified and beside herself with worry, and…"

He sighed for a moment before resuming.

"She needs to know about her father."

Lawson nodded again sadly.

"Indeed," he agreed. "However, before we begin the unfortunate responsibilities at hand, Nicholas, I must inform you of something that is of no small importance."

"Please, do," replied Nicholas after a thoughtful moment, his tone lilting with curiosity.

Lawson looked at him intently, then turned his gaze to Augee, before resting his stare on the peak of one of the distant western mountains whose summit spied over the surrounding forest.

"There is a place, Nicholas; known only to those most innately and faithfully connected with the Nexus; a place that transcends the tangible world and goes beyond the limits of time and the physical realm. It is an ancient refuge provided to us Hohalians, as the loyal and sole human subjects of the Nexus; a final sanctuary gifted to us to ensure that, no matter what destruction may befall our people, our spirit may be kept alive. It is a unique privilege endowed to us by the Nexus for our unwavering devotion; our reward for living with the faith that has been the cornerstones of our race for eons."

"I don't understand, Lawson," replied Nicholas doubtfully. "I've lived in Hohala my whole life, and I've never heard of such a thing; not from the priests, nor the elders—not even King Benjamin himself."

"That is because you were never entitled to know about it," interrupted the counselor, his tone mildly rebuking. "That is, until now. Such privileged knowledge is reserved only for the king of Hohala...and of his counselor who acts as a conduit between the Nexus and the king himself. I know that you've looked at me with exasperation many times in the past, Nicholas, when times were hard. Be aware that I did not mistake the frustration in your eyes when you wondered why I appeared to indulge King Benjamin when he stubbornly persisted in putting prayer before action, as it indeed seemed to you."

Nicholas felt himself blush, and his mind returned to the many occasions when he'd admonished the king and Lawson both publicly and in private.

"You see, Nicholas," he continued. "While it might appear that we have been abandoned by the Nexus in these trying days, the reality is that we have not. Of course, we do not—nor have we a right to—expect that the gods shield us entirely from the evils of creation. The reward for our faith and our enduring grace is granted to us after we have earned it in this world. Yet, unlike unfortunate races such as the Volcarons, who are denied the love of the Nexus, the gods have granted us—as their chosen people— one last safeguard against the final annihilation of our nation. It ensures that the spirit of the sacred tribe of Hohala will flicker on—no matter how weakly—and that, in turn, devotion to the Nexus and the dissemination of its teachings will never disappear from this world."

Nicholas listened wide-eyed, his mind racing to comprehend the immensity of Lawson's words.

"Now, my boy," the counselor went on. "King Benjamin's crown has been passed to you, and with it, both the privileges and responsibilities of that title. From now until either of us passes from this earth, I will be your devoted advisor and your link to the divine Nexus."

Lawson placed his hand once more on Nicholas's shoulder and bowed his head in a show of deference. Suddenly, Nicholas felt reassured, and the hesitant confusion that had plagued him since King Benjamin took his dying breath began to dissipate.

'"I have many questions, Lawson," Nicholas replied finally. "But I am aware that the time for lengthy discussions is not now. Given the threat we are facing at this moment, I must ask, about this place—this sanctuary. What is it?"

Lawson nodded.

"It is a passageway," he answered. "A shaft, if you will, that bridges the dimensions of the universe; it is a place where the physical and ethereal world intermingle and where spirits and shadows can pass freely. For the living of this world, it is a place in which to seek sanctuary and no more. It is but a final haven—a space to seek protection until such time that it is safe to venture back into the light of the sun."

Nicholas reflected quietly on Lawson's words. The solemnity of the counselor's tone and the seriousness with which he described the mysterious refuge underlined for him starkly the dire circumstances facing the Hohalians.

"Where is this place?" Nicholas inquired finally.

Lawson raised his eyes to the horizon and pointed to the same mountaintop that had captured his gaze a short time before.

"There," he indicated. "Located at the summit of the highest, most treacherous mountain visible from the Eternal Stream. At its peak, there is a sparse opening from which no light nor sound emanates. If one were to drop a stone inside it, they would wait an eternity to hear its echo."

"You mean it was there all the time while we were exiled in New Hohala and nobody ever knew?" question Nicholas incredulously.

Lawson smiled.

"Master Nicholas, it has always been there—long before any Hohalian set foot on this earthly terrain. But now, you see why King Benjamin chose such a place for us to settle after the Volcaron invasion. There are many more hospitable places in which to relocate a community; however, none of those are near to that final sanctuary in the event that such a last measure was required."

It was a bewildering revelation; one that unearthed as many questions as answers in Nicholas's mind. Nevertheless, the sun had begun to hover above the treetops, and the new king of Hohala was aware that time was of the essence.

"We must go," announced Nicholas after a pause of reflection. "There will be time for us to talk of this further when our people are safe. But now, we need to return to Hohala."

Lawson nodded, and both men picked themselves up from the warm grass. Augee, who had been patiently listening, growled softly to indicate that he too was ready. With a determined flap of his great wings, he hunched his body low to the ground, and Nicholas and Lawson clambered onto his back. Seconds later, they were airborne, and the minds of the three turned to the question of what remnants they would find of the Hohala they once knew.

57

A TERSE SILENCE hung in the air as Augee set his feet down on the scorched lawn of the royal mansion. The sky was overcast, and a chill breeze caused the fumes from the smoldering ruins to waft intrusively in every direction. In the somber daylight, the desolation of the scene was all the more tragically stark. Unsightly piles of rubble—the broken remnants of majestic marble pillars and the intricate creations of master craftsmen—were scattered across the gardens and walkways. What remained of the lavishly decorated platform where Nicholas and Caralisa were wed the day before was little more than a blackened, timber frame, the tattered fingers of ravaged, purple silk billowing morosely in the wind. Yet, despite the physical destruction at every angle, it paled against the human devastation. All around, the awful reality of the Volcaron offensive was visible by the bodies that littered the grounds. Bloodied, burnt, and abused, the remains of neighbors, friends, acquaintances, and strangers demonstrated the mercilessness nature of the aggressors' onslaught.

Nicholas swore at a roar as he surveyed his surroundings in disbelief. The royal seat of his people, once grand and welcoming, had been defiled beyond recognition—those people, so devout and peace-loving, had been set upon and crucified in the most depraved fashions. Augee, having grown to consider Hohala as his own home, began to groan and thrash his head in despair at the sight. Even Lawson, despite his years and experience, was frozen, dumbstruck and traumatized, his arms hanging limp and helpless by his side.

Unable to continue examining the ruination, Nicholas called out to Augee gruffly and the three of them took off into the air in silence. To their dismay, the remainder of the village offered little in the way of respite from the horror they'd witnessed within the mansion grounds, as street after razed street provided similar evidence of the cold bloodlust of the aggressors. Gliding silently across smoking cottages and pavements stained deep with the crimes of Volcaron knives, Nicholas attempted to fathom the barbarity of those foreign brutes and, in that moment, he chastised himself for the wanderlust and restlessness of his youth.

"Nicholas," came Lawson's animated voice from behind him, the counselor's arm outstretched and pointing toward the fringe of jungle by the eastern perimeter of the village. "Look, there!"

Between the twisted foliage of the forest and the gable of a tumbledown shed, a sudden darting movement indicated that there was some manner of stealthy activity occurring on the ground. With a flick of his arm, Nicholas indicated to Augee to go down low over the village for a closer inspection. As they flew nearer, a second figure bolted from behind the stable and into the thick vegetation of the jungle; a minute later, another did the same. Straining his eyes, Nicholas started as he recognized one of the men of Haven bounding into the foliage behind his companions, and it was clear that an escape or rescue attempt was taking place.

And then he saw her—Caralisa—busily directing a worried-looking trio of young children across the debris-littered street and into the shelter of the jungle. Nicholas's head swam, so glad was he to see that his wife was safe, but greatly unnerved that she had not continued her journey to the safety of the mountains as he'd believed. In that moment, the condition of the village and the matter of inspecting the coastline were of secondary importance; now, his focus was turned to immediately removing Caralisa from danger.

As Augee glided down to land on a green area by the edge of the village, they were spotted by one of the youngsters who cried out excitedly. Immediately, one of the Hohalian men in the huddled group was seen to throw his hands over the little boy's mouth, his eyes wild with alarm at the child's sudden exclamation. Below, the entire party of escapees turned their attention to the sky, and both Nicholas and Lawson began to gesture to them to remain low and quiet.

The crash of uprooting trees ripped through the silence of the village, and a shrill cry of "Look out!" caused Nicholas's heart to leap. He felt Lawson grip his shoulders rigidly as Augee deftly and narrowly dodged an oncoming flaming boulder that tore past them like a comet and ploughed explosively into a row of whitewashed cottages. A surge of dust and debris was thrown violently into the air as the compact homesteads were obliterated, with little more than a smoking crater was left in their place.

The reverberation of the boulder's impact caused Nicholas's hearing to dull, and the only sound that penetrated his ears was the beat of his pounding heart. In a daze, he barely managed to steady himself as Augee rolled in the air to avoid a second oncoming boulder that shot from another portion of jungle off to their right. In his peripheral vision, Nicholas could see fiery missiles of every size being hurled from multiple points within the jungle foliage, and it was clear that over the course of the previous night, the Volcarons had repositioned their arsenal of catapults to the cover of the jungle itself. No matter how hard he tried to discern the exact locations of the enemy artillery, the catapults were cleverly obscured from view by the tall treetops which bended and whipped with every missile launch. Shifting and darting at uncomfortable angles, Augee moved deftly through the air as boulder after boulder and shower after shower of flaming shrapnel whistled in their direction. It was an overwhelming ambush that none of them had anticipated and one that had been cunningly planned by their tormentors.

"Augee! Go higher!" roared Nicholas, at a loss as to what else to do.

With a powerful snap of his wings, Augee sent them hurtling upward, and Nicholas was forced to retain an iron grip around Lawson's torso to prevent the aged counselor from tumbling to his death. All of a sudden, Augee let out a sharp gasp as a shower of hot, jagged pebbles connected with his midriff from below, lacerating the pale, green skin of his lower body. Beneath him, Nicholas could feel Augee's muscles tighten as he winced in agony, but his friend maintained his steely resolve and continued to speedily climb higher. Eventually, with the village visible as a smoking blotch on the landscape below, Augee leveled out and hovered momentarily in the air to compose himself.

"Hold on!" Nicholas warned Lawson through gritted teeth as he felt Augee's body quiver and pulsate wildly.

Once more, Augee's skin blackened and tensed, and the light in his eyes turned blood-red as his rare metamorphosis took place. The features around his head and eyes hardened and grew sharper until his benevolence disappeared beneath a terrifying guise.

Without further warning, Augee pointed his fuming snout downward, and they began to plummet at breakneck speed toward the ground. As they came within meters of the jungle treetops, Augee levelled out, and with an intake of breath that almost knocked Nicholas and Lawson from his back, he let out an ear-shattering bellow; the cascade of fire that accompanied that deafening roar was vast and dreadful, and it rolled through the sky like an indomitable wave. Instantly, the jungle treetops in its path were incinerated, and a portion of jungle about an acre in size appeared to combust. From within the trees, the excruciated screams of hiding Volcarons could be heard as the tumbling inferno consumed them.

With the raging devastation left in his wake, Augee swept backward to consider his next attack. The smoke from the forest fire was thick and obscuring, and it billowed heavily in the coastal wind. A moment later, another torrent of boulders was fired from within an unscorched portion of jungle, forcing Augee to dive lower. Nicholas winced as shards of brick and stone sprayed himself and Lawson following the resultant impact with a portion of the village's perimeter wall.

And then, as Augee pulled up, Nicholas saw Caralisa. Below him, she stood alone at the center of a junction of wreckage-strewn streets, her hair disheveled and her gold wedding dress blood-stained and torn.

"Caralisa!" roared Nicholas as Augee jerked out of the path of a shower of smaller, high-speed projectiles. "Get out of there, *now*!"

At the sound of his voice, Caralisa raised her head in astonishment, the momentary relief at the sight of him etched across her haggard face. Suddenly, Nicholas grew alarmed to see his wife's eyes widen with fear. Flailing her arms wildly, the princess opened her mouth to cry up at him.

The oncoming boulder ensured that Nicholas never heard those words. With an impact that filled his ears with the sound of his own bones cracking, he was blown violently from Augee's back. His last sight before he plummeted limply to the ground was the horror-stricken eyes of Lawson as the counselor reached out in vain to prevent him from falling.

...

He didn't know how long he'd been lying on the ground or precisely where he'd landed. With a feeble groan, Nicholas attempted to lift his arms, but his powers of movement failed him, and his ears rang with a disconcerting blur. He twitched his eyes to the side, however, all that he could see were flames and smog, and he felt himself begin to be overcome by the fumes.

And then he heard Caralisa.

"Nicholas!" she screamed hysterically. He opened his eyes to see the princess crouched over him, her face ash-stained and streaked with tears. Next to her stood Lawson, and behind him, a visibly distraught Augee.

"Caralisa," he wheezed. "Go! You have to go!"

"No!" she wailed in devastation. "I can't leave you!"

"Please," implored Nicholas. "Get to safety. There's no time!"

"I won't leave you!" she insisted through howls of tears.

"I won't leave *you*," whispered Nicholas, the intent in his glazing eyes touching her heart where his fingers couldn't. "I'll never leave you. But please, you have to go now."

Suddenly, an ear-splitting boom in the near distance punctuated their exchange, sending rubble and dust raining in all directions.

"I can't go," whimpered Caralisa as she clutched Nicholas's limp and bloodied hand in hers and pressed it to her lips.

"Princess Caralisa, we must run *now*!" screamed Lawson above the delighted whoops and shrieks of the triumphant Volcarons who had re-entered the village from nearby.

Without waiting for her response, the counselor clutched her around the waist and dragged her to her feet as she clawed hysterically at Nicholas's charred clothing.

"I love you, Caralisa," he mouthed weakly as she was hauled away protectively by Lawson and ordered to crouch down beside a corbelled, stone wall.

"Lawson!" Nicholas moaned desperately. "Wait!"

The ringing in his ears prevented him from hearing Lawson's words to Caralisa, but the vehemence of his expression and his wild gesticulations told him that the counselor was demanding that she remain low. With a speed that defied his years, Lawson bounded back toward the prostrate Nicholas and dove to the ground next to him as the area was assailed by yet more catastrophic Volcaron fire.

"I'm sorry, Your Highness," he sobbed over the chaos. "It wasn't meant to be like this."

"Please, Lawson," wheezed Nicholas. "There's no time for words of defeat. The Volcarons are coming—you must get Caralisa and the other survivors to the hills; as many as you can save."

And then, Nicholas's expression hardened, and his eyes locked on Lawson's with a determination that unexpectedly put the counselor in mind of King Benjamin.

"Promise me, though, Lawson," he entreated the counselor with a labored rasp. "If the worst happens, you'll take Augee to the shaft you told me of. Hohala's only chance of salvation is through Augee."

Lawson's face was wracked with indecision as he glanced around him at all of the ruin and fire.

"Lawson!" growled Nicholas urgently. "Promise me! If the worst happens, you'll take Augee to the shaft. I need you to give me your word."

A tear dripped from the counselor's eyelid and landed softly on Nicholas's brow.

"I promise," assured Lawson, his lip trembling and his hand clutched tightly around Nicholas's.

"Thank you," replied Nicholas with a sigh before adding gruffly, "Now *go!*"

With that, Lawson scrambled to his feet and hobbled toward Caralisa as fast as his aged legs would carry him.

With all of his lingering energy, Nicholas then turned his head in the direction of Augee who towered above him, moaning in grief. His beautiful eyes sparkled with tears and emotion, and it almost seemed to Nicholas that the pain from his own brutal injuries had been inflicted on Augee also. Nicholas smiled at his friend in weak reassurance, his own ailing heart shaken by the bare devastation of his friend's demeanour.

"Please, Augee, save them," he pleaded breathlessly. "Get them out of here, and take them to safety."

Tears filled his eyes as Augee responded with a howl of mourning that gripped painfully at Nicholas's very soul. In that instant, his realization of all that they had been through together, and the unshakable bond that had grown between them cleaved at his mind like a razor, and their imminent parting of ways seemed all the more shattering.

"It's not the end, Augee," Nicholas urged weakly. "I'll always be with you."

In response, Augee lowered his giant head and nuzzled sadly at Nicholas's torso.

"There's the beast!" came a sudden, gleeful cry from the band of Volcarons who had emerged into the adjoining street. "Destroy it! Kill them all!"

"Augee, please, go!" growled Nicholas fiercely, drawing on his last store of energy.

With a final locking of their eyes, Augee whimpered sorrowfully, before raising his body and leaping into the air with a subtle, agile flinch.

As roars of the Volcaron horde advanced toward him, and the walls of Hohala continued to crash down all around, Nicholas turned his head at an angle and rested it on the grass. Through his rapidly blurring vision, he was filled with deep relief to observe Augee's sinewy outline rising through the air in the distance, the hunched silhouettes of two figures astride his back. And then, all of sudden, Nicholas became aware of the blistering pain that stabbed at every inch of his mangled body. With the mixed intensity of burning love and fuming, resentful anger in his heart, he sighed sorrowfully for a final time, long and deep. Finally, the light seeped from King Nicholas Stone's eyes, and the power of darkness held dominion once again.

58

THE HYSTERICAL WAILS of the princess seemed to vocalize Lawson's own broken spirit and his horror at all that had occurred. For the first time in his life, the counselor was empty of inspiration, and the inner strength that had served him so well throughout his life was gone. Flying high above Hohala, with the ravaged village now a glowing speck in the darkness below, Lawson felt suffocatingly alone, as if everything he'd known—all of the truths he'd once believed in—had been lies designed to set up the great fall of the Hohalians. There were no kind whisperings from the Nexus anymore; his soul had not smiled at the reassuring touch of the gods in so very long, and the great violence he'd just witnessed provoked him to question if his faith in the Nexus had been a delusion all along.

Perched in front of him, a distraught Caralisa held her head in her hands as she wept, and it was necessary for Lawson to keep a tight hold of her. So distracted was she by her grief that any sudden jerking movement threatened to unbalance her. For his part, Augee appeared to be struggling with the very act of flying as he moaned and shuddered at his own mental torment. Visibly heartbroken, Augee seemed to be flying directionless, drifting through the black sky without purpose or destination in mind. Above the world—away from a new reality where the embers of joy and hope had been stomped out by the invaders—the night sky was an empty vacuum; a hollow pocket of the universe in which to mourn and despair.

"Steady, Augee!" cried Lawson hoarsely as an abrupt swirl of wind threatened to upend him and Caralisa. "Please, focus until we can land safely."

Augee's response was a cry so loud and sheer in its suffering, that Lawson quickly sensed their grief-stricken companion was only partially in control of his faculties. As Augee quivered dangerously a second time, Lawson wiped the tears from his own eyes and scanned the landscape for any indication of a place to land. Unexpectedly, the counselor's heart jittered to spot a line of tiny, distant lights penetrating the darkness. They flickered like beacons on a lightless ocean, and as Lawson strained his vision, he could see that they were moving westward, away from the smouldering pockmark that denoted Hohala village.

"The Hohalians!" exclaimed Lawson, his animation more out of fear than relief. "Look, Your Highness!"

Caralisa turned her head feebly for a minute before burying her face in her hands again.

"What does it matter?" she hissed over the howling breeze, to which she could feel Lawson flinch in response. "It's all destroyed. Our future and our home, burned to ashes! Nicholas, my father, so many dead! Nothing matters anymore. There is no purpose in anything!"

"Your Highness, please!" beseeched Lawson, his own mental endurance too sapped to continue being strong for them both. "We must not give up. Those Hohalians you see fleeing yet again have not given up. *They* still have it in them to survive, and while they do, we have a duty to them."

An overwhelmed, breathless sob was Caralisa's only reply, and Lawson felt no choice but to take control of the situation.

"Augee," he called out with mock-assertiveness. "Take us down to our people. We must assist them immediately."

Augee emitted the feeblest whimper of acknowledgement and changed course in the direction of the drifting lights. Minutes later, as their altitude decreased, the make-up of the landscape became more visible. They could see that the pinprick lights were indeed those of torches, and that they were moving through a portion of thick jungle. Swooping in low, Lawson observed that the lights were moving more quickly than he'd first realized. Through gaps in the treetops, he could see the flash and swish of flame, and as the wind decreased, panicked shouts and screams reached his ears.

"Lawson?" Caralisa questioned fearfully as she clutched his arm. "What's happening?"

"I don't know," he answered warily, trying to pierce through the darkness to locate a place where they could attempt to land. "I pray that the Volcarons have not continued their pursuit of…"

The remainder of Lawson's sentence didn't make it past his lips. Without the slightest warning, the counselor felt his entire body being jolted as a boulder the size of a watermelon shot out of the trees below and struck Augee square on the head. Instinctively, Lawson clasped his arm around Caralisa's waist just in time to prevent her from being flung off of Augee's back. Simultaneously, Augee let out a shriek of alarm that chilled Lawson's blood, and in the barely penetrable darkness, his senses told him that they were careening sharply.

"Augee!" screamed Caralisa in terror as they began to angle downward ominously.

Clearly in agony, Augee thrashed his head from side to side, and his cries were like the howl of the direst storm. Breaking into a near-vertical dive, both riders held on as tightly as their exhausted arms would allow. Behind her, Caralisa felt Lawson stretch forward to touch Augee on the neck.

"Come on, old fellow!" he roared in a desperate attempt to incite Augee to take control. "You need to stay strong!"

As if Lawson's encouragement had shaken him to awareness, Augee's winced eyes flashed open, and his features tightened to a visible grimace. To the amazement of his two companions, they began to level out, and as they zipped across the pitch-black jungle, the flash of torches was visible throughout the dense vegetation below them.

"Look!" the counselor cried out suddenly, pointing toward a steep ridge that rose out of the tree tops.

In the meagre moonlight, they could see the outline of people—hundreds of them—scaling an extensive landform that appeared to bridge the frontier between the jungle and the highlands, and it was obvious by the haste with which they climbed that they were indeed the fleeing Hohalians.

"The people!" exclaimed Lawson so fervidly that he had to clutch Augee's spine to keep himself balanced.

"They look so frightened!" Caralisa lamented dejectedly.

Lawson peered across her and saw that Augee's neck had begun to droop, his skull gleaming with fresh blood.

"We need to land," the counselor announced firmly. "Augee is in a very bad way, and we *must* assist the Hohalians."

Without waiting for a reply, Lawson leaned forward and shouted to Augee to touch down on a wide, rounded ledge close to where the Hohalians were ascending in a meandering line. They climbed in precarious darkness, their lanterns evidently discarded so as not to draw the attention of pursuing Volcarons. At the first sight of Augee, the fleeing evacuees exclaimed and pointed at the sky in weary relief. Shuddering and groaning in pain, Augee swept downward and perched shakily on the wide-set rock ledge. To their alarm, Lawson and Caralisa were almost up-ended as the wounded Augee's legs buckled underneath him, and he collapsed with a moan of distress.

"Augee!" cried Lawson as he leapt to the ground with an urgency that his own frail legs were scarcely able to withstand. "Dear fellow, are you alright?"

A howl that prompted fearful gasps from the onlooking Hohalians emitted from Augee's jaws as both his grief and physical pain climbed to their apex.

"Is he going to be alright?" inquired Caralisa dropping to her knees next to Lawson. "Oh, Augee! Oh, Nicholas!"

At that, the devastated, young woman's powers of restraint abandoned her entirely, and she broke down in a torrent of weeping.

"Princess Caralisa!" called a male voice that shook with panic.

She and Lawson turned around in unison and were stunned to observe the harassed-looking figure of Hamar clambering down a gravelly embankment.

"Hamar, dear fellow!" gasped Lawson as their compatriot stumbled to where they were crouched by the collapsed Augee's side. "What is going on?"

Hamar's eyes shone with anger and agitation, and his frame quivered with emotion.

"We evacuated through the jungle," he stammered breathlessly. "There were many of us, but when we saw the Volcarons following, the people panicked, and some got separated in the darkness. I fear there have been many losses…"

"Dear Nexus!" breathed Lawson in dread.

"We have to lead the people far from here," continued Hamar as he glanced at Caralisa, before adding knowingly, "Too many loved ones have been taken from us tonight. There will be more deaths, if we do not move swiftly."

And then, as if prompted by Hamar's dire forecast, a frenzied shout went up from among the Hohalians.

"The Volcarons!" yelled a woman hysterically, inciting an instant commotion along the steep ridge. "They approach in the distance!"

Sure enough, to the dismay of all present, their tormentors' flaming torches could be seen drifting through the darkness of the jungle below them. Immediately, the hundreds-strong caravan of Hohalians began to surge forward, their panic over-ruling the need for caution. Amid the chaos, some of the weaker and less able-bodied climbers began to stumble and lose their balance, and in one horrifying moment, a man wrenched his young daughter back from the lip of the ridge, just as her foot slipped from under her.

"They're panicking," Hamar declared fearfully. "We have to take control of the situation, or few Hohalians will make it through the night."

He then placed his hand on Caralisa's shoulder.

"We need to show leadership," he insisted firmly. "*We* must take control."

Caralisa gave no acknowledgement. Instead, her face remained buried in her hands, her shoulders heaving as she sobbed.

The mayhem along the ridge was intensifying, and the bedlam was such that the slightest wayward movement threatened to unbalance entire swathes of climbers. As if to contribute to the grim frenzy, Augee continued to yowl in anguish.

"I am fearful that Augee's time may be short," interjected Lawson suddenly, to which Hamar and Caralisa turned around with concerned stares. "His spirit is most severely broken, and he needs help that none here can provide him. I must take him to safe haven."

"What?" snapped Hamar, alarmed by the thought of Lawson and Augee leaving their side. "Where do you speak of? Let us all go then."

The counselor shook his head as the chaos along the ridgeway continued behind them.

"It is not important where," he answered cryptically. "You and Her Highness must stay and lead the Hohalians away from harm. There is no time for discussion, Hamar. Those people need your strength and leadership."

Then, he placed his hands on Caralisa's shoulders, her swollen eyes glistening as she lifted her gaze to meet his.

"And they need their queen, now more than ever," he added, his tone soft but unmistakeable in its seriousness.

It was the first time that the realization of her new status among the Hohalians had dawned on Caralisa. It had been a nightmarish end to the happiest day of her life; her new husband and soul mate, her father, and the countless, undeserving victims of Volcaron bloodlust, all taken so barbarically. For a young woman well-acquainted with suffering, it felt that such a crown might be a weight too heavy.

"Lawson…" she breathed feebly. "I don't think I can. I'm not strong enough. I feel so lost. Please, don't leave."

And at that, the young queen's face collapsed into a sob. Before him, Lawson saw the child who he'd long loved like a daughter of his own, and the smile he returned to her was the comforting type that only a parent could truly provide.

"Your time is now, Your Highness," he whispered reassuringly. "We cannot know the hour when the true purpose of our lives will present itself. We can only embrace it, or allow it to pass us by. And I don't believe, my dear girl, that it's in your spirit to abandon the great responsibility and honor that awaits you. I *know* you are ready to lead our people through the immense challenge ahead. But without you, Queen Caralisa, I fear the Hohalian nation will eventually waste and disappear from the light of creation."

A fiendish cackle in the distance interrupted the counselor's eloquent appeal, causing every pair of Hohalian eyes to drop toward the jungle. The flaming torches of the Volcaron soldiers indicated their approach, and the crooked mountain ridge was now all that separated them from the Hohalians.

"Come, Your Highness," urged Hamar who had been listening distractedly. "Master Lawson is right. We have lost heavily this day. The people need you to stand with them. You are the only remaining pillar of the Hohala they once knew. Lead them, as is your birth right."

Sobbing, Caralisa deliberated the gravity of his words as the screams around them continued, and the lights of the stalking Volcaron pack floated ever closer

"What about Augee?" she inquired worriedly a moment later. "Please tell me he'll survive!"

Lawson turned to where Augee lay writhing in discomfort.

"I most deeply hope so," sighed the counselor. "He appears utterly debilitated by his grief at the loss of our dear Nich…"

Lawson's sentence was cut short at the look of distress on Caralisa's face as he stumbled over the deceased Nicholas's name, but he caught himself quickly by adding, "But we must go now—*all of us!*"

Caralisa's expression tightened into that of a woman on the cusp of capitulation, but the moment was interrupted abruptly.

"Please, Your Highness," interjected Hamar who was struggling to smother his own rising panic. "There's no more time!"

Queen Caralisa glanced up at Hamar resignedly before turning back to Lawson and throwing her arms around him.

"I pray this is not our final farewell, Lawson," she whispered lovingly. "I'll hold a flame of hope in my heart that I'll see you again."

Without another word, the young queen loosened her grip of the counselor's neck and took Hamar's impatiently-waiting hand. As she made to turn away, she glanced in the whimpering Augee's direction and wiped her streaming eyes.

"May the gods protect you, Augee," she breathed before disappearing into the mass of evacuating Hohalians.

For the briefest moment, Lawson stood and stared after them, contemplating the cruelness of so much uncertainty. Then, from a few meters below, a rasping voice called out sinisterly, interrupting his thoughts.

"Come back, cowards!" it mocked. "Where's your great beast to protect you now? Brought down by a mere rock! It, and every one of you, will die tonight. You can't escape Volcaron supremacy!"

Lawson turned to Augee who appeared to have become suddenly alert to the encroaching gang of Volcarons below, their knife blades reflecting the moonlight doomfully. Augee's skin was now an oily grey, and the wound to his skull was bleeding profusely.

"Can you fly?" entreated Lawson. "I know a place where you might have a chance."

Augee looked up at him brokenly as if his very life-force was wrestling against the crushing heartache of his loss.

"Come on, Augee!" cried Lawson, glancing across his shoulder with escalating terror. "Master Stone would not want it to be like this. Nicholas would not want to see you give up completely because of him. In his name we *must* survive! Let's do him that honor."

As if by some thread of a miracle, the counselor's plea seemed to rouse Augee's attention; the light in his eyes appeared to flicker with new urgency, and he returned an affirming growl. With a groan of exertion, he rose to his feet unsteadily and lowered his back for Lawson to climb across.

"The beast!" came the victorious roar of a pike-wielding Volcaron fighter. "*Kill it!*

Like a baying pack, the troop of Volcaron soldiers hoisted themselves onto the wide ledge, drawing their weapons expectantly as they rounded their injured and clearly struggling nemesis. With a pained flap of his wings, Augee leaped off the ledge. The wind blustered in Lawson's ears as they disappeared into the darkness, and the curses of the Volcarons that echoed from behind were the most vicious he had heard in his long life.

A moment later, the lights of their pursuers' torches were again pin-pricks in the gloom. Numb from anguish and the elements, Lawson buried his face in his arms and conceded that all had changed utterly. Across the void of sky, the counselor and a quaking Augee drifted toward their destination. As he stroked Augee supportively, Lawson wept to himself and reflected on so much loss, upheaval and thousands of shattered dreams. He wondered how any of it could have been real, and he acknowledged to himself that there would be many days of suffering ahead for the Hohalians.

However, in the darkest portion of sky above him, the flicker of a single star caught Lawson's attention. It winked with a strange luminescence that put the distraught counselor in mind of the star that had risen into the sky earlier that evening when he and Nicholas had laid King Benjamin's body to rest at the Eternal Stream. As he considered the lone, celestial light, Lawson reflected sadly on his fallen comrades—particularly Nicholas, who had done more than any Hohalian to deliver their nation from hardship and persecution. Even for the few hours in which Nicholas had briefly assumed the title of king, he and Augee had risked their lives against overwhelming enemy force. Indeed, through all of the Hohalians' ordeals, Nicholas had never once given up hope. Always a man of faith, Lawson wiped away his tears and reminded himself that as long as there was hope—however min-iscule—then surrender was a choice, rather than an inevitability.

And then, the counselor's mind turned to Augee whose pursed facial features suggested he was battling through searing pain. In silence, Lawson marvelled at the fortitude of the magnificent, otherworldly creature who had so bravely and willingly aided his adopted people. Suddenly, the counslor's exhausted soul felt thankful for the selflessness of strangers in the world.

"We must keep faith, Augee," he whispered, stroking his winged companion gently. "We *must* believe that the Hohalian story is not at an end."

In reply, Augee forced a whimper that indicated to Lawson that he somehow shared his hope.

A short time later, dawn colors began to infuse the sky, and the achingly beautiful country revealed itself below. Up ahead, the familiar, snowy caps of the western mountain belt stood stark against the peach-tinged sunrise, and with smoke from Hohala village still lingering across the horizon, Augee and Lawson ventured forward into their uncertain future.

COMING SOON

PART 2 OF
THE AUGEE SERIES

AUGEE
THE REAWAKENING

BY

PAUL STUEMPEL
& CORMAC LAMBE

For news and updates, check out:

augee.com

facebook.com/TheAugeeSeries

twitter.com/TheAugeeSeries

instagram.com/TheAugeeSeries

Want to share YOUR thoughts on *Augee: Guardian of Hohala*?

Go to augee.com to post a comment!

www.ingramcontent.com/pod-product-compliance
Lightning Source LLC
Chambersburg PA
CBHW030548180626
46816CB00005B/1448